Unexpected Tales From Beyond the Grave

Also from Chaosium:
The Antarktos Cycle
Arkham Tales
The Book of Eibon
The Complete Pegana
Frontier Cthulhu
The Hastur Cycle
The Ithaqua Cycle
The Necronomicon
Singers of Strange Songs
Song of Cthulhu
The Strange Cases of Rudolph Pearson
Tales Out of Innsmouth
The Tsathoggua Cycle

R. W. Chambers' *The Yellow Sign* (his complete weird fiction)

Arthur Machen's *The Three Impostors & Other Tales*
Arthur Machen's *The White People & Other Tales*
Arthur Machen's *The Terror & Other Tales*

These, and more, can be found on our catalog at
www.chaosium.com

Unexpected Tales From Beyond the Grave

by
C.J. Henderson, Cody Goodfellow,
Gary McMahon, Robert M. Price,
and others

Edited by
Brian M. Sammons
& David Conyers

UNDEAD & UNBOUND is published by Chaosium, Inc.
This book is copyright as a whole © 2013 Chaosium, Inc.; all rights reserved.

Cover art © 2010 by Steven Gilberts; all rights reserved. Cover layout by Charlie Krank.
Interior layout by Badger McInnes. Edited by Brian M. Sammons and David Conyers.

Similarities between characters in this book
nd persons living or dead are strictly coincidental.

Reproduction of material from within this book for the purposes of personal or corporate
profit, by photographic, digital, or other means of storage and retrieval is prohibited.

Our web site is updated frequently; see **www.chaosium.com**.

This book is printed on 100% acid-free paper.

FIRST EDITION
10 9 8 7 6 5 4 3 2 1

Chaosium Publication 6051
Published in May 2013.

ISBN-10: 1-56882-368-1
ISBN-13: 978-1-56882-368-3

CONTENTS

Introduction *by Brian M. Sammons and David Conyers* 6
Blind Item *by Cody Goodfellow* 9
Dead Baby Keychain Blues *by Gary McMahon* 25
A Personal Apocalypse *by Mercedes M. Yardley* 37
The Unexpected *by Mark Allan Gunnells* 51
Incarnate *by David Dunwoody* 63
Marionettes *by Robert Neilson* 83
Undead Night of the Undeadest Undead *by C.J. Henderson* 103
I Am Legion *by Robert M. Price* 121
When Dark Things Sleep *by Damien Walters Grintalis* 127
Descanse En Paz *by William Meikle* 137
Thunder in Old Kilpatrick *by Gustavo Bondoni* 149
Phallus Incarnate *by Glynn Owen Barrass* 163
Wreckers *by Tom Lynch* 177
Scavenger *by Oscar Rios* 187
In the House of Millions of Years *by John Goodrich* 199
Romero 2.0 *by Brian M. Sammons and David Conyers* 209
Mother Blood *by Scott David Aniolowski* 229
The Unforgiving Court *by David Schembri* 247
North of the Arctic Circle *by Peter Rawlik* 271
Contributor Biographies 276

INTRODUCTION

This book is a sign of our times. It was born in a world where the undead have never been hotter, or at least that's true for two flavors of the not-quite-dead. Everywhere you turn today vampires and zombies have all but taken over not only the horror-verse, but they have become pop culture icons. Movies, books, music, comic books, video games, t-shirts, television shows, they even pop up in TV commercials at an ever increasing rate. Simply put, though, both of these undying predators have been done to (un)death in every conceivable way. They have become stale, humdrum, and so very been there, done that. As for the other legions of horrors that mock death, with a few exceptions, they have largely been ignored.

Enter *Undead & Unbound*, a book looking to celebrate those that have returned from the grave in all their glory, in whatever form they take. Yes, you will find the famous blood-drinkers and flesh-eaters in here, but here there will also be ghosts, patched together re-animates, fiends of myth and folklore from around the globe and across the ages, and many not so easily identifiable creatures from beyond the grave. Hell, we think we even saw a good old Egyptian mummy in here somewhere. When is the last time you saw one of them?

That's the *Undead* part of the title, but what's *Unbound* all about? Well, not content to just provide a cornucopia of cavorting corpses of all walks of (un)life, we wanted to do something new with those very old monsters. With all the attention paid to some of the walking dead it was important to have them in new settings, doing new things, and in all ways staying as far away from the stale, humdrum, and been there done that as possible. So here you will find nineteen tales that take the undead and push them to their limits. From the distant past to the far flung future and from all corners of the Earth, or even locations far from it, the undead are eternal and everywhere.

From modern day Hollywood, Cody Goodfellow examines the symbiotic, sometimes parasitic, relationship between the famous, those that adore them, and the paparazzi that hunt them with "Blind Item".

Robert M. Price and Pete Rawlik both deliver two very different takes on a classic horror icon that in tone, style and plot could not be more different with their "I am Legion" and "North of the Arctic Circle".

Proving that stories of dead things, or in this case formerly dead things, don't have to be in all seriousness, C.J. Henderson delivers a delightful monster mash-up in "Undead Night of the Undeadest Undead" and Oscar Rios provides some ghoulish grins with his "Scavenger".

But less you think this book is all smiles, Robert Neilson delivers one of the bleakest, most horrifying tales of inescapable dread we have read in years with his "Marionettes". Not to be outdone, Scott David Aniolowski gives birth to "Mother Blood", a story about an ancient evil from a faraway land finding a new home for itself and its unspeakable dietary needs in a modern American city.

"Dead Baby Keychain Blues" not only has one of the best titles ever, but Gary McMahon uses it to show how very bad things can sometimes come in very small packages.

The horrors of war are the backdrop for two tales that breathe new life into two very traditional monsters of myth and legend. "Thunder in Old Kilpatrick" by Gustavo Bondoni is the touching tale of a boy and his...well you can bet it's not his dog. As for "The Unforgiving Court" by David Schembri, I'm positive that after reading it you'll never look at certain cute, winged-things the same way again.

History is brought to (un)life in William Meikle's "Descanse En Paz" and both John Goodrich and Glynn Owen Barrass use ancient Egypt as the starting point for their tales "In the House of Millions of Years" and "Phallus Incarnate". However from there, these stories vary quickly and greatly, proving that it's not where you came from, but where you're going that's really important.

Ghosts, specters, phantoms and haunts of every sort get some much needed love in Tom Lynch's "Wreckers" and "The Unexpected" by Mark Allan Gunnells. Both of these stories take the most traditional of all undead tales and run with them in exciting new directions.

Then there are the not-so-easily-classifiable stories that do new things with the very basic premise of what's alive, what's dead, and what's neither. "When Dark Things Sleep" by Damien Walters Grintalis is a disturbing story about the dead that just keep dying while David Dunwoody's "Incarnate" is full of black magic and is set in a true ghost town with a hero you'll not soon forget.

And yes you lovers of all things zombie; fear not for your favorite flesh eaters are here, but thankfully not exactly how you would expect them. Mercedes M. Yardley serves up a slice of suburban life and death in a world where the dead come back in "A Personal Apocalypse" while your editors do a futuristic homage to one of the greats with "Romero 2.0".

In selecting stories for *Undead & Unbound*, we have aimed to achieve a celebration of all things from beyond the grave. We have strived for the new and the different and hopefully, shown that no matter how old the bones, new life can be found in them if you look hard, and differently, enough.

–Brian M. Sammons and David Conyers, March 2012

BLIND ITEM
By Cody Goodfellow

If you know me at all, you know I'll publish anything. Doesn't matter if it ruins lives, or if no one believes it, or even if it's true. But I won't put my name to this.

If you don't know me, so much the better. I take pictures of celebrities, but not at fake publicity circle jerks where they stand around like action figures against that endless corporate logo wallpaper. I'm more of a big game hunter. I stalk the wily beasts in their native habitat. Nobody can read and none of the stars can talk, and every publicist uses the same robotic verbiage to honk out their empty spin, so my pictures *are* the story. When I drop shots of an A-list sitcom daddy with a reputation as a lady-killer gobbling WeHo hot dogs instead of tacos, my editors know they won't have to lawyer up, because I've got somebody's scalp in my teeth. The star's management can buy the shots and bury them, or let their guy go up in flames. I've burned more celebutards than tanning beds. It's the only thing about this job that still gets me excited, I freely admit. It almost reminds me why I used to love them.

I used to see those searchlights sweeping the night sky like God and his angels were expected any minute somewhere across town. Maybe it was just a movie premiere or a used car sale, but I ate up the hype like placebo vitamins. I vowed to do anything to get inside that light and see what all the fuss was about.

I'm not just a pest with a camera. I trained and worked for years as a fashion photographer. Nobody in this town knows more about how to make them look good. Nobody tries harder to keep them relevant, but they spit on us.

I eat their hate like Wheaties. I did not get into this business to be anyone's friend. And I sure as hell don't want to be famous, any more than the guy who shot that running, burning Cambodian girl would've wanted to share a napalm shower.

Undead and Unbound

We get the celebrities we deserve, and somehow, no matter how flashy the package, no matter how loud the crowd cheers, we know we're getting ripped off. Marilyn Monroe isn't as hot as most second-string underwear models, but that thing she became for 1/100 of a second at a time made her a goddess. Doesn't matter if she's dead; what you see in her eyes is still out there, looking for you.

They don't make them like they used to. Stars, I mean. Dead-eyed decoys are what they give us. Bait in a badly camouflaged trap.

But I digress. This is not a memoir. I'm only the camera, but I burned the original disks and I'll take the prints to my grave, so I have to tell it.

This is about her…

(I won't use her name. Don't need the headache, and don't need to, because you know her. Or you think you do. It's a lie that the name is the same as the thing. Call her name, and they know you want her, and something very different from the fantasy will come to collect. Names claim nothing in a place where everybody drops Ecstasy and renames themselves before they sober up. There is no name, no word, for what she really is now, anyway.)

A perennial star of tube and screen a few years ago, but now the queen of tabloid smears, superior court dockets and basic cable reruns. Whether she's getting caught shoplifting on Rodeo Drive or puking in the River Phoenix memorial gutter out front of the Viper Room, she's still America's crab-infested sweetheart. For a culture conditioned to crave fame, she's a career-long car crash, and nobody looks away, nobody learns a thing. Tabloid snaps of her three-way coke orgy at the Satori rehab chalet in Sedona opened bigger than her highest-grossing feature. The bitch ran over my foot and broke my toe in her Maserati at Coachella last year, but I didn't press charges, because her dumb, drunken antics bought me a BMW.

She came out of the Marmont an hour before last call Friday night, alone and unstable. A sure sign of impending drama. She was still supposed to be in rehab. Her erstwhile girlfriend was spinning at Cannes, and she'd been implicated with a married *X-Games* athlete two weeks before. She'd dyed her hair red again. I'd hated her as a blonde. I remember I felt like singing.

The usual goon squad followed her to the curb, snapping taunt-pics and shaking her down with ugly, blunt questions. You never know when you'll hit a nerve and get the target to go Full Metal Britney

Blind Item

on your ass. But she just weathered the lightning flashes and hit her cigarette like sucking venom out of a snakebite, her glassy rape-gaze orbiting the moon. The valet brought her silver Italian snob-coffin and she peeled out east on Sunset to turn north up Laurel Canyon.

I followed her into the hills. She didn't see me, but she drove like she did. She scorched the wafer-thin racing tires on the hairpin curves and blitzed every stop sign to the top of the hill, leaving a mile-long burnt-rubber autograph. I followed her through the last stop sign before Mulholland, and the dark of One AM turned into a red and blue high noon.

Down in the flats and in the Valley, it's a nonstop demolition derby, but go up into the hills in a cheap piece of shit car or a Mazda pickup full of lawnmowers, and you'll find the cops thicker than lawn jockeys. A cloud of fear-piss hangs around every half-hidden stop sign.

My BMW should've earned me a pass. But the cops all know her, and if I was following, they knew me, too.

The cop——young, chiseled Latino sportscaster type——rapped on my roof with his baton, then on the glass to show me he'd chipped my paint.

He spared me the speech, wrote me up for Failure To Stop, Reckless Driving and searched my car. Unscrewed the telephoto lens of my Nikon and dropped it in the gutter. Blar-har-har, no coke in here…

Finally, when our little make-out session was over, he advised me to go home and stop stalking respected citizens, smashed one of my taillights, and wished me a magical evening.

I didn't ask them why they didn't pull her over. That would've nailed her down for me to shoot, and any way they handled it would reflect badly on the sterling LAPD rep. The class chasm is so deep and so wide, you can't hide it, so why try? But the groundlings in the cheap seats want to see up the skirts of the immortals, and all the other side really has to sell is carefully orchestrated peeks behind the curtain wall. It's why I pull down 200k per annum and spend so much on lenses the size of elephant trunks.

I sat parked on Mulholland for a while, letting the dregs of adrenaline cook off before I did something dumb. I should go back down the way I came and take the 101 home to Studio City, but the mark they put on my car might get me pulled over by Highway Patrol. The only smart play was to take the narrowest, darkest side street into the Valley. I decided to risk slinking down Mulholland to the 405, instead.

Undead and Unbound

Ogle the palaces, chateaus and fuck-fortresses of the gods, and try to remember why I once wanted to be like them.

The view was for shit, the sparkle of the Valley lights drowning in smog and brushfire smoke, an attention-starved nebula of nobodies twinkling like they were further away than the stars.

It's still beautiful. It can still knock you sideways and make you fall in love with it all over again. Just to set you up for the next time it fucks you.

Mulholland wriggled and noodled to its terminus at Skirball and the 405, but all the onramps were blocked off and a Caltrans crew was tearing up the Sepulveda Bridge. I stayed on Mulholland and crossed the gridlocked river of diamonds and rubies. Getting worked over by fascist cocksuckers always brings out the aesthete in me.

West of Sepulveda Pass, the hills get even wilder, and the McMansions retreat behind shaggy landscaping and rusty wrought-iron gates. The high tide of TV's golden age crested here and rolled back to leave a lot of aging B-listers in their crumbling stucco villas, popping pills and watching their cracked swimming pools turn into primeval swamps. Past a couple megachurches and a fire station, the scrub brush and coyotes take over. I could've turned down Calneva into the Valley, but I didn't want to go home. Something didn't want me to. It wanted me for what I saw when I came around the turn overlooking the vacant lot behind Bel Air Presbyterian.

Pepper trees and scrub pines crowded the edge of the lot, but they didn't quite hide the squad car parked under them with its lights off.

I looked away and hit the gas and then the brake. If it was the same cop, I was already boned. But then I saw I'd struck lucky. He already had someone pulled over. In the split second before I passed it, I almost gave myself whiplash.

Her silver Maserati.

There's no place to park out there, so I just pulled onto the shoulder around the next bend. Traffic? There was none. I got my starlight lens and my stealth Nikon. It's covered in matte-black grip tape, and it can render a clear image in pitch blackness that makes the *Pam & Tommy* sex tape look like the Paris Hilton sex tape.

The sandy shoulder rose up into a ridge that overlooked the dirt lot, but there was no cover. Odd thickets of exotic wild grasses rose almost shoulder-high on the other side. Scottish heather, Russian thistle and bamboo linked arms and tried to tear my clothes off like

Blind Item

adoring fans with thorns for fingers. My leather jacket fared okay; my jeans and running shoes, not so much. I made enough goddamned noise the cop should've spotted me, but when I finally got within fifty yards of the parked cars, I saw he had his hands full.

And she had her mouth full.

She gets arrested a couple times a year, but the cops pull her over a dozen times a month. If there're no paparazzi around, they let her off with a warning. She's beat every rehab program in the country, and her stupid soap opera saga clogs up the courts and the jails like a kilo bindle of coke passing through a smuggler's gut.

Every peeper on my beat knew the cops had to get some kind of payback for letting her slide, and now I had proof.

The setup was so perfect, I would be looking for Satan's lawyer with a contract to sign, if I were a religious man. But I told myself it was just the dumb luck of the doggedly obsessive, and started shooting.

The cop could've been the same asshole who shook me down, in the ghostly greenish light of my light-gathering lens. He leaned against her door with one hand clamped on the back of her head. Deep auburn hair veiled her face, but there was no mistaking that profile.

Saying something nasty to her in a throaty growl, he thrust into her until she choked on him. Her hand came up, but circled his thigh, clinging to his utility belt, pulling him deeper.

I switched the camera to video and tried to creep up close enough to capture the audio. I got something better. For just a second, her eyes lock on the lens and she slowburn bats her lashes, as if to say, *you're next, little boy…*

God, what a magnificent whore. It must've chafed her to turn down that Vivid contract last year. She loved it like only a tranny who's fooled a drunken sailor can love it.

The cop had to work pretty hard, to remind her she wasn't supposed to.

"Watch the fucking teeth!" he shouted and tried to pull back, but she wouldn't let go. "Your mouth feels like a frozen turkey's asshole, what's the matter with you?"

I had edged up until I was twenty feet away, propped in the fork of the pepper tree like a nearsighted sniper. I was watching the action, not my footing. A fallen branch or some such shit crunched underfoot. I dropped to my knees and dove into the brush, but he saw me.

Undead and Unbound

"Freeze, fuckhead!"

I started to run, but what was he going to do, shoot me? Shoot both of us, with his dick hanging out? I turned to advise him of my rights as a representative of the fourth estate, but he didn't come running. Not right away.

She wouldn't let him go. Her tiny fingers hooked in the leather loops of his belt. He slapped her sideways so hard her head rebounded off the steering wheel, but he was the one screaming like a car alarm. He backed up tucking his dick in with one hand and trying to draw his gun with the other, and tripped on his own feet.

I came back down the slope into the trees, shooting video of the cop trying to get up. His legs were like noodles, but superior training won out, and he managed to draw his gun and point it at me, then her.

"Out of the fucking car!" He ordered me to get on the ground, but by then, I was halfway to the next zip code.

Deciding not to shoot me in the back, the cop finally came loping after me. He let out this low, tortured moan when he ran, with one hand holding his junk and the gun swinging like a winged thing on a tangled string.

He popped off two shots, wild and into the air. I juked left towards the road and a huge stand of prickly pear cacti, then turned right and tumbled down a loose gravel slope.

Camera in the air, I skidded down the rock-studded cheese-grater slope on my right side. Thunder crashed and a blinding flash took my eyesight. It was all so fucking ridiculous…she bit him, and he was shooting at me?

I rolled rolled rolled, and the cop came tumbling after. I hit my head, my shoulder, my ass, but I kept the camera safe. I am a fucking professional.

I crashed feet-first into a sagging chainlink fence shaggy with high weeds and wild cucumber vines and was overwhelmed with relief for about three seconds.

The cop avalanched into me and tried to grab me with blood-slathered hands. His gun was gone, lost somewhere on the slope. He was like a last-call drunk, ridiculously strong but totally uncoordinated, trying to wrestle me to the ground and get an arm around my throat. All his authority in shreds, all the wonderful toys on his Batman belt forgotten, he was just a big man who wanted me dead.

I've got into more shoving matches with bodyguards and publicists

BLIND ITEM

and event staff than I can remember, but I've never had to physically fight for my life. The cop had me pinned against the fence and put every ounce of his huge, donut-batter ass behind strangling me.

I hit him with the only thing I had. My camera is a digital, but the casing is carbon steel and graphite. You can bust a padlock with it, and still shoot a decent fashion spread.

The first hit split his eyebrow. His head whipped back, his fist spasmed and tried to tear my trachea out. I hit him again, again, I don't know how many times. When I finally stopped, my camera was slick with blood and bone chips. The cop wheezed into my face like the last squeeze of syrup from Aunt Jemima's head. I pushed him off me and then fell on top of him. He didn't get fresh with me again, but his corpse twitched under me like a Magic Fingers bed for a while. His little partner still stuck out the flap of his fly, leaking blood like a garden hose. It wasn't just scraped; at least half of it was missing.

"You fucked up everything," she said, right beside me. I jumped back and brandished my camera. I almost threw it at her, but she had the cop's gun. It took both her little hands to hold it up, but they didn't tremble. It might've been resting on a surveyor's tripod.

"I didn't do shit," I shot back. "This is your mess, this is, this is——"

I was knee-deep in a dead cop. His blood was all over my camera. His blood, hair and brains were under my fingernails.

She cocked the gun. Wiping white powder from under her nose and blood off her chin, she looked nothing like the doe-eyed lost little girl fame had thrown under so many buses. This was the Teflon-coated nymphet with a safety razor under her tongue, the brazen bitch-goddess she fleetingly channeled for a fistful of fashion spreads and a couple movies, before it burned her out.

"It's *our* mess, now," she said. "You've got to help me…"

"You're out of your fucking mind! This is a cop! You couldn't pay me to——"

Barefoot, she leapt down the slope to give me a quick master class in swallowing unwelcome cylindrical objects. The hot barrel raised blisters on my lips. "You're gonna help me make this right, and you'll get what you want…"

"I can go home?"

She looked up at the stars, then smiled at me…not the dazed smirk she mustered for red carpet petting sessions, but a real smile. It looked like something stolen. "You don't want to go home."

Undead and Unbound

We took a while dragging the cop up the slope, because *we* didn't do it. I pulled him up by his ankles. She supervised.

I followed her Maserati in the squad car. The dashboard camera was, obviously, disabled, and the radio was pinging with calls for the car I was sitting in. I didn't pick it up. I just drove the car, and she drove me.

We went west on Mulholland for another mile, where the only signs of humanity are the realtors' signs offering undeveloped lots on the wild, coyote-haunted hillsides. We turned up an unmarked private road and passed through an open gate that swung shut like a varmint trap when we passed through it. The Maserati bounced and fishtailed up the narrow, rutted dirt track, and I stayed close.

She said she knew what to do, and where to go. She had a plan. How stupid was I to buy into that? I'd made a fortune off her harebrained coke-whore clown show. She had a plan, and I had second degree murder all over me.

The road squeezed through a narrow, wiggly canyon for a quarter mile, then emerged into a bowl-shaped valley filled with gray water, enclosed in high steep sandstone cliffs crowned with windowless castles. It hugged the shore of the reservoir until the far side, where it curved up to terminate before an old Spanish bungalow that looked like the last of the red-hot lovers' silent era love nest. Even under the too-bright starlight, it had that weird, amputated glamor of a locale from old movies. I knew I'd seen it a hundred times. But no one came out here, and even the palatial houses on the peaks looked away.

She got out of her car and stepped into her punish-me pumps, lit a cigarette as she hobbled down the cobblestone driveway to wave me out of the cop car. "Get him in there… Leave the keys in it…" She sounded spacey again, lost little girl coked out of her mind and playing director. "They got me into this mess, they can fucking well get me out…"

"Where the hell are we? Who's going to fix this? You can't even get into Disneyland anymore, I don't think anyone's gonna help you cover up a murder——"

Her eyes went glassy and her bottom lip trembled, just like a baby's. Screaming, "WHY ARE YOU ATTACKING ME? WHO'S SIDE ARE YOU ON?" She bashed me in the ear with the cop's gun. I got out of the car. Enough of her shit, gun or no gun, she was going down.

She backed away, that weird, cold calm back in control. "You're

Blind Item

just like the rest of them, then. Fine, no skin, you'll get what you want. You'll get what everybody wants. Pop the trunk."

I did like she told me. Dragged the body out of the trunk. I didn't remind her cop cars had GPS and Lojack and shit, and I didn't remind her that we were both looking at capital murder. I just nodded in time with her wound-up whining about how nobody understood how hard it was to be 'on' all the time, nobody cared what it did to you, they just howled for more and then laughed at you when you crashed to earth. But she knew what to do. She had a plan. They finally let her in on the secret, and if I hadn't fucked it up for her, she would already be golden.

Wonderful. Cult bullshit, the only thing in Hollywood more boring than drugs.

The doors and windows were boarded up, but the storm cellar doors stood wide open, and a buttery yellow light spilled out from somewhere deep inside, like someone had set it up for us. I looked around again for hidden camera crews and found none, but the place we were about to enter now looked like the one-room schoolhouse from *Little House On The Prairie*.

The stairs were too steep, and I dropped the body when I saw the man waiting at the bottom.

The cop somersaulted down the stairs, leaving splashes of blood on each tread, and did a hilarious faceplant on the checkerboard tile floor of the cellar.

Old and unbearably familiar——that one old guy in all those old movies——and dressed in a vintage black wool suit and jodhpurs. He stepped back to keep his patent leather shoes, like little shiny hooves, out of the mess, but otherwise, he seemed cool with the dead cop. Looking right through me, he nodded at her as she prodded me down the stairs.

"We're expected," she said, in that flat, tone-deaf tone she used whenever she read her lines from off-camera cue cards. "I come here of my own free will, and I will leave when glory is finished with me."

"As you will, Madame," the butler replied in a dusty Prussian purr and clicked his heels, then backed into an alcove. He didn't help.

Did I say it was a cellar? It was fucking Carlsbad Caverns. Crimson flocked wallpaper and gilded mildew and legions of faded, stained headshots covered the walls. All the great ones from the last eighty years. Uprooted fixtures and piles of crushed velvet furniture under yellow sheets made a mountain range against the far wall, but the main attraction was long gone.

A huge sunken circular dent marked where something impossibly heavy once sat in the center of the room. Only a rusted drainpipe, about eighteen inches wide, stuck knee-high out of the floor.

"All the great ones came here," she whispered. "They had secret parties here, can you imagine? Only the greatest stars, and they came down here and they climbed into a huge marble bath together. Fuck, what must that have been like?"

"Silent movie orgies, great. Buster Keaton and Fatty Arbuckle pouring the pork to Clara Bow and Lillian Gish. So what?"

"They weren't just orgies, shut the fuck up…they were offering themselves up to something greater than their own greatness, okay? My agent told me it was the reason the movies came here in, like, 1910…they woke it up and it made them bring it, like, offerings? Some were sucked dry and eaten up, but the others——the crème de la crème——they were *remade*, right? Into *stars*…"

Scanning the Dorian Grey headshots grinning through mold and cracked glass, I saw nothing but Hollywood royalty. The great old ones…

She knelt before the drainpipe, then spread her long, slender legs and wrapped them around it suggestively. I hated myself for wanting her.

Her eyes went crossed for a moment, method acting bullshit, summoning the Muse. Finally, she stuck her fingers down her throat.

"Bulimia? Really? And me without my camera." She flipped me the bird and retched up a lawyer's paycheck's worth of booze and sushi. Something bigger choked her for a second, clung to her teeth when it came out. I guess we all know what it was.

For a long time, she just sat there wrapped around that pipe like a crackhead, making some ugly red noise down below her diaphragm over and over, like it had to be some kind of name. Occasionally, she gagged herself again and spat down the pipe, but nothing happened for long enough that she began to think this was some kind of horrible mistake. Whatever magic might've granted wishes and made superstars there once, you only had to look at *TMZ* or the *Enquirer* to know it was long since out of business.

"What was supposed to happen, honey?" I asked, real soft, in my warmest, fuzziest personal assistant voice.

Blind Item

She pointed the gun at me like she'd never seen me before, and how did I get in her bedroom? Then, finally finding her method, she split wide open. "I DON'T KNOW! I did everything right, but the stupid cop wouldn't come up here with me, and then you showed up…"

"If you don't want people like me to follow you, you could always go get a real job."

"You think this is funny? I'm just a big joke to everybody… I suppose I deserve this, though fucked if I could tell you why…" She dropped the gun and crawled across the floor like a broken-backed cat. "I just wanted to be something, just to feel for real what all those assholes thought they saw in me… Everything I did, was just to keep up with it, to capture it and become it… I just wanted to be loved… by something larger than myself…"

By now, she was at my feet on hands and knees, and she started climbing. I don't need to tell you, this is the moment most paparazzi fantasize about. These out-of-control beauties are all flaming bags of damage, and the worse they get, the harder they look around for someone to save them, and anyone they've seen more than once starts to look like an anchor.

All I ever wanted was to capture that momentary flicker of beauty and make it immortal. If she only would have let me in before, I could have saved her career with a photo shoot…or at least saved for history a snapshot of perfect beauty on the edge of the ledge.

Broken, weeping, she was crawling to me, her hands searching up my thigh and seeking my belt.

The perfect shot I'd thrown away my life for, and I had no camera. I tried to kneel and pick her up. We should get the fuck out of here. Set the cop car on fire and run away to Mexico and then the Maldives or somewhere else with no extradition treaty…

I thought that. Believed it. I saw it in her eyes when she looked up at me, saw the glossy blackness of her pupils as holes only I could fill, felt her needing me to protect her, reverence her, possess her…forever.

I fell hard to the floor and she swooped down on me, ripped my pants down and descended on my cock like a hawk on a squirrel.

Her mouth was colder than it should be, yes, and I could feel her teeth, but that cop was clearly some kind of blowjob snob. With her breath, she transmuted it to a bar of gold, and with the merest stroke of her tongue, she quickened it into a solar flare of pure plasma energy. I like a good blowjob as much as the next guy, but this was something else. This was the fulfillment of the promise those lips had made to every man in the free world, and delivered only to a lucky few whenever she blew an audition or her meds ran out. And it was, it really was, too good to be true...

I'm not ashamed to say I didn't last as long as it took you to read this sentence. But she didn't let go, and I didn't get soft, and it only got better.

Someone was watching us. I know that feeling. I cause that fucking feeling. I looked around just like the cop did in the moment before he saw me.

Something had answered her call. Maybe not what she was expecting, but I don't think she cared.

They came out of the drain. They looked like the fat, corrugated hoses on honeywagons, the trucks that drain port-a-shitters. But they also looked like the soft, stinging things on a sea anemone. I saw inside them, saw the light they were pumping out, and the stuff they were taking in.

One of them coiled around the cop's body like an anaconda, and went down his throat. Something came pumping out of the drain at high volume, bloating the cop so his chiseled face bulged and his badge and buttons popped and skipped across the checkerboard floor. I watched it and did nothing because...you have gotten a blowjob before, yes? You're familiar with the transaction, at least? Okay, then.

Abruptly, it stopped filling him up and suddenly reversed the flow, sucking out the fluid and everything else, the liquefied insides of the cop, left only a knurled rag of jerked skin and soft, floppy bones in the blue-black uniform.

Another colorless, see-through cable snaked across the room to disappear behind her. Still shaky from grand mal orgasm #4, I got up on one elbow to see where it went.

For a silly second, it looked like she'd grown a tail. It glowed like radioactive maple syrup was coming out of it, like pure golden light, and the thing was literally shining it up her ass. Whatever it was doing to her, it wasn't trying to digest her.

I pulled myself back, but stopped when I felt her nibbling teeth get serious, her tongue making me forget we were ever two separate animals. I started wondering what was really blowing me.

I looked around for something to persuade her to let me go, when

Blind Item

I saw another cable rearing up behind me like a cobra. Its mouth looked like a lamprey without the charm. Hooks bristled as it turned itself inside out and lunged for my mouth.

I caught it in my hand, but it was slick with eely slime and sludge from the dissolved cop. Pouting, collagen-pumped lips blew me a sulfuric kiss, wafted stench like the ocean floor and the grease pit of a deep fryer up my nose. Even so, I almost let it do what it wanted.

It slithered through my grip, but I pinched it and twisted it around until, writhing and puckering like a sphincter with teeth, it latched onto her throat.

Teeth gouged me but let me go as she gagged on the acidic torrent pumping into her neck. Rolling away from me and she tried to tear the lamprey-mouth off even as the fragile contours of her face swelled to the shape of a baked potato.

At the other end of her, the changes were just as drastic. Flabby jailbait legs ripened with well-marbled muscle and strained out, growing longer and stronger out of a perfectly toned, heart-shaped ass. Her rack had always been pedoliciously underdeveloped, which deficit of maturity she'd attacked with typically unsubtle D-cup bolt-ons. Now, her renascent cleavage ejected the saline and silicone implants like lanced boils, then regrouped and swelled into bouncing, perfect natural breasts. Her ribcage unhinged like a snake's jaw to make room for new vertebrae to support the udder perfection up front, and the two extra ribs she'd need to do that impossible thing Marvel superheroines and Varga pinup girls do with their hips.

From the neck down, my trashy nymphet had been remade into Raquel Welch. Upstairs, though, the skin split like a rotten rubber mask and red-gray bile soup jetted out to scald her shaking, maddeningly expressive hands.

And here, I'd always thought she couldn't act.

I crawled backwards across the checkered floor, watching it try to eat her and perfect her at the same time.

The whole cellar shook in the grip of at least a 5.0 tremor. Headshots fell and shattered and mirrored glass rained down from the ceiling like a blizzard of black ice.

I thought about getting the gun for all of two stupid seconds. I wasn't going to shoot anyone, but anything between me and the door was going to get fucked up. The butler stepped out of his alcove with his hands out like he was catching a little kid. My windmilling fists crowned his head and chest and sickeningly soft belly. He didn't just drop, he imploded. His head deflated and shrank into his shirt and his hands sucked up his sleeves. The moth-eaten old suit slouched to the floor, hiding whatever had filled it, now slipping down the Romanesque rathole in the back of the alcove.

I ran up the stairs on all fours into the dishwater predawn light. Down the road past the Maserati and the squad car. Not stopping to look behind me at the chateau/prison/castle/Gothic manor house that collapsed into itself with a sigh like an Oscar envelope filled with anthrax tearing open, or the gray reservoir slopping over its banks like a tub full of fat asses. Down the dirt road and over the gate. Down Mulholland past the white-haired lady jogger, the retarded cyclist and the blind dog-walker, each of whom stopped to take my picture. Hiding my face, I ran past them all, to where my car still sat parked on the shoulder.

Home.

No cops were waiting. No detectives came to my door. I didn't go outside. I thought I could outrun it, but the *E! Breaking News* came on while I packed my suitcase. In three minutes, I decided I was not going anywhere.

She was out of rehab early, and looking better than ever. TMZ's sheet-sniffers pimped rumors she spent the time in a spa and under a surgeon's knife again, but by God, she got it right, this time.

"She's back, rested and ready for a second chance," the closet case anchor snorted, but it wasn't a recovery. It was a goddamned resurrection.

Rosy cheeks, clear green-gold eyes without a trace of baggage, nic-stained fingers or ghastly pallor that we'd all come to know and loathe. No protoplastic lampreys wriggling under those intriguing, engaging, perfect features.

I switched to the local news and waited. A brief, heartfelt eulogy for LAPD officer Charles "Chip" Salcido, nine-year veteran, killed instantly just before 4AM, when his patrol car went off the dismantled bridge at Skirball Drive and plunged into early pre-rush hour traffic on the 405. The bridge, which was in the process of seismic retrofitting, will be renamed the Charles "Chip" Salcido overpass when it's completed in 2014.

I know I'll never leave here alive. When it gets dark, I can see the searchlights out there, searching for me. The soft-focus spotlight

BLIND ITEM

starshine glow is coming from the storm drain out front of my apartment.

I don't think it'll make any difference, but I deleted all the pictures, after making a couple prints. The compositions are nice——*Rodney King Behind The Green Door.* If anyone in this shitty city deserved to know, or if it would make any difference, then I'd send them to somebody. This thing is old and sick, and more than half forgotten by a new Hollywood that goes through reality stars like lightbulbs in a bug zapper. She's revived the old school of stardom, and her rise will be christened with a revival of the sirens and chanteuses of the Golden Age of the studio casting couch system…the return of the Great Old Ones. You will all fall down and worship her, and it won't need to hide what it does to me when it finds me, because the world will only have eyes for her.

Undead and Unbound

DEAD BABY KEYCHAIN BLUES
By Gary McMahon

I once wrote a hit record about this but nobody joined the dots or made the right connections. I didn't expect them to, not really; the names were changed to protect the innocent and the tune was one I borrowed from a long-dead bluesman with a better, prettier tale to tell.

I'm not saying this is exactly how things went down, but it's how I remember the events unfolding. And when reality fails us, sometimes our memory is all we have left, however unreliable that may be.

This story, then, is about the shadow that hangs over me, the darkness that's always behind me when I'm playing my guitar up on that lonely stage. Here is the origin of every song I ever wrote, each bluesy ballad and electric balls-to-the-wall rock anthem that ever helped make me famous…

Here's the low-down on Dead Baby Keychain Blues.

~*~

Uncle Dave usually came for a visit about twice a year. Although I always liked to see my father's brother, I also found him a bit strange. He rarely looked anyone directly in the eye when he was talking to them, and he always wore weird jewelry and clothes that never quite seemed to fit. He was a travelling man: he had a job in engineering that allowed him to go to a lot of places——Europe, the U.S., Asia, and South America——and he collected exotic items from all the places he went. Often he would bring me back a gift; if he knew that one of his family visits was set to occur close to one of his trips, he'd make sure he picked up something special just for me.

I was his only nephew, and even though he rarely showed any sentiment about anything, he sometimes told me that he believed our relationship was special. His wanderings, he said (usually when he and my dad had been drinking), reinforced to him the fact that family ties are the only ones worth a damn.

Then Uncle Dave stopped coming to visit. He and my dad had some kind of disagreement, and it felt like my uncle had been banished from our home. Dad drank more than ever, and he didn't cope well with the normal problems life threw at him. He seemed to withdraw, turning in on himself like a coiling snake, and his temper snapped more often than it had before.

He coped even worse when my mother died of a congenital heart condition when I was eight years old...something inside him was broken that day, and although his bad temper seemed to vanish overnight, so did his essence, the part of him that made him tick.

Two years after Mum died everything changed.

Uncle Dave started coming around again, but now he too was less vital, less colorful, as if a part of him had been erased. He still brought me gifts from his travels, but they were stranger, darker...sometimes it felt like he was testing me, just to see how hard he could push. What Uncle Dave failed to realize was that I preferred these bizarre gifts to the ones he used to bring me before Mum died. To a ten year old boy, they possessed a certain kind of magic.

The particular time I'm thinking of——the visit when Uncle Dave presented me with the gift that changed all our lives——it was not long after my tenth birthday. I was still a child, more or less, but when he arrived at our house, Uncle Dave, for the first time, shook my hand like I was a man. Every time before that he'd tousled my hair, given me a pat on the head, or hoisted me up onto his broad shoulders; but this time was different, he was different. And so was the gift he delivered.

"You've grown," he said as he bustled through the door and into the hallway. "My God, how you've grown."

I didn't know what to say so I just smiled and nodded.

"Let your Uncle in before you start pestering him, son." My dad rested his hand on my shoulder and maneuvered me roughly out of the way so that Uncle Dave could haul his oversized duffel bag to the bottom of the stairs, where he dumped it on the floor. Dad's grip was too tight. He left his hand there, squeezing me, for a long time after Uncle Dave went through to the untidy lounge.

After a lengthy pause, we followed him, my father and me. He let go of my shoulder and I went in first, eager to talk to my uncle.

"I have something for you," he said, sitting down on the armchair by the window and reaching into the pocket of his scruffy leather jacket. "It's from the Amazon jungle. I was there for a year, land-surveying for a big engineering project."

My hands began to tingle; my cheeks flushed hot.

"This," he said, pulling something wrapped in pale blue tissue paper from his inside pocket, "is very special. I'd never seen one of these before until a shaman gave me this one, and told me that it would protect me from evil spirits." He was smiling but he wasn't teasing me. The gifts Uncle Dave brought were never less than interesting and there was always some kind of story behind each item. I remember the blood-or-rust-stained machete he brought me back from Papa New Guinea; the tarantula under glass from East Texas; the human finger bone, a supposedly holy relic he'd somehow managed to smuggle into the U.K. from a village in Mexico.

"What is it?" My voice was tiny, barely filling my mouth let alone the room.

"Take a look," he whispered, clearly enjoying the atmosphere we'd created.

I took the package and opened my hand, staring at the wad of pale blue paper on my palm. Then, slowly and carefully, I began to unwrap whatever it was Uncle Dave had given me. It didn't take long; the wrapping was meager. At first I thought it was a small piece of stone, then a large piece of dried fruit——perhaps a plum——and finally, when I saw its face, I realized that I was holding what seemed to be a tiny human head attached to a silver keychain.

"I put it on there so I could get it through customs. I had it hanging from my belt all along, and nobody batted an eyelid. The idiots…"

"Is it…?" I could say no more.

"It's a shrunken head. The tiny processed head of a baby."

I stared at the thing. It was about the size of an egg, but raisin-black and hard as stone. The texture felt leathery against my fingers, and the small eyeholes and mouth had been sewn up tight with some kind of twine.

"It's a charm," said Uncle Dave. "The Shuar tribe decapitate their enemies and shrink their heads, using them as trophies. Sometimes, as in this case, they're used as protective talismans."

"Dave…" my father stepped forward, moving further into the room. "I think that's enough. He's only a kid, you might scare him."

I shook my head. "No. This is cool."

Undead and Unbound

Uncle Dave laughed. "I think your Dad's probably right——we can talk more about this stuff later, after dinner." The atmosphere in the room had shifted once again, but this time it was thick and heavy. In later life I'd recognize the sense of impending violence, but not then, when I was just ten years old and holding a treasure in my fist.

"Why don't you go upstairs so Dave and I can talk?" My dad didn't mean it as a question; this was a command.

So I left the room and climbed the stairs, opening my hand and staring again at the shrunken head. Then, once I was safe and sound in my room, I hung it from a nail on the wall above my bed. I sat on the mattress, staring at the small, wizened thing, wondering what kind of people would do this. Who would cut the head off a baby and then shrink it down, dry it out, and make it into a souvenir. I felt no horror as I examined the thing, only a vague sense of excitement, as if I'd been gifted something incredible.

The head gave no hint regarding its origin, it didn't let on at all. Its eyes were pinched and sightless and its mouth was never going to make another sound.

I took out my undersized six-string from beneath the bed and hammered out a few chords, never taking my eyes from the wall, and the thing that hung there, its sewn-shut eyes watching me. The music I made on the little guitar sounded different, it felt strange. Looking back, I think that was the first time I ever believed the people who told me I had something special. It was the first day I ever heard what they heard when I played that battered old acoustic guitar.

My own little eureka moment, watched over by a shrunken head.

Later, over a dinner of chicken pasta, a heavy silence seemed to grow and hang between my dad and my uncle. They didn't look at one another throughout the meal, and often one of them would touch me in a casual yet loving manner——a hand on the arm, fingers through the hair, the back of a hand pressed against my cheek——as if they were trying to prove some obscure point or compete in an unspoken game.

"So," I said, primarily to break the silence. "What's it like along the Amazon?"

Uncle Dave smiled and put down his fork. He took a drink of lemon cordial and pushed back his chair an inch or two so he could lean back in an expansive manner. "It's amazing. There's constant noise——the trilling of birds and insects, the sounds of animals moving through the undergrowth——but at the same time everything seems so still, like the whole jungle is just about to let out a breath."

I listened avidly. I loved it when he started telling stories.

"You don't see any big animals, because by the time you've paused to examine the details they've moved on, unseen. All you see are the smaller things: a procession of ants carrying huge leaves, dung beetles rolling their balls of waste, big hairy spiders looking for the next meal. And everything is capped off by the canopy, this huge green roof that seems like it's miles above you. Everything is in green shadow; a strange murky half-light."

Dad coughed into his fist. Because of the tension between the two men he clearly didn't want to speak, and I could tell that he was unhappy about the direction our conversation was taking.

"What about the Indian tribe…and the shrunken heads. The one you gave me. How did they do it?"

"I was told that it was taken from a newborn——the baby of a rival tribal leader. They lopped it off and skinned it, then placed a wooden ball inside the flesh. It was treated with berries and special herbs and spices and dried out with hot rocks and sand. They smoothed it down, molding the features, and then finished it off by rubbing the whole thing down with charcoal ash."

My right leg was twitching. I'd never been so excited, and yet so utterly terrified. "So it is real? It's not a fake?"

My dad coughed again into his fist.

"Yes, it's real, pal. I only stuck it on that keychain to get it home. So I could bring it back…just for you."

Dad jumped up, his chair jerking sharply backwards across the floor. There was a pause then, just a second or two, when nobody did or said anything, and then Dad stalked off out of the room, slamming the door behind him.

Uncle Dave wasn't looking at me; he was staring at the closed door. "You still play that guitar?"

I nodded, then realized that he wouldn't have noticed. "Yes. The one you bought me——I still have it. I play it every day."

"Are you any good?"

"People tell me I am. They say I have talent."

He nodded. "It runs in the family."

I had no idea what he meant——not then——because my dad had never played an instrument in his life. My mother had been tone deaf.

"Keep at it, son. Don't let your dreams die, and never, ever let anyone try to kill them." He was still staring at the door, as if he were talking to my dad and not me. "People——family, even——will try to hold you back, to spoil your ambition and take away the thing you want most. Just…just keep at it. Never quit." Then he went silent, and put his head in his hands. I wasn't sure if he was in physical pain or just trying to stem the flow of tears.

I went out into the hallway and found my dad standing there, with his back up against the wall. He was balling his fists and staring at the floor. His face was paler than I'd ever seen it.

"Dad?"

He shook his head and lifted his eyes. "It's okay, son. Don't worry. Your uncle and I…we've had a little argument. Adult stuff. Things you won't understand."

"I'm sorry, Dad…"

He took a step towards me, moving away from the wall, but stopped short of reaching me. His eyes were moist, shiny. I looked back at the kitchen door, behind which my uncle's eyes were the same. "You don't have to be sorry. This is…it isn't your fault. None of it. It's our fault——all of us. Me, your uncle, your mother…"

"What? What's Mum got to do with all this?"

His eyes widened. He realized he'd gone too far, said too much. When he stepped back against the wall I heard a soft thump as his heel clipped the wooden skirting board. He started to chew on his bottom lip. "Nothing, son. I'm just tired. My head's all over the place right now. Me and your uncle, we have things we need to talk about." Again, he started squeezing his hands into fists. The knuckles went white and the skin around them was bright red.

I decided to get out of there and leave them to it, so I went back upstairs to my room. Once I'd closed the door, I picked up my guitar and started to strum. There was a tune there, I knew it, even at that age, but for the moment it was lost to me, buried by layers of something I didn't quite understand. I looked up at the wall, where I'd hung the shrunken head key chain, and it was no longer there.

Panicked, I put down the guitar. It was dim in my room; I hadn't bothered switching on the lights. The last of the day's illumination bled through the window blinds, but it was only enough to allow me to see the shape of my environment and not the details. I remembered

Dead Baby Keychain Blues

Uncle Dave saying something similar about the Amazon jungle.

Movement behind me, and a faint scurrying sound. I turned around, dropping my shoulders, and could have sworn that I saw a tiny puppet-like figure with a too-large head scuttling across the floor at the base of the wall. It vanished under the bed, lost in shadow, and I crept towards the spot, holding my guitar like a weapon.

I approached the bed on my knees and once I got there I gently lifted the edge of the quilt, the part that was trailing on the floor. Nothing moved under there; the darkness was still. Then, sickeningly, I heard it again, the sound, but this time it was over on the other side of the room.

"Where are you?" My voice was soft, scared. "Why are you here?" For a second I thought it might be my mother's ghost.

I heard laughter, soft and muted, and for a moment my entire body froze. I gripped the guitar tighter, hugged it to my chest. It was no longer a weapon, but a comfort, something to hold on to while I waited for the thing in the dark to go away.

Then a strange thing happened. The fear receded and I remembered what Uncle Dave had said about never quitting, keeping the dream alive. I plucked a chord, and heard laughter again, and then the sound of small scampering footsteps faded as my visitor ran out of the room.

When I looked up, at the spot on the wall where before I'd seen only a bare nail, the charm, the fetish, the shrunken baby-head was once again hanging in place. But this time, bizarrely, there was a small, rudimentary body dangling from its neck. Somehow the thing had changed; it had begun to form a torso and a set of spindly arms and legs. It should have been funny, but it wasn't. It wasn't funny at all.

I stood and walked towards the wall, stepping up onto my bed. The old springs sang a whiny tune. When my nose was level with the creature, I paused. "What are you?" My voice was louder this time, but sounded no less afraid.

I could have sworn that the thing twitched against the wall as I spoke, pressing its stick-like limbs against my woodchip wallpaper as if it were afraid of me reaching out to touch its withered form. But when I stared at it, the thing didn't move again. It just hung there from its nail, the new body that could just have easily been some strands of dark matter that had broken loose from the neck, adhering to its wrinkled flesh.

Undead and Unbound

I wanted my mum; I needed her then more than I ever had before, even when she was alive. But she was dead, and not even her spirit remained.

~*~

Dad tucked me in that night, as usual. He didn't say a word, just kissed me on the forehead and shut the door tight to the frame as he left. I listened to his footsteps as they descended the stairs, and then instantly I was asleep. What felt like seconds later I was awake again, and I could make out raised voices downstairs. I glanced above me, at the shrunken head, but it looked just the same. Then I slipped out of bed, padded across the room, and quietly opened the door.

I crept along the landing and sat on the top step, listening. I could tell they'd been drinking because their words were slurred, but still I got the gist of the situation; that they were having a proper argument this time.

"I've had enough of travelling. Of running." That was Uncle Dave.

"Then run the other way," said my dad. "You're not welcome here, not anymore."

"I need to put things right. I want the truth to come out. I'm sick of lying. I can't live like this any longer."

The sound of something being pushed or pulled, or simply shoved violently across the floor. "Then stop living." My dad sounded furious. "Nobody would care if you died, anyway."

The voices stopped and there was a moment when I thought I could hear every timber in the house begin to creak; then that moment was filled with the sounds of scuffling, of heavy breathing, of physical contact. Furniture shifted; there was the sound of a slap or a punch. Then the kitchen door flew open and Dad stumbled out into the hallway, clutching his cheek. "Get out!" He opened the front door and I could feel the draft of cool air even from upstairs. "Get the hell out and don't come back."

From where I was sitting they couldn't see me, but I could see them. I watched as Uncle Dave emerged from the kitchen, his arms hanging loose at his sides. He was looking at the floor, or at his feet. He walked slowly to the door, grabbed its edge, and slammed it shut, wrenching it from my dad's hand. "No," he said, softly but firmly. "Not yet."

I rose into a crouch and headed back across the landing, not knowing what was going on down there yet certain that I should not get involved. There were things beneath the surface, under and between the words, that I had a feeling it would harm me to know.

The small, dark shape of the fetish was propped up in the doorway when I got to my room. I could see it there in the darkness, wavering on its narrow legs, its head slightly bigger than it had been before. As I watched it reached out with liquorice-lace arms and seemed to gather the air towards itself, in a motion not unlike somebody folding sheets. The head bulged; the limbs swelled. It was taking on sustenance, becoming slightly bigger and more solid as the bruised emotions raged on downstairs. Once again I was put in mind of a puppet, something controlled by unseen strings and pulleys——an avatar of some greater darkness.

I blinked, trying to either dismiss the sight or cement it in my mind.

When it saw me, the thing darted off towards the bathroom. I ducked into my room, grabbed my guitar, and followed it. This thing meant us all harm; I could see that now. Whatever its purpose, there was no good in that withered, shrunken soul——if it even had one. This wasn't a charm, it was a curse. And whatever animosity and bitterness I'd glimpsed hiding in the gaps between my father and uncle had woken it, somehow returning it to life. Because that's how magic works; it seeps through the gaps. Particularly bad magic, the kind that likes to destroy rather than create.

I had no time to turn on the upstairs lights, and I didn't want to summon the men from downstairs. I still couldn't quite believe what was happening, and even then part of me suspected that I might be dreaming or going mad. I was a precocious ten year old kid, my imagination had gone into overdrive, and some family feud had stoked up weird fires inside my heart. Nothing was certain.

I stepped softly into the bathroom, hanging on to that guitar for dear life. My bare feet made hardly a sound on the floor tiles and I was holding my breath as I crossed the threshold. I saw the shadowy thing hanging from the shower rod, the keychain looped around the stainless steel pipe. It was dangling, its legs a little longer now but still as thin, and as I moved towards it the creature laughed again.

"Come on, then," I whispered. "Come on, let's have you."

It swung twice, looped through the air, and landed on the edge of the sink, flailing the keychain behind it. Then, moving swiftly, the thing leaped onto the floor and raced between my legs. I swung the guitar, but missed. The strings twanged as the thing vanished around the doorframe, heading for the top of the stairs.

"Dad!" I ran after it, unconcerned now by the noise I was making. When I reached the top of the stairs I almost fell down them, taking the steps two or three at a time. Something small and black and skittering moved towards the lamp by the front door, and then the light went out.

I stumbled down to the ground floor and through the hard bright square of the open kitchen doorway I could see my dad and my uncle wrestling soundlessly across the dining table. It was like a silent film: there was no sound, not even that of their breathing. As Dad turned I could swear that I glimpsed the creature——demon, imp, whatever the hell it was——sitting atop his shoulders, riding him like a tiny jockey. It's hideously thin arms and rail-like legs were gripping the collar of his shirt, and its head——now almost the size of a tennis ball——bobbed obscenely, like a water-filled balloon held between sticks. But as quickly as it appeared, the vision was gone.

"No!" I screamed as I ran into the kitchen, and both men turned to face me. Dad's eyes were wide and white and bloodless, and Uncle Dave's cheeks had turned purple because of the grip Dad had on his throat. The nondescript creature was gone, but it was laughing, laughing, and I'm sure that only I could hear the sound——maybe it was just inside my head.

I swung at it with the guitar, breaking the fluorescent light and catching my dad a hard blow across the shoulder. Dad's grip relaxed; his knees buckled slightly, and he tipped backwards, crashing into the upright refrigerator. The damaged light flickered madly. Uncle Dave acted out of pure instinct——I'm sure of that, even now. There was no premeditation, no intent behind the action, just a reaction: one of self-defense. He had a carving knife in his left hand. I hadn't seen it before because his arm had been obscured by my father as he leaned across man and table, trying to throttle his brother.

Uncle Dave lashed out with the knife. The strobing light created a scene from a flicker book. Dad was standing closer than any of us had anticipated——and I thought I could see the tiny black bobbing head, the jittering threads of limbs that were wrapped in his hair, as the creature forced him to take that single step forward, towards the killing blow. The blade cut through the side of his neck, catching and severing the carotid artery. Blood spurted like water from a tap. He didn't last long, even when Uncle Dave realized what had happened and tried to staunch the flow with a handful of tea towels.

The lights continued to flicker.

~*~

Afterwards, as we waited for the police and the ambulance to arrive, Uncle Dave gave me the first solid clue as to why he and my dad had grown apart, the nature of the wedge that had come between them.

"I loved her," he said, cradling my dad's head in his arms. "I loved your mother, and I love you. We never meant any harm…sometimes things just happen, feelings come alive that should have stayed dead."

He didn't come right out and tell me that I was his son, but it was clear enough, even in that dim little kitchen with the light flickering like bottled lightning over our heads. He'd given me a guitar because he hoped I'd inherit his talent, and all the little trinkets from his travels were designed to keep him in my thoughts, to ensure that he was never truly absent from my life.

Without saying a thing I went back up to my room. I was crying but I felt strangely calm, as if the facts of my dad's death hadn't quite sunk in. The top floor lay in darkness, as though whatever powers were present here had brought with them a slice of their night-black world. I stopped at my bedroom door and looked inside. Hanging on the wall, from that single nail, was a small, blackened baby's head. Writhing beneath the weathered head was a bunch of spidery limbs, far too many of them to be human. It cackled as it hung there, pressed up against the wall, and, still laughing, it turned its awful, desiccated face towards me.

The thing had fed. It was sated. Now it could die again.

I ran my shaking fingers across the guitar strings. For some reason it felt like the right thing to do. Still does. The sound it produced was odd and tuneless, but there was a depth to it——a sense of potential——that stopped the breath in my throat.

I stood there and watched as the limbs withered, dropped away like autumn leaves, and the bloated head shrank, returning once more to its original size. It was over in less than a minute. That which had been dead, and had lived again, was now once more without life. In truth, I wasn't even sure if what I'd just seen had been real or a particularly vivid figment of my overactive imagination——I even tried to tell myself that it was a stress demon brought on by the emotional damage let loose by the violence I'd witnessed.

My face was wet with tears. My heart was clenched like a fist inside my hitching chest and I knew it would never open again. I hung my head and let the horror pass over me, washing me clean.

As I stood there shivering, I considered burning the damned keychain or throwing it away, but as the sirens approached along the street I simply took the charm back down from the wall and tied it to the splintered neck of my broken guitar. I knew then, right then, that whatever I had or had not seen this moment was now the source of my music. This creature was my muse; it represented the depthless darkness from which every tune I ever played would be born.

~*~ .

It hangs there still, the same dead baby keychain on the neck of my shiny new guitar. I carry it everywhere, a reminder of the people I left behind; it goes with me on each coast-to-coast tour and into every sweaty recording studio.

It's still dead, hasn't moved a muscle since that night. And if I keep on playing my blues, paying my dues, and never let my dreams curl up and die, I might just be able to keep it that way.

A PERSONAL APOCALYPSE

By Mercedes M. Yardley

The doorbell rang on a sunny Saturday morning, and I cracked my back before I answered it. Outside stood a zombie in a ragged brown suit and jaunty fedora.

"Yarga eigga blaaaaaaah," the zombie began in a friendly manner. He held a business card between his rotted fingers. I took it.

'Gregory P. Mills,' the card stated. 'Slicey! Dicey! Knives!'

Egads. "Not interested, thanks," I said, handing the exuberant card back, but the zombie was already reaching for his briefcase.

"Who is it, honey?" My wife Marian peeked over my shoulder. "Oh, hi, Greg. What are you selling today?"

The zombie brandished a knife, and grinned widely.

Marian nodded. "Ah, knives. We could use some. We could," she told me sternly, obviously watching my eyes roll. She put her hand on my shoulder and whispered, "Greg and Katherine are going through a hard time right now, honey. Why not help them out?"

The dilemma was this: Greg had been dead for four years, and his wife was just getting ready to remarry. And then the zombies rose. Greg had pigeon-toed up to Katherine in the chapel, pointed at his oxidized wedding ring and whimpered. The groom had fainted dead away and Katherine and Gregory had decided to work it out.

"It's awful," Katherine had confided to Marian. "Communication is simply nonexistent. And…things…have a tendency to just fall off." Marian's eyes had gone wide.

"Get some knives," she insisted again, and smiled at Gregory before scurrying off.

I turned back to Gregory, who was flashing the knife this way and that in the sun. "Aah? Aah?" he kept asking invitingly. Time was when a knife-wielding zombie would have inspired fear in the stoutest heart. Now it just made me want a drink.

"How much?" I asked, but Greg was in fine form. He probably couldn't hear me anyway, what with his eardrums all rotted out.

Next door the Gallagher girl was fighting with her mom, as usual.

"You don't like Jacob because he's a zombie!" The girl screamed. "Face it, Mom, you're a hater!" She stomped down the driveway.

"Sweetheart, it's not because he's a zombie! It's because, well…he's just so dumb! What kind of life would you two lead?"

Gregory was busy showing me how slicey and dicey his fabulous knives were. He was slicing through tomatoes with the greatest of ease. Aluminum cans. Filleting fish.

"I'd like two sets, Greg. Two." I held up my fingers, but Gregory was on a roll. He was humming some sort of song to himself, like he was a cheesy magician dazzling me with his showmanship. Suburbia fell away only to reveal the Las Vegas stage. Da da daaaaaa, da da daaaaaaa.

My next door neighbor shambled outside with a chainsaw in one hand. I waved at him. He gurgled something brightly and saluted before the chainsaw roared to life. The kids screamed and ran around in frenzied circles. My neighbor ambled over to the old dead tree in his yard and cut it down.

"Too many movies, kids!" I shouted, but they couldn't hear me over the grating buzz of the saw.

Greg's head flipped up in surprise. I smiled and waved my hand to encompass the neighborhood. He grinned back, and dropped his head down to his work.

I thought of my daughter, Sandra. I thought of how many of her young friends had died in the last few years. A case of leukemia, a couple of drunken car crashes. Three suicides. People that she thought she'd never see again, and here they were, all hanging out at the bowling alley today. A couple of them were even fairly chatty, not dead very long so their tongues and brains were pretty well intact. They'll never be nuclear physicists, of course, but that's another positive about zombies: they tend to be a pretty happy-go-lucky bunch if they're well fed.

We did not have a stray animal problem, that's for darn sure.

I brought my attention back to Greg, who had one last trick to show me. He took the knife, and pantomimed a man perplexed by having something specific to cut, but alas, nothing Slicey! and Dicey! enough to do it. What should he use? Gregory shook his head and threw imaginary less desirable knives over his shoulder, and then his face lit up when he discovered Slicey! Dicey! Knives! He took the thickest and sharpest out of his briefcase. He gazed at it in delighted wonder, and tested its blade with his thumb. He winced and shook his hand theatrically. I made a mental note to clean up the pieces of flesh that flew off. Then Greg brandished the knife in the *coup de grace*, the ultimate demonstration of the knife's power.

"No, Greg, no! That's not necessary."

Gregory P. Mills sawed his left arm clean off.

~*~

I threw the knives on the kitchen table and leaned against the counter.

"I will see that in my dreams, Marian. In my dreams!"

Marian slipped her arms around me. "I'm sorry, honey. But I appreciate it. You're a good man."

I snorted and she hugged me harder. "It's true," she said. "How many other men would even be willing to give Greg a chance?"

"I didn't want to give him a chance. You made me do it. You're a tyrant. A Nazi." I kissed the top of her head. "Greg was a good guy. Is. Is a good guy. There's just not much of him left."

"I know, Sweetie."

"I think…that they're coming for him. All of them. I've heard that they're going to do a Clean Sweep."

Marian went still. I heard the sound of her breath stop abruptly. It was a very long time until it started up again.

"Are you sure?"

"No, I'm not. It's just some rumblings that I've heard."

"Martin, we can't ignore this." She squeezed her arms around me tighter. "We can't."

I wasn't so certain. I'm not a straight up Necro, which is what they call the Zombie Lovers, the people who advocate for the living dead. But on the other hand, I don't hate zombies, either. They're basically harmless. Not all of them, of course. There are occasional zombies who make it tough for the rest of them, but that's just like the rest of us. One or two serial killers tarnish the good name of humanity as a whole. That's just the way it is.

"Martin." Marian's voice was firm, almost steely, and that wasn't like her. I focused on her brown eyes.

"What?"

"We have to do something about this. You know that we do."

Again, I was silent, and I could see that Marian was frustrated.

"They're our friends. They're our neighbors. We can't just stand by while a bunch of vigilante 'Protectors' roll around and kill the people of our community! What are they supposed to be protecting us from?"

"Marian, I don't want to get involved."

Her eyes caught on fire. It's the only way to describe it. "You are being lazy and a coward, Martin Fitzgerald, and I won't have it. It's Greg. It's Gregory and Katherine that you're turning your back on!"

Maybe I shouldn't have said it, but I was tired and frustrated and annoyed that I'd brought the concept of a Clean Sweep up in the first place. "Marian, you can't kill somebody who is already dead. Gregory P. Mills died over five years ago. Katherine is living a miserable life with a corpse. If we save him, are we really doing anybody any favors?"

In all of our years of marriage, Marian had never, ever walked out on me before. Until now.

~*~

"So. Clean Sweep Friday night. Be sure to keep your daughter home."

"You ever try to keep a teenage girl at home on the weekend?"

"If I were you, I'd try awfully hard."

I slammed my work locker closed. It gave me a second to think. I turned to Jimmy Tumble, a guy that I'd been working with for years.

"Homes?"

"Not yours."

We were buddies, in a way. Which was probably why he was telling me about the Clean Sweep in the first place. My daughter Sandra was a Necro in the first degree. She was always hanging out with her dead friends. Jimmy had just saved her life.

I met his eyes, tried to keep my voice as light as I could, but it didn't work. There was still emotion there. "Thanks," I said, and had to clear my throat. I looked down at my work boots so I missed Jimmy's nod, but I didn't miss his bear-like hand clapping my shoulder.

"She's a good kid," he said, and left.

He's right. She is a good kid. And so were the rest of them. I knew most of them since they were little, and they were still little in my eyes.

A Personal Apocalypse

The fact that they had died and somehow come back, well. That didn't change anything. I thought about Sandra, the way that she squinted when she was really thinking hard. I thought how I would feel if she had been in that car crash that took her best friend Veronica. I thought about how happy I'd be to have her come back to me, no matter what state she was in. I'd be the biggest Necro of all Necros if it meant that I could have my daughter sleeping in her bed every night.

These parents had lost their kids once before. I decided that it wasn't going to happen again.

Usually I head to the pool hall for an hour or two after work to wind down, but today I drove right past it and ended up at the bowling alley. Sandra was usually there in the evenings. Tonight was no different.

"Hey, Dad," she said, and gave me a surprised hug. Her friends waved. A couple of Living, a new guy that I'd have to quiz her about later, and the zombies. Veronica gave me a bright smile, and pointed at her hand.

"I lost two fingers in the bowling ball today, Mr. F. It was pretty gruesome." Veronica had a slight lisp due to her swollen tongue, but other than that, she was pretty much the same as she had always been. A little skin discoloration notwithstanding.

I swept Veronica up into my arms, too, and the slightly moldy smell of the grave only made me hold her harder. Sandra's eyes were wide with shock.

"Dad?"

I set Veronica back down, and looked at all of the kids. They were eying me carefully.

"Gaaarrggggg," a boy in back mumbled. A couple of others nodded.

"You know something."

It was the new boy, a living, breathing boy. He put his arm around a couple of the zombies, and his black eyes bored in to me. "What do you know?"

I knew that this kid was a punk. And I'd have to let him know that later. But right now, maybe he could be useful.

"You guys need to come home with us. Right now. Something big is going on the day after tomorrow, and we need to talk about it."

"Yeah? What?"

I looked at the Punk. He stared back at me.

"You, especially," I said. I needed to assert who was in charge here. "Don't forget to wipe your feet when you enter. My wife keeps a clean house."

There. That'll show him.

I'd called ahead so Marian wasn't bowled over by a gaggle of kids wandering into the house. They all wiped their feet carefully. Zombies can be an obedient bunch if they want to.

"So. Tell us," Punk said. He stood in the middle of the room, his body buzzing with energy. The rest of the kids sat down on the couches and floor around him.

"They're doing a Clean Sweep on Friday."

There was a gasp from everybody that breathed. I waited a second for it to sink in, and then I said the rest of what I knew.

"They're coming into homes, looking for zombies."

"Into homes?" This was Marian. "What a violation! There are laws…"

"What, for zombies?" The Punk again. "They're second class citizens. The Living can do whatever they want."

Marian stared him down. "Technically, they can't."

"But realistically, they can."

Marian's eyes softened. "Who's undead at your house?"

The Punk glared back at her. "My mother. Died when I was a little kid."

"And she came back to find you?"

"Yeah."

Marian smiled. "Good mama."

The Punk looked taken aback. "Well. Yeah. She is."

"Sit down, Jeff," Sandra said, and pulled him onto the seat next to her. They looked at me.

"So, what do we do, Dad?"

That's the thing. I had no idea. I go to work, I come home. I like to take care of my yard; I love my wife and kid. That's who I am. I'm a simple guy.

But I know right from wrong. And I know that a group of hoodlums racing around decapitating about fifty percent of our town's population isn't in the right.

"We do something." I said. Jeff the Punk stood up again.

"We fight."

Telling a bunch of zombies to fight against humankind, that wasn't in my plans. But then I'm not sure what my plans really were. To have everybody holed up in my basement until Saturday, I suppose. But

A Personal Apocalypse

then what?

"They're never going to leave us alone," Veronica said. She looked sad. "I mean, it's true. I can't get into college, I can't get a job. I'm smart. I work hard. But that doesn't matter." She looked ready to cry, but she had no fluid to spare.

Sandra put her arms around Veronica. Veronica turned to look at her.

"I never wanted to die," she said. That did it.

"You're right," I said wearily. Marian flicked her eyes to mine, but I didn't return her look. "We fight."

~*~

They went home and spread the words to their friends and family. That night in bed, Marian asked me, "Are you certain this is the right decision?"

I said, "When am I ever certain about anything?" I was planning the battle inside of my head. In the movies you light a cigarette and zombies shrink back from you in fear. But in real life, that wasn't the case. They needed a good bash in the head or decapitation to die, and then you burn their bodies to make sure they can't rise again. But humans? We can be hurt any which way. We're really very fragile. It would be easy to defend ourselves. To take the Living out.

I heard Marian whispering something, but my mind wasn't on it. I was too busy concentrating on our survival.

"I don't know what to do," is what she said. "Martin. I don't know what to do."

~*~

The next day there was a hush on the house. Sandra was over at Veronica's, and I was checking out our garage for heavy arsenal. Tools. Lots of tools. I grabbed an armful and brought them inside. Marian was washing dishes in the sink. I dumped the tools on the kitchen counter, and my eyes caught sight of something shiny.

"Thank goodness we bought those Slicey! Dicey! Knives!" I said with appropriate jubilation, and wiped my hands on my jeans. Marian didn't turn to look at me. I picked up a wood axe from the pile on the table and took a few practice swings.

"What?" I asked her. She didn't answer and I was getting angry. I was working hard here, and she didn't appreciate it.

"Fine," I said, and left to go back to the garage. "Don't help me."

Marian threw her plate down in the sink, and I heard it shatter. She whirled to face me.

"What exactly do you think you're doing, Martin?" she hissed at me. I was surprised to see her so furious. "Who do you think you're going to be attacking? Jimmy Tumble? Our pastor? You're suddenly so eager to fight, but you don't seem to realize who you'll be fighting!"

I drew myself up to my full height. She snorted.

"Are you trying to intimidate me, Martin? Are you going to attack me now?"

She sidestepped past me and ran up the stairs. I started to say something cutting to her, but then I caught sight of myself in the hallway mirror. I was wearing a cheesy shirt that said *World's Greatest Dad*, holding an axe, and had my mouth open to yell at my wife. I shut it, but it didn't seem to make a difference. She already knew everything that I was going to say.

Sandra bounded into the house right then. She paused, testing the ambiance. Then she looked at me.

"Can I see that?"

I automatically handed her the axe. She felt the heft in her hand, and tried a two armed swing like she was holding a baseball bat. I tasted acid.

"Give that back," I said softly. I was thrumming with a rage that I couldn't put a name to.

"Why?" she asked me, and took another clumsy swing.

"Right. Now."

She glanced at me, did a double take, and handed the axe over.

"I wasn't hurting anything," she said.

Not yet. But she planned to. She planned to take that axe and bring it down on the head or hands of somebody that she's known since birth. And she had picked it up from me.

I got Jimmy on the phone.

"Jimmy. This thing going down tomorrow. You can't do it."

"What's that, Martin? Got a lot going on. Can't hear ya."

He wasn't alone and obviously didn't want to go in to it. I talked fast.

"I've thought about it and it's crazy. A lot of people are going to get

A Personal Apocalypse

hurt."

"Good talking to ya but this dang phone reception…"

"Jim. They know."

He paused. "They do?"

I nodded although he couldn't see me. "They do. Call this off. It's going to get bloody."

His voice changed. "Thanks. You're a pal. Gotta go." He hung up.

I slammed the phone down in frustration. I turned around and saw Marian standing in the doorway. She held out her arms, and I walked into them.

"This thing," I said. Sandra with the axe. Jimmy with who knows what. My head was going to blow. "They're all going to kill each other."

"I know."

"We have to get out of here. Warn who we can, and then leave. Tonight."

"I'll get the bags."

I made a few more phone calls while Marian grabbed Sandra and started throwing things in a duffle bag. I was hoping that we had more time. But we didn't.

I heard the screeching of wheels outside, and Marian was screaming, "They're here! They're here!" Car doors opened and slammed, and I ran to the front door and threw it open.

It was chaos.

Trucks and cars had parked randomly all over the street, blocking all access. People spilled out of them, some wearing bandanas, some wearing baseball caps, some not bothering to cover their faces at all. Each was armed with something heavy or sharp in his or her hand. People streamed across lawns and into homes like ants.

A heavy figure strode purposefully up my steps. It was Jimmy Tumble with a red bandana pulled over his mouth and nose. In his hand he held a wooden baseball bat with nails driven through it.

"Cripes, Jimmy!" I swept Marian and Sandra behind me. Jimmy shook his head.

"I'm not here for you or yours, Martin. I'm just checking for Undead."

I still kept my arm between him and my girls. "I thought you weren't going to search my house."

"Things changed."

I nodded, and stepped aside to let Jimmy in. He did a cursory glance around the place, threw open some doors, and then he smiled at us. It was bizarre, seeing my old friend standing in my living room crudely armed. His smile didn't make me feel any better.

"You're good, Martin. I knew you would be. I just had to…you know."

"I understand."

I didn't. I didn't understand any of this. I looked outside and saw a group of men pull a zombie and her small son kicking and screaming out of their house. They held her down while another man sawed off her head, and then they started on the little boy.

"That's Gloria and Howie Kenvall! He's only seven years old, for crying out loud!"

Jimmy didn't even glance over his shoulder. "He was seven when he died, Martin. He's an abomination, is what he is. We're giving him and his mom a little peace is all."

Sandra was crying behind me, and Marian was trying to soothe her as best she could. I watched Howie Kenvall kick once more and then lie still. The man put down the saw and started the zombies' corpses on fire. He stayed to watch them burn while the others ran off to search for more victims.

My eyes met Jimmy's. "Howie wanted to be Chuck Norris when he grew up. You were at their funerals, Jim."

"The first time, yeah."

Sandra suddenly screamed. Jeff the Punk was running down the street, firing a gun at anything that moved. If it was a zombie, then it would live. If it was human, it wouldn't.

Two men fell to the ground. Jim said, "Stay inside," and charged after Jeff.

I grabbed Sandra from Marian and pressed her face against the front of my shirt. I didn't want to see what I knew would happen.

A man in a baseball cap threw him arms around Jeff the Punk and knocked him down. Jimmy and another man caught up to them and started beating the boy with whatever they had in their hands.

A nail-filled baseball bat. Something that looked like a pruning hook.

I couldn't stop staring. This was madness. I could hear screams and snarls and the sound of flames from zombie corpses all over the neighborhood. It was our own personal apocalypse.

My neighbor from next door was hauled out of his garage. He

A Personal Apocalypse

growled and bit the shoulder of one of his captors, who swore and punched him in the face. The zombie spit out teeth. He was dragged over to the stump of the old dead tree that he had cut down yesterday. They forced him to kneel over it while a wiry man severed his head with an axe uncomfortably similar to mine. I had to close my eyes.

"Dad! Look!"

Sandra pointed, and my heart dropped.

They had Veronica.

The principal of the middle school had her by her beautiful dark hair, while an oversized woman was trying to bash her in the head with a gardening hoe. Veronica grabbed the end of the hoe and there was a brutal tug-of-war.

"My baby!" screamed a voice, and there was Veronica's mother, all 5'2" of her. She ran to Veronica's side and grabbed on to the hoe as well, yanking back as hard as she could. The heavy woman staggered forward.

The principal pointed at Veronica's mother.

"Get back," he said. "We don't want to hurt you, just the monster."

Veronica's mother turned and faced the man squarely. "My daughter," she said calmly, "is not the monster here."

The hoe was torn from her hand and came down heavily on the back of her head. She crumpled. The lawn turned sticky with blood.

"Mom!" Veronica screamed, and turned back toward the woman who was staring at the lifeless form in shock. With a snarl unlike anything that I have ever heard, she lunged at the woman. The black hair tore out of her head and the principal was left holding a large clump. The heavy woman hardly had a chance to make a sound before Veronica killed her.

It seemed like everything had happened in slow motion, but I hadn't even made it across the street by the time Veronica had stepped over the woman's body and started in on the principal.

I dropped by Veronica's mother's body and checked her pulse even though she was obviously dead. Veronica growled and whirled at me, but I raised my hand in defense.

"It's me, Sandra's dad," I said. "I'm not the one that you want to hurt."

She stopped for a second, and then suddenly blood was spurting from the stump of what used to be her neck.

One of the guys from work ran by with something that looked like a machete. He was in the zone, decapitating zombies left and right. I thought I was going to be sick.

A zombie covered him with his huge body, ripped his head apart, and licked the inside of his skull. Then I really was sick.

The zombie turned to look at me.

It was Gregory P. Mills.

"Greg," I said in relief. "This is nuts. You have to hide!"

He lumbered toward me.

"Quick! Run to my house, they've already checked inside of there. You should be safe."

Greg loped clumsily toward me. I slid back on the grass, too stunned to get to my feet.

"Greg, no! What are you doing? It's me! You know me! I bought your stupid knives!"

Gregory was howling now, and that galvanized me. I lurched upright, but I wasn't fast enough. Greg pounced me, and I felt a splitting pain in my skull.

And then Greg fell away.

I saw Katherine behind him, exhausted, holding the biggest and baddest Slicey! Dicey! Knife! that I had ever seen. Greg's head hung by his hair from her other hand.

"Katherine," I whispered.

"It's a relief," she told me. "A relief." She closed her eyes.

Screaming brought me back to reality. I held my hand out to her.

"Come with me," I said. Dreamily, she gently set Greg's head down and took my hand. I dragged her back across the street and into my house.

Marian threw the lock behind us. "I think that we should get into the basement," she said. "Sandra's already down there."

Without a word, I pushed Katherine toward the stairs, and took one last glance outside. Carnage. There was so much smoke that I couldn't see who had been pushed to their knees on my front lawn. It wasn't simply zombie versus the Living anymore, though. That much was for sure.

I grabbed the axe from the kitchen and joined the ladies in the basement.

"All this time, they've been restraining themselves," Katherine was saying. "Greg has worked so hard to be so decent, to fight against his nature so that he didn't scare anybody. But look where it got him." Her eyes were strangely glassy. Shock, I suppose. "It got him killed. It turned him into a victim." Her mouth hardened. "They're not going to restrain themselves anymore. This night has changed everything. Everything."

I knew that she was right. I knew that we were experiencing an event that would be remembered forever. It was like 9/11. Like the day the zombies rose. Today was the day that they threw off their humanity and turned against the Living. It was the new apocalypse. I looked down the axe and hated the thing, but I still didn't put it down.

Undead and Unbound

THE UNEXPECTED
By Mark Allan Gunnells

Hudson was halfway down the stairs, on his way to the kitchen for a midnight snack, when someone began pounding on his front door. He halted, stood as still as a statue, and glanced down into the darkened foyer. He could see the door rattling with the force of the pounding. There was no pause in the assault, just a continuous hammering that boomed through the house like small explosions. Hudson was just considering going back upstairs for his pistol when he heard a familiar voice call his name from outside.

With an exasperated sigh, Hudson continued the rest of the way down the stairs. Unlocking the deadbolt, he left the chain on and opened the door a crack. Through the gap, he could see a tall, scrawny man with thin brown hair and an acne-scarred complexion standing on the stoop. The man continued battering the door for a full minute before realizing it had been opened.

"Oh, thank God!" the man gasped, sagging against the doorframe. "I was afraid you wasn't home. Hud, man, you gotta let me in."

Hudson cocked an eyebrow. "Do I?"

"C'mon, man, it's freezing out here."

"It's late, Pete. You shouldn't be here."

"I didn't know what else to do. I done left you about a half dozen messages."

"And the fact that I didn't answer them should have been a clue."

"Don't be that way, Hud," Pete said, shivering in his light camouflage jacket. His breath steamed out of his mouth in little puffs. "We brothers, after all. Family ought not treat each other this way."

"But family should show up uninvited at almost one o'clock in the morning and expect a warm welcome?"

"I didn't know where else to go, man. I got a real emergency."

"Then I suggest you call 911."

"It ain't that kind of emergency."

Hudson had started to close the door but stopped, his curiosity aroused despite himself. Finally he said, "What kind of emergency is it then?"

"*Your* kind of emergency."

Hudson closed the door, leaned against it for a moment, then released the security chain and opened the door wide, letting in a cold gust of wind and his brother. Pete was jittery and fidgeted around the foyer, a bundle of nervous energy as if he were amped up on caffeine or some other stimulant. "Nice place you got," he said, bouncing around like he had springs on his heels.

Hudson, wearing only a pair of boxers, crossed his arms over his bare chest and pinned his cousin down with a sharp glare. "You've got five minutes."

"It's Shelia, my old lady. She's…well, there's just some strange shit happening to her, Hud."

"I didn't realize you were married."

"Married? Hell no, but we been shacked up together going on six years now."

"And what is this 'strange shit' you say is happening to her?"

Pete ran a shaky hand through his mousy hair and let out an even shakier breath. After a momentary hesitation, during which Hudson grew increasingly impatient, Pete finally said, "I think she's possessed, man."

Hudson couldn't suppress a derisive snort. "That's impossible."

Pete's face fell and for a moment he looked as if he were going to cry. "I thought you of all people would believe me, Hud. I mean, this kind of freaky clusterfuck's right up your alley, ain't it?"

"I guess you could call me an expert in freaky clusterfuck situations, and I'm telling you as an expert that it is impossible."

"Why?"

"The spirits of the dead do not possess the bodies of the living," Hudson said mechanically, as if reciting facts memorized for a lecture. "That just isn't the way ghosts work."

"Well, maybe it ain't a ghost. Could be a demon or something."

"Demons are merely myths; I've seen nothing in all my years in the field of the paranormal to suggest that they actually exist."

Pete twined his fingers into his hair and looked as if he were at the point of ripping it out by the root. "Look, I don't know exactly what's happening to Shelia, okay? But something's happening to her, and whatever it is, it ain't natural. All I'm asking is for you to come take a look at her. I live no more than twenty minutes from here. C'mon, Hud, just come look at her."

"You have any money?"

Pete blinked and actually recoiled a step as if slapped. "Money? You gonna charge me?"

"Well, this is what I do for a living."

"Yeah, but I'm your bro, man."

"So if I were a doctor, you would expect free medical care?"

"Of course."

Hudson opened the door and said, "Goodnight, Pete."

"No, man, you gotta help." Now Pete was crying, and he made no move to leave. "I ain't got much. I got laid off from the textile plant last month and I ain't been able to find work nowhere else. I got nothing to give you."

"Like I said, Pete, good——"

"My car," Pete practically screamed. "It's all I got to my name besides the trailer, and the trailer ain't paid for yet. I'll give you my car."

Hudson glanced out the door and saw a bucket of rust on wheels parked at the curb, the engine sputtering while thick smoke coughed out of the exhaust. Hudson turned back to his brother to say no, but what he saw there made him pause. He felt no sense of family loyalty——he and Pete had never been close, and the two rarely saw one another these days——but the desperation and fear in Pete's eyes was quite real and difficult to ignore. Hudson looked back at the car; maybe he could get a couple hundred bucks for it by selling it for scrap.

"Fine," he said, turning back to his brother. "Wait here while I throw on some clothes."

"Oh thank you, Hud, thank you." Pete made as if he were going to embrace Hudson, but Hudson sidestepped him and hurried up the stairs.

~*~

Less than five minutes later, they were in the car, pulling away from Hudson's house. Hudson sat in the passenger's seat, feeling the car shudder and rattle around him. He wouldn't have been surprised if the car had simply fallen apart; it seemed to be held together by nothing more than glue and hope. If he'd had his own car, he would have insisted on taking it, but it was in the shop having work done on the transmission.

Pete, seemingly oblivious to the fact that his car was on the verge of utter collapse, gripped the steering wheel so tightly that the veins in the back of his hands stood out like ropes beneath the skin. He stared out the windshield with a look of fierce determination. The road ahead was illuminated by only one working headlight, and Pete inched the car's speed up ten miles above the speed limit, causing the car to shudder even more violently.

Hudson said nothing. He wanted to ask about Shelia, get a better idea of what kind of situation he was about to walk into, but he sensed that Pete was not ready to talk about it. Whatever it was, Hudson was confident he could handle it.

"You know," Pete said suddenly, not bothering to look over at Hudson, "I been thinking a lot lately about back when we was kids."

"That was a long time ago."

"Yeah, I know. Remember when we used to spend the summers at Grammy Bethel's house?"

"If you can call a four-room hovel a house."

"Better than the shack we lived in, huh?" Pete said with the ghost of a smile. "We had to share a room and a bed."

"A bed?" Hudson said with a humorless laugh. "It was just an old mattress laid right on the floor."

"Yeah, and at night the rats would come out. Remember, we came up with the system where we'd sleep in shifts to keep 'em off us."

Hudson didn't reply, but his silence had substance and filled the car with a dangerous atmosphere like the electricity that charges the air before a storm. Idly, he rubbed at a faint scar on his right elbow. He'd fallen asleep on watch one night when he was nine, and a rat had sneaked up and sank its teeth into his flesh. No trip to the hospital for a rabies shot; his grandmother had merely slapped a Band-Aid on it and told him to stop being such a crybaby. Hudson didn't like to think about those times, had built a wall out of time and money between himself and his past.

"Anyway," Pete said, apparently sensing his brother's desire not to go down this particular branch of Memory Lane, "I been thinking about that summer at Grammy Bethel's right after Grandpa Earl passed."

The Unexpected

"I was seven," Hudson said right away, surprising himself. He remembered that summer well; it was the summer that changed his life, that set the course for who he would become as an adult.

"Yep, you was seven and I was five. When we first got there, Grammy told us that even though Grandpa was dead, he wasn't gone. That if we saw him roaming around the house, we shouldn't be scared of him. 'Course, we thought she was pulling our legs at first."

"Grammy Bethel always was a strange one. With her homeopathic remedies and astrology charts, I used to think she was a witch."

"Me too. But she was right about Grandpa. The first time I saw him, I'd got outta bed late at night to use the outhouse, and I saw him walking along in the field behind the house. I wet my pants right then and there. I was terrified for the rest of the summer."

Hudson laughed again, this time with genuine humor. "I remember. You made me follow you out to the outhouse every time you had to take a piss."

"But you wasn't scared, I remember that. Even that time we woke up and saw Grandpa standing in our room, just staring at us, you wasn't scared. You just said, 'Hey Grandpa Earl,' rolled over, and went back to sleep."

Hudson shrugged and said, "Grandpa Earl had never hurt me when he was alive; I had no reason to think he'd hurt me now that he was dead."

"And then near the end of the summer, he disappeared. Grammy blamed you, said you'd sent him away, and she was royally pissed."

"Gave me the worst spanking of my life with that old wooden paddle she kept next to her bed. Hell, sometimes I think my backside has never stopped stinging."

"What really happened? Did you send him away?"

"He made his own decision; even ghosts have free will. I simply told him that he wasn't needed anymore, that his work here was finished and it was okay if he wanted to move on."

"And he listened to you?"

"Grandpa Earl was always a reasonable man; death hadn't changed that."

Silence settled back between them like an old friend. Hudson glanced surreptitiously at Pete, musing that his brother was like a stranger to him. They'd had little contact with one another over the past three years, ever since Pete had asked for a loan of four thousand dollars and Hudson had vehemently refused. That was the reason Pete had kept his distance all this time, but Hudson had distanced himself from his family ever since he left home at the age of seventeen, just after he graduated high school. They were nothing but a reminder of a life he'd rather forget. Still, Pete was his blood, and he thought maybe he would help out without demanding the car as payment. After all, there was a time when they'd been willing to help each other out. Like with the rats. Perhaps Hudson still had some sense of family loyalty, just buried under a heap of time.

"So you and Shelia have been together for six years?" he asked, trying to sound interested. It had been so long since he'd taken a genuine interest in his brother's life that it felt a little odd, like walking backward.

"We been dating off and on since high school, but we been living together for six years, yeah."

"Why not get married?"

Pete looked at his brother as if Hudson had just asked him why he didn't shave with a chainsaw. "Why rock the boat? You know how the saying goes: if it ain't broke, don't fix it."

"I hear that."

Pete got quiet for a few minutes, his eyes fixed straight ahead but looking somewhere a million miles away. "I gotta say, though, I did think about asking Shelia to marry me when I found out she was pregnant."

"You two are having a baby?"

"*Was.* Shelia lost it in her third month."

"Oh," Hudson said softly, wishing he'd never brought up the subject. "Sorry to hear that."

For a frightening moment, Hudson thought his brother was going to start crying again, his face working as if overcome with muscle spasms. Finally he seemed to regain control of himself and said, "I wasn't there when it happened. I'd gone out hunting with some buddies for the weekend. Shelia was all alone, and I came back to find out I wasn't gonna be a Daddy no more. I ain't never gonna forgive myself for not being there with her when it happened."

Hudson could think of nothing to say, so he opted to say nothing. He had never been good at giving comfort, and he figured it would be best not to even try. Besides, what comfort could be given in a situation such as this? None that he could think of. Time was the only

The Unexpected

panacea for that kind of pain.

Silence filled the car once again, and this time it stuck around. After a while, Pete turned the car onto a narrow road of loose gravel. A faded sign at the head of the road read, 'Happy Valley Trailer Park.' Hudson stared out his window as they bounced along the rutted trail. The land was flat for miles around, they certainly weren't in any valley that Hudson could see, and there was nothing about the dilapidated mobile homes they passed that seemed remotely happy.

The gravel road continued for almost a mile then abruptly dead-ended at a rock pile. To the left was a lone trailer sitting several hundred feet apart from the others. It seemed to be slanted, the right end slightly higher than the left, cardboard and plastic covering over one of the windows.

"Ain't much, but it's home," Pete said with an embarrassed laugh, apparently reading the disgust on Hudson's face.

They got out of the car and headed across the dirt lot to the trailer. Cinderblocks had been laid underneath the door to create a makeshift set of steps. Pete unlocked the door, having to jiggle the key in the lock for a full minute before getting it to turn, and Hudson followed him inside. They were in a cramped living room stuffed with thrift store furniture, dirty dishes and empty soda cans littering most surfaces. Inexplicably, the far side of the room was dominated by a large, flat-screen television which Hudson was sure must have cost close to a thousand dollars. The room was dark except for the muted light from a lamp in the corner.

"She's in the bedroom," Pete said and led Hudson through the living room into a small kitchen approximately the size of a postage stamp. Pete stopped at a closed door, knocked lightly and said, "Baby, it's me, I got my brother with me," before opening the door and stepping inside.

Hudson crossed the threshold then stopped rather abruptly. The overhead light was on, shining down on a room that looked like a cyclone had hit it recently. Clothes——clean and dirty——strewn about the floor, more dishes crusted with old food sitting on a simple wooden desk, an old exercise bike with clothes thrown over it, a bed with no headboard shoved against the wall by the closet, a woman with stringy blonde hair and a careworn face lying atop the bed in a shapeless housedress.

But what had stopped Hudson in his tracks was the woman's

stomach. In all other proportions she was a small woman, petite even, but her stomach was large and swollen, a huge mound bulging at her dress.

"Hud," Pete said, "meet Shelia, my old lady."

"I thought you said she miscarried," Hudson said, turning toward his brother.

"She did, six months ago."

"I don't understand. She got pregnant again?"

"Guess again?" Shelia said, pushing up on her elbows until her back rested against the wall behind her. "I been to the doctor; he insists I ain't pregnant."

"He said it was something called a 'hysterical pregnancy,'" Pete said. "Something about her being so traumatized from losing the baby that her mind and body are reacting as if she still was pregnant."

Hudson nodded, unable to take his eyes off Shelia's stomach. "I think I've heard of that before."

"But that ain't what this is," Shelia said, wincing as she readjusted her position. "I can feel the fucker moving around inside me, kicking up a storm. Come feel for yourself."

Normally Hudson was not the type of person interested in touching pregnant women's stomachs, but this time he hurried to the bed, sat down on the edge, and placed his hand over Shelia's belly. After only a few seconds, he felt movement beneath her flesh, a distinctive kick.

"Incredible," Hudson mumbled to himself. "When was the last time you saw a doctor?"

"Four days ago. I don't think he was even buying his 'hysterical pregnancy' theory anymore, but all his tests showed that I wasn't pregnant. Think I freaked him out, he couldn't get me out of his office fast enough."

Pete had walked up to the foot of the bed but seemed reluctant to come any further. "What is it, Hud? Any ideas?"

Hudson realized that he still had his hand splayed on Shelia's stomach and he removed it. "If I had to hazard a guess, I'd say that the ghost of the child Shelia lost has not moved on but has stayed behind."

"*Inside me?*" Shelia yelled. Sweat had broken out on her face, dampening the hair at her temples and beading on the tip of her nose.

"Ghosts tend to haunt the places where they died. Technically, this child died inside you."

The Unexpected

"Can't you perform an exorcism or something?"

"This isn't a demon."

"Well, *something else* then. Can't you do *anything* to get rid of this thing?"

"I'm not sure." Turning to Pete, Hudson said, "If this has been going on for six months, why did you only now come to me?"

Pete glanced at Shelia then quickly away, as if the sight of her hurt his eyes. "Something, uh, something happened tonight."

"What?"

Shelia suddenly let loose with a high-pitched scream that reached a crescendo that could surely have shattered glass. Hudson looked down at her, and she was writhing on the bed, clutching her stomach. When the episode passed, leaving her even more drenched with sweat, she lay gasping for several seconds. Finally she turned to Hudson and said, "Two hours ago my water broke. I'm in labor."

~*~

"I don't get it," Pete said for the hundredth time.

He was sitting on the edge of the bed next to Shelia, who was propped up on her elbows, her knees bent and legs spread wide. Hudson kneeled on the bed between her legs, with no idea what he was going to do.

"I don't get it," Pete said again.

Hudson growled in frustration. "I told you, this baby is ready to come out, and since we can't very well take Shelia to a hospital to deliver a spectral infant, we're going to have to take care of it ourselves."

"But you said there wasn't no baby."

"There isn't, not in the physical sense, but the child's spirit is still here, and it has manifested itself through this phantom pregnancy."

"Oh God it hurts!" Shelia moaned. She was soaked with sweat now, looking as if she'd been dunked in a pool, and she seemed weak, on the verge of collapse.

"What's gonna happen?" Pete said to Hudson. "I mean, when the baby comes…what's gonna happen?"

Hudson just shook his head. "I don't really know, Pete."

"You ever done anything like this before?"

"As far as I know, no one has ever done anything like this before."

"I'm being punished," Shelia said suddenly. "That's what this is,

I'm being punished."

Pete took a damp washcloth he'd brought from the bathroom and began dabbing sweat off Shelia's forehead. "Shhh, don't be silly. You ain't done nothing to be punished for."

Shelia looked up at Pete, and her eyes were glassy with pain. "I got to confess something to you."

"We can talk later——"

"No, *now!*" Shelia said, and there was steel in her voice. "I didn't miscarry."

Pete leaned away from Shelia. "What do ya mean?"

"I never wanted no kid," she spat. "You were all excited about it, but I certainly didn't wanna have some little parasite leeching off me for the rest of my life. I ain't never wanted to be no Mamma. Then you went off with your buddies for the weekend, and I saw my chance."

"What are you saying?" Pete said, and Hudson noticed that he was squeezing the washcloth so hard that water was dribbling down his arm.

"I had an abortion," Shelia said through gritted teeth, cords standing out in her neck as another labor pain wracked her body. "I had an abortion then told you I'd lost the baby when you got back."

Pete looked too stunned to speak, and Hudson was pretty damn stunned himself. This changed the equation quite a bit. Spirits by and large were benign entities, but the ghosts of murder victims could be vengeful, looking for payback from those that murdered them. Hudson wasn't some right-wing nut who equated abortion with murder——as far as he was concerned, until birth the baby was part of the woman's body and she had every right to do with it as she pleased——but from the baby's perspective, Shelia could be construed as its killer.

Pete opened his mouth, seeming about to say something, when Shelia let out her loudest scream yet, arching her back and digging her nails into the mattress. Hudson could see her opening up before him, skin ripping at the edges, and he thought he heard the distinctive crack of breaking bone. Blood and mucus sprayed his hands. It was time.

"Can you see anything?" Pete asked, an edge of hysteria in his voice. "Can you see the baby?"

Pete's may have seemed like a stupid question, but Hudson knew it wasn't. Some ghosts manifested themselves as fully corporeal, others were insubstantial wraiths, and still others were completely invisible.

THE UNEXPECTED

There was no way to know how the ghost of the baby would appear, or if it would appear at all.

Shelia continued to scream, and Hudson leaned forward, snatched the washcloth from Pete's hand, and stuffed it in Shelia's gaping mouth, muffling her cries.

"What'd you do that for?" Pete asked.

"Do you want the neighbors calling the police on us? She's screaming like someone's killing her, and if things don't go well…"

"If things don't go well *what?*"

Hudson looked his brother steady in the eye and said, "We'll have a dead body on our hands."

Even in the grips of her pain, Shelia seemed to hear this and started thrashing her head back and forth, hair whipping around her face, biting into the washcloth. Blood and other fluids continued leaking from her as her skin stretched wider, and Hudson held out his hands. It was instinctual but impractical; he knew that ghosts had no substance, so even if the baby was corporeal, he wouldn't be able to touch it.

A shrill crying filled the air, and for a moment Hudson thought Shelia must have spit out the washcloth, but then he saw that her stomach was rapidly shrinking back to its original proportions, like a deflating balloon. The crying was all around him, coming from everywhere and nowhere at once. The baby had been born.

Shelia lay flat on the bed, panting and feeling her stomach. She removed the makeshift gag and started laughing, the sound hoarse and raw. "It's over, it's out."

Hudson looked up at his brother and was shocked to see him staring down at Shelia with unadulterated hatred and rage; it was rather frightening. The crying continued around them. "Pete," Hudson said tentatively, "you okay?"

"Give us a minute," he said flatly, not taking his eyes off Shelia. "I wanna talk to my old lady alone."

Hudson didn't argue. He climbed down off the bed and left the room, closing the door behind him. He stopped in the kitchen and washed himself as best he could in the sink before going into the living room and sitting down on a hard futon that smelled unpleasantly of sweat and Cheese Doodles.

Hudson could still hear the crying even in the living room. It seemed to fill the whole trailer, having no particular focal point of origin. After ten minutes, Pete joined him. He looked exhausted, as if he were the one who had just given birth, and there was something dead in his eyes.

"Everything okay?" Hudson asked, and was surprised to find that he was sincere in his concern.

"Told her I wanted her out. I'll give her a couple weeks to heal up then she can pack her shit and get out."

"Where will she go?"

"You think I give a fuck? She knew how bad I wanted to be a Daddy, and she took that from me."

The two sat together for a while without saying anything, nothing but the phantom crying breaking the silence.

~*~

When Pete pulled up to the curb in front of Hudson's house, Hudson turned to his brother and said, "I'll try to figure out some way to get rid of the baby."

Pete jumped as if he'd forgotten Hudson were there. "What?"

"Well, ghosts can usually be reasoned with, convinced to move on, but this is the spirit of an infant, and infants lack the intellect for advanced reasoning. But don't worry, I'll find a way."

"Don't."

"Don't what?"

Pete looked over at Hudson, and the deadness that had been in his eyes earlier had been replaced by need and longing. "Don't get rid of it. I don't want you to."

"Why not?"

Pete said nothing for a moment then looked away and muttered, "I always wanted to be a Daddy."

Hudson got out of the car without another word. He stood on the sidewalk and watched his brother drive away. After the taillights had faded in the darkness, Hudson turned and went inside.

INCARNATE

By David Dunwoody

On a dawn in mid-September, a man crossed the train tracks at the mouth of Hatchet Ravine, so named because it rested in a narrow, sloping valley which resembled a great hatchet-blow in the earth. He was covered from head to toe——hat, scarf, charcoal duster with straps and buckles running in and out of the material to secure various items in their respective pockets, heavy shirt and pants and knee-high boots. Beneath the hat, a steel mask with a beak-like protrusion covered his face. He paused before a freight car which sat a dozen yards from the tiny station. It was an ore jenny, wheels sunk into the earth, rust-eaten body cradled by weeds. There were letters scrawled on the side in stark white paint. The man withdrew a small notepad and pencil from his strange coat, copied down the words, then continued into the sloping forest.

I.

The man seated himself at the counter of a small café. The place was dark, boarded-over windows affording just enough daylight for him to maneuver about the room, and the counter was layered with grease and dust. He folded his gloved hands there and sat for a time. Then he rose, walked the length of the counter, stepped around the register and flipped on the lights. Fluorescents stuttered to life, throwing into sharp relief the creased face of a very tired and frightened woman.

She was at the grill, staring at the man through the window where servers slapped down orders and cooks clapped down plates of steaming food. The lip of the window was as filthy as the counter, save for the smudges where her fingers had gripped it before the lights had come on and she'd recoiled.

The man tilted the brim of his hat in greeting and asked, "Do you sell cigarettes?"

She didn't say anything. Thinking it might be the mask muffling his voice, he repeated the question louder. She still didn't answer. Maybe it was the mask's appearance, like that of an emotionless mechanical bird. Its curved steel beak was framed by eyes of orange glass obscuring his actual gaze. The man walked back around the counter and took the same seat as before.

The woman's expression was blank, but he could see her color slowly returning, and after a few minutes her mouth trembled with a barely-audible response. He leaned his head forward.

"Piper?" she croaked, as if she hadn't spoken in a very long time.

He shook his head. "No, ma'am. I can't risk removing the apparatus from my face, you understand——after being outside and possibly exposed to the plague which has confined you here. Who is Piper?"

This time the frailty in her voice was that of a woman in terror. "Him," she hissed, as if she regretted having spoken the name.

"I assure you I'm not that man," he said.

She nodded slowly. He couldn't be certain if she were reassured or not. She seemed to be in a state of shock.

He took out his notepad and the little pencil. "First name?"

"Mine or his?"

"Both, if you don't mind, in reverse order."

She thought for a moment. "William, William Piper. I'm Mary Nelson."

He muttered the names while jotting them down.

Mary came out from the back and took a dingy cloth from her apron. She tried to cut through the grime on the countertop.

"Do you have fresh coffee?" he asked.

She nodded and turned, then said, "I'd like to leave the lights off."

He grunted. She turned from him to reach the switch, and the room went dark. The sound of the percolator made him grunt again.

The woman asked him if he was the Devil. He said no, and she——in a more hesitant tone, as if this question were more foolish——asked if he was an angel.

"I'm a man," he said. "If I weren't a man I wouldn't need to wear this. It's protection against Piper's plague."

His garments were similarly strange. At least he figured they must seem strange to Mary Nelson, though in fact her uncovered face had been something of a shock to him. That anyone still alive in Hatchet Ravine didn't at least wear a kerchief over their mouth was extraordinary. She was clearly aware of the plague which had been visited upon her small town, given that she'd sealed herself up in here. In truth it was more of a curse, and not likely airborne, but it was equally unlikely that she understood that fact.

When she poured him a cup of coffee, he requested two spoonfuls of sugar and a straw.

"We only have artificial sugar now," she said apologetically.

He waved his hand in defeat, and she emptied two pink packets into the cup. Once he'd stirred the noxious poison in with the straw, he adjusted his mask so that he could place the straw through one of the beak's nostril-holes and drink that way. He felt her watching him, hunched over the cup in his bizarre garb, and his eyes studied her hands on the counter. They were young, delicate hands. He'd thought her to be in her late forties from the sight of her face, but realized recent events had probably aged her a decade or two.

"Are you here to help us?"

He pulled the straw from the mask and wiped the beak down with a kerchief from his coat. "I'm going to try." He handed her the cloth. "Your nose and mouth should be covered."

She took the cloth, turning it in her hands, likely searching for a monogram or label. "I didn't think the sickness was carried on the air," she said.

"I don't know that it is or that it isn't, but you shouldn't chance it, particularly when I've just come in from the outside. My gear protects only its wearer. It may still become contaminated."

Her head jerked up. She was staring past him; he knew at what, and took another slow draw from the coffee cup.

"How did you…"

She dropped the kerchief. "You said you were a man."

He grunted, slurped.

"What sort of man walks right through a boarded-up door?" Her voice broke as she answered her own question.

But he said, "I'm not a ghost," and continued drinking.

"I don't understand. I'm sorry but I don't understand." She was wringing her hands. He saw the thumb and forefinger of her right hand worrying at the spot where a wedding ring would have been.

"I travel along different thoroughfares," he said. "Time and space have very little meaning where I come from. Neither do 'where' or 'from', in fact, until I get here and then I'm from a place where I have been."

She gaped at him.

He said, "Let's call me a warlock."

"Why?"

"Because that's what I am."

"Do you have a name?"

"Gault." He flipped back through the notepad. "*Aid Lo Drub.*"

She refilled his cup. It was all she could do, he supposed, the only thing keeping her mind anchored in what she knew to be reality. "Beg your pardon?" she said with a saccharin edge. She was trying not to frustrate him, but that sweetness made him think of those pink packets and his stomach turned.

He cleared his throat loudly. "*Aid Lo Drub.* It was written on the jenny car out there. Piper did it, most likely. Maybe Gaelic?"

She shrugged at him. He drummed the little pencil against the paper and said, "He's the one responsible for the sickness, you understand? If he's left this as some sort of message, it's terribly important I decipher it."

"Of course I know he's responsible," Mary shot back. "Why do you think I spoke his name to begin with?"

He raised a gloved hand in concession. "Very well then. When does he come?"

"Just after dusk."

"How many hours does that give us?"

"Four or so." She pressed the kerchief over her mouth and stifled a fearful sound.

"I'll try to put this in layman's terms," Gault said. "Mister Piper was something of a warlock himself. By virtue of his unusual return, he has broken a number of rules. I'm here to assess the matter, then settle it. I'm not necessarily here to save you or anyone else. I'm not omniscient either, so I require some assistance. You'll help me?"

Mary Nelson nodded.

"Why haven't you tried to leave?" he asked. The tip of the pencil rested on a blank page. He waited.

"I don't know," she said.

II.

"Gail Millard called this morning," Mary told Gault as he stared at his notepad. "She said Piper went to the Eagan house last night. Jim

Eagan and his boy. Hasn't seen either of them today."

"Dead," Gault remarked softly, and made a few scribbles.

Mary sat at the end of the counter with a glass of water. She watched the ice melt and said, "People beyond the ravine, they must know, and have just left us for dead. The operator doesn't pick up anymore. Train used to come through every Monday, like clockwork. Hasn't come in a month. Roger Durrance used to sit out on the little platform there, every Monday, and he told us the train had stopped coming. Then he hung himself."

"Saw him," Gault mumbled absently.

Mary slammed her palm down on the counter. Gault adjusted his mask and looked up.

"Don't you *care?*" she cried.

He cocked his head just like a real bird, glass ports unblinking, then set the notepad down. "*Aid Lo Drub*."

"I don't know what it means!" Mary yelled, then shrank down, startled by her own voice and the way it bounced around the empty room. She shut her eyes and clasped her hands. The man in the bird mask stared.

"When did your husband die?"

"Oh." She shook her head, laughed a little. "That was long before all this. He was down in the mine——this town was built on top of a big iron vein, now there's no iron vein. Anyhow, there was an accident and he's still down there. Maybe that's why I've stayed up here."

"That and the train's stopped coming," Gault said.

She looked about to yell again, but the lines in her face smoothed and water began to fall from her eyes. Gault grabbed the notepad and re-read his scrawl.

After she stopped crying, he said, "I'm sorry about your husband."

"Thank you." She picked up his kerchief from beside her glass and blew her nose into it. "Oh…I wasn't even thinking."

"Keep it," Gault said. He removed his hat, massaging a head of thin gray hair with gloved hands. "Undead like Piper have a hard time communicating in modern tongues. That's why I thought maybe the phrase on the car was Gaelic. I don't know Gaelic." He lowered his head and swung it from side to side, stretching his aching neck, and continued kneading his scalp. "It could be something else though. Sometimes they try to write in the King's English and it just comes out a jumble."

Undead and Unbound

Gault replaced his hat and said again, "Aid Lo Drub…" he traced letters in the air before him. "*Rail.*" He wrote hastily on his pad.

"You think the letters are just mixed up." Mary started writing on the counter with her fingertip.

"Rail," Gault repeated. "That leaves…is there anyone here named Bud? Buddo? Odd…wait." He scratched through letters, wrote.

"*Odd Burial*," they both said at once. Gault cocked his head again. Mary smiled a little. "I like puzzles."

~*~

She'd tied a big dish towel over her face, and she looked like a bandit, only she was trying to break *out*, prying the boards away from the door with a hammer.

Gault paced behind her. "Tell me about Piper."

"I don't know much," Mary said. "I only knew his face. Everyone did. We all knew not to look at it, even before all this started, when he was alive. That hateful stare of his, he just waited for someone's glance to meet it and then it was off to the races." Boards clattered on the floor. "He was a drunk and a braggart. But he was more than that. He was evil. I always knew. Tom knew too. He told me to stay away from Piper. Whenever Piper came in to eat I made Eddie come out from the back and get his order. I could feel him glaring at me the whole time."

Mary turned and tucked the hammer into her apron. "Six years ago he died alone in that shack of his. We all figured it was his heart. Put him in the churchyard that same day, no service. A few people did drop by to spit on his coffin. They're all dead now. They were the first. But he keeps coming back, night after night. From the dead, I mean. I feel like I can say that to you and you know I'm not crazy."

He didn't nod, but said, "And?"

"Don't you know?"

He did, but he wanted to hear her account anyway, so she told him. "He stops at a house and beats on the walls. He hollers in this awful voice, like his throat's full of grit and mud and worms and maybe it is. He hollers for hours, going up and down the street. Then dawn comes and someone's dead. Whichever house he pounded on. Last night it was the Eagans."

"He's come back as a 'revenant,'" Gault said. "Do you know that word?"

Mary shook her head no.

"They usually don't cause this much trouble," Gault said. "They're usually after just one family, maybe two. A revenant is a sort of ghost, usually driven by a specific purpose. Some have been known to imitate corporeal form in order to fulfill their goal——often, revenge. Piper doesn't seem to have a clear agenda."

Mary shivered. There was a draft coming through the door now, and with it open just a crack they could see the sky stained reddish-orange above the trees as the sun began its descent.

"It's too late to go out," Mary said, and shut the door.

"The churchyard can't be far. I only need to see his remains——"

"You'll see more than a corpse if we go out there now!" Mary hissed. She started gathering boards. "Stupid, this was stupid." She began hammering frantically. Gault jumped as she let out a scream of pain. She spun at him, shaking a bloodied hand, and tore the towel from her mouth and shouted, "*Why me?*"

"I don't know," he said.

III.

"When the body dies, the spirit migrates to a new place," Gault explained. He and Mary were seated in darkness, behind the counter. His breath rasped within the mask.

"Sometimes it leaves this world entirely. Other times it will come to occupy a new body, or a place. But a spirit's former identity is not meant to return once cast off.

"The problem with Piper," Gault said, "is that we can't get a clear read on him. By all accounts, he seems to be a common heretic, an occultist who fancied himself something greater, but…his spirit is incomplete, scattered. The revenant——a sort of flesh-and-blood ghost, a walking plague——is only one piece of this puzzle."

"And you say you're a warlock…but you're good." Either she didn't understand the idea or just didn't buy it.

"There's nothing to be gained by probing my backstory," Gault said. "I'm an agent assigned a task. This isn't about me."

"It is to me. Just as much as it is about Piper. Try, just for a moment, to look at things from my side." Her eyes were pleading, so he sat back and opened his hands, to say *go ahead*.

"He's killing us all house by house, family by family, and you show up dressed like——like *that* with nothing but more questions."

"I've answered some of yours."

"Some isn't enough with what's going on out there!"

"Make do," Gault said, and looked down to fuss with a glove.

Her arms dropped at her sides. "Gault. I just need to know you're telling the truth——"

A distant howl sounded, a strangled curse that rent the silence. Gault heard Mary drawing herself into a ball. "*No, no, no.*" The breath from her nostrils grew labored as she clamped her hands over her mouth.

Gault listened to the night.

"*Maaaaaaaaaaaaa. Maaaaaaaaaaahh!*"

Mary had said the churchyard was in the deepest hollow of the ravine, and that had to be the thing's point of origin. Gault, however, wasn't sure which direction the sounds were coming from, nor how close or far away they were, not until the noise was right outside.

Mary sucked air into her lungs and held it. Gault heard her toes scratching across the floor as she trembled. Outside the door, the one they'd hastily boarded up an hour earlier, Piper moaned.

"*MAAAAAAAAAAAAAAAAAA…*"

It was an angry, infantile sort of sound, one devoid of any reason. Gault folded his hands across his knees and drew thin tendrils of breath into his lungs.

Another moan. Piper hadn't moved from the door. *He knew.*

Mary made the smallest, softest sound in her throat. She sucked in another breath. Again, "Mmm. Mmm." Somewhere in her viscera, behind those trembling hands, she was screaming. Gault's eyes had adjusted enough that he could see her entire frame shaking. If the vise-grip over her lips broke, and Piper heard, it would happen all at once.

She stared through the shadows at Gault. Her right hand slipped and her eyes went wide.

Both of his hands shot out and locked her wrists in place. He pressed until he could feel the grinding of her teeth through her bones. Through the cold glass eyes of the mask he willed her to remain silent and still.

Piper roared. The sound turned from the door, and Gault heard feet shuffling into the dirt road. Still he did not release Mary. Her fingers were crushed against her nose and he knew she couldn't breathe. Still he did not let go.

Feet shuffling back. A low murmur outside the door.

Behind glass ports, Gault closed his eyes. It was too late.

Then Piper moved away again.

They heard the pounding begin on some other building, someone else's shelter, and Gault very slowly relaxed his arms so that Mary could catch her breath. He waited until her shaking lessened before dropping his hands.

A female scream cut through the night and Piper bellowed.

"*GO AWAY! GO AWAY!*"

Mary clutched her legs to her chest. "That's Gail Millard," she whispered. Gault pressed an urgent finger beneath his beak.

The ringing of the phone was like the sky being ripped in two. Every buried scream exploded from Mary's body at once and she flung herself at the jangling, banging thing, tearing it down from the wall with a cry of "GOD DAMN YOU!" and slammed it against the floor. Gault threw himself atop it——it had stopped mid-ring but inside the mask all he could hear was that clattering death-knell echoing between his ears. He smothered the thing and then Mary's face was in his back. They lay stock-still. Gault blinked his eyes and gritted his teeth and tried to force the ringing from his brain.

Gail Millard wailed at the top of her lungs. Piper beat on her walls, and she beat back, sobbing, and then there was only the mad percussion of Gault's and Mary's hearts. No ringing. No moaning. Mary slumped to the floor beside Gault.

He lay awake until sunup. The time passed quickly, and he wondered if he had actually at some point fallen asleep. Picking himself up off the phone, he nudged Mary.

She looked at his strange visage and frowned, as if struggling in dream's veil; then she burst into tears.

"She just wanted help. I was her friend. I was all she had."

"There's nothing you could have done."

"She's dead now." Mary sat up. "I want to see."

"You shouldn't."

"We'll see her." Mary got to her feet and walked purposefully into the back. Gault heard splashing in the sink, clothes hitting the floor. "We'll see," Mary choked.

"All right." Gault rose and checked his buckles. He made his own coffee while Mary wept.

Undead and Unbound

~*~

"I haven't been outside in five weeks," Mary said. She stood still in front of the café, taking in the morning air, surveying the treetops. "It almost looks the way it used to. It looks exactly the same, really, but…"

Her voice trailed off. She started down the dirt road at a brisk pace, Gault following. He couldn't read her any better than he could Piper. She'd accepted that he was here to help, but seemed to resent his presence. He supposed she had simply resigned herself to numbness before he'd arrived and upset things. Strange how people came to prefer the devil they knew.

Gail Millard's house was just around the corner, nestled in the trees which encroached everywhere but the main street. It was a little box of a place, like all the others, with a single door and a single window. With the dish towel still covering her nose and mouth, still uncertain of whether the reach of Piper's curse was limited to his nightly haunts, Mary took Gault's kerchief and used to it take hold of the doorknob. She then stood in silence.

"We can skip this and go to the churchyard," said Gault.

She went in.

The front room was dark but for the shaft of light through the door. There was a small kitchenette in the back, stovetop piled with hand-washed dishes and a large towel draped across the sink. There was a narrow door which presumably led to a bathroom or closet. On a card table beside the icebox sat several half-melted candles and a stack of paperbacks. Besides that, on a Murphy bed, cradling a telephone, was a form tangled in a blue sheet.

Mary stood over the body. It was covered from head to toe, but the sheet was spotted with fluid and the creases of Gail Millard's body were drawn in blood.

"Don't look," Gault said.

"I have to."

"Don't punish yourself. It's pointless."

He thumbed through the paperbacks. They were all decades-old pulp thrillers. He opened the first one and began tearing pages from it, laying them atop one another on the edge of the table.

"What are you doing?" Mary asked.

Gault took his beak in both hands and gave it a sharp quarter-turn, counterclockwise, then removed it. Turning so that she couldn't see the hole in the mask, he unceremoniously emptied the beak's contents onto the floor. Crumpled balls of yellowed paper bounced over the carpet. He began stuffing new pages into the beak.

"Some use spices or dried flowers," he said, his voice oddly distorted even to him without the beak in place. "I like old books."

"Is that supposed to help protect you from the sickness?"

Gault snapped the beak into the faceplate. "No," he replied, "I just don't care for the smell of death."

"Why was she washing herself in here?" He plucked the bath towel from the sink. It was still slightly damp; he wrung a bit of water out and watched it run down the drain.

He barely managed to catch Mary's arm before she went through the narrow door. Pulling her back, Gault shook his head. "She had a husband?"

"No, not for a year now. She saw John Ayres a bit but that wasn't a romance, just keeping company."

Gault opened the narrow door and poked his head in. He saw the naked body of a young man, mottled with sores, lying gray and bloated in a bathtub.

He shut the door and turned to Mary. "John Ayres' home must have been struck some time ago. He came here before the plague finished him."

"Is he——"

"Take my word for it."

"She never told me they were together."

"Hmm." He went back to the card table and pocketed several of the remaining books. "Good ones. Strong smell."

IV.

Down into the hollow, past the tiny chapel to the shrouded graveyard.

Odd Burial. Gault surmised the body of William Piper had been buried facedown or otherwise defiled by his spiteful neighbors. Or perhaps it was just the opposite——perhaps he'd left behind unusual instructions for his interment, blasphemous rites, only to have them ignored by the people of Hatchet Ravine. There was only one way to know what had gotten his ire up and spurred his comeback.

As Gault and Mary made slow progress through the underbrush——ducking gnarled branches and stepping over crumbled headstones, searching the canopy above for any bit of sunlight——they heard a shout up ahead. "*Get out of here!*"

"Who is that?" Gault demanded, reaching into his coat.

"I think that was Mister Scrimm. The caretaker!" Mary took off past him. He started after her and caught his boot on a twisted root jutting from the earth. "Damn!" Gault pried himself loose and stumbled over a grave marker into the weeds.

He thrashed his way to a standing position and tried to orient himself. All the trees looked the same, haunted copses with diseased, drooping limbs. Then he heard the shout again. "*Go on, get out of here!*"

Then Mary: "*Wait!*"

He followed the commotion and emerged in a small clearing which looked to be the sunken, tapered end of the ravine. A few headstones dotted the barren earth, and Mary stood before one of them. A young boy cowered behind her, and leering at the pair was a man with wispy white hair and filthy coveralls. He raised a shovel threateningly——

The man stopped when he heard the cock of the hammer on Gault's gun, and slowly turned.

His angered expression went slack. "Who in the hell are you?"

"Set that shovel down," Gault said.

The man didn't move.

"He's a friend, Mister Scrimm," said Mary. "His name is Mister Gault."

"Is that a flintlock?" Mr. Scrimm squinted his eyes and wiped his forehead. "And what's on your damn face?"

"It's for protection," Mary interjected again. The towel she had been wearing was draped around her neck. She waved it at the old man.

"Oh." Mr. Scrimm seemed no less aggravated, but turned the shovel in his hands and stuck the blade into the soil. "What's everyone doing out here anyway? Are y'all loony?"

Gault put the pistol back in its pocket. "I've come to exhume Piper."

"You and the lady and a boy?" Scrimm's face twisted in confusion.

"The boy's not with us." Turning, Mary tousled the child's dark hair. "He's just frightened. I think he's lost his father."

"What makes you say that?" Scrimm asked. Gault stepped forward, equally interested.

"This is Boyd Eagan," Mary said. "Remember Gault, I told you Piper went to the Eagan house the night before last?"

Gault fished out his notepad and pencil. "Eagan. Right." To the boy he said, "Where were you then?"

"Please, he's afraid." Mary said.

"No he isn't."

Nor did he seem put off by Gault's lack of sympathy. The boy stared unabashedly at the mask; perhaps he didn't even know the man was a man. Gault knelt, and Boyd Eagan left Mary's shadow to study the beak more closely. He reached to touch it and Gault flinched away.

"If Piper was at your house, and you're alive, then you weren't in the house. Where were you?"

Boyd shrugged. "I dunno."

"You're lying." Gault said.

Scrimm nodded.

Mary crossed her arms and sighed.

"What?" Gault asked her.

"You're not going to get any answers by interrogating him. Boyd, were you out playing the night before last? Were you with somebody else?"

Boyd looked at her, and his gaze fell. "I runned away."

"Why did you run away, Boyd?" Mary asked softly.

"Daddy didn't want me around no more. Said he'd of killed himself already if he didn't have me around."

Mary took the boy into her arms. "You know he didn't mean it, don't you? He was just afraid like everyone else."

"But he did it."

"No he didn't. He didn't kill himself. He got sick."

"From the loud man?"

"That's right."

Gault looked past the scene to the gravestone where the confrontation had taken place. *William Piper.*

"I'll need your shovel," he said to Scrimm.

"No!" Boyd broke away from Mary and raced into the woods. She took off after him. Gault threw his hands in the air.

"If you think it'll put an end to all this——if you *know* so——I'll help you," Scrimm said. "I've got another shovel."

"Good." Gault pulled out a pocket watch. "We should have plenty of time before dark."

"They wanted to dig him up before, when it started, but I wouldn't let them near him." Scrimm tossed the shovel, brushed his hands on his thighs and pressed them into the small of his back. "I thought they were all crazy, saying he'd come back. I told them they couldn't disturb hallowed ground. See, I been laid off from the mine a good fifteen years now, and this is all I have."

Gault nodded, taking the shovel.

"Those men tried to kill me just for standing in their way. I was trying to be damn reasonable. The constable turned on 'em then. They killed him instead. Then they left. I guess most of 'em died off pretty soon after that."

Gault stomped the rusty blade into the ground beneath Piper's name. "Better get that other shovel."

"Gault?" Mary called from the woods.

"I'll be back," Gault said to Scrimm.

Scrimm headed in the other direction. "I'll get it started, but I don't have much of a back for digging anymore. Father Hale did most of that before the sick took him."

"Piper's curse."

"Call it what you want, he died like the rest."

As he reached the top of a steep slope, Gault found Mary standing with Boyd Eagan and a blonde-haired girl who looked to be about the same age. "This is Amanda Keller," Mary said. "Both of them have lost their parents."

"They've been running around in the night, then?"

"They were afraid and lonely," Mary said. He knew she was still offended at his attitude toward the work, but it was just that.

A crow cawed incessantly overhead. Gault looked the two children over, then said to Mary, "You should take them to the café. Let them eat."

"Of course. You'll be back soon?"

"Before nightfall."

He turned to head back to the churchyard, then glanced over his shoulder. "Boyd Eagan!"

The child turned. "Yessir?"

"How old are you?"

Boyd held up six fingers.

Incarnate

~*~

Scrimm watched while Gault grunted and growled and hefted the pine box out of the hole. Pushing it across the earth, Gault lost his footing and fell back into the grave. Landing hard, he felt the air blown out of his lungs and gasped for breath inside the mask.

"Why don't you take that silly thing off?" Scrimm grumbled. "That fiend walks past my place every damned night and I haven't got so much as a runny nose."

Gault heard the cawing of crows again and peered up at the sky. Orange-red. He checked his watch and saw it was seven.

"Not much time," he huffed, and swung an arm at Scrimm. "Help me out!"

Scrimm muttered a few complaints, but hauled Gault up with surprising strength.

Gault pried at the coffin lid. The nails, most of them only hammered halfway in, popped off with relative ease. Scrimm backed away as the wood groaned.

"The revenant itself is a spirit," Gault panted, "but proper treatment of the corporeal body will cut it loose from this plane." He tore the lid away completely.

There wasn't much left of Piper but bones and rags. He was lying on his back, arms folded, head at the top and feet at the bottom. So he'd been given a proper Christian burial. Only a black magician would have been offended at that. So it was, then. Piper may have been something of an amateur, but he'd known enough to lay a curse on this town.

"No heart to cut out." Gault drew a long knife from his coat and placed its teeth against the skeleton's neck. "Only——the head——" and the skull came free. He set it outside the coffin, replaced the knife and took out a black vial.

"Step further back," he said to Scrimm, and himself did the same as he emptied the contents over the skeleton. Flames leapt into the air. "Let it burn itself out. That's it."

"That's it? You're sure."

"Should be." Gault tossed in the skull. "If not…"

"If not what?"

"Nothing. Go home."

V.

If not.

Gault peered through a crack in the boards covering the front window of the café——he couldn't see much, but he was able to make out Piper's shambling form. What he could see of the man's visage was ugly and alive with rage. Piper's eyes were glowing embers, and there was something moving behind him——he was dragging something; that was why his walk was so curious.

The moon broke through a blanket of clouds, and Gault saw that it was Scrimm's body.

Gault gritted his teeth and kneaded his knuckles. What was he missing? Why had he failed?

An odd hunch had struck him earlier, one which he'd dismissed, telling himself he was overthinking the matter. But now he was convinced of it.

Piper's face remained in shadow. He dropped the body in front of the café and stood motionless.

Gault could hear the children whimpering behind him. Mary had her arms around them, but she couldn't keep their mouths covered. No matter. Piper already knew one of them was in here.

Gault drew his knife.

"The uninitiated warlock, he with the blood of the ancients but little knowledge, sometimes makes mistakes when trying to extend his life." He spoke softly, stepping gingerly across the room. "Sometimes the spirit is broken, one part bound to the former identity while the other migrates to a new body."

He came around the counter. Mary saw the knife and stiffened. "What——"

"Boyd Eagan," Gault whispered, and pointed the blade at the boy. "Six years old. William Piper, half-reincarnated. It's his life keeping the revenant tethered here."

Mary opened her mouth in protest, but he cut her off. "That's why he survived when his father didn't. It's the only reason. I knew it when I saw him, Mary. I've been doing this for well over a lifetime. Don't question my intuition."

"No, Gault."

"You know I'm right. Let him go. Give him over to me."

"He's a child, an innocent child. You're wrong."

"Keep quiet," Gault rasped. "Give me the boy!"

Amanda Keller grabbed Boyd's arm. "You're mean!" she snapped at Gault, then pulled Boyd into the back. The darkness swallowed them both before Gault could even raise the knife.

Mary seized his leg. "Let them go!"

He kicked her off and ran into the kitchen. Banged his knee on the corner of something, grabbed it and shut his eyes tight. Damn it, he'd almost forgotten that Piper was out there listening for them. Gault slowly felt his way along a counter. Nudged a pot, caught it before it went over, swore under his breath. He had no idea what the layout of this room was. They could be right under his beak, or behind him... no, there was a sliver of gray up ahead, an open door, and the night beyond that.

He stepped over fallen boards and out the door, looking from side to side. They'd likely gone into the woods.

"*Maaaaaaaaaaaaaaaaaa.*"

After the moan, a soft sound, one that could have been either a laugh or a choke.

My God.

Gault crept along the side of the café, stopping at the corner. He saw the edge of Amanda Keller's blue dress. She was standing in the street. He inched forward and saw Boyd Eagan in front of her, standing face to face with Piper.

"You kilt my daddy," Boyd said. He was trying to sound brave, to sound angry, but Gault could hear the roiling terror just beneath.

Piper stared down at the boy, unspeaking, unmoving.

"He didn't wanna die before. You did it. You're an awful thing."

Boyd stepped forward and screamed, "*An awful thing!*" and jabbed his fingers into Piper's substance. He dropped dead instantly.

A crow lit on the roof above Gault and screamed. Gault spun out of view, racing for the trees, heart thundering in his chest. He cried at himself to turn back, to save the girl, but his legs carried him so fast he felt like he was going to be thrown right off his feet. Then he was hitting the dirt with a *CROINK* as his beak was bent in half. The notepad fell onto the ground. In the moonlight he saw *Odd Burial.*

CAW!

Rolling onto his back, he saw the crow trotting toward him and, behind it, Amanda Keller.

Not *Odd Burial. A Loud Bird.*

It must have been Amanda's familiar, an otherworldly companion to the girl whose spirit had once belonged to William Piper. The writing on the car——intended as a message to her? She was Piper incarnate——had to be, if it hadn't been the Eagan boy. The way she had just watched that poor child go to his death…gods, she had used the boy as a red herring and Gault had fallen for it. He should have seen it in her eyes at the first. He should have known. Fool!

Boyd Eagan hadn't been some bloated corpse Gault had discovered. This was a child he had doomed. His frame sagged in the dirt.

Amanda approached slowly.

He raised the knife. "Monster. Not a child. Monster."

"I thought you were going to help us," she said.

The knife wavered. Gault said, "What——"

The crow lifted into the air and settled on her shoulder. Gault let out a wail as he saw its touch radiate through the child's body, her eyes filling with tears and then going blank as she died before him.

It was *the bird*. The goddamned bird.

Piper shuffled into view, his glowing glare fixed on Gault. "*Maaaaaaaaaaaaaa.*"

"A bird," Gault stammered, and chuckled. "You came back as a goddamned bird. You'd have been better off a pile of ash."

He saw Piper sneer, and the crow's beak split in a raucous laugh. Two halves of a wretched whole. The crow hopped toward Gault's feet. He kicked madly, screaming. He hurled the knife and missed by a yard. It passed through Piper's substance and clattered against the building.

Then Mary ran out the back door, snatching it up, and charged at Piper's back.

"No!" Gault cried. "*Not him!*"

Piper and the crow turned. Gault whipped the pistol out and fired. Black feathers sprayed through the air.

Mary slumped to the ground. Feathers settled around her. Then the air was clear——of birds, of spirits. There was only moonlight.

Gault crawled over to the woman, patting himself in search of his kerchief. It looked as if the lead ball had torn out of the bird's back and glanced off her arm.

That's right, she had the kerchief. He found it in her apron and pressed it to her arm. The pain stirred her eyelids, and she looked at him.

"*A Loud Bird*," she said. "I heard the crow and I knew."

"You meant to kill the crow?"

She nodded. "Piper would have gotten me first. Still I had to try." She smiled at Gault. "You look like a bird too."

He lowered his head. "Yes. I should have figured it out long before now. The message on the car *was* for me. I think Piper wanted me to figure it out, to rectify his blunder and free his spirit. But even proper warlocks make mistakes."

He grasped his beak and bent it back into place. "His bodies, the former and the latter, are both destroyed. He's gone. No one else will die."

"Does that mean you'll leave?"

"Yes." He lifted his gloved hand, her blood glistening on his fingertips. "But your kin will always be safe. Your children. I'll see to it. Just remember, none of us have ever known how to shoot."

"Us…?"

"The name was Nilsson in my time, not Nelson," he said. "But you remind me very much of my own daughter. And hers, in fact, and on down through the generations. All your kin did enjoy a puzzle."

There was a smile in his voice when he said that, and Mary was able to laugh a while, even after he'd gone.

Undead and Unbound

MARIONETTES
By Robert Neilson

From where he sat Redmond could see about a third of the doorway into the hall. Sometimes it was left open. Those were the good days. The dog would often come in. There had been others but the current one was the spit of Toto from *The Wizard of Oz*. Over the years the dogs, more than anything, had kept him sane. The old man never spoke to him. He hardly ever even came into the room. If he could have taken it all back he would have. A thousand times. He often wondered if maybe Smoky had been the lucky one after all.

~*~

The *White Horse* was never much of a pub. In the old days it had been a real kip; a place you only went if you knew the barman or were well armed. Then they turned it into a yuppie designer pub that no yuppie in his right mind would drink in. It was at the wrong end of the quays on the wrong side of the river. But it was near Redmond's bus stop.

Smoky was already at the bar and with a pint under his belt when Redmond arrived. "Redmond Clarke in the full of his health and the prime of his life. How are ya?" Smoky roared, slapping him on the shoulder.

Redmond smiled and shook his outstretched hand. "Good, Smoky," he said, his voice sounding low after his friend's vocal onslaught. "And yourself?"

"Never better. You'll have a pint?"

"Does the pope shit in the woods?"

They exchanged small talk while their pints settled. Smoky nodded towards a table at the back, near the wheelchair toilet. The tables around it were empty. "I need an electrician, Redmond," he said as they sat.

"I'm your man. I could do with the work. The moths in my wallet have turned cannibal."

"I know what you mean, bud. I've been doing a bit here and there trying to make ends meet. But there's not too many bits these days."

"If you're broke how are you going to pay me? I'll do you a good deal but I need to get paid."

"It's not that kind of job."

"What kind is it then?"

"I was doing some deliveries off a van and we dropped some stuff to this house. Huge place it was. Stuffed with antiques. You want to see it."

"I don't think I like where this is going."

"Hear me out. It's easy."

The legs on Redmond's chair screeched sharply as he edged away from the table. "Isn't it always?"

"It's not as if you haven't done it before."

"I was desperate. Jen was about to have our first baby. I hadn't even a quid in my pocket for bus fare. Never mind food, and stuff for the nipper."

"Well I'm desperate now and I need your help. I owe a bloke a lot of money. He's not the sort of bloke who'll wait. He wants the money or he'll send the boys around to mess me up."

"Oh Jesus, Smoky, I promised Jen I'd never do it again."

"It's a simple alarm. Nothing else. Take five minutes to crack. It's like he's askin' to be robbed."

"Please Smoky." Redmond hated the whine in his voice.

"You owe me." Smoky's voice was flat, matter of fact and brooked no argument.

Redmond knew he had no choice. He owed a debt and it was being called. He would be no sort of mate if he refused.

~*~

The dog limped in and lay on the floor in the center of Redmond's field of view. It was getting old. Soon, as before, the dog would disappear to be replaced by a pup. The pups were always lively and fun to watch though he didn't like the way they would sometimes worry at the cuff of his trousers. It was unnerving; he couldn't see the floor at

MARIONETTES

his feet because of the angle at which he sat. He would miss this one more than most. Some of the dogs had pretty much ignored him, though they had all come in to check him out occasionally. It broke the monotony.

Even the old man's appearances did that. Every so often he would run a vacuum cleaner over the floor and do a bit of dusting. Redmond knew there was staff in the rest of the house. Sometimes he could hear distant voices and sounds of domestic activity. But no-one except the old man came into this part of the house.

~*~

The break-in was, as promised, easy. The alarm was a joke and the locks on the windows were cheap jobs from a DIY shop. Once they were in all Redmond had to do was haul away the contraband. Smoky had very definite views on what he wanted and rejected every item Redmond shone his torch onto. "Just hold the sack open," he hissed.

"I'm only trying to help."

"Well you're not. I know what I can sell and what I can't."

"From watching the *Antiques Roadshow*?"

"Very funny. I have a contact in the trade and he's shown me what he can move. It's all going overseas."

"But not today," a voice said.

Both men froze. The overhead light switched on. A figure stood in the shadows just outside the doorway. Only his revolver intruded into the light.

"Place the bag carefully on the floor," the man in the shadows said. Behind him it was possible to make out other vague man-shapes.

When Redmond complied he continued, "Now, put your hands on your head. Both of you." The gun jerked at Smoky as he was slow to follow the instruction. "Interlace your fingers."

A tall, well-built man stepped into the room. At first glance he appeared to be fit and in his forties. But his face was a lattice of fine wrinkles with hair so white his scalp shone pink through it. Redmond had read in books about characters with eyes old beyond the evidence of their owner's appearance. Those that watched him from behind the revolver looked like they had been robbed from Methuselah.

The old eyes twinkled with malicious amusement. Their owner slowly shook his head. "You have no idea how much trouble you are in, have you?"

Smoky began, "Look, mister…"

A swift jerk of the gun cut him off. "The question was rhetorical. I don't want to hear your stupid voices unless I specifically ask you to speak. So shut up."

A bodyguard stepped into the light, maybe five feet eight tall, shaven head, squat body-builder's muscles squeezed into a dark suit. He held an automatic across his chest, tapping it meaningfully against a lapel.

The old man regarded them for a moment. "Drop your hands. You look ridiculous." He stepped closer and cocked the revolver. "Now, I'm going to explain something. Try to keep up." He subdued a chuckle. "You have come into my house to steal from me. You don't know who I am and for that I cannot blame you. I keep my life out of the public eye. But despite that, I am a very powerful man. In fact, I am the most powerful person you will ever meet in your sad short lives. The truth is I can do anything I wish. So I am going to shoot one of you." He paused archly then added, "Dead."

Redmond felt his bowels turn to liquid. In a very short time he was going to embarrass himself totally. But he was too scared to worry about that. He looked into the ancient eyes and saw truth and certainty in them. Hot tears burned down his cheeks. He began to mumble a string of Hail Marys under his breath.

Smoky began to protest. "Now hold on a…" A gunshot interrupted him. A flower of blood bloomed in the center of his thigh and he crashed backwards onto the floor like a toppled wardrobe. A second bodyguard moved into the room, looking as though he had been bought as the second one of a pair from Russian Thugs Is Us Dot Com. He blocked the door as though Smoky's fall had been the precursor to an escape attempt. Redmond's legs gave out completely, as though the hamstrings had been cut. He crumpled to his knees beside his prostrate friend. All the fight had gone out of Smoky. He curled around his shattered leg and cried, huge wracking sobs. The desolate sound of his friend only served to make Redmond more frightened. He squeezed his eyes shut, unwilling to face the reality of their terrible predicament.

"Now my cowardly friends, I have a gift beyond value for one of you. And I give it because I can." He knelt beside Redmond and slid the gun barrel beneath his chin, forcing the terrified burglar to raise

Marionettes

his head. Unwillingly his eyes ratcheted open and he looked into the face of his death.

The old man smiled. His ancient eyes remained frigid as the surface of Pluto. Redmond stared into those searingly cold orbs searching for a shred of humanity. There was none. He remembered to breathe. Somewhere in the back of his mind a voice began to count the breaths that would take him down to his inevitable death.

"So," the old man said, "which one should I kill? Either of you have any thoughts on the subject?"

Smoky groaned and unfolded a little. He looked directly at the old man. His brow furrowed slightly. He glanced at his partner then rapidly back to their captor.

Redmond knew the way Smoky thought. He was calculating what to say in order to give himself the best chance of survival. He had never been an intellectual giant but he had always been cunning. Redmond was too tired to play. The adrenalin that pumped through his body in the past moments had drained away. His impetus to flight or fight had ebbed. Now he was simply tired.

Smoky spoke through gritted teeth, fighting the pain for each word. "Redmond has more to live for. He has two little girls. A wife that loves him. Take me."

The old man laughed long and loud. He shook with amusement though his eyes remained frozen. He straightened then bent slightly to catch his breath. "I don't think I've heard one as funny as that in years." The laughter subsided to a faint cackle. "Take me," he repeated, mimicking Smoky's voice. "Take me." Then he laughed loudly again. "Very well," he said, shooting Smoky twice in the chest and once in the head.

He turned the gun on Redmond. "Get up before I lose patience with you."

The tremulous burglar struggled to his feet.

"I took your friend's life because I could. You understand that, I think." He opened the revolver and emptied the bullets into his palm, flipped it closed and held it out to Redmond. "This has my fingerprints all over it." He rummaged in his trouser pocket and came up with a tissue. Wrapping the tissue about the butt of the revolver he again held it out, like a birthday gift from the devil himself.

"This is all the evidence you will need. However, I must tell you, it will do you no good whatsoever. Bring it to the police with your tale about a bungled burglary and they will arrest you. No matter how careful you are the police will arrest you for the murder. They will tell you that the only prints found on the gun were yours. You might go to jail for a long time. I'm telling you this because it is the truth. I am above the law. I am beyond the law." He paused to give his words emphasis and whispered: "I am older than the law." His lips curved into a smile devoid of humor. He continued in a conversational tone, "Your friend's body will be found elsewhere. The police will never come here. They would never trouble me. Naturally you won't believe me without proof. So you'll go to the Garda and tell them your, frankly, fantastic tale."

Redmond opened his mouth but the man with the ageless eyes held up his hand. "I told you not to speak. I don't want to hear your stupid whining voice, ever." He turned and walked out of the room.

From the hall the old man's voice called, "Are you going to stand there all night?"

Redmond slowly followed him into the hall on legs that would have struggled to carry Bambi. The old man crossed to the door and opened it. Holding it wide he said, "Go. And take your most precious gift with you. If you ever come back here that gift is forfeit. Do I make myself clear?" after a moment he added, "You may reply."

"I understand," Redmond said.

"Good." The old man stood holding the door open until Redmond passed through. Then he gently closed it.

As Redmond stood in the driveway the house lights extinguished one by one. In the far distance he could make out the pale glow of streetlamps.

~*~

The dog, whose name was Fergie, sat up and began to indolently lick his genitals. Redmond averted his gaze as a matter of politeness. He strained to catch a glimpse of movement through the door but, as usual, there was none. It was winter. Redmond could tell because the room was cold. There was no artificial heating in this part of the house. He reckoned it was probably December. January and February were colder. March could be a killer too. If he was offered a wish it would be a close choice between extra clothing in the winter, a meal or human companionship.

Marionettes

The old man never spoke to him. He had not conversed with a human since the last time he saw his wife. That had been, by Redmond's rough calculation, fifty years before. He knew that there had been periods of extended unconsciousness. So he was really only guessing. Time had long ago ceased to have meaning. He didn't feel any older or any different from the first moment he was placed in the chair. His hands, sticking out from the sleeves of his black jumper, were the only part of his body he could see. The hands did not appear to have aged; there were no liver spots or wrinkles and the skin still looked pink and healthy. Even the hope of dying from old age seemed to have been stolen from him.

Fergie stood and yawned widely. "The old man is considering having me put down," he said in a curiously dispassionate voice. Redmond never got over the fact that the dog spoke with a distinctly Scottish burr.

"Does he think you're in pain?" Redmond asked.

"Naw. I crapped on the carpet in the hall outside his bedroom."

"That's not much of a reason for taking a life."

The little dog laughed. "Now that's funny," he said, breathing hard. "You above all people should know how little he values the lives of others."

"I guess," Redmond said.

"He thinks I did it on purpose."

"Why would he think that?"

"Because he's one smart old bastard," Fergie said.

"Huh?"

"I did do it on purpose you moron. God, it's easy to see how you got yourself into this mess."

Redmond ignored the dog's jibe. "Why don't you run away?" he asked.

"Why don't you?" Fergie replied.

~*~

As the old man had known he would, Redmond went straight to the police. He told them his story without lying to hide his guilt or omitting anything to try to cast himself in a better light. The detectives placed him in an interview room while they followed up on his unlikely story. They left him sitting there for seven straight hours. Eventually two of the detectives returned. The one who had introduced himself as Detective Sergeant Fallon said, "We have three problems." He held up one finger. "Firstly the only prints on the gun are yours."

Redmond had taken pains to ensure that he only held the gun with the tissue the old man had supplied. There was no possibility his prints were on it.

The sergeant held up a second finger. "Secondly, there is no victim."

"But Smoky's missing. Ask his wife. Ask his parents."

"Mr. McBride's wife told us she hasn't seen him in a year. His parents are dead. His brother says he might not see him for a year at a time. We went to his last know employer who told us he believed Mr. McBride had emigrated."

"But he was with me last night. I spoke to his wife on the phone six months ago. She called him to the phone."

"Sorry, Mr. Clarke. None of this adds up. I don't know what it is you're at but you'd better give it a rest before we lock you up for wasting our time."

Redmond felt himself awash in feelings of dread and resignation. He mumbled a question apologetically.

"What? I didn't catch that." Sergeant Fallon asked, an edge of aggression to his voice.

"You said there were three things."

"Yes. Of course." He held up three fingers and smiled. "Third. There is no house at the address you gave us. We looked. I don't think we could have missed a big place like that. Even if we sent P.C. Plod himself." He and his colleague had a good laugh at this police witticism.

Redmond mumbled something else.

"You'll have to speak up, Mr. Clarke."

"I said, the old man said this would happen."

"Really?"

Fallon leant across the table and slapped Redmond hard across the face. It happened so fast and with such ferocity that Redmond was as much taken aback as hurt.

Fallon leant in close and said, "Now fuck off out of here and don't ever let me hear your name again. If we ever have words again I'll make trouble for you that you'll never forget." Fallon smiled. "You wouldn't believe the sentence for being arrested after I warned you."

MARIONETTES

"But everything I told you is true."
Moving closer to his ear Fallon whispered, "I know."

~*~

It is said that blind people's remaining senses become sharper than normal. Redmond had discovered that he could hear minute sounds from within the house and his sense of smell had improved beyond recognition since his confinement. He could track the old man as he moved around and for a long time had been able to distinguish between different members of the household staff by their footfalls. He had never seen most of them but he had built up a picture of each one, even giving them names. He had an awful lot of time to indulge in such fancies.

He worked out that there were four bodyguards whom he thought of as the goon squad. At least two of them had been the shadows in the hall on the night he had broken in with Smoky. They had looked huge. They worked shifts so that there were always at least three of them on duty. The only thing Redmond couldn't work out was what they were needed for.

Redmond also followed the movements of the domestic staff. The old man had a personal servant who waited on him day and night. There was a heavy-set woman who did the cleaning and a tiny woman who did the cooking. She was the one who fascinated him most. He could not make up his mind whether she was anorexic or some sort of midget. Her tread and her touch were so light he found it hard to build an accurate sound picture. But he knew her through her cooking. In the beginning, the smells had driven him half crazy. He did not eat; did not need to eat and was not allowed to eat. But there was a psychological need for food beyond that of mere sustenance.

Over the years he had developed his sense of smell to the point where he could distinguish the components of the meals she cooked. Some of the spices and herbs he couldn't name but he soon came to know their individual aromas, and gave them his own names, for ease of identification. The one he thought of as rosemary was a particular favorite. And she used a lot of basil. The cuisine was mostly Italian in origin but she occasionally spiced it up, quite literally, with Indian and Thai dishes. They were his favorites, their pungency delivering a sensation as close to taste as he had experienced since his captivity.

Fergie was sure if the old man knew how much of a kick he got from the spicy aromas he'd cut it from the menu. He was nothing if not spiteful.

"You're telling me?" Redmond said.

~*~

When Redmond Clarke's eldest daughter disappeared he, naturally, went to the police and reported it. The officer on duty diligently took his particulars and reassured him that she would turn up at a friend's house or something equally mundane.

His wife rang the hospitals but there were no reports of an unidentified fourteen-year-old girl being admitted. Redmond plagued the Gardai with telephone calls. They dealt with him patiently and with great sympathy.

After she had been missing for a week he was at the end of his tether. He went to the local Garda station and demanded to see someone in charge. The station sergeant brought him into an office and sat him down. He told Redmond very calmly and still with great sympathy that they had made a short investigation of the situation and that the case was closed.

"Closed," Redmond yelled, jumping from his chair. "How can it be closed? My daughter is missing."

The sergeant appeared genuinely saddened. He placed a sympathetic hand on Redmond's shoulder. He said, in a quiet voice, "You have no daughter."

The gentle words smacked into Redmond like a steel toe-capped boot, driving all the breath from his body. He bent at the waist and sagged at the knees, holding himself up by balancing his hands against his thighs. The sergeant grabbed his shoulders and helped him back into the chair.

"I thought I'd seen just about everything in my years as a station sergeant. But you, Mr. Clarke, are something new," Sergeant Ganley said. "You obviously believe you have a teenage daughter and that she's missing. But all the records plainly show that you've only one child, a nine-year-old girl, and little Alice is safe at home. Maybe I'll call the hospital. You're clearly in need of psychiatric help."

Redmond realized he must sound like he was raving and so stayed silent.

Marionettes

"Maybe," Ganley said, "the best thing for everyone would be if you went home. You're not a criminal; you don't deserve to be locked up. Maybe you're having some sort of breakdown. But the best place for you is in the bosom of your family. I'll get a car to drop you off," he said.

Redmond looked up at him blankly, without hope.

~*~

Redmond could never be sure of the stuff the dog told him. Fergie had a perverse sense of humor and it was quite possible that a lot of it was fabrication. For instance, he claimed that the old man's favorite dish was seafood chowder that was made to a secret recipe known only to the cook. Fergie swore that the most secret of the ingredients was the cook's own urine.

Another of his stories concerned the old man's sexual prowess. The dog swore blind that no woman came into the house, except for servants, who were not subjected to his unusual demands and desires. He further asserted that the old man's penis, when erect, though thin, stood well beyond his navel in height. How the dog could know this was beyond Redmond but he found the conjured image difficult to dismiss.

"Has it got a barbed tip?" he asked the dog. "Is he, like, the devil?"

"Are you trying to sound more stupid than you look?" The dog licked his balls contemplatively. It appeared to be one of his favorite past-times. "He's just a man. But a very powerful man. You get to be smart and powerful when you've been around as long as he has." The dog cocked his head to one side. "Or maybe it's the other way round." He scratched behind his ear with grave concentration. "You think the government runs this country? It's people like the old man who let them. For show. So eegits like you don't get the wrong idea." The dog tilted his head as though listening to music outside a human's audible range. "Or is that the right idea?"

It was unwise to challenge Fergie over the veracity of his tales. The first time he had done so the dog failed to speak to him for a year by his best estimate. The only other time he had expressed doubt the gap in contact had been months. Fergie was merely a dog, but he was Redmond's only source of information about the world beyond his narrow field of vision.

~*~

Smoky's brother was a journalist. At the end of his tether, Redmond called Dom and begged for help.

"I write articles for technical journals," Dom protested after hearing Redmond's unlikely story. "How can I help?"

"You have contacts. You know how to track down information. I've got to find the old man. The house. Prove they exist."

Redmond knew Dom could hear the desperation in his voice. They had always got along well enough but he knew Dom would try to check with his brother before doing anything. He wondered what Dom would find.

"I can't promise anything, Redmond, but I'll make some calls."

When Dom called back he sounded calm, but Redmond was sure he could detect strain behind the façade.

"What's happened to Neil?"

For a moment the use of Smoky's given name confused Redmond. Dom continued' "I can't find a sign of him." He paused for a time. Redmond remained silent and waited for him to speak again. Eventually Dom said: "It's like I imagined him. I didn't though. Did I, Redmond?"

After a while Redmond said: "You find anything for me?"

"I checked the newspaper archive in the National Library," he said, brusquely. "I'll give it to you short and sweet then you'll forget we ever spoke. Right?" When Redmond failed to respond he repeated, "Right?" much louder.

"Right."

"The house exists though I could find no records for it later than 1937. The last and only listed owner is a Howard Crandell. Mr. Crandell was not a very nice man. He owned a slew of tenements in the city. He was murdered by two of his tenants in 1852. This is all a matter of public record. The tenants were never brought to trial——it was never clear in the newspapers why——but both of them were the victims of violent death within six months. There was one investigative story about the deaths. The journalist suggested——this was the Nineteenth Century remember?——that Crandell had returned from the grave for his vengeance.

"I checked for follow-up stories but the reporter was arrested shortly afterwards for stealing a pig and transported to Australia.

"I found two other mentions of Howard Crandall in the papers in 1933. He was in an altercation in a tavern in Fishamble Street. The fight was reported to be over a woman. Crandall had his head split open by a blow from an axe. According to witnesses the axe was embedded six inches into the skull and Arthur Stokes and Daniel Murray claimed that his brain matter could be seen through the hole. They claimed Crandall laughed and pulled the axe free. What happened next is not clear and the reporter apologized that the witness statements varied so dramatically he could not in all conscience choose one version above the others. But when the dust settled Crandall was gone and the guy with the axe had had his head torn completely off his shoulders and most of his blood drained.

"The story from 1852 and the one from 1933 both featured artist's impressions of Crandall. I'll email them to you. But they're definitely the same man.

"The only reporter to follow it up was from the *Irish Times*. He wrote a piece demanding that Crandall be arrested for the crime and he made a reference to several stories from the previous thirty or forty years about the Fishamble Blood Fiend. But mostly he had preyed on indigents and travelers so there were no real investigations by the police. The bloke from the *Times*, by the way, turned up dead a couple of weeks later. I'll send you his obituary.

"I cross referenced the Fishamble Fiend and got several hits between 1871 and 1958. One of the hits was Abraham Stoker. Ol' Bram was very interested in Crandall at one time. I tracked down a guy who had been mentioned peripherally in one of the reports. I've never met a more frightened person. When I mentioned the fiend he shut the door in my face and screamed threats and abuse. One odd thing though. He threatened to call the police, 'And you know who they work for,' he yelled. That was his ultimate threat."

Dom was finished so he stopped talking. After a moment Redmond said, "Did you come to a conclusion?"

"Just two things, Redmond."

"Yes?"

"Firstly, whatever sort of undead monster this Crandall is, you should get as far away from him as possible. Cut your losses."

"I can't do that, Dom. My daughter…"

"Second, you don't know me. We never had this conversation. If you weren't Smoky's mate we never would have had it. We'll never speak again."

"Dom…"

"I did what you asked. Now I'm out of it."

The phone line went dead. Redmond tried to call back a couple of days later but the line had been disconnected. The email attachment came as promised. It was two drawings of the old man.

~*~

Sometimes Redmond sat for days without trying to move; there was just no point to it. The night his foot lifted off the floor he wasn't even aware of why his muscles or mind attempted the movement. He wasn't straining against his imprisonment or aware of more than the usual discomfort his immobility caused. It simply happened. And when it did he was afraid to replace the foot. He held it in mid-air and lifted the other one. When it came off the floor he tried pushing his body off the seat. It lifted. Gingerly, he placed his feet back on the floor and attempted to stand. Nothing prevented him. For the first time in years he could move.

His head swirled. His balance was askew; it had been so long since his body had been perpendicular. His knees felt like those of a newborn foal. He leant an arm on the back of the chair. Listening intently for the sound of movement elsewhere in the house, he could hear none. His trembling legs walked him to the door. The hallway to the stairs was dark. For this he was thankful; it would increase his chance of escaping undetected.

Redmond used the walls to stay upright; he couldn't afford to wait for his balance to return. The stairs seemed Himalayan. Each step was a struggle as his knees attempted to fold. The front door felt like it was in the next county. Every painful stride toward freedom seemed to echo sharply in the silence of the slumbering house. The door, when it opened, creaked and rattled like a horse and cart clattering over the polished parquet floor.

Outside the night was cloudy and starless. Redmond staggered down the winding driveway. The road beyond was empty and black as pitch. He walked in the direction of the nearest lights. Turning onto a wider road lined with streetlamps he saw a car approach. It had a light on its roof: a taxi or a police car, either would do. He stepped into the middle of the road and waved it down.

It was a squad car. The guards were helpful and solicitous. Even to his own ears it sounded to Redmond like he was raving. He took several deep breaths. "You've got to help me," he said.

The passenger opened the back door and pushed it wide for Redmond to climb inside.

"That's what we're here for, Mr Clarke," the driver said.

The guard in the passenger seat turned from the waist. "The old man will be worried about you." He pulled the door closed.

"What? No. I…"

Both guards laughed. "Did you really think you would be allowed to escape?" They looked at one another and giggled harder. Redmond placed his hands over his ears to keep out the wretched noise. They collapsed into paroxysms of laughter, slapping their thighs, lolling helplessly in their seats. Redmond screamed at them to shut up. He was ignored or unheard. The laughter continued. He closed his eyes. His forehead sagged to his knees.

~*~

When his second daughter disappeared Redmond knew it had to be the old man. There was no other possible explanation. Once again the Gardai informed him in calm measured tones that he did not have a daughter to disappear. The school had no record of her. Her friends gave him sad distant looks of incomprehension. People in general began to treat him like a harmless lunatic.

Jen cried virtually all the time.

He went back to the old man's house. It took him days to find it. A butler opened the door before he had a chance to ring on the bell. Wordlessly, the servant led him through the labyrinthine ground floor to a library. The old man sat before a roaring fire, his back to the door, a leather-bound book balanced on his bony knees. Without looking around he said, "I knew you would come back."

Redmond stood in the doorway as the butler backed away down the curved hallway. He struggled to keep his voice even and rational. When people treat you like a lunatic you can begin to doubt your own sanity.

"You took my daughters."

The old man rose from his chair. "I gave you your life. Everything else is mine."

"Where are they you bastard?" Redmond crossed towards the old man, his hands bunched into fists. His attempts at a calm demeanor had deserted him at the first stress point.

The old man smiled and said, in a conversational tone, "Stop."

Redmond stopped.

"Turn around and walk to the door."

Redmond obeyed. Refusing never crossed his mind.

The old man directed him through the house and up two flights of stairs, taking him to a soon to become familiar room. A chair stood in the center of the floor. "Sit in the chair and don't move."

Without further conversation the old man left.

A week, a month, a decade later, Redmond could not be certain, the old man re-entered the room. Redmond's wife was with him. The old man whispered in her ear. She threw her head back and laughed, her long black hair flowing in slow motion about her neck and shoulders. Redmond ached to touch her. The old man began to slowly remove her clothing, sighing appreciatively at each tiny revelation.

Redmond screamed: "No!"

His wife looked directly at him. Their eyes locked. Hers were pools of infinite sadness shot through with soul-crushing dread. "Please, Redmond," she said in a high, cracked voice. "You must be quiet. For me."

The words sounded as though they came from a long way off. In her voice, abject terror was laced through with an absolute absence of hope. Redmond gritted his teeth and closed his eyes.

"No," she said. "You can't close your eyes." She sobbed but quickly caught herself and her voice steeled. "You must watch. The alternative…" She seemed to shrink in the old man's arms, like a balloon with a slow puncture. Her voice cracked as she continued. "The alternative is…" a tear rolled slowly down her cheek, across her top lip then dropped to the floor. "…not something you want to think about."

The old man smiled lasciviously over her shoulder as he slid her blouse along her arms. The ancient eyes glittered like ice on an airplane's wing. Redmond forced himself to stare into their putrid depths. Had there been anything in his stomach he would have vomited. His throat worked to emit imaginary bile. The performance had only begun but already his wife was being subjected to humiliations

MARIONETTES

he had never imagined. Already the pain was beginning to show on her face. Redmond could imagine no torture worse than that to which she had already been treated. Yet he knew the surface had only been scratched. He could only presume she was doing this to protect their daughters. So they had to be alive. Nothing else could explain her sacrifice. A thrill of elation swept through every cell in his body. He looked at the old man. Saw the calculated evil in his eyes, the tiny smile in the corners of his mouth. The old man was reading him. Oh God, she was protecting him. Or thought she was. He gulped air, preparing to shout at her——tell her to save herself. He couldn't speak. His throat flexed and rippled but no sound emerged. He felt a tear slip down his cheek.

Today he was going to discover how much he could be hurt without having a finger laid upon him. He was about to find out how far his mind could be stretched before it broke and gave him ghastly relief. There was only so much pain he could absorb before he became inured to it. He hoped.

~*~

Fergie trotted into the room, tail wagging, brow furrowed. "I think the old man's finally cracked."

Redmond was used to the dog's arbitrary remarks. "Yeah?" he said without a shred of interest.

"He's dismissed the kitchen staff and he's cooking."

"So?"

"He's stirring pots and humming away to himself and smiling like he's Martha frickin' Stewart on uppers."

Redmond's level of interest remained close to non-existent. He repeated, "So?"

"I've never seen him like this. I wandered into the kitchen by mistake and he threw me scraps of meat, like I was the family pet. As if he liked me."

Redmond remained too wrapped in his own pain to respond.

"He didn't even kick me." The dog stared up at the captive man and wagged his tail hopefully. Redmond remained closed off. "Humans," he said loudly, turned and trotted haughtily back the way he had come.

Later in the day the old man entered the room carrying a tray.

On it sat a bowl of steaming hot soup. The old man placed the tray carefully on Redmond's lap and stood back as though waiting for a reaction. It was the first time since he had been taken that food was offered. Redmond knew that for whatever reason he didn't need food to sustain him. But his hunger knew no bounds.

The smell of the food was overwhelming. Redmond's mouth watered like a leaky tap. Without conscious command his hand lifted the spoon and dipped it into the liquid. It was thick and green——pea and ham he reckoned.

The soup tasted, as any food would have right then, like the nectar of the gods. He ate it greedily, splashing drops across his shirt. The old man watched silently and removed the tray when he was finished. Twenty minutes later he returned with another tray. On it was a plate of roast meat, with mashed potato, cauliflower and peas, generously covered in gravy.

Redmond Clarke had never been a glutton but he felt like one as he shoveled the meat and veg into his mouth, chewing maniacally, stuffing in more before finishing the last mouthful. Somewhere, far in the back of his mind, a tiny voice yelled that it was a trick. At every mouthful he expected the tray to be whipped off his knees. With the speed of desperation he cleaned the plate. By the end he was panting like a wolf at a kill. His stomach felt stretched. He slumped back into the chair. For the first time in his captivity he felt close to content.

The old man retrieved the tray without a word. Shortly, he was back with another tray. The dish, this time, was covered by a domed, metal lid. "The *piece de resistance*," the old man said, his French accent faultless. "I must apologize for the one-note meal," he smiled. "Each course is based on the same ingredient," he explained. "But that is the beauty of it." He lifted the dome with a flourish and stepped back.

Sitting on the plate in front of him, Redmond's wife's head stared at him with boiled eyeballs and overcooked lips. Flesh dripped from her cheekbones. As he watched, her tongue slithered across her teeth, lolling down her chin. His entire body convulsed but the restraint that had kept him trapped in the chair over the years prevented him from dislodging the hateful tray. His hands pushed at it. Liquid skin sloughed across his fingers. The head tumbled down his shins and across the floor to stare at him with a mixture of resignation and resentment. The eye sockets were empty now, staring emptily. The mask of flesh began to slip. The skin on her forehead tore raggedly. A cap of

Marionettes

stringy hair remained incongruously atop the skull.

Redmond began to scream. The old man grinned. He pulled up a chair and sat down. Lighting a cigarette he crossed his legs and relaxed. Redmond's screams paused only while he gasped a new breath. The scream reflex continued long after his vocal chords shredded and lost their ability to turn his pain into sound. Unconsciousness claimed him for the first time in over half a century.

When he came around, Redmond's first coherent thoughts were of his daughters. He screamed soundlessly for a full hour. After a while he began to pray. Not for death, for the old man would not allow it. He prayed for madness. Or sanity. Only one could save him.

Undead and Unbound

UNDEAD NIGHT OF THE UN-DEADEST UNDEAD

By C.J. Henderson

"Everybody loves a sequel."
—— Jim the Ripper

"What do you mean, we're going back to Wixom?"

Marvin Richards' confusion was understandable. In the producer's mind, the quaint town of Wixom was a played out story——finished. Used up.

"You're right. What I actually meant to say was, you're going back to Wixom."

Now, it was true, the quiet little Michigan town had been an utter sensation in its time, but Richards' work was not writing history books, it was television, and the life expectancy of anything on the idiot box was not something recorded for the ages, but rather measured in nano-seconds. Which was exactly what the executive producer/anchorman of the much beloved news show, *Challenge of the Unknown*, tried to explain as he said;

"Gerber, have a heart. The attention span of the American public——God bless 'em——is shorter than a wino's average bowel movement. They want something new——"

"They always want something new," interrupted Maxie Gerber, the network liaison to Richards' show. "But sadly, there is nothing new right now, and you know it. Not anything that your show can exploit, anyway. I mean, com'on, Marv, you look me in the eye and tell me, what topic have you guys ever covered that comes close to an actual outbreak of 'one hundred percent, genuine, guaranteed, son-of-a-bitchin' zombies?'"

Richards had to stop for a moment to marshal his thoughts. It was going to be hard to find a way around Gerber's thunderous logic.

Undead and Unbound

Hell, the producer mused to himself, the liaison had just quoted his own words on the subject from when he himself had first learned of the outbreak.

No, he had to admit that Wixom had been a blessing beyond belief. Not that the *Challenge* team had not found plenty of great stories in their time. They had shown the world actual UFO footage, had brought their vast video audience vampires on the hunt and werewolves in full transformation. They had been on top of things in the leprechaun uprising, shown the world the cockroach fairies and even presided over the destruction of a minor deity, all to satisfy the American public's need to be entertained by the bizarre, the bug-eyed and the blasphemous.

But Wixom and its zombies, well, that was special, even for the *Challenge* team. The cold, hard truth was that the whole world, for some unknown reason, was simply in love with the idea of the walking dead. Books, movies, television shows, rap lyrics, comics——whatever, it did not matter——zombies were everywhere, all the time. They were the number one unreal attention grabber in the world, and if that was the case, then *Challenge of the Unknown* had to stay on top of all things zombie.

And, sighed Richards to himself, if that meant a return trip to Wixom, the site of the only actual zombie outbreak the world had ever known, to try and squeeze some more life out of the story, well that was what was going to have to happen. Not that it would be easy.

During the original outbreak, Marvin Richards and his executive assistant, Lora Dean, had almost died. Instead, at the last moment, when they were surrounded by brain-craving zombies, the producer had been struck with an unbelievably ludicrous show-stopper of an idea. Capturing the undead horde's attention, he had convinced them that what they really wanted——rather than the chance to chew on his gray matter——was to be celebrities. To make a long story short, Richards convinced the shamblers to allow themselves to be shipped to Universal Studios' Orlando theme park where they became an overnight sensation, performing 'Thriller' live three times a day.

It had been a ratings stunner. The commercial footage had stayed over-the-top dramatic for two weeks, convincing America that Marv and Lora would be torn apart——on screen. Having the producer con the zombies, instead of ripping them limb from bloody limb, to stage an impromptu rendition of 'There's No Business Like Show

Undead Night of the Undeadest Undead

Business', there on camera, instantaneously became one of the greatest moments in television history.

The network had instantly signed *Challenge* for two more years. The show was guaranteed an Emmy if Richards would agree to perform at the next ceremony, bringing one of the Universal zombies with him to do a duet of "Can't Get A Head Without You." Richards had raked in the perks, including new carpeting for his office from the network, a new Mercedes from the production studio, and a life-time supply of Bacon In A Can!, the wonder snack from Treats-Fer-Geeks that was sweeping the nation.

And that, for Richards, was the problem.

"But, Maxie..." the producer pleaded, "don't you get it, we just pulled off the greatest live moment in television history——"

Yes, he was perfectly willing to admit that any competent newsman could drag more of a story out of Wixom. But that's what it would be doing, raking the ground, looking for kernels of entertainment, scraps of novelty——when the entire world was waiting to see what wild and zanily over-the-top spectacle he would pull off next.

"How...exactly," Richards asked quietly, his voice filled with an earnest amount of plea, "am I supposed to top that?"

"You'll think of something," answered Gerber with a wink so insincere it looked as if it were being produced by a wooden puppet, "you always do."

And that, as they say in the business, was that. The network liaison departed for a round of martinis, his one exhausting task for the week finally accomplished, and Marvin Richards was left to stare at the far wall in his newly carpeted office, wondering just what might be left in Wixom to exploit. After a while——a while consisting of a nosh platter from Sunseri's Sushi Summit, and a half bottle of Scotch——the producer belched out a forlorn sigh and finally settled down to work.

In dread anticipation of the moment which had been forced upon him that afternoon, Richards had kept several members of his staff hopping since Wixom was a special project. Their job had been to monitor all media, including the Internet, searching for every rival bit of coverage of the events of Wixom. When he called for their results to be brought to his office, even he was surprised at what they had found.

Of course, the bulk of it consisted of television segments and radio programs, all of which were delivered to his computer. The physical coverage——newspaper articles, magazine features, hastily produced paperbacks——filled eighteen Xerox copy paper boxes. Even Richards was staggered by the overwhelmingness of it all.

"How," the producer sighed with weary exasperation in the general direction of his assistant, "could an industry, even one as venal as ours, have produced this much crap about a subject, in such a short time, without coming up with one iota of truth?"

"This is television we're talking about now——right?" responded Lora, only slightly amused at her boss's plight. "That can't possibly have been a real question."

"Spare me your pointed barbs, foul beast. Just please tell me you've been keeping track of all this…this…" Richards spun his hands in futility at the wall of boxes before him, finally adding, "Oh, just tell me that I don't have to start from scratch."

"Now, would I be the loyal, long-suffering, best-in-the-business executive assistant the wonderful world of production has ever known if I allowed something like that to happen?" When Richards merely stared blankly, a small ring of hope circling his normally carnivorous eyes, Lora sighed softly, then said;

"Yes, it's already broken down and coordinated so you can——"

Those were all the words the young woman was able to get out before her boss's yelps of glee drowned her out entirely.

~*~

Even with the quite efficient manner in which Lora had organized the transferred video, as well as all the print materials, it still took the pair all of that work day, as well as a number of hours into the night before Richards had a true handle on everything spread out before him. His office had become a maze of mounds constructed from newspaper and magazine clippings, these adorned with Post-It notes of various colors.

The sticky squares were detailed with references to video entries corresponding to the print pieces in each pile. This allowed the pair to have a solid, real-world grouping of each subject the media had covered in relation to the Wixom zombies. Eventually, even Richards was slightly amazed at the lengths to which various outlets had gone to keep the Wixom story alive. Holding one article in his hand, he murmured;

"Fashion choices of your favorite Undead…I mean, seriously, has

Undead Night of the Undeadest Undead

the world really, actually, finally taken leave of its goddamned senses?"

"You forget, chief, people love them some zombies."

"Yes, I know, I know, Klingmeyer's theory on personality displacement and identity transference…blahblahblah…fine. Society is filled with morons who feel so ignored by the world around them that they internalize their own sense of self in place of that of a construct which can't be hurt. The dead have no feelings, so now everyone identifies with zombies and vampires. Which means, basically, as we've always known, people are stupid. But how does that help us here?"

"Actually, it might…"

As Lora's voice trailed off, Richards' eyes sparked with interest. He knew each individual tone and cadence of his assistant's voice. His every instinct screamed at him that she had somehow, in all the morass of information around them, spotted the one thing that everyone else in the media had missed. And, if he was gauging her pause correctly, this was not just another nonsense angle on which boy band this or that zombie-of-the-week should join, this was something solid, something with non-maggot-infested meat on its bones. As he sat transfixed, actually forgetting the tumbler of Scotch around which his fingers were clenched, Lora mused;

"You know, I think the most important angle of this story has been totally ignored by everyone."

"I like the sound of that, darling…"

"Oh, I'm no longer a foul beast?"

"Consider it an upgrade in title. Now spill, what has that marvelous brain of yours uncovered just in the nick of time to keep you employed for another week?"

"Tell me, Marvin…what caused the zombie outbreak in Wixom, anyway?"

"Well, there was, I mean…didn't they——"

The producer paused, not quite able to remember what scientific explanation had finally been attached to the first——and only—— actual outbreak of the walking dead in all of recorded human history. He could remember some chatter about it early on, this or that scientist offering possible explanations. The randomness of their theories, however, had reminded him of nothing more than the opening of one of Romero's *Walking Dead* pictures, where a voice on a television somewhere in the background was spewing possible answers for the terror walking the streets. The announcer was simply reading off a laundry list of unexplained ideas and hunches, none of which actually told anyone anything. And, building atop that image, Lora's point finally crystallized within Richards' mind.

"That's it. Oh…my…God in Heaven…that's it! I can't believe it, but you're right. You're absolutely right. No one has yet explained how the hell this happened!"

"There have been a few who have tried," Lora was quick to point out. As the producer turned toward her, she added, "but sadly, for others, not us, no one really seemed to pay attention."

Richards nodded, his mind whirling. Obviously the government was working on the problem. There had to be an army of biologists, chemists, and who knew what else digging, poking and prodding every inch of Wixom looking for an answer. The remains of those zombies blown apart by the military must have been shredded into microscopic pieces for analysis. Whether, of course, the government would share such knowledge in a manner that would make outstanding programming was always a dicey question, however. Turning to Lora, the producer said;

"All right, that's our angle. Once again you've earned your pay for the week. Now, drop everything on me connected to the cause, get someone in here to cart the rest of this crap the hell out of my sight, order me a corned beef on rye, brown mustard, with an ice cold seltzer…and for Christ's sake——"

"Don't let them forget the pickle. Relax, chief," sighed Lora, the speed dial number of Richards' favorite deli already punched in on her cell phone's key pad, "you think I don't know your moods by now?"

Ignoring his assistant's comment, as she knew he would, the producer began flipping through what the other networks, news shows, and entertainment outlets of any kind had served up so far on the actual cause of the Wixom outbreak. While he did so, Lora ordered his all-nighter snack, as well as something for herself, then phoned the airport, knowing they would be flying to Michigan in the morning. If she could manage it, she would not only book them into the same hotel as last time, she would secure the same rooms.

He had been satisfied with them, which was always a plus. The real benefit in doing so, however, would be watching his face when she told him that, of course they had the same rooms since she had booked them in advance before they left the last time. Richards was no idiot. She knew he would not believe her. But, she also knew he was

Undead Night of the Undeadest Undead

best kept on his leash if she could shake him up once in a while.

Little did she know at that moment exactly just how shaken both of them would be by their return to Wixom.

~*~

Some twenty-eight hours after confirming both their flight plan and room reservations, Richards and Lora were walking down the main street of Wixom, along with their film crew, reacquainting themselves with the city. Walking with them were two police officers, and the mayor, one Agnes Gooley, answering what questions they might have.

"So, Ms. Gooley, nice of you to meet us, and with a protective escort no less."

"You know us here in Wixom, Mr. Richards," answered the mayor pleasantly, though somehow seeming a trifle nervous. "Nothing is too good for our friends in the media."

"Really? Well, tell me, what's changed in Wixom since we were here last? Much?"

"Oh, no…same old, same old."

The woman's nervous laugh did little to convince the producer she was not hiding something. Smelling the beginnings of an up-until-then unsuspected lead, he asked innocently;

"But, no more zombies——yes? All the walking dead were rounded up, shipped out, graves all secure, hospitals in no need of shotgun-totting guards——"

"Oh, there might be…"

"No more curfew, police not specifically listening in on ambulance radio traffic——"

"I'm not certain that…"

"Military all packed up and gone home, no more threats of city-wide sterilization by fire——"

"Okay, I get it." Gooley's shout stopped everyone in their tracks. Keen to play the mayor for all he might be able to pry out of her before she realized she was being played, Richards assumed his most doe-eyed expression, then asked;

"I don't understand, your honor…what's the matter? Have I done something wrong?"

"Don't play innocent with me," snapped Gooley. Wheeling on the producer, she pointed a finger at him accusingly, saying, "I knew you'd be back. I knew you'd be the one to figure it out." Trying not to allow his genuine puzzlement to show on his face, Richards asked;

"Figure out 'what,' ma'am?"

Lost in her own little world, the mayor ignored Lora's question, forgot about the cameraman following them, forgot even about the producer. As Richards lifted a finger to his lips, cautioning all the others to silence, he lowered his voice to its most sympathetic register, then said;

"It's all right. Why don't you just get it all off your chest? You'll feel better."

"What's there to tell, it's the damn vampires."

"Vampires?"

All eyes turned toward the cameraman——including the mayor's. Chet Winston was new, had been grabbed at the last minute, did not know how the *Challenge* game was played. Richards immediately refocused his energy on Gooley, but it was too late, the damage had been done. Even though only the mayor of a small, mid-western town, Gooley was politician enough to realize she was being handled. Weeks of stress had made her vulnerable. When she had discovered Richards was returning, she had accepted that the game was up, and surrendered within her mind to the inevitable. But, Winston's one-word question had shattered her capitulation, letting her know that the producer did not know nearly as much as she had worried herself into believing he did.

"I do believe this meeting is over, Mr. Richards," said the mayor, unthinkingly beginning to walk away from the others, including their police escort. "I have duties to attend to, a town to run——"

Running herself at that point, she shouted;

"So sorry to have to dash, but——"

Whatever less than honest excuse she was about to make the others would never know for, at that moment, a zombie staggered forth from an alleyway, cutting off Gooley's retreat. Catching her plump body in its outstretched arms, the horror leaned forward and snapped its still functioning jaw closed on her neck before the group's pair of escorting police officers could even unholster their weapons. As they did so, the creature turned toward the small group, holding the mayor's nearly severed head aloft, pointing at it with a kindergartner's pride as it shouted;

Undead Night of the Undeadest Undead

"TV...me on TV? Me on TV?"

The officers turned toward Richards, hesitating to shoot. Mildly surprised, the producer pointed toward the zombie as it began moving toward them, dragging Gooley in its wake, telling them;

"Gentlemen, if you please..."

Gunfire followed, several bullets shattering the zombie's brain, dropping it, several more pumped into the mayor's head even as her eyes reopened. Looking around nervously before reholstering his weapon, the taller of the two policemen said;

"I really hate this job anymore."

"You mean," asked Richards innocently, "since the vampires showed up?"

The two cops stared at each other, wondering what exactly they should do next. Their first instinct was to go silent until they had checked with their superior. But, both men knew all the chief of police would do would be to check with the city council, which would want to check with the mayor. And, since that option was no longer open to anyone, the pair knew such would just be wasting everyone's time.

"Mr. Richards," said the shorter of the two finally, "can we trust you? And, before you go all Hollywood on us, do remember you're talking to two men with guns, who could just walk away and leave you in more shit than you could imagine."

Richards smiled, delighted at the man's honesty. Giving them the most guileless facial expression he possessed within his storehouse of well-rehearsed expressions, he responded;

"Since we both know that I can imagine a whole whirlwind of shit, and that you can't trust anyone in television further than you can throw a Buick, how about this? You report to whoever needs to know that the mayor is dead. You further tell them she spilled the beans about the vampires, and then just put us all into a meeting together and walk away. How's that sound?"

The two looked at each other for only a moment.

"Sounds like about as good as this town's gonna get from anyone," answered the taller officer. Nodding, his partner added;

"You will not believe what's been goin' down around here, Mr. Richards."

"Yeah, tell him about the damn Chihuahuas."

"Yes," agreed the producer, "by all means, tell me all about the damn Chihuahuas."

Undead and Unbound

~*~

In less than an hour, the two officers had rounded up all the members of the city council that had not left Wixom for good, put them together with Richards and his crew, and then returned to the streets where they could go back to their current favorite hobby of trying to figure out what to do next with their lives now that their home town had descended as far into the crapper as seemed possible to them.

"Welcome back to Wixom, Mr. Richards."

The speaker was a middle-aged man——slightly graying, slightly balding, slightly over-weight——by the name of Bradley Crenler. Spreading his arms wide, he asked;

"What can we do for you fine people this time around?"

"You could tell us what's going on. I mean, according to all reports, Wixom is supposed to be zombie free. 'Welcome back to Wixom,' that's the new town slogan——right?"

"Yeah, that's true, that's true," agreed the councilman. "So, tell me…how much do you know?"

"I know about the vampires." When his statement received no immediate response from those present, Richards added;

"And the Chihuahuas."

That news sent both a shudder and a stir around the room which, from the expressions on the councilmen and women's faces, pleased no one. As the producer calmly waited, the assembly conferred amongst itself for a moment. Finally, after a great deal of whispering, then sighs, shrugs, and some extremely defeated head-nodding, Crenler chewed on his lower lip for a moment, then said;

"Aw, Hell by the bushel, you're here. You're in the middle of it… and with night comin', wouldn't be fair to not tell you what comes next. But…ah…could we possibly do this with the cameras off?"

"Now, ladies and gentlemen…we could do that, soldier forward under a veil of secrecy, but…as you know…nothing in this great land remains hidden for very long. And politicians with secrets don't seem to keep their jobs anymore." As the assembly began to fidget, Richards added;

"But, politicians who maintain control of information for the benefit of all, who sacrifice themselves for the greater good, like your own brave Ms. Gooley, well…those are the folks who serve multiple terms. Am I right?"

After the council members took turns giving one another meaningful looks, the nod went to Crenler who said;

"You're slick, Richards, I'll give you that. But what can we do? This is a small town. And a poor one. We've been limpin' by for some time now. But, we do need the tourist dollars this could bring in if we could fix it…" The councilman let his voice trail off for a second, then suggested;

"How's this, we throw our cards on the table, you throw the might of your cameras behind us, and we try to figure out what the hell's gone wrong in this town. Wha'cha think?"

"Anything for America, boys and girls. Let's find us a barn and put on a show."

Taking a seat before the council table, the producer listened as the laundry list of horrors roaming the streets of Wixom was tabulated for him. At first, everything had seemed fine. Richards had marched all the zombies off to Florida and peace had been restored. For a while. It was not long after that, however, when the vampires had begun to appear.

These were not any kind of modern leeches, though——no vegetarians, no opera capes, no conflicted morals, and certainly no runway models. The vampires that had shown up were leathery, angular, sinister things, as given to crawling along on all fours as they were to ambling along in an upright position. They did not fly, change into bats, disappear in clouds of smoke or perform any of the other Hollywood parlor tricks. They did fear sunlight, at least. And, they murdered people for their blood, which was more than enough to get them labeled as vampires in Wixom.

"Also," a small woman from the end of the table interjected, "I don't know if this is important or not, but the vampires…they didn't seem, from the pictures taken…it's like…"

"They all appear to be Indians," Crenler explained, "ahhh, you know, Native Americans."

Richards nodded, as if he heard such things all the time, and told the council to proceed. They did. After Wixom had supposedly been cleared of zombies, to help entertain the tourists flocking to see the only place where the undead had actually walked, the town's museum had arranged to play host to a quartet of Egyptian mummies. The rag-wrapped royals had stayed on display for only six days before they began to stagger around on their own. The quartet was quickly joined by a new wave of zombies. And…

They were not alone.

Across town, a Mrs. Gertrude Spilbee died in her home. Being old and on her own, she was apparently dead some time before anyone knew about it. Long enough, at least, for her pack of Chihuahuas to go hungry enough to begin feasting on her remains. After a while, it seems not only did Gertie reanimate and wander off into the streets moaning about brains, but her hairless little dogs followed. They had also mutated, becoming something more akin to Chupacabras that Chihuahuas.

After that, no one was certain of the order of happenings. For instance, did the eyeball slurping hummingbirds appear before or after the brain-craving porcupines? No one could remember. What they did know was that no sooner would they patch up one outbreak, when another would wander onto the scene. At that point the council had been plagued by everything from spiders the size of Volkswagens to ghosts coming to the town meetings to complain about the lowering of the local property values. And there were other problems.

The scientists left by the government had not been able to pinpoint the origins of their problems. They analyzed the air and the water, the ground, the electrical towers, the tar content of the roadways' asphalt, everything of which they could think. But, nothing gave them the slightest clue as to why any of Wixom's problems were occurring.

On top of that, the rich from around the world were petitioning for the right to be buried in Wixom in the hopes of resurrection. Right behind them, the Catholic Church had sent representatives, escorted by a contingent of Swiss Guards, to decide whether or not Wixom could be classified as Lourdes II. The town simply did not need billionaires or papal dignitaries being chewed upon by their former citizens.

"It's all just craziness. Nothin'll stay dead in this damn town no more. Which would be fine," mused Crenler, "if you could pop off one night and then just get up in a few days, dust yourself off and get back to livin' your life. But despite what most of the wealthy nincompoops in this world think, that ain't what's happenin' here, now is it?"

Nodding in agreement, Richards struggled to pull all the pieces together he had been given. Closing his eyes for a moment, he told himself;

Undead Night of the Undeadest Undead

"Think, you slug. Put it together. Somewhere in the world's catalogue of horror movies there's a clue as to what went down here. Zombies just don't up and start walking around. Something has to trigger it."

"True enough," another voice within his mind admitted, "but if the best scientists in the world can't figure it out…what makes you think you can?" And then, snapping his fingers, Richards shouted;

"Show me the money!"

"Excuse me…"

"The only possible reason the test tube jockeys haven't cracked this case is that they must be looking in the wrong places. Wixom has been in financial trouble for some time——right?" When the council members all nodded, Richards said;

"But, when the zombies first arrived, this town was solvent——yes?" As hope began to filter into the nodding heads all around him, the producer said;

"Boys, grab the record books. I'm thinking Gooley pulled some kind of under the table deal, introduced something new into the environment around here that set off your walking dead beach party. The science boys can't uncover anything because it's not something that's in the normal records. So, city treasurer, let's start scanning those ledgers, shall we?"

And, it was just as Mr. Fred Ortiz, city record keeper and owner of the local KFC franchise, dumped the record books for the year before the first zombie outbreak on the council table that the sounds of the walking undead and those citizens foolish enough to be out after dark began to filter upward from the streets below. It was only ten minutes after that when the noise of most of the things those in the Wixom Council Chambers could hear became unmistakably focused on the council chambers themselves.

"Focus on the records, people," shouted Richards.

"But, goddamnit——those things are comin'!"

"Then focus quickly," added the producer. Turning to the Mutt and Jeff of the Wixom police department, he shouted, "Fellahs, ahhhh… just spit-balling here, but how about barricading the door, wha'da'ya think?"

As the two officers rushed to jam a table and then some filing cabinets against the only entrance to the council chambers just as the hideous sound of yammering three ounce dogs began to filter under the door, Lora began passing out ledger books to the politicians too old or feeble to help in their common defense.

"Com'on, people," snapped Richards, "dig through, look for the hidden object. Something irregular got hidden somewhere in those books——"

The sound of splintering wood overpowered the producer's voice for a moment, all heads turning to see terrible sets of clawed fingernails slicing their way through the door. As the sound of tiny teeth gnawing on the bottom of the same panel joined in, Richards added;

"And I need the bunch of you to find it and find it fast!"

As the producer marched up and down in front of the council table, peering over each of the record books, throwing out managerial bits of encouragement as best he could, Lora crossed to the doorway where the officers and three of the stouter council members were holding the tide as best they could. Reaching into her over-sized shoulder bag, she pulled out an orange-colored weapon, one quickly identified as a squirt gun. As one of the clawed hands broke away a dinner plate-sized section of door, she aimed and fired, receiving a piercing shriek for her efforts. Giving the taller cop a smile, she said;

"Holy water mixed with garlic powder and bug-killer."

"Bug-killer?"

"Vicious if it gets in their eyes."

As those throwing themselves against the make-shift wall all nodded in approval, Ortiz raised his hand, calling for Richards' attention. As the producer galloped across the room, the older man said;

"Sir...I think, maybe..."

Not waiting to hear any more, Richards grabbed up the ledger and began reading. As he did, searching for what the city record keeper had found, Ortiz added;

"It's the entry about accepting waste from New York City for burial here. It's this other note here, explaining what it was...like I said, I think..."

Richards snatched the note away from the older man, scanning it quickly as the terrible sounds from the hallway threatened to overwhelm the sanity of those trapped within the council chamber. As Lora stared at her boss, hoping for the best, suddenly the producer turned away from the table, his expression one his executive assistant could not read. Then, as the pressure from the other side of the door began to grow to the point where it could no longer be contained,

Undead Night of the Undeadest Undead

suddenly, Richards did the one thing no one had expected.

He laughed.

As those in the assembly forward-thinking enough to have already prepared wills patted themselves on the back for such forethought, Marvin Richards, anchorman and head producer of *Challenge of the Unknown* got himself under control, straightened his tie, and then said;

"All right, let 'em in. I'm ready for them."

~*~

"Marv, I've said it before, and I'll say it again, you are one slick fish."

"I'm certain that's a compliment back in whatever podunk it was from whence thou sprang, my fair Lora," answered Richards, "and so I shall not have thee flogged. Not today, anyway."

Feet up on his desk, tumbler of Scotch in one hand and a cigar the size of a breadstick in the other, the producer appeared more at ease than his assistant could remember ever having seen him. Giving him a small curtsey, she added;

"No really, it was one thing for Ortiz to put together the fact that Gooley had been accepting the remains of destroyed vampires for burial in Wixom. With their DNA seeping into the water table there, it's no wonder the dead started to walk."

"Yeah, I like the way our science guys worked it out," interjected Richards. Taking a long drag on his cigar, he exhaled while saying, "first the buried dead started to walk, then as mosquitos and the such started feeding on them, anyone they bit after that acquired the re-animation gene——god I love that phrase, put whoever coined that down for a bonus——anyway, after that, anyone that died just didn't stay dead."

"True enough, but the way you handled the vampires. I mean, those cops were ready to dump a load. Everybody's sweating, screaming, crying…and you, cool as ever——"

With the ringing of line three on his red phone, conversation ceased. Taking the call from upstairs——that-which-had-to-be-answered——Richards said;

"Hello…yes, sir…it's all been handled, sir…yes…well, thank you, sir…yes, the vampires are all Native Americans. Well, that's because the toxic vampire waste Wixom accepted was stashed in an old Indian burial ground. Yep, biggest cliché in the world, but...what can I tell you?"

Lora headed for the door, knowing that her boss's current conversation would most likely last for several hours.

"Oh yes again, sir, they were happy to sign waivers. Yep, indeed, they hate everything about the modern world, but they do seem to understand that they ended up dead in the first place because the modern world has bigger and better weapons. Yep, they really loved the idea of a leveled playing field."

Pausing at the door, Lora took one last look at her boss, smiling as she did so. He was crass, cynical and as opportunistic as a hungry cat let loose in a mouse farm——

"Oh, yes, sir, they understand they're only allowed to hunt zombies, designated mutants, oh, and of course, the contestants from our new show. And, trust me, sir, with zombies, hummingbirds from hell, vampires, the Swiss Guard, roaming packs of Chihauhau Chupacabras, and even those damn mummies, *Extreme Survivor* is going to be the highest rated reality show ever!"

But he was all hers.

"I'm telling you, they're looking forward to it."

And for the moment, anyway, she told herself, that really was good enough.

I AM LEGION
By Robert M. Price

My name is Martin Steils, and I am by occupation a parish priest in the village of Frankenstein in the state of Bavaria. Some may understandably discount my narrative as a bit of tasteless fiction, taking advantage of a tragedy, or rather a series of tragedies, that have ruined the lives of many and stolen peaceful sleep from many more. But my Christian conscience would never allow me to take such liberties. By the same token, honesty compels me to admit that these blows struck pious and impious alike, the believer and the unbeliever the same. Thus I cannot call the destruction wrought by the hulking juggernaut of Heinrich Frankenstein, son of the old baron, a judgment wrought by God, as some have, some who have not learnt the lesson taught to Job's comforters in olden days. My wish here is simply to add to the public knowledge concerning these terrible events, as I am privileged, or rather cursed, to possess special knowledge of these matters. I will for the moment withhold the source of this information. But I must hasten to record what I know, what I have seen, before circumstances prevent me. My reader will very likely, as I say, reject my report as preposterous, but I can only remind him that to be forewarned is likewise to be forearmed, and that if the master of the house knew to expect the thief, he would be prepared for him, as the gospel also says.

Many comfort themselves with the lie that the Frankenstein behemoth was no more than a murdering madman escaped from confinement in one of those awful dungeons to which we consign the insane, as if the Middle Ages still lingered, and in there, they do. This would have been bad enough, but the reports of those present at the events, survivors of the monster's fury, tell us of feats of fantastic strength and of near-invulnerability to harm impossible for any human being. Admittedly, the whispered tales of Frankenstein's creation of the thing do not account for these facts much better, but, as you will shortly see, they point in the direction of the truth.

The story has it that young Heinrich Frankenstein, called 'Doctor' despite his expulsion from the medical college, had sunk to the level of England's 'resurrection men', filching fresh corpses from cemeteries, lingering like a vulture to appropriate the bodies as soon as their mourners had all departed. Accompanied by his furtive servant Friedrich, 'Fritz', he would lower himself to manual labor as the pair of them displaced the moldy graveyard soil tamped down only minutes before by workmen who had the right to be there. Digging till their shovels struck the coffin lid, they chortled like a man whose spade had disclosed buried treasure. And indeed this is what they imagined they had found, for every corpse, or what they could salvage from it, was another building block in the hideous fortress of flesh they were constructing, like a medieval structure made from Roman ruins.

From one body they took a hand or leg, but, finding its mate too corrupt already, they would steal another from a second body, matching and mismatching as they went. (This must have accounted in some measure for the shambling gait observed in the resultant monster.) The facial features of their cadavers had suffered the most, and a new mask of a face had to be stitched together from the incongruent features of several corpses. Perhaps the most distinguishing thing about the monster of Frankenstein, the first thing people recognized upon his lumbering approach, was the cranium. Frankenstein was in truth a genius, the mad application of his talents notwithstanding, and he did contrive, more or less successfully, to transplant a brain from one dead man into another's skull. But given the disparity in size and shape (he had only so many pieces from which to make his puzzle, after all) he found he had to reshape and enlarge the cranial cavity by some means I cannot guess, though I suspect metal casing to have been involved. But the result was plain, as the crown of the creature's head rose up to meet a flat lid of a scalp at right angles, as if the brain were carried around in a bucket atop the thing's massive shoulders. And, good God!, the nail-head bolts protruding from the fencepost neck! He had employed them in his Galvanic method of stimulating the dead tissues and did not bother to remove them following surgery.

Frankenstein might have had better luck with the brain had he simply murdered some poor victim and transferred the fresh organ into its new, moldy prison. But to this he would not sink, still flat-

I Am Legion

tering himself that some vestige of professional and personal ethics remained in him. And, to be fair, we must remember that he never intended to create a murdering marauder. Nor was such even the result of his using a rotting brain. The worse that should have come from that error was that his creature should have remained stretched out upon his operating table, breathing but inert, with no mental activity outside the automatic nervous system. In fact, this is why most men of science take refuge in the theory of an escaped madman, as they cannot credit the notion of a patient with a necrotic brain even moving, much less killing and terrorizing. This is where I am able to shed some light on the matter. A priest can afford to entertain certain possibilities that a conventional man of medicine will not consider, or if he does, he will be laughed out of his profession.

You will ask me how I can possibly know what I am about to reveal, but again I beg your patience.

As a Roman Catholic priest, I teach the existence of an immortal soul. I was catechized not to believe in ghosts lingering after the death of the body, for this contradicted the doctrines of the Church. Souls were sent, upon death, to Heaven or to Hell, except for those with unfinished business, and they were consigned to Purgatory, as the gospel says, till they should pay the last farthing. They were not at liberty to circulate among the living, seeking vengeance or righting old wrongs. That, I long believed, was mere superstition.

It is not, or else I am superstitious.

The truth is that the Frankenstein monster, having no real consciousness of his own (such being impossible for a dead brain no matter how many volts one shoots into it), was animated and driven by——forgive me——the spirits of the dead whose body parts Doctor Frankenstein had defiled. As long as their bodies were forbidden proper rest, their spirits must seek recompense. Perhaps the horror would have been mitigated had Frankenstein not relied so completely on the bodies of recently hanged criminals. But he did, and their spirits, trapped within the patchwork carcass of the monster, continued their habitual abominations beyond the grave through its scarred and crudely stitched hands. Their wrath is what bade the shuffling bulk rise off the table, snap the leather restraints, and strangle poor Fritz, who had sought to hold him at bay with a smoking torch. Their rage was what sent him slaying and crippling through the countryside.

The first of his outrages of which we are aware was, of course, the drowning of little Maria. I conducted the funeral mass for the innocent child and sought in vain to console her weeping parents. And yet her fate might have been worse yet. For one of the felons who had involuntarily contributed to the monster's anatomy had been a child predator. He had violated and murdered several children of both sexes before the mob overtook and dispatched him. But now, in a new and ghastlier form, this devil prowled again. As he stumbled through the woods, he saw the rising smoke from a lakeside cottage and made his clumsy way to it. The little maid sat on the shore making daisy chains until she saw a shadow looming over her, blocking the last sunlight she would ever see. The hulking form sought to kneel beside her but fell to his knees with surprising impact. Maria reached out to steady the poor fellow, in her naïve kindness, lest he fall on his face. The molester was accustomed to beguiling his little victims with tempting words of candy or pets, but he found he was inarticulate, able to do no more than groan. But this touched the pure heart of the simple girl, and she took pity upon him. She held out her flower chain to him, but he brushed it aside, dealing her a glancing blow to the head. His perverse lust aroused, he seized the helpless child. But he found his loins to be frustratingly asleep. In his rage he raised the girl above his flat head and cast her like a rag doll into the pond where she thrashed briefly before expiring in a fountain of bubbles.

But it was not only his victim that sailed through the air to a watery grave. One of the hands that had thrown her came loose and followed its burden. The slightest hint of surprised dismay flitted across the hideous countenance of the monster. Then he turned and lurched back into the woods, just as Maria's father was returning from the neighboring farm, his peace of soul forever lost.

It would be a mistake to imagine that the murderer pondered what had happened to him. There was not enough of a central mind, no core of thought, to allow that. The truth is, I am sure, that, the evil deed done, the offending member abandoned the composite body and the corrupt soul who had possessed it fled away. The maimed automaton simply made for the village as the dusk gathered.

Mere moments later, Maria's father, whose name, God forgive me, I can no longer recall, returned home. Receiving no reply to his frantic calls, he searched the place. Shortly afterward, he came walking with leaden pace into the village, through the square, holding the dripping body of his lost daughter. I can never forget the sight, as I struggled to

I AM LEGION

penetrate the crowd that instantly formed around him, spectators at a harvest festival now gone sour. After a tearful explanation from the poor wretch, it took but minutes to form a search party. Even the young Baron Frankenstein was eager to take part, no doubt to help atone for the sin of fashioning the death-dealer in the first place.

The first to come upon the monster was the doughty Police Inspector Krogh. This man should have known enough to wait for help. He did indeed call to the others, but he had already made himself known to the monster, who made for him with murder in his mismatched eyes. But there was more to it than met the eye, as horrifying a spectacle as it was. You see, the Inspector had been the one to arrest more than one of the criminals whose members now cohered in the creature towering above him. The object of their vengeance had obligingly come to them. At this point any observer (I was not one of them) would have expected an attack on the Inspector by the one-handed menace, but the manner of it was wholly unexpected when the creature snatched his own handless arm from its stitched mounting and used it to bludgeon Krogh to death. As the gathering searchers answered the Inspector's call moments too late, their quarry lumbered away amid the boulders long ago distributed on the mountainside by the passage of sovereignly indifferent glaciers, monsters in their own right. Incredible as it seems, the villagers, their torches, rakes, and clubs forming a moving forest above their heads, could thereafter find no trace of him. Some echo of the stealth one of the ghostly felons had practiced in life must have served to help him find concealment.

The reign of terror had only commenced. Despite the terrified vigilance of the local populace, the next to die was Herr Ullmann, a village apothecary who had testified against one of the murderers now animating the Frankenstein monster. It seems that the creature contrived to hide itself beneath some blankets on the bed of a wagon, which someone had then pulled up to the rear of Ullmann's shop. When left alone, the monster arose from beneath his coverings and easily battered the door down. Ullmann came running, clad only in his nightshirt, to intercept the intruder, then nearly fainted at the sight of him. Of course he had no idea why he should have attracted the monster's attentions; he probably thought himself no more chosen than the victim of a bear in the forest. He was just in the wrong place at the wrong time. So he thought. His attacker flung the old man's fragile form to the floor and proceeded to stomp and kick him to a bloody death with his giant, anvil-like boots, leaving behind not only a clear trail of splattered blood but his stamping foot as well! Had the force of his attack loosened the links that had bound his borrowed foot to his stolen leg? His progress thereafter was difficult, and even so, no one could find him once the red tracks gave out in the nearby fields.

Frankenstein's bastard spawn lost its other massive hand when Dr. Niemann lost his life. The irony in this case was great indeed, though only I have realized it. Niemann had been a fellow medical student with Frankenstein and had similar inclinations, at least insofar as he was not above stealing cadavers for his own unorthodox experiments. He was one of those who presumed to stretch the medical code in order to dare experiments which might advance medicine at a more rapid pace. Should their gambles pay off, such radicals would be hailed as heroes and pioneers, and such was Niemann. Though largely unknown outside of the immediate area, he had actually pioneered some new treatments for the sick. Perhaps Heinrich Frankenstein would enjoy like esteem had his delvings turned out differently.

One of the dark spirits indwelling the monster had, in life, discovered Niemann's appropriation of his wife's remains and tried to kill him for it. He failed and was arrested on his would-be victim's word. The man finally died in prison. Now he sought to finish his old mission, and he succeeded. Yet in the process, the slaying fist, which had belonged to the avenging widower, fell from the monster's rotting wrist joint like a piece of bad fruit. The creature did not bother trying to retrieve it but instead stalked off to his next appointment, seeming to know that his time was short.

Strauss was the village undertaker. Death was his friend, he thought, until it came looking for him. The monster visited him by night, heedless of any who might interfere, though none did, from either ignorance or stark terror. A grotesque sight, the creature hobbled through the burst-in door, dragging himself unsteadily with what tenuous limbs remained to him, and managed to prop himself up long enough to aim a mighty kick with his other great foot, this one built up with an inches-thick sole to compensate for the leg having been shorter than the other, fetched from a different corpse. It was the last thing he did with it. As for Strauss, his pot-bellied bulk bounced down the worn steps to his basement storeroom where he kept his embalming chemicals. Someone else would have to administer them to him. He never had an inkling that he was paying with his life for once having discovered an assistant

I Am Legion

fondling one of their cold charges and driving him out.

The death of the undying monster came about in this wise. His mobility was by this time practically nil, though 'his' lust for vengeance blazed unabated. A diabolical providence must have assisted the creature, for the final victim on his list came to him. For some years, one Professor Lampini had made the rounds of the region's villages, providing rare entertainment, albeit such as caters to immature minds. He operated a rolling freak show replete with obvious frauds and pretended horrors, including sets of crimsoned vampire fangs, stuffed bats, fake mummies, and such like. As his horse-drawn trailer made its slow way along the muddy road, returning to the village of Frankenstein, he thought he spied a lone traveler in the ditch, like the Jew in the Good Samaritan parable, of which Lampini now thought with a pang of conscience. He brought his weary horse to a welcome halt, then dismounted and made his way over to the injured man.

Of course it was the Frankenstein monster, lying there, blankly staring, missing limbs, as if some passing highwayman had robbed him of them. He groaned, unable to speak to his rescuer. Now thinking perhaps he should not have stopped, Lampini gave a shrug of his shoulders and half-hoisted, half-dragged the massive form to the rear of his wagon and helped him in. But Lampini was not all compassion. He saw an opportunity. He recognized the figure he had retrieved from the mud and rain. He did not particularly fear him, incapacitated as he was. He hoped to capitalize on the monster's notoriety and to exhibit him in the manner of a jungle ape or a caged bear. The law might not allow this in his own village, where memory of the monster's recent crimes was still a gaping, stinging wound. Surely the police would take the murderer from him. But he hoped he might escape police interference if he displayed the thing in the surrounding villages of Vysaria, Mendendorf, Läthos, and the rest.

What the doomed man could not have guessed was that the monster he planned to exploit also recognized him. For the last of the vengeful spirits energizing him had once served as Lampini's hunchbacked assistant, and Lampini had severely lashed him when he found him forcing his attentions on a gypsy dancer. At the time he did not dare oppose his master, but for that very reason the anguish and resentment had only smoldered hotter and hotter, finally breaking into a raging fire only now, after death.

The foolish Lampini did not count on word of his new exhibit getting around, for he was not the only one who recognized the monster. As it happened, the news reached little Maria's grief-stricken father, who decided he could not wait for the judicial system to give him satisfaction. So he managed to secure a stick of explosive charge and crept one night into the trailer of Professor Lampini. He shone his shaded lantern in the face of the monster and found its eyes open and staring. He had the outlandish notion that the thing had been waiting for him, even that, paradoxically, it meant him no harm. Nor did it. The man set the fuse, then stuffed the explosive between the monster's chest and arm. He hopped from the wagon and started running. Lampini, meantime, roused from sleep in the next wagon, entered this one to see what the matter might be. He had supposed the monster to be near immobile, but perhaps he was not?

Poor Lampini crossed the threshold into a blasting inferno, itself the threshold of the greater Inferno into which he at once descended. The monster, of course, though amazingly resilient under gunfire, flew to atoms. All his animating spirits had flown, some measure of satisfaction theirs at last. Did they return to Hell, to join their last victim, having enjoyed this short respite? I do not know.

But I do know something else. I know that the reign of bloody ambushes, assassinations and molestations continued on even after the destruction of Frankenstein's misbegotten creature. There was a brief period of restored peace, and all finally allowed themselves a sigh of relief. But that interval was sadly short lived. Who was guilty this time? I know.

I can explain the following as little as I can explain the preceding, but I now believe, nay, I am certain, that the fiercest, most vengeful spirit survived: that of the Frankenstein monster itself. It seems he was after all more than the sum of his parts, no mere empty vehicle for restive ghosts in their foul missions. Had their possession somehow awakened, or even created, a new and twisted soul within him, a soul of his own? Or had their volitional activity called forth some echo of the brain's former tenant? Who knows? Even Doctor Frankenstein does not. Or rather *did* not, for he was the first to die in this new wave of hellish violence.

You have been patient to learn how I can possibly be in possession of the information I have recorded here. Well, 'possession' is the word, for the risen shade of the monster, lacking any physical shell of its own, has passed into *me*. It directs me, it corrupts me, it makes my members its servants, and, God help me, I do its bloody work.

WHEN DARK THINGS SLEEP
By Damien Walters Grintalis

The sun set at nine o'clock on a warm night in Arcadia, Maryland. By the time it rose the next morning, everyone in town was dead, or dying, or worse.

Everyone except the four people huddled close in the back office of the town's bar. From their hideout, they could hear the groans and screams of the dying——their friends and family members, people they'd known all their lives. And they couldn't do anything but hide and wait and, perhaps, pray.

Paul had stopped praying hours ago. He suspected a God who'd allow something like this to happen in a small town of no importance wasn't listening anyway.

"Do you think my mom is really dead?" The youngest of the four, a kid named Kevin hovering on that awkward line between childhood and the teen years, choked out.

Laura, the only woman in town not dead or dying, put her arm around the boy. He didn't pull away. "I think so," she whispered.

Paul looked down, away from the lie. Kevin's mother, along with the rest of them, had died, but she was still dying, and terribly, judging by the sounds.

"Why are we still okay?" Paul asked. "Has anyone thought of that? I mean, whatever caused it, why didn't it do the same thing to us?"

The fourth person in the room shook his head. "Does it matter why?" Vic, the owner of the bar, unclasped his calloused hands and raked his fingers through hair speckled with traces of grey at the temples.

No one answered.

Paul shivered, even though their combined body heat had turned the small room warm. Not long after sunset, he had been with his wife and daughter in their living room, getting ready to put a movie in the DVD player. A normal Sunday night. "Daddy?" his daughter whispered, and that caught his attention right away. She gave up Daddy for Dad three years before. Five minutes later, both Helen and Eve were dying, clutching their throats, unable to breathe, their skin turning dusky shades of purple, while their eyes rolled back until only the whites showed.

And it became worse, so much worse. A half hour later, only minutes after he stopped trying to revive them, they… What? What exactly? Woke up? Rose from the dead? Recovered? For almost fifteen minutes, Paul held both of them in his arms, sobbing and laughing, ignoring the sour-milk stench rising from their bodies and the dull confusion in their eyes.

Then Helen asked, "Paul, did you remember to turn the lights off?"

Eve giggled, a strange sound suited more to a doll with dying batteries than to a teenager.

They died again, this time drowning, their lungs filling up with water——real water, not imaginary. It poured out from their mouths and noses. When they finally stopped thrashing on the living room floor, the rug beneath them was soaked with an improbable amount of water and the air filled with a hot, brackish smell.

He kept his distance when they sat up.

Helen cocked her head to the side and smiled. Eve blinked several times, held her hands out and clapped three times, a line of drool dangling from her lower lip.

"Daddy, push me on the swing," she said, in a high-pitched sing-song voice.

Then Helen reached out and slapped him across the face, a heavy blow that left his skin tingling. "Your fault," she shouted and lifted her hand again. He grabbed her wrist, and she shrieked into his face——a long, wordless cry filled with a horrible, stark awareness.

And again, they died, their skin pulsing with fevered heat, their brows dripping with sweat. When they both dropped to the floor in convulsions, Paul had fled out of the house, into the night, to discover his wife and daughter had not been the only ones.

Some of the dying had taken to the streets, and they reached for him with pain-filled eyes and mouths opened in hideous, watery gasps.

He ran with no destination in mind, just a desperate need to get away. Away from his wife of fifteen years and away from his baby girl.

When Dark Things Sleep

He stumbled across Laura first, and the relief had been clear in her shocked eyes. They took refuge in the church until the boy ran in with several of the dying (That death a macabre tableau of open wounds weeping pus and a foul stink.) following close behind, their hands outstretched and their mouths contorted in agony.

Paul couldn't remember when their group of three turned four. It was lost somewhere in the night's blur as everyone around them died again and again, each death more tortured than the last. Paige might have joined them after they'd fled the church or perhaps the supermarket.

But he remembered all too well when the four turned back to three. Paige had fallen, a stupid stumble off a curb that could have happened to any of them. By the time they'd realized what happened, it was too late. The dying came, too many swarming (Searching for help? Trying to hurt?) over her before any of them could help. Her screams had echoed in their ears even after they'd run, even after Vic had shouted at them from the door of the bar, even after he'd ushered them into the office. They hadn't spoken of her since.

Outside, the screaming had reached a fevered pitch, and Laura closed her mouth with an audible click. Kevin buried his face in his hands. The others looked down. When the screams turned to moans and chaotic ramblings, Kevin wiped at his eyes. "Why won't they stay dead?" he asked, his voice hollow.

Laura hugged him tighter. "I don't know."

"So what are we going to do?" Kevin asked.

"We wait," Paul said. "And when it's done, we leave."

Kevin frowned. "And how will we know when it's done?"

When they stopped screaming, Paul thought. When they all stopped screaming for good.

"What if they never stop?" Kevin asked. "What do we do then? We can't wait here forever."

The question hung in the air like a bad smell.

"Maybe the phone's working now. You should try it," Laura said.

Vic lifted up the phone receiver, listened for a moment, and shook his head. Laura gave a soft sigh. Paul picked at a hangnail. Helen always got on him for it, silently handing him nail clippers with a small smile. Maybe when it was all over, when they stopped dying, they'd be okay. Maybe it was something like the flu and had to run its course. Tears burned in his eyes.

Vic cleared his throat. "I think we should try and get out of here——"

"Get out?" Paul said, his voice hoarse. "Are you out of your mind? You know what will happen."

"Why don't you let him finish before you jump down his throat?" Laura snapped.

"I wasn't jumping down his throat."

"My house is only three blocks away and my car is in the driveway." Vic lifted one shoulder. "I only drive here when it rains or snows. I can run like hell to the house, get the car, come back, and pick you all up. Then we'll get out of here."

Paul grimaced. "They'll grab you as soon as you go out the door."

"I'll use the back door. I don't think any of them are out that way."

"I want to go with you," Kevin said.

"Kid. I can go faster on my own."

"I don't want to stay here anymore."

"It's better if I go alone." Vic gave Paul and Laura a small nod. He stood up, stretched, and reached for the doorknob. "Make sure you lock this behind me. I shouldn't be too long." He slipped out, shutting the door behind him.

Laura jumped when Paul turned the lock.

The three of them sat in silence while the wall clocked ticked away the minutes.

"I know why he wanted to go alone," Kevin said. "Cause if they catch him, we'll still be safe. But we won't be. Not really. We're stuck here." He picked up the phone and punched numbers at random. "Why isn't the phone working?"

"I don't know," Laura said, taking the phone from his hand.

"I can't believe Mr. Vic doesn't have a computer in here. You can make phone calls over the internet, you know. That's how I talk to my Dad. He's supposed to come home from Iraq in two months." He yawned. "Maybe everything will be okay tomorrow."

"Maybe it will," Laura said. "Why don't you close your eyes and take a cat nap?"

"You'll wake me up when he gets back, right? Promise?"

"Of course we will. Close your eyes."

He did. Within a few minutes, his breathing leveled out. Paul watched the clock. Five minutes passed. Then ten. Then twenty. Then thirty.

Laura rubbed her upper arms. "Vic should be back by now. He said his house was only three blocks away. It shouldn't take this long."

"I know."

"Do you think…?"

Paul shrugged. "I don't know. I don't know anything anymore."

"What do we do if he doesn't come back?"

"We wait. It's Monday. People are going to wonder why folks aren't showing up to work. They'll make phone calls, maybe call the police. Someone will come here and figure out what's going on. They have to."

Another fifteen minutes ticked by. Outside, the dying shrieked on and on. Kevin moaned in his sleep.

"I am so tired," Laura said. "But I feel like I'll never be able to sleep again."

"I wish they would go to sleep," Paul muttered.

"What if it isn't just here?" Laura whispered. "What if it's everywhere?"

"Don't say that. Oh, God, don't say that."

"But the phone isn't working. Don't you think that's a little strange?"

Paul picked up the phone; nothing but dead air answered back. The silence caused an uncomfortable twinge in his abdomen. It didn't mean anything, he thought. It didn't mean anything at all.

A huge thud sounded not far from the locked door. Paul jumped. Laura stifled a cry with her hand, and Kevin sat straight up, his eyes wide. Paul held a finger to his lips and shook his head, hard.

The soft sound of someone crying drifted in the space between the door and the floor. Paul put one hand on the doorknob.

"Don't," Kevin said. "It might be one of them."

"But what if it isn't?" Laura twisted her hands together. "What if it's someone real, like us?"

The cries continued, soft and muffled, and then a voice spoke. "I can't find my keys. Bobby, where did you put the damn remote?" Glass shattered.

"They're inside the bar," Paul whispered.

Laura shuddered. Kevin hunched up his shoulders and turned toward the wall.

"Bobby, come out now. I'm ready to go home."

Another thump. A tinkle of broken glass. Then heavy footsteps leading away and a door slammed shut.

The three of them all sighed, the exhalations adding even more warmth to the stuffy room.

"I don't think he's coming back," Kevin said.

The chaotic voices beyond the door turned to screams again. A loud thump at the door pulled a cry from all three of their mouths.

"It's Vic. Let me in," he said, his voice thick and ragged.

Paul flipped the lock and opened the door. Vic stood in the doorway, his shirt torn and a long scratch marring one cheek. His lips were set in a thin, grim line. "Let's go," he said. "The car's right outside the back door."

"What took you so long?" Paul asked.

"It doesn't matter. Come on. We need to go now."

They filtered out of the office. A table lay on its side, the chairs tossed this way and that, and broken glass littered the floor. The front door was closed; beyond the bar's front windows, a scene from hell itself played out. The dying, clustered in small groups, moved like dark clouds in the street. Screams like banshee wails punctuated each movement, and their flesh bore traces of each previous death.

A louder scream, made all the more unspeakable echoed by hundreds of open mouths, shook the glass in their panes. Bodies tumbled to the ground on legs with too many bends. Bones splintered through the skin with a sound of breaking twigs. Arms raised up, folded this way and that. Cries rose and fell.

In unison, the living inside the bar turned away.

Vic pushed the back door open, checked outside, and nodded. Paul stepped out first, followed by Kevin and Laura. Vic closed the door quietly behind them, and without a word, they piled into the back seat of his still-running car, a four-door sedan redolent with the stale scent of cigarettes. Vic ran around the car and climbed in. Once he engaged the locks on all the doors, Paul sighed in relief.

Vic pulled away from the bar, turned the corner, and slammed on the brakes. A crowd of the dying had gathered at the end of the street, all twisted limbs and misshapen skulls. Kevin covered his eyes. Paul stared over the back of the seat, his mouth open.

Vic put the car in reverse, moved back a few feet, and slammed the brakes again. "Shit."

Paul turned around. Another group had gathered at the opposite end.

"What are they doing?" Laura whispered.

Vic drummed his hands on the steering wheel. "I don't know. They weren't here a minute ago."

"They don't want us to go. They aren't going to let us go," Kevin said and burst into tears.

The group in front moved closer, shambling forward with awkward, limping steps. The bright white of bone peeked out from split skin. One man, Paul thought for sure it was old man Thompson who'd lived on his street, crawled forward on his elbows, dragging his legs behind him.

And underneath the horrible sounds of shuffling feet and moans of pain, whispers emerged.

"Help us, please."

"Won't hurt you."

"Make it stop."

A young girl's voice lifted over the others. "Please, oh, please, oh, please."

"Go away and leave us alone," Kevin shrieked, his voice filling up every empty space in the car. He strained forward, the muscles in his neck tense. "Go away."

Laura put her arm around Kevin's shoulders. "It's okay."

"No, it isn't okay. It isn't at all. Let's go. Please, let's go."

The crowd moved closer.

A woman, as broken as the rest, stepped forward, away from the crowd, her arms open.

"Paul, I want to go home. Come take me home."

"Oh, God, that's Helen. That's my wife."

Laura grabbed his arm. "Yes, but you can't help her. We'll get out, and we'll get help."

"How do you know there's anyone out there left to help?"

"Of course there is. There has to be."

A young girl moved out of the crowd and staggered toward the car. "Daddy!" she shrieked.

Paul shook his head. "Oh, no, oh, no. Eve, I'm so sorry." His little girl, the one he'd held by the hands when she was too tiny to walk, but he held her up and bounced her feet on the ground, the little girl he'd held at night when she'd had bad dreams, the little girl he'd loved——

"Let it go," Vic said. "Let her go."

Vic moved the car back another foot. And the dying died again.

The crowd stopped moving and fell silent, eyes widening in fear and dreadful anticipation. Inside the car, Laura moaned. Orange-red flames flickered from nowhere, reaching up and out from under their skin. The dying dropped, writhing on the ground. Their screams took flight. The flames burned brighter, licking skin and melting flesh; filling the car with a flickering glow.

Kevin dug his nails into his cheeks, pulling his face into a Halloween scare. Laura screamed, brittle and high-pitched. Vic and Paul shouted.

And Paul's little girl screamed in agony, batting her hair and her face with her hands.

"I can't just sit here. I can't," Paul whispered.

"Everybody close your eyes," Vic said.

Paul flipped the lock up and gripped the handle of the door. His baby girl was burning out there. He couldn't just let Vic drive him away. He opened the door. The smell of burning hair and skin and the sharp tang of smoke flooded into the car. The taste of dying flesh filled Paul's throat.

"What are you doing?" Laura screamed.

"Shut the goddamn door," Vic shouted.

"I can't, I'm sorry," Paul said. "Go without me."

He got out and moved away from the car, toward Eve, his Evie.

"It hurts, Daddy. It hurts. Help me," she cried.

Paul sobbed. "Evie, baby, I'm so sorry." He moved forward.

Behind him, the engine gunned in reverse, tires screeched, and the air filled with the liquid squelch of flesh striking pavement, the snap of bones breaking, and horrible screams.

"Evie, Daddy's here, okay?"

The dying charged.

They surged forward, screaming and shrieking behind the flames. Eve reached him first. When her hand touched his arm, all the hairs sizzled down to dark nubs.

"Let's go see the fireworks," she screamed into his face, her own face alight with tiny flames and wisps of smoke.

Paul opened his mouth and the heat scorched his throat. Dimly, he heard the car engine roar again.

"Daddy," Eve whispered, her eyes blank and inhuman. She smiled through blackened lips. "Stay with me."

Hands gripped his shoulders, pushing, pulling, grasping. He fell to his knees. The flames flickered away and the dead fell on top of him, pushing him down until he was drowning in a sea of charred flesh.

From far away, he heard Eve's laughter, but she was missing from the sound. It was a madwoman's laugh. His daughter was gone. He couldn't help her.

Paul dug up through the bodies, his fingers tearing and ripping. He shoved arms and legs out of the way, flesh raining down in black chunks on his hands. A clump of liquefying fat landed on his shoulder, burning hot through his shirt. He screamed and the dying mimicked his cry.

Helen's voice broke through the screams, a stranger's voice, all thick vowels and slurred syllables. "Paul, did you remember the milk?"

He scrambled to his feet. The dying fell to the ground around him, crying out as their ruined bodies began to shake in convulsions.

"Daddy," Eve cried out, her voice twisted in pain.

Paul ran away from his daughter, away from his wife, with tears blurring his vision.

Behind him, the screams went on and on and on.

Undead and Unbound

DESCANSE EN PAZ
By William Meikle

Pastor David Smith took one look at what passed for a town and shook his head.

I travelled two thousand miles for this?

It certainly was a far cry from his ministry in Boston. There were no fine ladies here, no men with European overcoats and expensive walking canes sauntering casually on an evening stroll. Instead there was mud and slurry, threadbare clothes and a sense of urgency and panic that was almost palpable. The houses, if they could be called that, were little more than ramshackle huts and tents strewn along what had once been a riverbank. The whole site was sunk deep in a narrow canyon. Where water had once flowed freely there was now an open scar on the landscape crawling with scrambling miners, each trying to outdo his neighbor in the rush for the small fragments of yellow stone that could be extracted from the soil and gravel of the old riverbed.

And not a one of them has a thought for God in their heads.

It was obvious that Old Jock, his driver on the long hard trail to get here, had exactly the same thoughts.

"Say hello to your new flock Pastor," the Scotsman said, and cackled before having to spit out a glob of blood. "I wish you luck, for you're surely going to need it."

It took the older man several seconds of coughing before he was strong enough to take the reins again and urge the horses down into the narrow sided valley that bounded *New Hamilton*. Every foot closer made the Pastor's heart sink further. Each twist and turn down the gully brought some fresh depravity into sight. Those miners who were not working were drunk, or fornicating openly with grubby saloon girls, or both. There looked to be at least half a dozen establishments; some no more than tents pitched at opportune spots, offering gambling, drink and women for anyone able to pay. He guessed that a lot of the gold went straight from the riverbed to the brothels with nary time for a breath to be caught in the process.

The Pastor had a tent of his own in the back of the wagon; wrapped up as a nice clean bundle of canvas that was going to look too white when pitched in this place. He had few illusions as to the enormity of the task ahead of him, but the Lord had spoken to him. He had a *mission* in this place, one that he had no choice but to see to the end.

They had to ask nearly a dozen people before they found one who was both sober enough and smart enough to show them to the spot that had been allotted to them. It had cost him nearly two hundred dollars to buy the small patch of land, but he would consider it money well spent if a single soul could be saved from what was coming.

That *something* was coming he had no doubt whatsoever. While Old Jock made camp and arranged to have the tent pitched the Pastor sat quietly on the wagon, smoking his long clay pipe and remembering; the night of *the dream*, the one that had brought him all this way.

It was the dreams that had led him to take the cloth in the first place, back in the days when his own soul had been in as much danger as those of the gold-seekers here. After the first one he'd left the Navy, after the second he went to a church, and after the third he took the orders of his ministry. That had all been many years ago now, and he *had* thought that the Lord, having shown him the path, had moved on to worthier men. But he had been wrong.

It came on a Friday night, after a particularly uneventful day in the church. He had just taken to bed, and drifted off to sleep only to be thrown into the most vivid of nightmares. Afterwards he remembered few of the specifics——just the blood, the gold and the name *New Hamilton*. But that was enough. The very next day he had started the proceedings that had brought him here, to this seat, on this wagon, to arrive in this den of iniquity.

I have souls to save. It is time to begin.

He barely gave Old Jock time to get the tent pitched and the benches in place before he made his start. He strode out to stand on a small ledge above the riverbed and, with a voice trained by years of preaching in the big church in Boston, called the faithful to prayer.

At first no one paid him any notice, but he was on a *mission*, and would brook no refusal. He continued to *insist* at the top of his voice, issuing dire warnings against the wrath of God, reminding them of fire, brimstone and the gnashing of teeth waiting for unrepentant sinners.

Finally they came, in dribs and drabs at first, and mostly more curious than in any great haste to meet the Lord. Among them was a group of swaggering youths, none of whom looked ready for shaving yet but all with the blank stare and cold eyes the Pastor knew well from his fighting days in the Navy.

Spoiling for a fight, and no sense of right and wrong. I will need to watch these ones closely.

"We don't need your holy-joe shite," one of them shouted, and the rest laughed. Several of the older men tried to hush them into submission but they kept catcalling and laughing long into the Pastor's sermon. They only moved on when they got bored…which thankfully wasn't too long into the service.

The Pastor looked over his remaining *flock*. In truth not many of them showed much enthusiasm for the word of the Lord.

But they have come. And I can make them listen. It is what I am here for.

~*~

The Pastor wasn't too surprised in the morning to find Jock reeking of liquor, asleep and fully clothed in the back of the wagon. He had guessed when the man left the tent the previous afternoon that he wouldn't see him for a while, not sober anyway. He didn't begrudge the Scotsman his drink, even if it was a sin to give in to the flesh quite so openly. No, the old man deserved it for the times he'd spent coaxing tired horses over mountain passes, endless prairies potted with gopher holes and across swollen rivers.

I owe him a great debt. I can scarce repay him with a sermon at this early hour.

Instead he busied himself with preparing what would have to pass for a breakfast——dried beef jerky and coffee. Later he might venture forth to find bread and maybe even some fruit, but for now he made do with what the Lord had seen fit to provide. He was still filled with the excitement of yesterday's first sermon. He'd *felt* the Lord move through him, had seen on the faces of his new flock that he had reached them. He still did not know why he had been brought to this town, but he now knew for sure that he'd made the right decision in coming.

But tell me Lord, what would you have me do now?

He had to wait less time than he had anticipated for his answer. Just as he thought it was time to rouse Old Jock, circumstance did it for him. A loud *blast* rocked the canyon and the air was suddenly filled with smoke and dust. When it cleared he saw Jock sitting up on the bed of the wagon blearily looking around.

"You needn't have been quite so loud about waking me," the old man said, laughing then holding his head. The Pastor wasn't listening. He looked up the slope to the source of the blast. The dust had already cleared and he saw a small crowd of miners scurrying over a new scar on the hill. A loud cry echoed down the valley as someone called for a doctor.

And where they need a doctor, they might also need some spiritual guidance.

He left at a run, only vaguely aware that Jock was following along, but already some way behind him. He was among the first on the scene. A large area of steep hillside had been split open. If those involved had expected to expose a new seam to mine they were to be bitterly disappointed, for instead of gold they got bodies. Or rather, they got bones; skeletal remains, many of which wore metal armor tarnished and rusted after what must have been centuries in the ground.

They have uncovered a mass grave.

He did not have time to inspect the old bones, for there were new ones that needed more urgent attention. Two men lay sprawled on the hillside, the rocks around them splashed red with their blood. The local doctor was tending to one of them who had white bone protruding from his thigh. The second was alive, but surely would not be for too long. Smith bent down and cradled the lad's head, trying to ignore the wet heat of brain tissue and blood that immediately filled his palm.

"Do you repent your sins boy," the Pastor said, whispering.

The youth, barely into his teens by the look, mouthed his reply through tears. "I don't need your holy-joe shite," the lad said, and died before waiting further reply.

The Pastor laid the boy down. He turned to see if the doctor needed help but the second injured man was already being carried off down the hill. The Pastor was left alone with the dead boy and the scattered remains from the disturbed graves. He was suddenly aware of the red

Descanse En Paz

gore that was plastered over his palms. He was loath to rub them clean on his own cassock, and to use the dead boy's clothes would feel like desecration. He looked around for something to use. It was only then that he realized the scale of the grave that had been exposed.

Bones, weaponry and armor lay strewn all across the hillside; as many as thirty fighting men had been interred here and it looked like they had merely been thrown in a heap together and covered quickly. There was no sign of any funereal vestments and no indication that the ground had been consecrated in any way. There was a fragment of what might at one time have been a cloak just to his left but to use that would have been just as much a desecration as using the dead boy's clothes.

Instead he bent and rubbed his hands in the dirt, over and over until all the blood was hidden under brown smears. When he stood it was to find Old Jock struggling up the hill towards him.

"Give me a hand Jock," he said. "We'll get the boy back down and see that he gets a Christian burial."

Jock looked around.

"We could just inter him here with the rest?"

At that a trickle of stones came down the hill from higher up, pebbles running around their feet.

"No," the Pastor said. "I'll need to come back and tend to these poor souls here, but for now we need to see right by the boy. Let us take him down."

More stones trickled down from above as they hefted the lad between them and made for the town. As they neared their tent the Pastor's gaze was taken by a shifting shadow back up the hill but when he looked again the sun was in his eyes and all he saw was a rock tumbling over and over down the slope.

By the time they laid the boy down on a pew in the prayer tent the Pastor could see that Old Jock himself was near to collapse, his face as white as the dead boy's and fresh blood flecked at his lips.

"I'll take him from here Jock," he said softly. "You get some rest."

The old man didn't complain, just shuffled off. The Pastor wondered how long Jock had left. For the whole duration of the long journey he'd coughed blood into his handkerchief. *Black Lung* he called it, but whatever its name, it was surely killing him, and the Pastor knew he'd have more than just the boy to bury soon enough.

But not yet Lord. Please not yet. I've grown fond of the cantankerous old man.

The Pastor turned his attention to the dead boy. No-one had as yet turned up to claim him and, judging by the fact that the panning and digging activities had already started up again all over the site, it looked like no-one was likely to do so.

But he is somebody's son. I need to do right by him.

He started by washing the blood and grime from the body. More brain tissue coated his palms until he had it cleaned away to his satisfaction. He leaned down and closed the boy's eyes.

Dear Father, take this soul to your bosom and...

"I told you afore," an indignant voice said, clear as day. "I don't need your holy-joe shite."

The Pastor was almost afraid to open his eyes, but when he did he was still looking down at the dead boy.

So you're hearing things in daytime now as well? Are you sure it is God's voice you are hearing and not just delusional mania?

He's asked himself that same question several times on the journey here, and had no answer to it beyond the depth of his faith.

That will have to be enough.

He went back to his prayers. There were no interruptions this time. He reached the end and made the sign of the cross over the dead boy. He had just turned away when the first screams rang out over the valley. He turned towards the source of the sound and could scarcely believe what he saw.

Delusional mania?

The miners were running down the gully, fleeing in disarray ahead of a score or more figures. At first they were only dark outlines on the skyline, strangely thin and drawn, but as they started to move down the hill it was obvious that whoever had been buried in that long unmarked grave was no longer resting in peace. Some clad in armor, others wrapped in the remains of cloaks, but all carrying rusted and tarnished weapons, they moved like warriors, herding the miners ahead of them. There was only bone and strips of skin inside the clothing but it did not slow them down any. The *clack* as their loose joints worked, echoed, loud even above the fearful yells of their prey.

The Pastor did not stop to think. He strode out onto a shelf above the gully. From here he could see that the skeletal attackers would soon have herded the miners into a narrow ravine from which there would be no escape from their blades. In his mind's eye the Pastor once again

DESCANSE EN PAZ

saw his dream——the too red blood, the screams, the carnage.

"Stop, in the name of the Lord."

His shout echoed the length and breadth of the encampment. The miners kept running, piling into each other in a tangle of legs and arms as the ravine narrowed and funneled them into a panicked thrash of limbs.

The skeletal attackers did not follow, seemingly struck immobile by the Pastor's words. A tall figure at the front of the group turned, black shadows moving in empty eye sockets. The Pastor felt the gaze like a physical blow, one that sent him immediately down into blackness.

Someone spoke to him.

He listened.

~*~

If there is a hell on Earth then surely it is in this place. No God-fearing man should have to face the horrors I have led my men through to reach this pass. My name is Juan Santoro, Captain of these brave men here. On the 3rd of April 1535 we set forth from San Diego into the mountains looking for gold for the cause.

I would be remiss in my duty to the Church if I did not report on the things that plague this new land. If the Crown wishes, as I have been told, to colonize this place, then the king must know what manner of things lay claim on it at present.

In truth, I know not what we have found. The natives died bravely defending it, and for most of the day we thought that we had stumbled on a great treasure; that the gold we had sought for so long was within our grasp. We fought through their defenses, hacking and slashing our way through the savages to the mouth of this dark cave.

As I have said, we expected treasure. And we found it. Gold lay strewn across the floor, no more attention paid to it than if it had been pebbles for the amusement of children.

An ancient native sat there cross-legged, just staring at us.

"If you want this earth so badly, you may have it. But as the earth stays where it belongs, so you too will stay."

And at that, I felt my will escape me. I tried to pray, but God would not hear me, not in that place, not in the dark. The grip on my mind grew ever stronger.

I saw vast plains of snow and ice where black things slumped amid tumbled ruins of long dead cities. My head swam, and the walls of the cave melted and ran. The firebrand in my hand seemed to recede into a great distance until it was little more than a pinpoint of light in a blanket of darkness, and I was alone, in a vast cathedral of emptiness.

A tide took me, a swell that lifted and transported me, faster than thought, to the green twilight of ocean depths far distant.

I realized I was not alone. My men were with me.

They are still with me. We float, mere shadows now, in that cold silent sea. I am aware that others I knew as brothers are nearby, but I have no thought for aught but the rhythm, the dance. We dream, of vast empty spaces, of giant clouds of gas that engulf the stars, of blackness where there is nothing but endless dark, endless quiet.

And while our slumbering god dreams, we dance for him, there in the twilight, dance to the rhythm.

And here we have been, through all the long passage of time, until now, when our eyes have opened, and the glory of the voice of the Lord has finally spoken to us.

Give us rest Lord.

Dear Lord, give us rest.

~*~

The Pastor came out of it slowly, aware that someone else was now speaking to him, but at first the accent sounded strange and uncouth after the soft Spanish from the dream.

"I said, are ye all right Pastor? You gave me a hell of a fright."

He looked up into Old Jock's face, only then becoming aware that he was lying on his back on the ground. He sat up, too fast, and the world swam around him. He tried again, slower this time, and managed to get carefully to his feet, helped by Jock giving him a shoulder to lean on. He looked down into the ravine.

It was empty of people, no sign of either miners or *skeletons*.

"What happened?" the Pastor said.

"I was hoping you would tell me," Jock replied. "Them *haunts* were running down the miners, you commanded them to stop, and the next thing anybody knew the *haunts* were heading back up the hill and you were flat on your back on the ground here."

The Pastor's head was clearing slowly, but he could still hear that

Descanse En Paz

soft Spanish voice in his head.

Dear Lord, give us rest.

"Where are the miners now?"

Jock pointed down to the village.

"They've called a town meeting. I think they mean to go back up the hill and do something about the *haunts*."

The Pastor laughed. "What, kill them you mean?" He started to walk down the hill. "Come on. If there is a meeting, then I have something to say."

He strode off, leaving Jock to follow behind as quickly as he could manage.

There was indeed a meeting in progress. The youths——the same bunch who had heckled so loudly at his sermon the day before, seemed to be holding forth, loudly and obviously drunkenly.

"I say we go up there and show them who the boss is around these parts," the ringleader shouted, and to the Pastor's dismay there was much drunken agreement in the crowd. He pushed his way to the front.

"And what will you do when you get there? These are troubled souls. They need to be met with the Lord's voice, not violence."

The ringleader turned, spittle flecking his lips.

"Violence is it? Haven't they already killed young John Sommers? You yourself brought the body down."

That drew more shouts of agreement in the crowd.

I'm losing them.

"That lad died from his own misuse of powder. Whatever these... these skeletons, might be, all they want is to be left alone to make their peace with the Lord," the Pastor said.

The youths all laughed at that.

"And I suppose you've been talking to them Pastor? How's that working for you?"

The crowd laughed along loudly. Whisky bottles were being passed freely, as were rifles and ammunition. The Pastor was pushed aside.

"You can say your prayers when we're done," the leader of the youths said. "Your holy-joe shite won't be needed until then."

And with that the Pastor and old Jock were left alone. It seemed that almost everyone else had fallen in with the youth's plan. A drunken mob, little more than a rabble with rifles, started to climb the slope out of town.

"Just as well I did not mention the gold," the Pastor muttered. That got him a quizzical look from the old Scotsman. The Pastor put a hand on the old man's shoulder.

"I fear this is not going to end well," he said. "Promise me that you'll continue to do the Lord's work should anything happen to me?"

Jock nodded. "I promise to try. You're a good man Pastor. But maybe this is not your fight?"

The Pastor was starting to believe otherwise.

Maybe this is exactly my fight. Maybe I have been tending to the wrong flock since I got here.

Without another word he started to stride up the hill after the mob. He was still a long way back when the gunfire started. The screams came quickly afterwards.

~*~

He took the hill at a flat-out run, but was still too late. The scene that met him came straight out of the dream that brought him here in the first place. Men lay dead and dying all over the hill as the skeletal *Conquistadores* hacked and hewed gaping wounds into the miners' flesh with weapons too blunted by age to do the job quickly. Volley after volley of rifle shots rang in the hills, punching holes in rusted armor, shredding cloth made threadbare with age and sending chips flying from old dried bone. But the *Conquistadores* kept on hacking, and the miners kept dying. Blood ran in streams over the dry stones.

The previously cocksure youths stood in a circle, pumping round after round into advancing skeletons that had them almost surrounded. The Pastor strode forward and raised a hand to begin a prayer. But before he could speak the ringleader saw him coming and raised his rifle.

"You see what happens when you bring your holy-joe *shite* here Pastor? See what you have done?"

And without warning he fired, the shot taking the Pastor full in the chest and sending him to his knees. Old Jock bellowed in rage and moved to run forward. The Pastor was able to put up a hand to stop him.

"Help me up Jock, one last time," he said. He put the hand to his chest. When he lifted it away his palm was fully coated, red with blood. Jock put a shoulder in the Pastor's armpit and together they managed

Descanse En Paz

to get him upright. The Pastor's sight had already started to dim.

"Remember your promise Jock," he whispered. "I'll be watching you."

He raised the red hand and called out.

Anima eius et animae omnium fidelium defunctorum per Dei misericordiam requiescant in pace.

As one the *Conquistadores* paused. The youths kept firing, but still their shots had little effect. Once again the lead *Conquistadore's* eye sockets turned towards the Pastor.

Anima eius et animae omnium fidelium defunctorum per Dei misericordiam requiescant in pace, he called out again, and this time Jock's voice was raised alongside his own. Although there were only the two of them, the chant took on depth and substance, ringing and echoing around the canyon until it seemed that a vast throng called out with them. The Pastor stumbled, almost fell, but Jock held him up, and kept up the Latin chant going, keeping the echoes running around the canyon walls.

The Pastor took a last look over the scene before him. The *Conquistadores*, as one, dropped their weapons, sank to their knees and raised their palms together in prayer, bony fingers pointed skyward.

The Pastor was almost blind now, and the fire of pain in his chest threatened to burn him out completely. His voice failed him and his last words were whispered, in Spanish.

"Descanse En Paz."

The skeletal *Conquistadores* fell face first to the dirt.

The Pastor fell forward to join them.

He had found his flock.

Undead and Unbound

THUNDER IN OLD KILPATRICK

By Gustavo Bondoni

The skies came alive with a drone like a disturbed beehive and Richard glanced up at the heavens.

But only for a moment. There were more pressing things occupying his attention on Earth, wonderful things that he'd never imagined possible back in boring old London. Fluttering on the ground in front of him was a bird, red-headed and angry, dragging a broken wing through the heather.

Richard wondered what to do with it. There was no question of just letting it be, not after he's spent all afternoon trying to bring one down, but he was torn between the sheer delight of tormenting it, taking revenge on all of taunting, elusive bird-kind, or of nursing it back to health and having it for a pet. These weighty meditations were the reason that Old Tom managed to sneak up on him.

"I see you've got your first grouse, laddie."

"A grouse?" He'd heard some of the men talking about grouses, and sometimes they even went out to hunt them. The guns they carried were so big that Richard had always imagined that a grouse would be something huge, with hide, tusks and a temper to match. The thing wriggling forlornly on the ground certainly didn't look the part.

Old Tom nodded towards the bird. "They're hard to bring down, especially with a sling. You've the makings of a hunter, boy." The groundskeeper's craggy face never showed any emotion, but his voice seemed to radiate approval. "But stones won't save you if Hannah finds you out here. The wireless says that the sirens have gone, over in Clydebank, and she's ordered everyone into the cellar."

"The sirens are going all the time. We're too far away for it to matter," Richard replied, half-mutinous. He knew that Old Tom wouldn't report his words, but there was always the chance that Hannah would appear from out of the underbrush. The plump, grandmotherly woman was lightning-fast with a switch. "And I'll tell her I ran all the way back, but I was too far away."

The old man pursed his lips to speak, but suddenly stopped and looked into the air. Richard realized that the drone had grown louder. But he still didn't worry. It was probably just an RAF defender, reaching the scene of the bombing too late to be of any use.

A rough, calloused hand pressed into Richard's shoulder. "Get down, lad!"

Tom pushed him down into the heather, right beside the struggling bird, and lay on top of him. Or at least it felt that way to Richard. Before he'd finished falling, he felt the Earth around him shake. Then he was deafened by a sound of thunder and thrown some meters clear. He hit the ground hard, and didn't hear the second bomb.

~*~

The pain in Richard's hand became more and more urgent, and he came back to his senses with a gasp. A voice, shouting in a closed, unintelligible Scottish brogue sounded distantly through the ringing in his ears. He turned his head and saw Old Tom brandishing a thick branch in one hand. The groundskeeper's other arm hung, bloody and limp, at his side.

At first, Richard wondered whether the blast that had thrown them across the moor had also finally driven the old man insane. The servants muttered about Tom's lonely life and bleak disposition all the time, not caring that the young master might hear. Now, though, the man seemed to be incoherent, bracing for an attack.

The doubts were short-lived. A lumbering form, wearing rags and some rusted metallic fabric, came into view. The strange figure uttered a low moan, a sound that——even through the buzzing in Richard's ears——felt like the lament of a lost soul. He paused in front of the groundskeeper, and them lowered a shoulder and advanced.

Tom made a valiant effort to stop the second man, advancing grimly and breaking the branch——a dry, infirm weapon——over the other man's head.

The blow was completely ignored by the second man. Moaning

Thunder in Old Kilpatrick

continuously, he struck once, with his hand, and sent Tom head over heels to the ground. Then he waited, as if to see what the groundskeeper would do next, until satisfied that his opponent was not going to move again.

With slow, deliberate motions, the man turned to where Richard was lying. The boy felt the fear rushing into his gut and tried to stand, tried to run. But it was impossible. His balance abandoned him, and he stumbled onto the floor, able only to lie and watch as the figure of Tom's assailant advanced.

The other man bent and picked Richard up by the shirt. The scent coming off of him was of earth and mold. The man pulled him up to face him, and Richard nearly fainted when he saw the eyes, they were white, milky, the eyes of a blind man. The man's skin was grey——almost white——and there was an open cut running across the length of his forehead, but the open flap of skin showed no blood, just more white-grey.

Richard opened his mouth, but the scream came through his deafened ears as a pitiful whine. The man held his gaze for just another second before dismissively tossing the boy to the ground. When Richard's head hit, the darkness descended once again.

~*~

The next time Richard opened his eyes, he found himself in a bed. He was in a wood-paneled room, with sunlight streaming through a window. A glass of water sat in a tray beside him.

So, it was all a dream, he thought sleepily, and decided to go out to see what delights the moors held in store for him.

He never managed it. As he attempted to sit up, a strange bundle around his chest impeded his progress, and it was a good thing, too. Pain shot up from his ribs, and he fell back to the bed with a gasp.

"Richard! What do you think you're doing, young man?" Hannah entered the room, her dark blue uniform immediately filling it, leaving little room for anything else. Hannah was supposedly head of the household staff——not quite a housekeeper, not quite a member of the family——but, in reality, she ran the house with an iron fist, and anyone who wasn't an adult member of the gentry would do as she ordered or feel the sharp sting of her tongue. Richard thought there must be a bit of bear in her makeup. "Near broken in half by the bombs, and trying to get out of bed without a by-your-leave. I'll not have it."

He nodded dumbly, as was his custom whenever she asked him a question, but the tactic——usually infallible——was wasted on her.

"Now tell me how you're feeling. Those ribs all right? Doctor said you'd be feeling the break for a few weeks. No tree-climbing for you, lad."

"Break?" Richard said. He was relieved to find that speech was possible, and that the pain had subsided.

"Broke a rib, maybe two. I'm surprised it wasn't more, fool lad, playing out on the moors in the middle of a German attack. How many times have I told you to get inside when the alarms sound? The cellar is the only place to be in a raid. But do you listen? No. No one ever listens to me."

That was so ridiculously untrue that Richard nearly interrupted her, but caught himself in time. Even so, it was unlikely that Hannah would have paid him the least attention. She had a full head of steam.

"And that old man is the worst of the lot. Just because the master is fond of grouse hunting and he's the only one who can keep his grouse moors clear, he thinks he's above the law. Well, you see where it got him?" She paused to give Richard a questioning glare, to which the boy could only give a confused look in response. "It nearly cost him an arm——and it did cost him his sanity, not that there was much of it to begin with. Do you know what he's been saying?" This time she didn't stop to ask for Richard's opinion, she just went on. "He's been saying there's a wight loose on the moors. That's Old Tom for you. He'd never be content to be bombed by the Germans. No, he has to bring ghouls and ghosts into his story as well."

Hannah sighed in disgust and left, muttering something about getting the young fool something to eat, if the old fool had left anything at all. Richard ignored her completely.

He was thinking about a wight.

~*~

The next few days were torture. Even though he hardly felt any pain, Richard was forced to stay in bed, under strict guard and the threat of lost privileges, as life went on around him. That, in itself, would have been enough to make him chafe. Who knew how long the

THUNDER IN OLD KILPATRICK

war would last, how long the German bombs in London would allow him to remain out there in the Scottish countryside? His freedom from the grey limitations of life as the son of a wealthy city merchant might come to an end at any time.

But this was not the main reason for Richard's restlessness. There was a darkness in the house that made the weeks before——when German air raids were a daily occurrence——seem like a light-hearted time of happiness. Maids, whispering as they approached, would immediately fall silent when they entered his room to clean or to leave his meals on the bedside table. Even Hannah, forbidding as she was, seemed to be showing chinks in her armor. Once, during a particularly windy day, a sudden gust closed one of the room's shutters with a loud bang, causing Hannah to start and drop a tray complete with Richard's breakfast. The woman had tried to hide her fear under a veneer of anger, but her face had remained white as a sheet for the rest of the day——and she'd ordered all the shutters on the ground floor to be closed as soon as dusk began to fall.

Frustration mounted as the days went by and no one gave him any indication of what was going on. Day after day he suffered until, one afternoon, bored of the illustrated books that had kept him sane to that point, Richard stole out of bed. He reasoned that, if discovered, he would simply say that he was on the way to the restroom——his only permitted excursion——and hadn't told anyone in order to avoid being a nuisance.

The door of his room was about halfway down the hall on the first floor of the house. Richard made his way silently down the corridor, towards the flight of stairs leading into the entrance hall. He stopped dead. Below him, two of the maids were in earnest conversation.

"They say the wight's not been seen for two days," one said. She was the scullery maid, married to a clerk in town, so she was the source of any and all information in the house.

"Must be hiding."

"No, they say wights don't know how to hide. They're just dead flesh, and they have to keep moving. They have unfinished business, that's why they can't really die."

"But this one was from years and years ago. How come it's just come out now?"

"Old Tom says that they must have buried it under tons of stone, and that the bombs set it free."

"*Pshaw*. Old Tom ain't right in the head since he lost 'is arm. Anyhow, if the wight's gone, the army probably got it."

"No. You can't kill a wight with guns. It can't rest until it does what it has to do. That's what I told Emma when she said that it had probably thrown itself into the sea. I told her that wights have to do what they have to do. It's silly to think they'd go throwing themselves into the sea."

"Why not? Must be an awful way to live, being a wight."

They continued this line of conversation for some time, repeating themselves over and over again. In time Richard realized these two would not give him any more useful information. They knew less about the monster than he did. Just from looking into its dead eyes for that single instant, he could have told them beyond any doubt that the wight was still out there somewhere. The mere suggestion of its throwing itself into the sea was ridiculous. He moved back to his room, undiscovered.

~*~

It took the full force of the doctor's command——and Richard managed to overhear the phrase: "I don't care if the armies of Hell itself are out on those moors. The boy needs to be allowed to recover in the fresh air,"——for Richard's personal Cerberus to allow him freedom.

At first, the command was taken literally, with supervised strolls along the terrace being deemed sufficient contact with the elements to be going with. But even Hannah quickly realized that this was impracticable. People busy making certain he wasn't being attacked by ancient monsters were often needed in the kitchen or elsewhere. And the fact that they avoided any mention of it was even worse. They pretended to be concerned that he might fall, or that he would move in the wrong direction and hurt himself. Richard fantasized about asking the scullery maid that was with him that day what, exactly, she would do if the wight attacked them.

He kept silent, and on the third day they simply left him to his own devices.

Richard knew that there was a fine line between freedom and obedience that had to be observed. If he disappeared into the moors for too long, Hannah would cause his freedom to end in a complete way——and besides, he still wasn't in any condition to be overly frolicsome. But there was one thing he had to do, despite the darkness of the day, and the fog that hadn't quite burned away even though it was nearly noon.

The place where the German plane had dropped the bombs was about half a mile away, just beyond one of the small hills that dotted the estate.

Richard set off, and soon found the wight sitting in the shadows of the crater. It looked up as he approached, and Richard was again surprised by the lack of life in its eyes. He knew what people were saying about it, knew that it was supposed to be the walking dead, supposed to be able to tear strong men apart without even making much of an effort, but he felt no fear. He'd moved on, and was no longer the shell-shocked bomb victim the wight had encountered previously. Even injured, Richard knew he could run faster than it could stumble after him.

They studied each other in silence for a moment. The wight's dead eyes seemed to have grown glassier since they'd last met, but other than that, it didn't seem to be the worse for wear. It was still wearing the rust-colored shirt whose unused hood fell behind the creature's head. Now that Richard had time to observe more carefully, he saw that the shirt reached its knees, and was held in place at the waist by a rotted belt which couldn't possibly hold out much longer. The cloth rags which it had been wearing over the shirt on their first encounter were gone.

Somehow, this creature, this dead man from another age, looked perfectly at home standing in a bomb crater in the gloom of the overcast moor. It looked natural, making Richard feel like he was the otherworldly intruder.

Without warning, it emitted the moan again. It wasn't a loud sound, but the thing cut straight to the boy's soul, passing through his physical body as if it were made of spider silk. Richard nearly turned and ran, but held his position until the wailing stopped and they stood facing each other again, with Richard feeling just slightly wave-tossed.

The wight clearly didn't see him as a threat. Whether something had changed since their last encounter, or whether it simply remembered the ease with which it had handled him, Richard had no way of knowing. But the creature simply turned, without so much as a shrug, and began methodically lifting stones that it found in the scarred earth where the German bombs had fallen. There seemed to be no point to what it was doing——every rock it took into its arms was then dropped back into a seemingly random place as it picked up another. It wasn't piling them up, nor was it organizing them in any way. It didn't even seem to know which ones it had already discarded. In the ten minutes that Richard watched, he saw the wight pick up one particular stone no less than eight times before tossing it back to the ground.

Richard took two steps forward, trying to get a closer look at what was happening, but suddenly he heard a familiar drone, high in the skies.

He didn't stop to think that it might just be an RAF patrol, he didn't stop to hear if the sirens were going. He just ran as quickly as his battered body could take him for the imaginary safety of the house.

Richard only turned back once, when the wailing of the wight hit him from behind. He turned to see it waving its arms frantically at some unseen enemy above, as if it were being attacked by bees. Richard stood for a second, thinking how much it looked like some of the engravings of old Scottish knights in the books in his father's library.

Then he turned back to the house and ran from the sound of the airplanes.

~*~

The raids continued, around the clock, for two days. This time, it was no incidental thing, with bombers dropping a load or two on their way back to Germany. This time, the target was Clydebank, and Richard could hear the distant rumbling whenever he left the bunker. They were tense times——but all of them knew, at least deep within themselves——that the shelter would protect them. It might have been a false belief, or even completely mistaken, but it kept them from going mad. And the thunder from the bombs never came too close again.

On the third day, the bombing stopped, and thunder of a different kind, full of blowing gales and rattling windows took over the land. Richard was confined to the house for yet another spell. By the time the storm blew over, he was nearly completely recovered, and fit to burst from the combined effects of cabin fever and the secret he'd managed to keep to himself in the shelter. As soon as it dawned sunny,

Thunder in Old Kilpatrick

he was off into the moors.

The wight hadn't gone far. It was standing nearly in the same place as he had left it, almost as though it hadn't moved.

But it was clear that it must have. The place where the bombs had fallen had been churned into a muddy mass, of deep footprints and the wight itself had half-dried clods sticking to it as high as its knees.

And it had found a sword.

Well, perhaps the word 'sword' is a bit generous for the rusted piece of metal it held in one hand and whose edge lay on one shoulder, but it was clear from looking at the wight that for the undead creature at least, it felt that the sword was no less than Excalibur. It seemed to stand taller, prouder, and a sense of calm that hadn't been present in their earlier encounters filled the moor.

It watched Richard approach but made no move towards him. When it was clear that the boy would come no closer, the creature simply turned away, sending its gaze back up into the heavens. It seemed to be waiting for something, and its posture made it extremely clear that it was prepared to wait as long as necessary.

What exactly it was waiting for was more of a mystery.

Richard wondered whether it believed that the noisy, dangerous metal beasts that ringed the sky were dragons——or whether they were angels sent to take him to his promised land. One thing seemed certain: a dead creature from the deep past armed with a rusted sword was unlikely to understand the Luftwaffe. The boy took another step towards the wight. And then another. A third.

At the fourth, the wight turned its attention back to the ground and gave him a look that froze Richard in his tracks. It raised its sword——not at the boy, but at the sky, and grunted. Then it pointed at the countryside, indicating everything around them: the moors, the overcast sky and a distant copse of trees, and tried to speak. The sound that came out was completely impossible to understand, but the message was clear. What was out there belonged to the wight——and all challenges would be met by the sword, rusty or not.

Richard halted, but held his ground, anger welling up at the implied message. "All this land belongs to my family. And it has for hundreds of years." He puffed up his chest. "My grandfather said we took it from another clan back when Scots still ruled themselves."

The wight seemed to study him intently, to use its glazed eyes to stare deep into Richard's soul. Then it turned its attention back to the sky.

"I think you're one of my grandfather's grandfathers. Or maybe you were one of their servants. In any case, if you want to stay here, you have to listen to me."

The wight glanced back at the boy for just one instant, then dismissed him completely. Richard tried to get it to respond again, but no matter what outrageous claims he made, it staunchly ignored him.

That night, the boy's dreams were haunted by wights in armor. Every time he closed his eyes, undead from enemy clans would be chasing him through the heather. Each dream ended in a cold sweat, with the feeling of a mesh gauntlet closing around the back of his neck.

~*~

When Old Tom finally became ambulatory once again, Richard was certain the wight, still standing where he'd left it, would be discovered. But the groundskeeper seemed to have little inclination to leave the house, and spent his time drinking broth in the kitchen and telling the maids wilder and wilder tales of undead creatures that made Hitler's armies seem like a thing to be laughed off.

Though the old man stayed away from the moors, Richard still kept him in his sights. He didn't want to find that, in a careless moment, the groundskeeper would sneak up on him like he had that very first day. That would be a true catastrophe.

But Richard's presence seemed to be discomfiting to everyone in the servant's hall. Eyes shifted, and people found other things to do when he walked in. The pall seemed to grow and grow until, late one day, Old Tom, well into his drink, finally spluttered. "Don't you follow me around all day, lad. T'ain't my fault the Germans killed your parents in the last attack. Why if it hadn't..."

But Richard heard no more. Now he understood the freedom he was given, understood why Hannah hadn't even chided him when he'd returned late for dinner the night before. It was no comfort to him that he now owned the house and the surrounding countryside for miles around.

Blinded by tears, the boy ran off into the moor, and whether by design or by accident, he soon found himself face to face with the wight, just as night was falling. Overcome by tears, he had ignored both the sound of distant sirens and the commotion caused by Old Tom's sudden outburst. It was only under the supremely sobering effect of that undead gaze that he realized what was going on around him.

The air-raid siren——a new one that had been installed following the bombing incident——could be clearly heard, its wail only slightly distorted by the distance. And, in sharp barks and cries, the shouts of the household calling his name.

He debated whether to return to the open arms of his own people or to stay there, alone on the moor, surrounded by nothing that was alive.

The memory of his servants' betrayal, of their refusal to do what was right, made the decision for him. As night fell, he stood next to the wight, on its seemingly eternal vigil. He wondered what it was thinking about; he himself was wondering how long they'd known without telling him.

The darkness was soon complete. If he hadn't known what the thing standing beside him actually was, he could have easily pretended that it was just a silent man. "My dad and mum are dead," the boy said. And with that, the emotion he'd been holding back spilled out. "Killed in this war. I don't understand it, I just want it to end. But now it's too late... too late..." And he broke down completely even going as far as to lean on the wight's leg.

Shouts in the darkness got nearer, and then farther away as the household staff crisscrossed the moors in search of the wayward boy who was now their master. Richard wondered if he would have to wait to grow up before he could sack them all. He went back to gazing at the sky, tears flowing down his cheeks——starting hot before chilling in the wind.

The air above seemed somehow full of anger, despite the fact that little could be seen save directly above the city of Clydebank, where fires on the ground turned the clouds above into unnatural shades of pink, orange and purple. The distant droning and occasional booms that descended upon them created the sensation of a clash of unseen titans.

But the light was distant, and hardly illuminated the boy and his unusual protector, meaning that, when the household staff finally stumbled over them, it was as much a surprise to the searchers as to Richard.

Warren, the kennel keeper, a stout fellow of around twenty, faced them in the flickering light of an old-style lamp that hadn't been modified to Blitz black-out standards. Hannah herself held the lamp, trying to keep her face composed.

"It's all right boy, come here," she said. Her attempts at sounding gentle and soothing would have made Richard laugh, had he felt capable of it. Instead, the mere sight of her brought the anger, and the helpless sense of having been betrayed back to the fore.

"No!" He turned to the wight, and implored. "Save me from these people, kill them for me. I am the lord of these lands."

But the ancient knight ignored him.

"What are you doing, Richard?" Hannah screeched. "Get away from that ungodly thing!"

"Ungodly? Who are you to talk about ungodly? You're just…" But that was as far as the boy got. In his attempt to turn and face the woman, Richard stumbled and fell to the ground.

As soon as he saw that Richard was no longer at the wight's side, the kennel keeper raised a shotgun——the Mossberg which all his father's friends had told Richard was completely wrong for shooting grouse, and was therefore used by the staff——and fired without preamble into the creature's chest.

The wight stopped, raised its head into the air and keened, the sound of eternal torment.

Richard recoiled from the blast. He was close enough that the sound of the gun left his ears ringing, and close enough that the servant should never have dared fire in his direction. This fact proved the man had shown just how afraid he was.

For a second after the blast, they all stood silent, contemplating each other, before Warren began working the bolt for another shot, and Richard acted. He closed the gap between himself and the wight, placing his own body in the line of fire.

"Get out off the way, Richard," Hannah hissed. "We just want what's best for you."

But the boy remained in place, even stepping towards the gun, hearing the wight come up behind him. He stopped when the shaking barrel was just inches from his chest and looked into Warren's eyes.

It was too much for the man. The Kennel keeper broke and ran into the dark moors, ignoring Hannah's enraged commands.

Richard ignored her and looked into the warrior's eyes. "I've done my part." He didn't know whether the creature could understand the words he was saying, and he didn't really care. The words were unimportant. Both of them knew what had happened, knew what it meant. Some bonds had to be respected.

"Now, kill them all," Richard said.

This time, the long-dead warrior moved to obey, and though Hannah stood her ground defiantly, as if she believed that God Himself would intervene on her behalf, Richard knew that the rest of the scattered servants would be more difficult to track down among the dark moors.

Fortunately, they had all night.

Undead and Unbound

PHALLUS INCARNATE
By Glynn Owen Barrass

"This cannot be!" Unable to believe his eyes, Set approached the coffin slowly, warily. He waded barefoot through the swamp, the pungent water rising past his ankles, sloshing around his knees. Sharp bones crunched beneath his feet, the skeletal remnants of crocodile meals stabbing him cruelly. Set winced at the pain but continued. Alongside the bones, squishy muck, the shit of those ancient beasts, squelched between his toes, commingling with the freshly released blood. He cared not about the discomfort, for this coffin was most certainly the one he had trapped his brother within.

The dawn still hours away, the gilded form of the bandage-wrapped king carved on the coffin lid glowed dully in the cool night air. Set well remembered carving the lid, before he placed it atop a box made to the measurements of his maligned brother: Osiris, the King of Egypt.

"Isis, you bitch," he muttered, his mouth twisting into a wicked snarl, "this is your handiwork, isn't it?" Set hoped his curse would scar her dreams as she lay asleep nearby in her temple beside the Nile.

"Bes, Ptah, come!"

At his command, his huntsmen servants waded through the water towards him. Silent since his strange discovery of the coffin, with his scheme undone, they approached nervously, wary of his anger.

Once he had trapped Osiris within the coffin and abandoned it to the Nile, he was sure his future Kingship had been secure. Until now.

"Could it be," Ptah wondered, "that a water-lizard nuzzled the box here from the river?"

Set spat into the swamp, shaking his head, "No, this is certainly my sister's doing. Isis tracked him down the Nile."

Raising his spear, the shaft dripping fetid water down his arm, he poked the offending object. It swayed at his touch, slowly drifting away. "Oh, no, you don't," Set smiled, his scowl finally disappearing, "you don't escape this time."

His servants retrieved the coffin, dragging it from the swamp as he directed them towards the embankment. In the light of a waning moon, they hacked away the seal with their belt daggers. The lid cracked, and as it did the sky flashed, thunder rumbling far above. A strong, spicy scent followed: cinnamon mingled with rot. Set's servants cowered, but he spurred them on. Removing the lid, they revealed his brother's corpse.

The men gasped. Osiris looked to be sleeping, his green-tinged face calm beneath an ostrich-feathered crown. Crossed upon his white tunic, his hands bore a golden crook and flail, symbols of the station Set had stolen. Stamping forward, Set ripped them from his brother's grip and tossed both towards the swamp. A second slap of thunder followed, the outraged sky releasing a torrent of foul-smelling rain.

Ptah wailed. Bes crouched, covering his head. Unperturbed, Set unsheathed his sword. Mucky water, filling the coffin, turned reddish brown as he hacked away his brother's left hand. The right followed, then he cruelly castrated Osiris. He tossed the phallus into the swamp where a hungry fish, aroused by the torrent pounding its home, swallowed it whole.

When Set had finished, a bloody soup replaced his brother's corpse. Satisfied with his handiwork, he raised his sword defiantly against the lightning. His laughter filled the storm-wracked night.

~*~

"Fourteen pieces in total, including the cock he tossed in the swamp."

Reaching down, Tara's captor stroked his crotch for emphasis. It was an ugly sight. Bound at ankles and wrists, there wasn't much she could do but stare at the ranting maniac.

"Isis and Set's sister-wife Nepththys, they searched the world for the missing pieces, finding all but one. And that, my dear girl, is how I came to be."

Tara should have been terrified. She could feel sweat beading on her forehead, realizing her captor might rape or kill her (or both, and in what order?) any second.

"So," asked Tara, twisting her neck to lift her cheek off the dirty concrete a fraction of an inch, "you're the cock, yeah?"

Phallus Incarnate

"YES!" the man's voice boomed through the room, "when Isis stitched her dead husband back together, his resurrection invoked my transformation: an immortal, undead phallus!"

Fucking loony, she thought, and couldn't keep the sneer off her face. Returning her head to the floor, she closed her eyes as the madman walked closer.

This dirty freak is Nosferatu! Yeah right.

"Don't you dare mock me, young lady!"

The kick was unexpected, his bare bony toes knocking the breath out of her. Tara coughed violently, shuddering where she lay. Through glazed, watery eyes she watched a calloused foot readying for another kick.

It didn't come; his foot returned harmlessly to the floor.

Tara retched, then looked up. Past the brown cotton trousers and the tatty jumper with black and white checks, she reached her attacker's face. He nodded in satisfaction.

"Screw you, freak." She'd give him the finger if she could. "Don't beat me, just do it and let me go!"

"Me do unto you?" He grinned as if amused, yellow teeth appearing between his cruelly curled lips. He was missing the front two. Hawk-nosed, cheeks gaunt and shriveled, the man's eyes gleamed beneath black, dandruff-dusted brows. Unlike his face, his scalp was smooth as a hard-boiled egg. It reflected the bulb dangling from the cobweb-strewn, bare plaster ceiling.

"No, no, you have to do something for me," he said, his Adam's apple bobbing in excitement.

Oh, Christ. He's gonna make me suck him off.

Crouching, the man spread his legs.

Catching a strong, fishy odor, Tara's urge to retch returned.

She thought the bony knuckles of his hands, haloed in coarse black hair, looked too large for his thin, wiry limbs. He scratched fingernails thick with dirt over his worn jeans, then reached for her face.

Tara closed her eyes, flinching from the unwanted caress. She re-opened them as he said: "I've been watching you, you see, and know your kind very well. So I want you, just before I kill you," his face became a grinning rictus, "to become a werewolf."

Her jaw dropped in spite of herself.

~*~

Undead and Unbound

2 Hours Earlier:

The mornings were the worst. It had been two weeks since Tara had black bagged Alex's things and still she wondered: 'did I do the right thing?' Her constant, depressive mood said no, as did the sleepless nights and mornings alone. Today was no exception. She turned, stretched, and for a brief moment felt great inside, invigorated. Opening her eyes doused the sensation. Seeing the empty space to her left, the same pillow remained from the night she'd sent him packing.

And last night, a sweet-voiced prostitute heckling a man jackal-like for business had twice interrupted her sleep.

Closing her eyes with a sigh, she attempted further rest. Minutes of stubborn trying passed before she gave up the ghost. Reaching for her Blackberry, she examined the screen.

7:11 AM

Damn it! I'm sick of this! she screamed inside.

Rolling onto her back, staring upwards, Tara crossed her arms in frustration. The lemon yellow ceiling looked sickly in the post dawn light.

The color had been his choice, not hers.

"Screw you Alex. Silly Puh-rick!" Feeling marginally better after her outburst, Tara tossed the sheets aside. It was time she faced the day.

But...she couldn't get out of bed.

"Um, great."

Too wakeful to sleep, yet too fatigued to rise, she lay for a while doing nothing. A burst of energy later took her for a shower, then coffee.

Powering the PC, checking Facebook (no messages, Fuck YOU Alex, Silly Prick!) lowered her mood again. Finding the house keys then tugging on her denim jacket, Tara thought taking a walk might clear her head.

She walked along uneven pavements flanking gutters cluttered with last night's trash, down tawdry streets lined with cramped, terraced houses. Crushed beer cans, mountains of cigarette stubs dumped by lazy cabbies: she registered the sordid scene with distaste. A spent condom, shriveled and yellow, appeared across her path, given momentum by a gentle breeze. She gave the offending object a wide berth.

Parked cars were sparse. A few stood mounted on mortar-caked bricks, their tires sold or stolen. Still the air bore a salty exhaust fume taste.

Two blocks from home and already the area had degraded into somewhere Tara wouldn't dare venture at night.

Her Blackberry became a welcome presence as the streets grew scruffier and the litter increased. The majority of the houses were boarded up behind green metal shutters, scratched, mottled with graffiti, mute witnesses to evictions and drugs raids. Passing an alleyway, she glimpsed black bags, a sodden discarded mattress slumped against a wall lined with jagged fangs of glass. The dusty pavement ended a few yards later. Another street followed this, rowed with yet more green-shuttered houses. Should she turn back, return to bed? It was that or turn the corner, continuing on her tedious trek.

Turning right, Tara encountered the crippled urban sprawl's first living denizen. On the doorstep of a house ahead sat a hunched, sleepy-faced drunk, his head bobbing sluggishly. He didn't seem a threat.

Should I cross anyway? You know I don't even know where I am. She considered retrieving her Blackberry, checking the time but…'Scuse me, can I borrow your phone,' would be the vagrant's perfect excuse to address her.

Almost upon him now, *Hell he's not wearing shoes, what a scruff!* Tara veered left, leaving the sidewalk for the opposite side of the street.

In the peripheral of her vision, the man climbed quickly to his feet. Shuffling movements followed, bare feet scraping across dusty paving slabs.

I should just run!

She sped up, getting halfway across the street. Sensing him close behind, Tara wanted to look back.

Stupid idea. Don't attract his attention any more than you have already!

The bag came as a complete shock. Pulled over her face, the thin, blue carrier obscured her vision in an instant of ugly surprise.

She breathed polythene.

Strong hands, gripping her throat, had Tara struggling in manic terror, her panic hastening her asphyxiation.

Fighting for survival, she kicked, flailing for release. Breathing in her own exhaled fumes, black dots formed across the blue consuming her vision. She fought for breath now, futilely trying to remove herself from her attacker's clutches.

I'm going to die here.

The iron grip tightened. A moment later, consciousness departed.

~*~

An unknown period later, hours or minutes, Tara couldn't guess, she awoke. Head pounding like a drum, her throat felt sore, raw inside. The smell of motor oil permeated her nostrils, issuing from the bare concrete pillowing her head.

Her prison: a small room walled with bare brick foundations. Her arms were tied tightly behind her back, ankles equally bound. She'd never been so confused and angry. Then the leering presence appeared, the not-so-harmless drunk obscuring the room's emptiness.

"Yes!" he said in way of introduction, before commencing his insane mythological tale; and now, the werewolf thing.

He's insane! There would be no reasoning with him, none whatsoever. Tara had thought for a second she might be able to negotiate her release, but knew now, with a sinking heart, that it was impossible.

"A werewolf? Really?" Mockery filling her voice, Tara sent him an undisguised sneer. "There's more chance of you blowing a baboon out your backside than me turning into a wolf!"

He released her chin, his expression darkening with rage. Tara flinched and closed her eyes as his hand rose into a shaking fist.

Silent seconds passed. Footsteps, padding across the concrete, were followed by a sharp click. Reopening her eyes, she found a caul of darkness replacing the light.

His voice, low and angry, filled the void. "I'm going to give you time to consider your dilemma; but not too long. Then I'll start using harsher methods to reveal your true form."

Barely audible movements followed before a door creaked open. Slamming it closed, he left Tara alone with her feelings and the darkness. Confused. Despairing. Pissed.

"My true form," she sighed, exasperation replacing her anger. "I'm twenty-four years old and a former university student. I have pet rats at home that need feeding, and a bin bag filled with my ex-boyfriend's stuff that I intend to burn. I've been mugged and tied up by some demented deviant, AND LIKE FUCK CAN I BECOME A WEREWOLF FOR YOU!" Her shouts still echoing through the darkness, she struggled, panting, with her bonds. Her wrists twisting in pain, she felt tears trickle down: the bonds were tight and she wasn't getting out of here.

I'm going to die here. Fuck, if I could turn into a werewolf I would!

Twisting again, Tara rolled to her back and raised her knees. *My phone, where's my damn phone?* In her jacket of course, where she'd left it, and the jacket? While he'd been spouting Egyptian mythology, she'd seen a blue metal shelving unit against the wall behind him. There, stuffed between a cardboard box and a paint can, lay her jacket. And beside the shelves was a door, layered in chipped green paint.

Freedom.

So, before escaping, all I need do is squirm through the darkness towards the shelf, hop to my feet, remove the jacket using my teeth before nuzzling out the phone and dialing 999 with my nose...

Genius.

Christ, I'm fucked!

Sobs followed her tears, but she quickly quelled them for fear he was listening. Tara wouldn't give the crazy bastard the satisfaction. Bound and trapped... what could she do *but* cry?

She could never hope for rescue. No one knew she was here. Shout for help? Who knew what the freak might do in retaliation, in punishment? She was going to be raped, tortured to death: horror she couldn't bear to think of but couldn't get out of her mind.

I need to talk with him, convince him I'm not the werewolf he thinks I am.

Waiting in darkness, an indeterminable time passed while she rehearsed what to tell her delusional kidnapper. When the light came on again she flinched, issuing an involuntary yelp of surprise.

It wasn't only the light, but the face it illuminated. Drawn, haggard, even uglier in the Blackberry's wan illumination, his sunken eyes leered, cruel lips smacking around broken teeth.

"Peek a boo!" Grinning, her captor licked his wormy lips, "Come to your senses yet?"

His voice hissed the words, fouling the air with a sour, fecal stink.

Heart pounding, Tara swallowed, closing her eyes against the other's looming visage.

A large hand brushed her cheek, and clammy fingers traced her ear before pausing at her jaw. "I'm growing weary of your games, you know." The reek grew stronger, his rank breath filling her nostrils.

"Or perhaps," he asked, making a liquid sucking sound, "you require proof of my credentials."

The unwanted caress changed, her captor's hand squeezing tightly down. A sweaty palm, pressed against her mouth, flattened Tara's nose with a crunch of cartilage. His strong digits brutally squeezed her cheeks against her teeth.

Spasming, twisting her head, a disgusting sight followed the constricting pain.

Tara whined into his palm, the low squeal of a frightened animal. Inches from her face, the man's jaw had unhinged like a snake's gaping maw. Lips stretching to slivers, the skin tore asunder, revealing raw red flesh surrounding shrunken pink gums. Blood-tinged drool, dribbling down his chin, spattered her forehead with disgusting warmth.

No, oh no!

Between slimy yellow teeth the diseased mouth birthed something abnormal, alien. Instead of a tongue, a fleshy chunk of dark red squirming pseudopods came flopping down towards her.

Wormy nubs ending in tiny suckers slivered greasily across her brow. The disgusting sensation, wetting Tara's eyebrows, brushed uncomfortably near her eyes.

"Ah hah ha ha!" came his cackling voice as the moist spongy shapes molested her forehead. It was unbearable, so much so that pulling back, her head smacked loudly against the concrete. Through ringing pain Tara discerned a loud liquid gulp. The release of her face followed.

Gasping, she breathed a lungful of foul air. Her jaw aching alongside her head, Tara found him smiling smugly. "I can reveal more if you wish." A sliver of pink appeared between his bleeding lips. He licked them closely, wincing visibly from the pain, "even titillate you with my other assets." Reaching down, he stroked her thigh with obvious intent.

Flinching in disgust, Tara pulled away.

"But no, not yet," he continued, reaching around to clutch her left buttock. "My little display has attracted some unwanted attention."

Following his words, Tara discerned a low rumble. The floor vibrated beneath her, growing in strength with the sound. Her captor released her, backing away and taking the wan light with him to leave Tara alone in darkness. And the vibrations? The concrete literally quaked beneath her now.

PHALLUS INCARNATE

"You feel it, yes?" he raised his voice against the growing din. "She often does this, but not usually this quickly. Hmmm, perhaps she can sense you too, eh?"

Tara turned towards him. A new and unexpected light source, issuing from her left, illuminated his ghastly face.

"Now shush, sssh," he hissed, raising a finger to his lips "and watch."

Curiosity overcoming her fear, Tara raised her head. *I must be hallucinating*, her rationale said. The wall behind him was radiant, a rich orange halo surrounding a shimmering white blob. The light swelled as she watched, changing from a blob to an oblong that reached down towards the floor. A well-defined, human shaped silhouette appeared within.

The rumbling stopped.

Fear trickled along her spine. "Oh my god!" she gasped.

"My God, actually," her captor explained, "here she comes."

The silhouette transformed into a woman. Floating quickly from the light, short, slim, her naked, milk white flesh glowed from within. Her face was petite, elfin even, her bow-shaped lips dark like the mascara beneath her upward curved brow. She was the very vision of perfection, even though her shoulders ended in empty stumps.

Tara's heart thumped in her chest. Despite her beauty, the woman exuded a palpable aura of unnaturalness.

Eyes glazed, she stared forward blindly, her dark-brown, center-parted hair swaying as she approached. Toes scraping across the concrete, she appeared somehow elevated. *She's floating*, Tara thought with a shudder.

Then two massive, grey-feathered wings sprouted up from the empty shoulders and Tara lost herself, mumbling "ohmygod, ohmygod, ohmygod..."

A hand stroked her head, followed by her captor whispering in her ear. "Keep quiet and stay still, she's searching for me."

Her gaze transfixed, Tara nodded. Staring blindly forward, the winged woman paused before her feet. Upon closer inspection, below a dark pubic thatch her legs appeared fused together, sealed right down to the tips of her toes. The close proximity brought a bitter cold that throbbed from the woman in waves, permeating Tara's trainers and socks and numbing her to the bone in mere seconds.

"Isis, the protector of the dead, still searching for her husband's lost phallus." Her captor's words beat against her forehead with his warm breath. "I manifest myself, and she comes looking, sometimes." As if on cue, the woman's head twitched, birdlike, blank eyes darting about the room's small confines.

Panicked close to hyperventilation, Tara's fear grew with the numbness creeping through her legs. The goddess radiated death. Her twitching head only enhanced the terror.

Is she blind?

A gloating whisper answered her unvoiced question. "Years without worship has left her mind sluggish. Isis walks in a dream-state. But this... she isn't usually this coherent. Perhaps... it's because of you, again?"

When the cold crept up to Tara's stomach, the woman's head ceased moving.

Staring down, her glazed eyes widened, changing from dull to bright in an instant. Grey irises, visible between widened lids, turned a fiery glowing sapphire.

Their eyes locked, sending Tara into a spasm of shock. Ice filled her veins, her nerves, her very being as the woman's deathly, angelic face lowered.

A hidden knowledge, blasting her mind, sent Tara tumbling towards oblivion. But not before Isis Unveiled:

~*~

1716: Born in Augustow, Poland, Tara (then 'Tekla') lived a quiet, uneventful childhood. Her Roman Catholic parents raised her strictly, but with love. Everything changed near the end of her sixteenth year, when something terrible invaded Tekla's peaceful world: an 'Upier,' a devilish being believed to be the resurrected corpse of a man from a neighboring village, began systematically murdering the townsfolk.

Preying solely on women, the creature stalked the hours after dusk, leaving mutilated victims drained of blood. To her family's sorrow, Tekla's younger sister Miriam became the next victim. Then, five nights later, the Upier attacked her. The monster caught Tekla scurrying through the streets after dark, heading home bearing a pail of borrowed milk.

The following morning her parents found her sprawled in an alley, alive and quite well. Recalling nothing of the incident, neither did she know how the Upier's decapitated corpse came to be lying near her naked, blood-smeared form.

Not only was it dead and decapitated, it was literally dismembered, its guts splattered on the alley walls. Its purple, barbed tongue still twitched as the villagers burned the remains.

Proclaimed a hero, Tekla enjoyed many years of happiness, until folks began to whisper that she hadn't aged a day since her sixteenth year.

Faced with the rising suspicions of her superstitious neighbors, Tekla was eventually sent to live with an uncle in Hungary. There, in the village of Meduegna, she encountered her second vampire, the demented revenant Arnold Paole. Paole suffered the same fate as his predecessor, albeit more discreetly, decapitated in the yard behind her uncle's farmhouse.

After her uncle's death, she continued living in Meduegna for many years, until suspicions were again aroused regarding her youthful appearance. Deciding to emigrate to England, she sold off her uncle's property, and left quietly. Her family was long dead and their descendants had no knowledge of her. She thought it best things remain that way.

Tekla became Tara.

She encountered her third vampire whilst travelling through France, and yet another near her new home in Exmoor. She was a magnet to them, it seemed.

After decades of self-enforced spinsterhood, Tara fell for a man she met in Kilorglin, Southern Ireland. He died during their sixth year of marriage, his secret mistress proving to be a 'Leenhaum-shee,' a vampiric seductress.

Before her return to England, Tara quite gleefully dispatched *that* creature.

As she continued through the Twentieth and Twenty-First Century, Tara began to forget, her subconscious mind inventing new pasts as she continued living, never aging.

The vampires, along with her colorful past, eventually disappeared from the world. It took the mother of all vampires, the goddess Isis, to return her memories to the fore. One thing Isis couldn't reveal, however, were Tara's memories of wolf-form. A different deity reigned over those bestial moments.

As with her first transformation, three hundred years previously, Tara awoke feeling the exact same sensations.

Confused.
Disorientated.
Horny.

"Ugh, unh." Waking up on the concrete floor, full coherency betrayed her. It was cold, mainly because she'd awoken naked, her body smothered in a slick sheen of drying sweat.

Sprawled face down, Tara opened her eyes onto an uneven grey surface. Someone had switched on the light. Her, the vampire? Utterly confused, all the new/old memories swiftly integrated themselves into her brain matter.

People always say I act old beyond my years. But go figure.

Her whole body fatigued and wasted, with a groan Tara pushed herself to her knees. Seeing her hands, she gasped. It wasn't sweat that covered them, but bright red blood. She looked up to see a lot more. It surrounded her in veritable pools, alongside the torn remnants of her clothes. *Damn, did I do this?*

Tara's erstwhile captor lay to her right, the majority of him, anyway. The room, lit cruelly by the bare light bulb, was a charnel house. Bloodstains spattered the red brick walls, and in one cobwebby corner she found his head.

Shivering, and not from the cold, she covered her breasts with her forearms.

That head...the eyes bulged, dark red marbles within a face pallid in death. The monstrous tongue having reappeared, its pseudopods, grey and lifeless, dripped clear fluid into the blood pooling around the severed neck.

Turning from the head, she padded towards the matching corpse. Barefoot, she was careful to avoid the blood.

Tara noted three injuries, the first being the torn, twisted neck socket beneath which lay a wide, gory gouge. Ribs, bulging purple organs...her throat clenched, the bile bubbling through her stomach. Briefly inspecting her crimson-stained hands, Tara returned to her inspection.

"Guess I offed the Big Cahuna, huh?"

The third wound: pants pulled past his knees, a dark red rent replaced the vampire's phallus. It appeared she hadn't dispatched this monster alone.

"Cheers, Isis!" Tara smiled. "But if I can pass another hundred years without encountering one of these," she said, looking down at the corpse with distaste, "I'll die a happy lycanthrope."

Kneeling, she retrieved the remnants of her clothes. Beneath the jeans, she found her Blackberry's narrow, tablet-shaped form. Dressing herself in tattered ruins, she shrugged her jacket on to cover the rents.

Tara left the room looking ragged, bloody, and immensely pleased with herself.

Her enemy vanquished, the hunter was content.

Undead and Unbound

WRECKERS
By Tom Lynch

The rain soaked Massen till he felt he was wet enough to grow moss. He hated it. But he needed the rain. He scanned out over the choppy surf tasting the salt in the air, and checked that Clemo was keeping his eye on the donkey's rig. Clemo had neglected that once, and the ship had realized their plan and turned back out to sea. Sure they'd shouted that they'd have the law on them but how? By the time they'd put in to talk of it, it'd be days or weeks later. Still, though, they'd lost their quarry, and missed out on all that loot.

"S'posed to be the best 'un yet, eh, Mass?" Jago said from Massen's side, huddled away from the rain with the rest of the crew in their rude rock shelter.

"Mm," Massen grunted back.

"A John Company ship?"

"That's what I heard."

"Ah, should be your best yet, then Mass. Really, a triumph for us all. Take a ship like that. Think of the loot. Why I bet there'll be——"

"Oi!" hissed Massen. "Could ya shut yer trap? Sound carries over the water. You know that, Jago. You're supposed to be the wiser older brother, yet Jowan next to ya has made not a sound."

Jago bit his lip. He punched his younger brother, and Jowan shifted and glared back at him. Massen spun again and glared at them both.

"Are we even sure it's coming tonight?" piped up Santo, too loud.

All three of the others stared daggers at him, and Massen almost pulled his knife. Santo reeled back against the stone of the shallow cave, throwing his hands up.

"Another sound from any of ya, and ya join the crew of the ship." Massen's voice was ice. "And you, Santo…I could always have you watch the road and let young Jory join us on the beach. Not. A. Bloody. Sound!"

Undead and Unbound

Massen stalked out into the rain. Once he was halfway to Clemo, he turned, surveying their spot concealed in the rocks at the back of the narrow beach. It was hard to call it a beach, really, just a pile of smaller rocks. Walking in the area was treacherous in the rain, but that was part of the job. He and his mates knew how to handle themselves on this terrain, and were able to get out into the water when the time came. They may not enjoy the biting cold of the sea, but the payoff was good. Their spot was a good one: miles away from any houses, along a rarely-used road, and protected from view by a rocky hill by the road. They stood a point in the bay, deceptively far out in the water, and invisible to passing ships in bad weather. Satisfied, he grunted and went to check with Clemo.

"Heard ya," Clemo said as Massen approached.

"Yeah. Should be quieter now."

"Hope so. Almost time I reckon."

Massen didn't question Clemo. He had a feel for these things, and seemed to be able to predict about when they were going to happen. He nodded and moved on to make sure Jory was watching the road.

As he rounded the rocky bluff, he found Jory crouched on the road, spilling offal from a pig carcass. "Make sure to mash it up right," Massen said as he walked up. "Best if it looks human."

"Yah. I will. Gotta keep the rumors good about this place, eh?"

"Aye. It'll do us no good to have the King's men poking around here. Not many come this way these days anyway, but it's best to discourage the locals."

Jory grinned up from his gruesome work, stretching a length of pig gut and laying it artfully across the mud. "Think this'll be enough now?"

Massen surveyed the area. There were three gutted pigs, their blood and innards spread across the water-rutted road and the surrounding grass and rocks. He hoped this would help firm the stories of a restless spirit or a murderous madman in the area. They'd worked to spread both rumors, paying friends to 'see ghosts' or spot shadowy forms roaming the dark nights during bad weather. It had gotten to the point where some local mothers scared their children back indoors with "the Black Reiver will get you!" He grinned at his own cleverness. He hadn't even come up with the name. Local imagination had done it for him. "Next," he thought to himself chuckling, "I'll have to see if I can start everyone calling this Reiver's Point."

WRECKERS

"I think this will be just fine, Jory," Massen said aloud. "Fine job. Now watch our backs, Clemo says its close."

"D'you think——?"

"Jory," Massen said, cutting him off. "We've been over this. Your brothers want to look out for you. With your parents gone, they're who you've got to listen to. In a few years, maybe, you can join the others, but right now, you're the most help watching this side. Just imagine what would happen to us all if someone were to come upon us, eh? What then? No...you do this for now."

Jory heaved a sigh. "Fine." He wiped the bloody muck on his trousers, and went to look for a bit of shelter.

With only one more task to check on before watching for the ship, Massen turned away. He headed to check on the horse and cart. The horse was tethered as he'd left her, down the road, south of a small bluff to keep the worst of the wind and rain off her. The beaten down nag didn't have much left in her, but she served the purpose of carrying them on these midnight trips to the coast ever so often. He stroked her nose and fed her a clump of grass from his hand. He'd be sad to see her go, but figured he should talk to some horse dealers about a replacement, and perhaps even about a future for himself.

Massen made his way back to the beach and looked out over the water. The sea had been high. They'd gotten a lot of rain, even for Cornwall. The rough water easily covered the rocky shoals that stretched almost one hundred yards out into the surf. His face stretched into a dark grin. He crouched to pick up a few sharp, fist-sized rocks, and turned back to his mates in their shelter, snapping his fists out left and right to keep warm as he walked back up the beach.

Jowan appeared to be sleeping with his head slumped on his chest, while Jago was making faces at Santo to amuse and calm him. Massen shook his head and slid down the rough wall next to Jowan and elbowed him in the ribs. Jowan's head came up and his eyes opened, looking out over the water, and he turned toward Massen.

"No, not time yet. Just makin' sure you were awake."

Jowan ticked an eyebrow and leaned his head back against the rock.

What seemed like hours later, Santo shot to his feet and pointed, his mouth open to cry out. Massen hissed at him just in time to shut him up. There, through the gloom, were the lights of a struggling three-master. Its sails were being buffeted by the erratic winds, and the ship was being tossed about on the waves like an angry child's toy.

"Steady," Massen whispered. "Let Clemo do his part." With that, Massen's long-time comrade-in-arms did what he'd done countless times: he kept his pace steady as he walked the donkey back and forth along the beach, allowing the lantern on the donkey's rig to sway, fooling all but the most observant into thinking that a ship had docked safely in a harbor.

All present held their breath as they watched the reaction of the ship. At first, it appeared they'd pass by, but soon they managed to bring the ship around and point it directly at the beach. The men released their breath, but remained tense, hoping not to be spotted.

As the ship came closer, Massen noted the size and quality of the ship through the spray. He reached inside his coat and pulled out his father's old spyglass. The figurehead on this ship was no poor replica, but a genuine work of art, a woman leaping lifelike out of the prow of the ship. And the decorative carvings along the gunwales were breathtaking. If the workmanship that went into building this ship was any indication of the wealth of the passengers, then this would be the take to end all. He could secure his cut and retire up north in the countryside living like royalty.

He continued to scan the vessel, and the one nagging point finally became clear. Where was the crew? The ship was still coming, the course was still being adjusted, and the sails' trim kept changing, but the sailors themselves were nowhere to be seen. "It must be the light," he thought to himself. "Or I'm imagining…something."

"Here she comes, boys," Massen said aloud to his companions. "She's a beauty to be sure, a sight to behold."

"Can't wait to get meself in there, Mass. I jus' can't wait!" Jago said, rocking back and forth on the balls of his feet. His younger brother, Jowan, reached out and put a steadying hand on his shoulder. With the other hand, Jowan hefted a spearhead-shaped stone. Santo flexed his hands and cracked his knuckles. The four of them watched from their shelter as the ship pitched in toward the rocks.

Suddenly, with a tearing crunch of timbers, the ship stopped after riding up on jagged stones, and lay dead in the water. The men on the shore waited for passengers and crew to dive overboard and make for shore as the ship took on water. But nobody came. A time usually filled with screams and wailing was eerily silent, but for the wind and rain.

Massen knit his eyebrows and looked through the spyglass again.

All was quiet on board. "Well, they're not going anywhere, Lads. Let's go collect some booty."

They ran out and met Clemo at the water's edge. He had a hook and rope ready. All five of them now ran out into the chilling water, and as the waves rose up against their chests, they reached their quarry. Massen took the hook and hurled it over the gunwales, and climbed up.

Surveying it now in person, he confirmed that there was *still* no one on deck. Something was wrong. His throat felt tight. How could this be? How could a ship come this far with no passengers and crew? His mates joined him on deck. They too looked silently about. Perhaps they'd all moved below.

"Let's go down, and see what's what," Massen said quietly.

As they headed below decks, they stopped on the steps. Jago voiced it first, "Do you hear moanin'?"

"I do," said Massen.

"I call it, says I," Jago cried and ran around the other toward the nearest cabin.

Massen looked back at the others and grinned, relaxing. "This is more like it. Have at it, boys. And remember, no witnesses." He smiled as his crew of wreckers went about their grim business. He then turned and made his way to the captain's quarters, which was always his by virtue of their agreement and his leadership.

He gathered speed, and crashed through the stateroom door, raising the stones he'd collected on the shore. He found the room… empty. He whirled from corner to corner. "I know you're in here! Be a man and show yourself," Massen cried. "Stop being such a coward! No wonder we saw no crew! Their captain hides and they follow, eh?"

Cold fear gripped Massen tighter than ever. He fought the urge to flee like a woman and stayed at his post. He tore open desk drawers and cabinet doors. Papers. Most of them blank. There weren't even any maps worth spending time on. Tension built in his shoulders. He flexed his back and looked around. There had to be something here.

With that, he heard a rustling thump in the closet behind the door to the cabin. "Oh ho! There you hide, Captain Coward! I'm coming for you now, and my face will be the last thing in this life you s——"

There was no one there. The closet was empty. There weren't even any clothes or uniforms hanging. A chill started at the back of Massen's head and ran down to his lower back. What devil ship had they found?

Massen heard distant noises elsewhere on the ship. His mates running after their quarry. He had to know if they'd had better luck than he. Out he went down the hall. "Cooome here, sweeeetiieeee," crooned Jago. He came around the corner, tiptoeing after an unseen victim, his trousers hanging open. "Mass!" he cried, and jumped, pulling his garments together. "I was just after this young lady, but I can't seem to find her now. Can't find nothin'! What kinda ship you say this was?"

"Just keep lookin', Jag." Massen stalked off, swallowing. He hoped the others were having better luck. This pull was supposed to be the mother-load. After this he was going to retire as a horse trader up north. He didn't want to do this anymore.

He heard noises behind walls, and followed them. Soon, he realized the noises weren't from behind the walls, but were coming from the walls themselves.

Massen swallowed and shook himself. This was impossible. It was just a ship. It was just another pull for him and his mates, and he was going to do his job, just as he had countless times before.

Strong but quiet Jowan came out of a cabin down the hall, his eyebrows knit in consternation. His eyes met Massen's and he shook his head. Jowan continued down the hall the other way. Massen spat. Clemo came up behind Massen, and looked up at him.

"Well?" asked Massen.

"All wrong," Clemo said. "Should leave."

"Like bloody Hell, we'll leave," Massen said. "We're here to pick this tub clean, and that's what we'll do——" The floor lurched beneath them, and the ship began to rock slightly. "We're aground," cried Massen. "How are we movin'?"

Frantic cries came from outside. Massen bolted up the steps onto the deck and ran to the gunwales. There, on the top of the bluff, was Jory waving the lantern back and forth.

"Ye've cast off!" he cried from the shore.

Massen looked down at the water. Sure enough, the water swirled around the sides of the ship as it pulled away from the land. "This is impossible!" he shouted as he ran back below.

At the base of the steps lay Clemo, his short form crumpled on the ground in the middle of a glowing pool of crimson. Massen leapt down to his side and hauled him up. Clemo's head lolled to one side, the gaping wound opening on his throat still oozing blood. Massen clenched his jaw. Someone was playing games with him and his mates and they were going to be sorry.

He had to check below. Timbers had torn and broken when the ship ran aground, so there should be a hole with water flooding the bilge. They should not be seaworthy, and yet they were afloat. As he headed for the ladder, he heard gurgling noises from the cabin he'd seen Jago head into moments before. Fearing the worst, he opened the door.

There on the bunk lay Jago, clearly in agony. He must have lain face down on the bunk in pursuit of the lady he'd been chasing, only to be sucked into the bunk itself, midsection first. He was being slowly bent backwards like a bow, grabbing, pushing, pulling at the sheets and surrounding structure as he sank into the bed. His lower legs kicked and flexed as they began to follow his thighs into the impossible quicksand of the mattress.

Massen rushed forward to help his friend. He grabbed Jago's hands, and pulled frantically. He kept going down. Massen looped his arms underneath Jago's and heaved backwards.

Jago squealed in pain and slapped Massen away as a snapping, cracking sound came from underneath the mattress. Massen grabbed and pulled at Jago's clothing, trying desperately to pull his friend free. With a sickening pop, Jago's body went limp and slipped below the sheets.

Massen stood there dumbfounded, and blinked away tears. He had to find Jowan and Santo, and they had to get off this ship. Better they should survive and get back to shore to plan the next haul than die in this haunted trap.

He bolted out of the room. "Jowan! Santo! Where are ya, lads! Answer me!" His only response was the creaking of the ship's timbers.

The sound of weeping pulled him around the corner. There, with his back facing Massen, knelt Santo. "I can't get them out, Mass!" he wept. "It hurts! You have to come help——Ah! They've just gone further! They're crushing me!" Massen came and looked over Santo's shoulder to see his hands sunk into the decking up to his elbows. Massen licked his lips and looked around. He swallowed the bile that just started to come up and pulled out his knife.

"This is all I got, Santo," Massen said quietly. "It may kill ya, lad, but I might be able to cut you free."

Tears ran freely down Santo's face. "I don't want to die, Mass!

Undead and Unbound

AaaOW!" His arms had now disappeared beyond his elbows.

"Lad," said Massen gently, trying very hard to stay calm, "I'd better start now——" And the decking below Santo opened like a giant maw and bit Santo down so quickly and violently that all Massen had time to do was leap back and drop his knife.

Santo was gone. There was no trace left of him. Massen's knife had been swallowed up, too. Massen's eyes were wide and sweat trickled down his back. His breath came in gasps as he staggered away.

He found Jowan. He'd hoped to find him alive, but had known he wouldn't. As he looked down at his friend, his breathing slowed. He approached Jowan quietly. Only his head was visible, sticking up out of the decking, and just beyond him was the ladder to the hold and bilge below. He reached down to touch his friend's face, and his head rolled away and thumped sickeningly down the ladder. Massen retched. He couldn't stop himself any more.

His knees felt week, but he went below. Something told him he needed to be in the hold, so he went. He stepped down the ladder, stooping to keep from cracking his head on the low timbers. There was no damage down here. He'd heard and seen the ship run aground. Damage like that tears a hole into a ship that can't be mended quickly, and yet this had, or it had never really been damaged. He didn't know, but he knew he wanted to find who was responsible. He was practically numb from losing his comrades this night, but the part that kept him moving wanted revenge.

Massen's steps became more determined as his need for vengeance fueled him. He rounded a corner and spotted a figure walking back and forth. "Finally, you bloody COWARD! I've found you. You're mine, you MONSTER!" Massen roared at the uniformed figure, but then stopped himself from charging. Something was not right with this person. He was too small to be a captain. It looked as if a child were playing dress-up with very authentic clothing.

The form turned and gazed at Massen.

Massen's stomach lurched and dropped as his blood chilled. There, staring at him was a boy of no more than six with gaunt features that gazed out from under the captain's chapeau from blank, empty eyes. The boy-captain's frame was so thin that it looked as if a stiff wind would break him. He certainly couldn't draw or hold the saber at his belt. As Massen watched the skin on the boy's right temple tore open, the surrounding flesh bruising. Blood welled up and spattered out onto his shoulder and ran down the side of his face.

"Don't you remember me, Massen?" the boy asked with a voice of a multitude. "I was but one of your victims. This ship houses hundreds of others like me. Do you remember all of us? Bashing our heads in with rocks? Pressing our faces under the water to make us drown in site of land? Denying us the God-given right to live and grow? Or do you only remember the blood-money you've earned?"

Massen's stomach twisted, and his vision blurred. His knees buckled.

"You do remember then. I'm why you're alone. The ship you and your crew chose that night was this ship carrying your wife and son. And rather than tell us the truth about what you were, you murdered us to keep your secret."

Massen crumpled to his hands and knees. His breath felt shallow. He remembered pulling the woman off the ship, and the shock of recognition, and the almost physical blow when he turned to see his five-year-old son gazing up at him in confusion. He remembered. He remembered throwing his wife into the brutally cold waves below, and slamming the side of his son's head with a rock, beating his skull till the little boy stopped moving. He couldn't have told them what he truly was. He couldn't face them, having them know that he was nothing more than a pirate, not the sea captain he'd told them he was.

Now he recognized the ship. This ship was identical to the one where he stumbled across and murdered his own family to keep his secret. Part of him died that night.

The rest would die tonight.

UNDEAD AND UNBOUND

SCAVENGER

By Oscar Rios

Kevin Petersen unpacked his brown paper bag suspiciously, checked and rechecked its contents with growing frustration. The banana was there, as was the bottle of ice tea, but the half pastrami sandwich he thought he'd packed was missing.

His mind thought back to his morning, trying to remember if he'd simply not brought it to work with him. Maybe it was sitting on the counter in his kitchen, so when he returned home he'd simply have to throw it out after a day unrefrigerated. But that wasn't it; he remembered the weight of the leftover deli sandwich as he carried the bag into work this morning. He remembered how bulky the bag had been, with the clear plastic container inside, as he pushed it into the communal office refrigerator.

"Damn it… God damn it!" Kevin muttered, as he thumped his lunch bag hard onto the table. He went to the garbage and rummaged through it, despite the uninviting food scraps left by his co-workers who *had* eaten lunch today. He was sure he looked foolish, like some sort of homeless man, but he was beyond caring.

"What are you doing?" asked Ed, the marketing director, as he marched into the kitchen. Snatching his lunch from the refrigerator, he heated it in the toaster oven.

Without turning to face Ed, Kevin muttered, "I'm looking…for… Oh mother fucker!" Kevin spun around with a clear plastic container in his dirty hands, retrieved from the very bottom of the garbage can. He angrily slammed it on the communal kitchen table, causing it to open. He smelt the stone-ground brown mustard and pastrami wafting out of the now empty container.

The aroma propelled his mind back to last night. Kevin had not finished this sandwich for dinner so he could bring it to work. His car needed some repairs. His girlfriend's birthday was less than a week away. It was a tight month if he were to maintain his budget and pay for a mechanic and a gold necklace. The only reason he'd ordered this sandwich was because he knew he could get two meals out of it, but that wasn't going to happen now.

Ed said: "Okay Kevin, so you found some garbage?"

"No Ed, this isn't garbage, this is evidence. This was in my lunch bag, and it had *my* sandwich in it. Someone went into my bag, took out my sandwich, buried the container at the bottom of the trash and then closed my lunch bag up."

Before Kevin did something he would regret he closed his eyes, tried to breathe and control his temper. His therapist told him over and over again not to let little things bother him, to try to have some logical perspective and not overreact. But he was hungry. It was two days until payday and he'd used his last forty dollars to put gas in his car.

Before Kevin could say another word, Brett, the office director walked in. His concerned expression suggested he'd already heard most of Kevin and Ed's exchange. He coldly and dismissively said, "Kevin, look, I'm sure you just left it at home. Could it have fallen out in your car or something?" He was trying to diffuse the situation.

"No Brett," Kevin came close to snarling, "I didn't leave it at home. Here's the container. Someone stole my lunch, and this isn't the first time it's happened, either. Other people have had things taken from them, too."

"Who?" Brett asked.

Now more co-workers had entered the lunchroom. Each agreed with Kevin, offered their own stories of theft from the communal refrigerator. This was at least the tenth time this year it had happened. Many employees had taken to writing their names on their lunch bags. Some had even tried to hide things in the back of the refrigerator to make it more difficult for the thief.

"This is a serious problem Brett." Rebecca, a junior grief counselor who'd recently joined the company just before Christmas, spoke up. "The last time this happened you said you'd look into it and that it wouldn't happen again. You didn't even let me hang my sign."

"What sign?" asked Brett, looking nonplussed. He'd yet to have his lunch stolen, which Kevin surmised might change his casual attitude to the problem if he did.

Rebecca shrugged as if to say he should already know. "I printed

SCAVENGER

a sign, remember, that read 'If It's Not Yours, Don't Take It!', but you wouldn't let me put it up."

Brett shrugged, "Look, perhaps we're all over reacting. Sometimes things go bad and people throw them out because of the smell. I'm sure no one here is stealing from their co-workers, and if they were going to steal something it wouldn't be something as silly as lunches."

"None of us are overreacting, Kevin," answered Doug, the office IT manager who had just joined the conversation. He stood back, leaning against the wall behind the gathering crowd. His tone was even, his expression calm, but his eyes were sharp as if inviting a challenge to his statement. "This isn't about lunches, Brett. This is about respect. It's about being victimized. You don't think it's an important issue because it hasn't happened to you yet."

"Okay, okay," Brett raised his hands in surrender. "I'll send out an office e-mail addressing this——and you can hang your sign on the fridge, Bec, if you want to, but we're not starting some half-baked witch hunt. Some lunches have gone missing, I get that, but that doesn't mean anyone is stealing. Everyone needs to calm down."

"That's easy for you to say," replied Kevin, smarting. "You're not the one who has to have a banana for lunch."

"Somebody *will* do something about this," snapped Doug. "I'll make sure of that."

Brett folded his arms. "This conversation is getting us nowhere. Look, Kevin, I'll give you five dollars from petty cash. Will that be enough to buy lunch today?"

Kevin's frown should have been enough of an indicator to say that it most certainly wasn't, but five dollars was all he got.

~*~

When the arguing ran out of steam and work duties loomed, the staff of office workers slowly went back to work, everyone that was except for Sandy, the receptionist, who usually ate her lunch at her desk. Today she had packed a Greek yogurt and a small side salad——she had her figure to think of. But some days she couldn't help herself, and today was one of those days. All morning she'd been snacking on pastrami, pinching bits of succulent meat off half a sandwich that she'd stashed inside her desk. The meat melted in her mouth, thinly sliced like she preferred it.

She had heard Kevin's exchange from her desk, and somehow his anger just made everything taste so much better.

~*~

"We can't have this happen anymore," Brett quietly explained. "You understand that. It's gotten out of hand. You are disrupting things in the office."

The office had been closed for an hour and everyone was gone, except for Sandy and Brett.

"I told you that I'd buy you lunch, whatever you wanted, whenever you wanted, you just had to ask. Why are you still doing this?"

Sandy looked up from where she crouched between Brett's hairy legs, paused before answering. "Because I wanted it and it was there. Now excuse me, I'll go back to work." She resumed her task at hand.

"Sandy, it needs to stop. It needs to…" his voice drifted off, replaced by guttural animalistic sounds, followed by thrashing and a long sigh.

"There now, all better," Sandy replied as she rose from her knees before the chair of her seated supervisor. "Nothing is going to stop, Brett, because I will take what I want." She wiped her mouth with the back of her hand, and with the other hand picked up a family photo from his desk of a wife and four young children. She smiled, turned the picture to face inward toward her boss. "Besides, eating something that doesn't belong to you makes it taste so much better. Don't you think your wife would agree?"

Brett had no answer for her.

~*~

No one saw the two cars leaving the office, past the headstones and crypts, the mausoleums and monuments. It was dark and security let them out, opening the locked gates of the cemetery. Few people realized that in the center of the graveyard was an office not too dissimilar from most offices. A business was a business, billing was billing and paperwork was paperwork. Most people not in the industry of death would have been amazed at just how much paper followed a corpse.

But what even the cemetery workers didn't realize was that their place of business was like an embassy for the living in a nation of the dead. It was a safe zone, untouched by those who called the cemetery home. It had always been this way. It would always be this way, for that was as the Master commanded.

As the last car pulled away, as the sun set, the nocturnal residents of the cemetery awoke, rose from their hiding places and moved about their homeland.

Nightfall marked the start of their foraging. They were hungry. Hunger could only be resisted for only so long.

~*~

Cooking was a lot like alchemy, and in many ways like sorcery. It was a blending of elements, of rhythms and textures in the pursuit of creating something new. It was to make a thing that was much more than the sum of its individual components. It was very easy to do poorly, difficult to do well. But if you had a gift for it, the craft could be called an art. The man stopping by the farmers' market on the way home from the cemetery was one such artist.

Soup would have been easier, chili would have been ideal, but it was August. Slow cooking a pot of chili in the summertime was probably more trouble than it was worth. But the germ of Mexican food stuck in the man's head, and when he passed the avocados he was struck with inspiration. *Why not guacamole? Now that would be a challenge!*

So the man picked out a few nice looking avocados, a lime, red onion, a clove of garlic and a beautiful tomato. He knew this great salsa guacamole combo dip that was a real hit. Freshness counted for a lot, because the flavors came through. He'd need those strong flavors to mask the belladonna and foxglove, as well as the pinch of dried and ground poison dart frog and the nine drops of his own blood. None of those items would be found at the farmers' market, but he took pride in maintaining his workshop at home through various 'exotic' contacts across the globe——in Mexico City, Port-au-Prince and Hong Kong. His 'pantry' was always well-stocked for just about any task he might undertake.

When he returned home, he unpacked his supplies and mashed the avocadoes, smiling as he did so. He enjoyed cooking, just as much as he enjoyed alchemy. He never thought he would, or imagined when he started out that he'd be combining the two. His first master had been the one who introduced him to cooking. "So, you want to learn alchemy, do you boy?" the ancient mummified wizard had once asked him. "Well, let me see you make a pot of gumbo and then we'll talk." He remembered how silly it seemed but later learned how wise his master had been. If you couldn't master gumbo, you'd never master alchemy.

The last ingredient was a few drops of his own blood. He had a taste. The flavor was a bit off, so he tweaked the mixture with salt, ground pepper and lime juice. After the fourth taste it was perfect. He then made three small containers, labeling them Wednesday, Thursday and Friday. Tomorrow he'd get a nice big bag of nachos and just leave them on the kitchen table at work.

There was a little left over, so he ate it. It was quite a good batch, if he did think so himself. His own blood made him immune to its effects.

No one else would be so lucky.

~*~

The next day three small containers of dip——a delicious-looking salsa guacamole combo——were discovered sitting on a shelf on the door of the office refrigerator. Hanging on the refrigerator was a new sign, *If It's Not Yours Don't Take It! Please Have Some Respect For Your Fellow Co-workers.* People saw the owner of the guacamole enjoying it in the kitchen on Wednesday, and again on Thursday. However, on Friday, the man left the office and returned with a slice of pizza because the container marked Friday had gone missing. He wasn't the least bit disappointed, in fact, he was thrilled.

Later that afternoon he wrote a quick note on a Post-It and taped it to a rock. As he left work he drove through the cemetery, taking the long way around to the rear entrance. This led through Section One, long disused by the cemetery for fresh plots because there were none there. He slowed his car and tossed the rock with its attached message onto the steps of the Thurman family crypt: one of the biggest and oldest in the cemetery, and a place of long history and dark secrets.

He didn't wait to see who would retrieve the message, but he knew what would unfold. Sometime after dark one of the crypt's inhabitants would pick up the mail, and then share the good news with the rest of its pack.

Master had left a note! Master was sending them a gift.

SCAVENGER

~*~

Sandy spent a nice evening at home, watching the cooking channel and enjoying some amazing dip. The guacamole didn't belong to her. She'd taken it out of the fridge at work and smiled as she ate every mouthful. The nachos shaped like little bowls were perfect for the dip, and she'd picked up another bag on the way home from work. Her stolen treat was going to be the high point of her evening and it did not disappoint. As she was meeting friends at the lake tomorrow for a lovely summer Saturday in the sun, she turned in early.

By three in the morning she woke suddenly, because she was ravenously hungry. Her stomach growled so badly it was cramping up. She couldn't remember ever being so insatiable.

Downstairs, Sandy tore open her refrigerator and bit into a leftover drumstick of chicken, but immediately spat it out. It tasted sour, putrid, her mouth stinging from the mere contact with it. But still the hunger remained. She tried a piece of cheese, a handful of grapes and then a slice of hard salami, but everything tasted rotten. She looked to see if her refrigerator was turned off, but felt the cold wafting out the open door. How could everything inside be spoiled?

Her stomach clenched, she nearly screamed. She simply had to eat something! So holding her nose, she bit into a croissant and forced herself to swallow a mouthful, just to put something into her stomach and make the pain go away.

Suddenly, a whole new world of pain opened up to her.

Pain was redefined.

Sandy gasped and moaned as fire griped her belly and spread through her body. Her bowels voided before she could make it to the bathroom. She tried to scream, but her throat was choked as she vomited uncontrollably. Her legs gave out and she fell to the floor, landing in a puddle of her own waste. Her cellular phone was in the bedroom charging. She knew it might as well be on the Moon because there was no way she could reach it. She tried to scream, thinking maybe a neighbor would hear her, but all that came out was vomit, blood and gore.

Then she convulsed in a pool of her own filth. She felt slithering, crawling and squirming all around and under her. The vile puddle contained roaches and earthworms, small black snakes and tiny fiddler crabs.

She vomited again, tried to cover her mouth to stop it, but it was no use. In her hands squirmed worms and roaches. The creatures were coming from inside her body!

Death came slowly to Sandy, but mercifully it came. Eventually she stopped vomiting, stopped breathing. When her heart ceased beating she was finally able to lay still. The pain stopped…

…but only for a moment before it began again.

Only now she couldn't move. She waited for darkness or light, for heaven or hell to claim her. She begged God for anything to stop the pain, but nothing did.

~*~

Sandy waited a very long time before the police finally investigated, because of the smell, and broke in. She listened as they declared her dead and called for the coroner to come and pick up 'the body'. But she was alive. She could hear them, could feel their touch when they checked for a pulse then lifted her into a body bag, but she couldn't move, couldn't breathe. Sandy was trapped in the prison of her uncooperative body, filled with pain.

Before the zipper closed her in with the darkness, she saw that all the worms, insects and other horrors that had erupted from within her were gone. All traces of blood, vomit and waste were gone as well. Was it all a dream?

Yes, it had to be a dream!

Sandy tried to wake herself on the way to the hospital and during her time in the morgue, when thankfully she was out of the bag but stripped of her clothes. By the time the funeral director picked her up the pain had finally stopped. She was embalmed, dressed, and placed in a casket. All the while she screamed within her mind to just wake up.

The lid closed and she felt herself being moved. She was carried, driven, carried again. She listened to the muffled voices before feeling that she was being lowered. It became cold and quiet, before at long last, her mind faded into darkness. I'm finally dead, finally! She thought it felt like falling asleep. It was peaceful and she was relieved, until she suddenly woke up.

~*~

Awake again, she was still ravenously hungry. The pain that wracked her body at least was gone. She breathed a sigh of relief. For a moment she thought it had all been a dream.

Then she realized she wasn't in her bed. She was in a casket.

She looked around and saw no way out, nothing that could be used as a tool. She was about to scream when she smelled something... delicious.

She turned her head to her left and the scent grew stronger. Whatever it was wasn't far away and it smelled so good. She was so hungry, an all-consuming hunger. She growled and punched the side of the casket, causing the wood to splinter. Earth started to cave in on her but she frantically dug, pushed the soil away and behind her.

Sandy swam through the earth, her tunnel caving in on itself as she moved. After a few dozen yards she broke into a chamber. She hauled herself upright, rose to her feet. She was covered in soil. She shook her head hard, flinging dirt like a dog shakes off water. Sandy looked around the chamber, took stock of her surroundings.

The dark, subterranean place was wide and low——just a little above seven feet high, and maybe seventy feet across. There were plastic lawn chairs, a table made out of a board and some milk cartons, a pile of old magazines, a few boxes of board games and a mirror hanging beside a well-stocked bookcase. Then she smelled what had drawn her here.

There on the floor was a fresh human corpse. It was a man dressed in a suit, plump and probably only fifty-five or sixty. The scent filled her nostrils, set her blood on fire. A single word flashed into Sandy's mind: FOOD.

She rushed forward, grabbed the corpse's arm and bit into it, through the clothing. Sandy tore bite after bite from the arm, stripping the flesh and swallowing it down in wolf-like gulps. She feasted, felt the pain of her hunger slowly fade. When she was finally able to stop herself and catch her breath, she realized she'd devoured all the meat from the wrist to the shoulder, down to the bone. At some point she had somehow torn off the limb and backed into a corner, holding the skeletal human arm.

She wasn't alone.

Five figures surrounded her and were horrific to behold. They were nearly nude, wearing filthy tattered rags. Their hands were large and powerful, with thick curved claws. Their eyes shone purple, set back behind a long canine muzzle. The noses were large and bat-like. The ears swept back like frills on a reptile. The five figures simply watched her, made no moves, as if waiting. Sandy stood up slowly, her heart pounding in her breast. Slowly she began drawing a breath to scream.

"Okay now, calm down miss. We all understand. No one here is going to judge you," the largest one said.

Another, smaller creature spoke up, "Well, thank goodness. Another female, that will make things easier, we're evened up again."

"Hush now, all of you. You'll scare the poor thing. Don't be afraid. We're your friends. See, we left some food out for when you woke up," one of the males answered.

"I… I… Oh god, I don't understand. Please don't hurt me." Sandy said, as she started to cry.

The other female, who had yet to speak, came forward. "There, there now, no one is going to hurt you. You're our new sister, we're so happy to meet you. You're going to be just fine. It's always hard at first." The creature made to embrace her, and Sandy screamed. She lunged forward, pushing past the ring of figures to rush toward the far end of the chamber.

This positioned her squarely before the hanging mirror. Purple eyes looked back at her. She saw that she had a muzzle and it was caked with dirt, saliva and scraps of human flesh. Her skin was grey but her hair remained. She tried to brush the dirt from it, only to see her massive curved talons on her powerful-looking hand.

The newly-born ghoul turned back to her welcoming pack, and shook her head in confusion. They surrounded her again in a circle of welcome. Introductions were made and they asked her name. The pack then began their evening meal, by surrounding the corpse and feasting upon it. It all felt…*normal.*

Sandy only picked at the meat, as she'd eaten nearly her fill already. Afterwards they broke out a board game and played in pairs, happy to have an even number to their fellowship once more.

"So," asked the largest male in the pack as he moved his piece on the board, "what did you do to piss off Master Doug?"

IN THE HOUSE OF MILLIONS OF YEARS

By John Goodrich

Intef floated, free, in the current of the great lightless river. He had peace; no worries or cares, no regrets, no ambitions. Past and future were far away, inoffensive. Calm suffused him in an omnipresent, timeless now.

Something caught at his attention; a speck of light. He let his drifting turn him away. A tiny sound, a chant, annoyed his ears like the whine of a gnat. With the first effort since he had arrived in this nonplace, he ignored it. The drifting, the now, the peace, was everything.

The sound got louder, more insistent. The pinprick of light grew, like the golden bark of Amun-Ra surmounting the horizon. He again tried to turn away, to let the dark encompass him again, but the noise and the light would not let him go. The droning chant grew, became sinuous, entwined him like a snake. He was dragged to the light, away from the comforting calm.

"Mighty Pharaoh?" Hands touched his face. "Golden Horus?"

Intef felt old. His muscles and joints ached. He opened eyes that felt parched as a thousand years of drought. Akhetsau, High Priest of Amun-Ra, stood before him, flanked by two strangers. They chanted the damnable, snakelike spell that had called him from…somewhere. His memory of where was fading like a morning mist.

"What is this?" Intef croaked.

Now that he was awake, everyone on the room bowed before him. In the sudden quiet, the braziers hissed, billowing out noxious smoke. With slow effort, he worked himself into a sitting position, and discovered that he was in a sarcophagus. His coffin, with his name enclosed in the spells.

"Have I been ill?"

Akhetsau bowed his shaven head, unwilling to look directly at his god-king. Frowning, Intef searched his memory. What had happened? Where had be been?

The battle had been long and difficult. His men were tired from their long march, the pretender's troops fresh, their supply lines short. But the enemy was weak, without much stomach for the fight, where Intef's men were fighting for their true god-king.

The arrow had struck him cross-wise, entering his right shoulder. Intef curled in on himself, as the phantom of pain rushed through him. He remembered the confused shouting of his men as he was hauled from the battlefield, the arrow an agonizing brand.

His stench of remembered rot filled his nostrils. He read the truth in the grim faces of the royal physicians, that he was dying with his great work undone. He had sworn to unite Upper and Lower Egypt under one throne, as they had been a hundred years ago. Only then would the Empire be as it should, the most glorious in all the world. Would his son be a true son of Montu and take up this costly, difficult war to finally unite the Two Ladies?

Intef shook the past off and peered into the gloom that surrounded him. He was not on the Bark of Amun-Ra. But where was he? He knew the smell of the room; salt and strange, bitter herbs. He was in an embalmer's chamber. Though he could not focus on them, two indistinct figures, dressed neither as embalmers nor priests of Anubis, stood by him.

"Gods above, what have you done?" His voice was strange, a dry croak.

Akhetsau glanced at the dark figures. Intef could see a great, ashen stain on the High Priest's normally immaculate white robe.

"We have brought you back from the brink of death, Golden Horus." The man behind Akhetsau wore a black, concealing robe that was a mockery of the priest's pure white. "We were High Priest Akhetsau's last hope, and yours as well. You wish for more life, do you not, Great Pharaoh?"

His words were oily, and Intef disliked him.

"How long has it been?" He spoke to Akhetsau, ignoring the men. "Are my armies in disarray?"

"We have performed ceremonies over your holy body for more than ten days, mighty lord. Your armies returned you here, and remain encamped outside the city." The man's unctuous voice worked into his ear.

Intef turned a baleful eye on the men. "And who are you?"

"Heriabgher and Tehenraau, gracious lord."

"Where are we?"

"Thebes," Akhetsau cut in.

Only now did Intef realize how exhausted he was, as if he had been in battle for days. His limbs ached, his head was as heavy as lead. He knew that he should show himself to his troops. Let them know he was not dead. But the prospect wearied him. He had been in the field, chasing the pretenders and laying siege to their cities——his rightful cities——for years.

"Leave us." He did not care if this was Heriabgher and Tehenraau's home. He would not show weakness in front of them. Glancing at each other, they bowed, and left.

"Home." Even uttering the word was tiring.

"Golden Horus?"

"I don't wish to spend more time in this place of death. Take me to my wives and children."

He reached out, and Akhetsau took his hand. The High Priest of Amun-Ra helped him from his coffin, supported him out into the cool night as if the God-King were a common drunkard.

~*~

Intef drank in the sight of his palace like cool water in the desert. His wives, his children were there, beer and good food. Gleeful shrieks erupted from the serving girls as they went running to fetch his wives. Intef stood on his own, feeling his strength returning. He clapped the priest's shoulder.

"Thank you, Akhetsau."

The priest bowed low, then straightened.

"I endeavor to serve Pharaoh and the gods with my every breath." Akhetsau let out a troubled sigh. "I was afraid Egypt had lost her true King, the only one capable of reuniting her."

"Afraid enough to let two strangers work spells on me?"

The priest looked away.

"What choice did I have? To leave the land divided, with the madmen of Henen-nesut in power for another hundred years? I had to grasp the straw they offered me, no matter what the cost. With you restored, Thebes shall be the seat of power forever, the Two Ladies reunited."

Intef smiled, some of his weariness lifting.

"There is a still a lot of work to be done. I shall reward you as you deserve, Akhetsau. And the two strangers, even if I do not like them."

Light was coming down the corridors, and the gabble of voices as his wives and their ladies-in-waiting all tried to call him at once. The priest bowed and retreated as the tide of Intef's wives washed over him. There were nerves to soothe, rumors to lay at rest, attention to distribute, and he had missed it all desperately.

After his wives had been reassured and news exchanged, he chose his fourth and youngest wife Enehy to pass the night with. She was his youngest, married to him less than three years, as beautiful and flawless as anyone the gods had made.

"Intef, is that truly you?" She asked when they were alone, her khol-smeared eyes larger than usual.

"Truly me, daughter of Nefer."

Her smile brightened.

"Then you have tired of the company of your men?" Only she would dare tease him in such fashion.

"My empire is my work. You, my wife, are entirely my pleasure."

"Everything my mighty God-King, strong as a bull, wishes." Her murmur was breathy. Her linen dress slipped to the floor, and she stood before him clad only in the golden pectoral he had given her when they married.

Her delicate hand reached out and touched his chest, and her face clouded over.

"What happened to your heart?"

She took his hand and placed it over his heart. There was no beat. His chest was as still as stone.

"It changes nothing," he said to buy time. Nothing was wrong with him. He felt the same as he always had. Didn't he?

Almost concealing her fear and confusion, she touched him again, stroking his sides, avoiding his chest. He watched her with unwanted detachment. He had desired to be reunited with her more than anything else. She had never failed to arouse him with her youth and beauty. He had hoped for, longed for her while he had been on the campaign. Now, he felt nothing, as if her hands and mouth were touching another man. His body was like stone, incapable of reacting. Hoping against hope, he let her continue, but no pleasure came. She redoubled her efforts, as he watched, unmoved, incapable, until he pushed the tearful Enehy away.

Her failure betrayed not only him, but all of the kingdom.

"Sobekari!" He called for the night guard who kept watch over his bedchamber.

"Mighty Horus?" Sobekari bowed as he entered.

Intef looked at the pathetic weeping woman, huddled in the corner. He thought of the stillness in his chest, of her failure. All he had wanted was to return to his wife, and she had failed to elicit his interest, or his pleasure.

"Throw her to the crocodiles."

Sobekari was a loyal subject. He glanced to the weeping woman and back to Intef.

"Dread lord?" His voice quavered.

"She had failed as a wife, and I have no more use for her."

Again his eyes flickered to her. He bowed again.

"As Pharaoh wishes."

A scream tore itself out of her as Sobekari's large hand closed around her arm. Intef felt nothing. She screamed again, and now the palace was alive with the shuffling of bare feet on stone. Whispers flew, and people watched wide-eyed as Sobekari dragged Enehy along.

He led them, and a small crowd gathered in their wake, to the temple of Sobek, where the sacred crocodiles lolled sleepily in the night's cool air. If her screaming didn't waken them, the scent of a good meal would.

The priests came scampering out of their small cells, prostrated themselves before the terrible presence of their Pharaoh. The musky, reptilian scent that emanated from the enclosure was unmistakable, as was the carrion reek from their previous meals.

Intef strode to the stone lip of the enclosure, gazed down on Sobek's sacred predators. They were groggy from the chill air, but the scent and hubbub had woken them. Enehy knelt at the verge of the muddy pit, her flawless skin pale in the moonlight, arms mutely raised to him, begging for mercy.

Sobekari paused, his hope-filled eyes on his Pharaoh.

Intef placed a hand on his chest, felt the stillness. Enehy and Sobekari were breathing hard, but he was not. He was not breathing at all. His body was completely silent.

She sent him one last, imploring look. When he did not respond, she closed her eyes. She landed in the mud, and for a breathless minute, blunt, scaled muzzles snuffed the air. Then they were in motion.

Enehy was done with screaming. She stood, naked in the knee-deep water, her golden pectoral gleaming dimly in the starlight. As the crocodiles closed, she walked forward to greet them. Sobekari turned away, but Intef stood, watching. He could remember her touch, but not why it had thrilled him. The crocs tore into her soft body, her screams brief and then gone. Blood roiled in the water as the beasts hissed and snapped at each other, trying to steal another portion of bloody meat.

Intef could see the fear and hopelessness in Sobekari's eyes. For himself, he felt nothing.

~*~

With his heart still and his breath gone, Intef found that he could not sleep. He closed his eyes and laid his head to rest, but it did no good. After long hours, he simply paced the dark and empty corridors of his palace, waiting for Amun-Ra's golden touch to warm the land. The cold hours seemed endless, without his heart and breath to keep time. How had he not noticed his body's silence? Why did he feel nothing, when he had thrown his beloved wife to the crocodiles?

Across the silent morning came the chant of Amun-Ra's priests welcoming the god's life-giving rays, and Intef knew what he was. After endless, tortured darkness, the Golden Bark finally rose above the horizon, chasing the cold shadows from the land. But it did not warm him.

He summoned his scribes, and ordered them to take down his words.

"The necromancers Heriabgher and Tehenraau are to be treated as criminals. They have robbed me of the breath of life, and now I have no place in maat. They have violated the sacred precepts of maat by knowing what should not be known. I have no living heart to be weighed against the Feather of Truth. These traitors have done injury to their pharaoh."

"Find them and impale them on stakes. Find their families, and do the same. Destroy their houses, leave no brick standing on another.

In the House of Millions of Years

Burn what you find within, scatter the ashes on the Nile. Raze the villages they were born in, and allow none to escape. This knowledge is an abomination which must not be allowed to continue. No sacrifice is too great, no hardship too unendurable to bring lawful death to these men."

He paused. "High Priest Akhetsau brought these men of corrupt knowledge to his dying Pharaoh. He is to share their fate.

"This proclamation is to be sped to all the provinces of Egypt, even those in rebellion against their rightful king."

~*~

Intef had a tomb carved to inter his first life. Intef Seher-tawy, Maker of Peace in the Two Lands, was no more. He put away his wives, became Intef Wah-Ankh, the Strong in Life. And strong he had been. Untiring when his soldiers dropped in their tracks of exhaustion, never hungry, never thirsty, and unwearying in battle. His campaign against the rebels of Lower Egypt progressed, but always, somehow, victory slipped from his grasp. Taken cities rebelled, governors thought loyal betrayed him.

Fear was the common element. Fear of him. His body, withered by the rays of the Aten, had become a shrunken horror, detestable and inhuman. No one confronted with such a face would believe it was that of the Golden Horus, Pharaoh, Lord of the Two Ladies.

Intef had a golden mask made to hide his hideous visage, and buried his second life in a new tomb. He re-named himself Nakj-tneb-tep-nefer Intef, the strong and beautiful champion.

His scribes told him he had been on the throne for only seventy years. His work was nearly done, the land close to united. But Intef had watched the burning sun rise on more than twenty-five thousand days, and wandered sleepless and alone for twenty-five thousand endless nights. His children had all grown old, withered, and been buried. Their children had done the same as the hateful tyranny of years ground on.

~*~

Intef stood before the assembled crowd of his courtiers, as well as the people of Thebes, the light of Amun-Ra's glory reflecting off the golden mask which hid his features.

"Egypt, the long work we have begun is nearly complete. The Two Ladies will come under a single crown, but this work is not for me to finish. The gods have another task for me." He gestured to the resplendent figure of Mokhtar, High Priest of Amun-Ra, standing by his side.

"The gods have sent me clear signs," Mokhtar's rich voice filled the court. "The Pharaoh Nakj-tneb-tep-nefer Intef, the strong and beautiful champion, now has other duties to perform, higher duties that only a god such as himself may attend to. He is to become a priest of Amun-Ra at the House of Millions of Years at Karnak, the holiest of holies, and worship them for the peace and prosperity of all the land. In years to come, should a Pharaoh wish to consult Intef's great wisdom, it shall be preserved and cherished at Karnak." In truth, Intef had begged the priest to find some way of releasing him from the unendurable bondage of rulership. Mokhtar had received this timely command from the gods.

"I present to you Mentuhotep, child of my body, to rule over you as Amun-Ra is king of the gods." Intef stepped back, bowing his head. Mentuhotep stepped forward, already fitted with the double crown of Pharaoh. He was in the glory of his prime, with strong arms, muscular shoulders, and a resonant voice. Men would follow him to their deaths.

"My long work is ended." Intef imagined he heard a breath, long held, finally exhaled as he stepped into the shadows behind his great-grandson.

Intef was taken by litter to the House of Millions of Years, and he looked forward to a new day for the first time in decades.

~*~

Karnak was beautiful. A temple worthy of the gods, spotlessly clean, blinding white limestone in the glory of Amun-Ra's light. Intef found some solace there, his days now filled with the endless rituals, singing the hymns of praise, and washing the statues of the gods. But even the priests' life was centered around the bodily needs he no longer had. The sacred brotherhood ate twice a day, times during which Intef could either watch, or remain alone. During the nights, they slept.

The long, still nights left time for holy contemplation and study of the temple's library. He wondered what had become of his ba, his animating force. He did not sleep because he was an empty khat, a body without soul. He looked on living men with envy and a sense of loss. Had his ba been set free to join the gods and his ancestors? Did it live on without him? Or had the necromancers destroyed it? Was this shriveled body all of him that existed? When that was destroyed, would he cease to exist? His names were still carved on his tombs, and priests still said prayers in his honor, but without a ba to receive them, were they worthless? He should have extracted answers from the necromancers before having them executed.

Intef was seldom consulted by Pharaohs; they preferred to honor him from afar. What had been a single holy structure was now a complex with outbuildings, layer upon layer of pylon gates, enormous columned pillars, a towering facade, and enclosing walls. But the Pharaohs who built these new structures were not merely bringing glory to Amun-Ra, Montu, and themselves. They were erecting barriers to contain that abomination that dwelt in the holiest of holies, the thing whose dead heart would never be balanced against the Feather of Truth. Him.

And yet, the names of the Pharaohs were carved into the walls, where he would eternally see them, and by reading their names keep their memories alive.

He was abandoned, alone, unique. Every day Amun-Ra's Bark came over the horizon, and he bowed and scraped before the remote gods, hoping some favor would be granted him. As the endless days stretched into years and the years to decades, then to centuries, he heard nothing.

~*~

"Ever-living God, there is a visitor who wishes to see you." Intef had just finished the Celebration of the Awakening of Amun-Ra. Time had worn him down like a road rutted by stone wheels. He did not even know the name of the priest who spoke to him.

The newcomer was dressed strangely, and his accent atrocious. But he knelt with proper respect.

"Mighty God of the Golden Mask," the man mumbled, awestruck.

"I am." He'd had another name, once. The grinding of years had abraded that memory to nothing.

"I...I did not believe you were real."

Undead and Unbound

"And yet you sought me out."

The man tried to recover himself.

"You are said to an undying god, as old as this holy temple."

The God considered.

"I have watched more than eight hundred thousand days dawn in this House of Millions of Years. I have seen more nights than there are grains of sand. The Persian Darius came to murder me, thinking it would be as easy as slaughtering the apis bulls. He beheld me, and fell down in worship. As I watch, Pharaohs die, their children die, and dynasties pass into nothing. Nations have been born and passed away, and I remain."

"I have a son, Deathless One. His heart is quick, and I will send him to train as a scribe next year. He is a good boy who does what he is told, who will help his father any time that he can. He has a good heart and is the joy of his mother and beloved of his siblings.

"He fell from the rooftop as he was playing. The bleeding has stopped, but he has not woken for three days. The doctors mumble that there is nothing to be done. I came for a priest, but——" a choking sob interrupted him.

"Could you not spare him a portion of your eternal life? Only an eyeblink to you, twenty or thirty years. Or use my own life and give it to him? Please Great God, please."

The man wept, his shoulders shaking with his misery.

Intef knelt next to him.

"You are chained to your burden of years like an ox to its cart. Hope is a heavy burden to carry over such a stony road. Kill your child in the most painless way possible. Let your son go, and begin to heal your heart."

~*~

The House of Millions of Years was crumbling around him. The stone was worn, showing cracks at the seams. The statues were no longer washed in the sacred lake, the priesthood had fled. This temple, the holiest of holies, was falling to ruin. The people sang only the praises of Osiris, only with a strange, foreign name. They had scrawled new pictures over carvings more than two thousand years old. He alone chanted the praises of Amun-Ra, whose wrath could shatter the world. Even stars had changed positions, so ancient was he.

In the House of Millions of Years

"Dread God of the Golden Mask?"

He focused on the man who stood, fidgeting and frightened, before him. He wore a strange bastardization of Egyptian and Roman clothing. How long had it been since someone had come to speak with him?

"What do you want?" His voice was dry as the desert around him. Though he kept up the rituals, he had not spoken to anyone for close to a hundred years. The new worshipers ignored him out of fear. Even it its crumbling state, the sprawling temple complex was large enough to share.

"We are invaded, Dread One."

"I am neglected and ancient as the dust on the floor. The Greeks and Romans plundered the black land and no one consulted me."

"A family legend says that my many-times grandfather once spoke to a deathless god as old as this temple. When I heard of these Arab invaders, I thought that you could help us." His eyes were wild, like a panicked horse's. "Surely, none may stand against you who are deathless."

He pulled a sword from its scabbard and offered it. The god's wasted, leathery hand closed around it. He had not borne a sword since… the impossible remoteness of the past made it cloudy. Not something strange like this one, but a proper khepesh. This felt Roman; light, short, strange. But it would do.

He had welcomed the dawning of Amun-Ra more than a million times since coming to the temple's confining walls. The world outside had changed little, the small huts men lived in were much the same, as were the men who tended their small farms and water lifts.

They still bowed before him, too terrified to look at the golden mask he had never removed. His enemies would also cower before him. All men did. This was no army. They were a rabble, peasants determined to resist invaders. They had heart, but only the messenger who had spoken to him even carried a weapon. Any disciplined enemy would leave them trying to stuff their intestines back into their mutilated bodies.

And yet, these people needed him. For the first time in his sleepless ages, he felt needed.

He would lead these farmers to victory, for the preservation of sacred Egypt.

"Where are our enemies?"

Undead and Unbound

~*~

An enormous snake of men slouched in along the road. Mounted riders flanked them, keeping the soldiers in line.

A rider spotted them, and spurred his horse in their direction. Intef, the Undying One, stood his ground. Yes that had been his name: Intef!

He roared his recovered name to the skies, and the horse reared, nearly throwing the rider.

Intef lifted his sword and took off at a lope, unsure if his withered body would take a full run. The horse shuffled its hooves and rolled its eyes in fear as the rider fought for control. When they were dead, he would slaughter the entire army. He was Intef of Three Thousand Years, God of the Golden Mask, strong like a bull, the Undying. None could stop him.

The rider got his mount under control, and charged across the dry sand. The ground shook as the iron-shod hooves thundered toward Intef. The God of the Golden Mask braced for the impact, timing his sword thrust to take the rider full in the chest.

The rider whipped his curved sword up, knocking Intef's tip into the air, then swept downward. Intef spun to the ground, and saw, through the tilted eyeholes of his mask, his decapitated body collapse.

The horseman swung around, approached at a slow trot. Feet landed next to him. Rough, uncouth fingers grasped his neck, and Intef was hoisted into the air. With a wrench that tore his skin, he was pulled from the golden mask. A face considered Intef in one hand, the golden mask in the other. With a casual flip, Intef's decapitated head was discarded.

His rabble of farmers was nowhere in sight. He could not shout, could not speak. Moving his jaw didn't give him enough purchase to right himself, to move at all.

Amun-Ra abandoned the sky. In the dark of night, the wind buried Intef's still-conscious head under a tall, silent dune.

ROMERO 2.0

By Brian M. Sammons
and
David Conyers

Cory Alvarez wiped away the single tear to escape his eye. He didn't wish for the two Outpost Directors of Salvation Point to see how deeply Beth's death had affected him, especially when Beth stood before them, seen outside through the habitat portal. Frozen dust from the red desert blew around her, fluttered the tattered, torn clothes she had died in. Her skin had already greyed and was sloughing off her desiccated muscles. She stared with vacant eyes that no longer recognized anything in the Martian outpost, that a few hours earlier had been her home.

"How did it happen?" Alvarez asked as he wiped away a second tear.

"Does it matter?" The big bear of a man, Outpost Director Jeremiah South, placed his hand upon Alvarez's shoulder. Charity, Jeremiah's overfed wife and co-Outpost Director, gave her best sufficiently sympathetic face from her usual position at her husband's side. "All that matters is that she's in God's hands now."

"Bullshit!" Alvarez snapped.

Both Jeremiah and Charity inhaled sharply. "Swearing, Brother Cory, is not tolerated in our colony," snapped the wife. In a more conciliatory tone, she said, "We appreciate that Beth and you were engaged to be married, but still——"

"But still...what?" he snapped. "She's dead. She died on your fucking watch. What the fuck happened?"

"Language!" snapped Charity, whose pudgy skin was reddening with the heated discussions.

Jeremiah held up his hand, a command for silence. "Emotions run high in times of trouble, for all of us. Beth was a valued member of our family, Cory. Charity and I also grieve for her unfortunate, early departure."

Alvarez clenched his fists. He wanted to punch something. "I was the one who loved her."

"We all loved her."

He pressed his fists against his forehead and held them there. "Stop with all of this, please."

"Just trust in God, my brother."

Dropping his arms, he noticed the bulging veins in his forearms. The Sandhouse Serum that gave Beth a second, half-life, also lived inside his blood, as it lived inside every colonist who migrated to the Red Planet. Injection was a contractual stipulation enforced by the Mars-ruling Sandhouse Consortium. No serum, no entry visa. The stipulation was to ensure that dead colonists served a second purpose, as undead labor. With the future that awaited her as one of those slaves, Alvarez hoped Beth no longer felt human emotions.

"Can we at least put her out of his misery? The life she faces, this undead-like existence, Beth doesn't deserve this."

Jeremiah patted Alvarez on the back, hugged him tight enough that it would become a struggle should he try to resist. "I know you and Elizabeth felt like outsiders here. If you only embraced God, let him into your heart——"

That was too much for Alvarez, and he did struggle until the moment became more awkward than it already was, with Alvarez practically having to topple over using his body weight to escape Jeremiah's grip.

"You know the rules," Jeremiah said when a good distance again separated them, and he could pretend their past scuffle had never been. "Our colony, which is one of the remotest, needs as many hands as it can secure, alive or dead. We must mine oxygen. Crops need to be attended. Livestock needs feeding and milking, and pens need cleaning. Maintenance is an ongoing and constant problem. One major hull breach, and then we are all dead."

Alvarez was too angry to say anything.

"You'll need to fit her with the neural controller," said Charity. "You are our info tech officer, after all."

Stunned, he nodded.

"Get her working with the others. Then we will pray together."

"I'm not fucking religious, okay? So please, just drop it."

Jeremiah and Charity stared at him as if he had just murdered one of their children.

"That is sacrilegious talk there, young Cory," said Jeremiah in a more conciliatory tone than Faith had ever managed in the whole time Alvarez had known them both. "This is one of God's colonies, and here your words are an action worthy of banishment. However, we know this is your grief talking. Fit the corpse with a controller, as discussed, and we promise that your indiscretion will be forgotten."

Alvarez became numb. She was no longer Beth to their eyes, or Elizabeth as they had insisted on calling her, she was just one more of their undead.

He wondered if that was how they had always seen her.

"Whatever you say, Director."

~*~

Alvarez suited up his cheap Indian manufactured vacuum suit, pressurized then checked all his seals, electrics, heating elements and oxygen flow lines. Everything seemed to be in good working order, considering its quality. So he entered the airlock and waited until the pressure dropped to one hundredth that of inside their base.

Outside, Alvarez marched through the dusty desolate wasteland that had been his home for the last Martian year. The undead, wearing only the torn and dirty clothes that they had died in or nothing at all, stared at him from behind the five meter high wire fencing of their compound. It was late in the day and they had just returned from their work duties. Some roamed aimlessly or in circles. A few might have called out to him, but Alvarez could never really tell if they used real words or not because the atmosphere was too thin for sound to carry very far. If they could talk he didn't want to know if they had needs. If the undead wanted for 'things' that meant an element of their personality had survived. He didn't want to know that.

He should have waited until it was properly dark before he came outside, when the air temperature was too cold even for the anti-freeze in the undead's former blood streams and they lost their mobility, and ceased-up for the night.

When he found Beth, alone on the rocky rust colored sands, he burst into tears. She was wandering aimlessly, like a stunned survivor of a car crash who walks away from the wreckage. Her back was to him, and she seemed normal enough had he discounted that the temperature was minus eighty degrees Celsius and the super-thin atmosphere was devoid of oxygen. If there was any blood left in her, it would have already boiled into the atmosphere. Only the Sandhouse Serum gave her life now.

He walked up behind her, grabbed her gently by the shoulders and spun her around.

What he saw made him gag, and then sob hysterically.

The undead always carried the scars that killed them, and Beth was no different. Her nose, ears and mouth had bled out. Her eyes bulged and one had split open. Skin had ruptured and torn around her joints, where the outer layers had frozen and her constant movements had caused the flesh to crack.

"Beth?" he asked when he managed to control his sobs. "Beth, can you hear me?"

He switched on his speaker unit when he realized no sound was coming from him, and asked again.

"Beth?"

For one terrible second he thought she was going to answer him.

But there was no recognition. Nothing. It was a small mercy.

"I'm sorry this happened, Beth. I'm so sorry we came to Mars in the first place."

He stopped, took a moment to compose himself but sobbed again anyway. He realized that talking to her was cathartic, and this was a chance to say goodbye. "I know why we came. There is no work on Earth, at least not for an info technician like me, and definitely nothing for you as a geologist. Who'd expect that we'd end up here, in the middle of nowhere on some crazy religious colony on Argyre Planitia? I know you didn't want to be a farmer…"

Snuffling, he studied the horizon. He saw their modular habitats, the biospheres where the crops and livestock lived, hydrogen fuel tanks, a few all-terrain vehicles, and the outpost's single tethered vacuum dirigible. Beyond there was nothing but flat, rocky and boring Martian wasteland that the Sandhouse Consortium had done nothing to improve with terraforming.

If he kept thinking about his situation and how isolated he was Alvarez felt certain he'd never be able to get out of bed in the morning ever again.

ROMERO 2.0

"I need to inject you with this fluid, Beth. It will keep you warm, and protect you."

He took the anti-freeze gun from his utility belt. When the needle extracted from its protective casing, he was horrified by its size. Alive, the injection would have been extremely painful.

Lifting her thin, wasted arm, he found the remains of a vein, and fired the gun. Over the next few minutes as he fed her the anti-freeze, Beth inflated noticeably, commencing from her arm and then working its way across her body and into her face and legs. She began to look more human, but she still resembled the victim of a recent and horrible accident.

Afterwards he checked her body, identified points where anti-freeze leaked, mostly from cracks around her joints. Pinch clamps soon sealed those leaks. Then he noticed her split eye gushing more of the green liquid.

There was no other option: he had to clamp it shut leaving her half blind.

Through the process she said or did nothing, not even flinched when he eyeball was squashed. Her mouth worked up and down. She looked like she was trying to tell him something, but no sound would carry in the near-vacuum.

He sobbed again. He wished he could stop. Instead he switched off his radio link to the colony against the possibility other colonists were snooping. He didn't want anyone, especially Jeremiah and Charity, to know how badly he hurt.

"Beth." He could no longer look at her as he spoke. "Beth, I need to insert the neuralcomp onto your spine."

He spun her around, tore away the tatters of her t-shirt exposing her back. With the neuralcomp in hand, he checked that its circuitry clamps were all in working order. It would sit upon her spine and resemble a large, black matt centipede that fed instructions into the nervous system. He told himself the outpost needed these neuralcomps, because through them they could command all the undead to perform basic duties, such as cleaning, tending the crops and feeding the livestock. Duties Beth had been commanded to do when she was alive.

Just as he was about to apply the neuralcomp he noticed the puncture wound just below the ribcage on her left side. It was circular, and unlike Beth's other injuries the flesh was pushed inwards, not rupturing outwards.

He folded back the remains of her t-shirt. The puncture hole was there too. The shirt material was stained with blood that showed signs of congealing on her skin, rather than evaporating into the atmosphere had this wound occurred outside.

A thought occurred so he checked his multi-tool, the same multi-tool that everyone on the base owned, and set it to screwdriver setting.

There was no mistaking it; someone had stabbed her with a multi-tool.

He shuddered.

"Come with me?"

He grabbed Beth by the hand, led her to the base. They passed the compounds and he saw the undead versions of other colonists he had once known in their first lives. There was Bill MacKay, a human resources manager from Edinburgh; Josie Forrester, a former journalist from Imbrium City on Luna; and Carlos van Ghent, a publisher from Santiago. They had all died suddenly and unexpectedly. But that was the way it was on Mars, where a simple suit rupture, a bad oxygen line, radiation poisoning from solar flares, or a dozen other hazards that were part of everyday life in an environment not suited for human habitation, which could kill quickly. But when Alvarez studied each of the undead closely, he only saw people whose professions back before they arrived on Mars would serve no purpose in a remote and struggling colony. Here they worked as farmers, laborers, and in odd jobs.

Jobs the undead could do.

His fists tightened into hard balls. His teeth clenched. "You're a bastard, Jeremiah," he muttered to himself.

Alvarez had planned on placing Beth in the compound with the others, but not anymore. She didn't deserve this, not after what had been done to her.

Together they entered the airlock. Bringing an undead into the living habitats was a serious breach of their laws, but he was beyond caring about minor indiscretions any more.

In the base he removed his helmet, but kept it with him, and his suit remained on. Once again he was breaking operational procedures.

He took Beth to the server hub, the one room in the entire base no one else had access to——except for Jeremiah who never came in here anyway. He locked him and Beth inside. Then he called Jeremiah on the datacomms.

"Cory? You okay? Your suit comms were down."

"Yes, slight malfunction," he said biting his tongue. "I've got some news."

"I'm sorry about Elizabeth. Did you manage to fit her with a neuralcomp, or do you need assistance?"

"She has anti-freeze, and is clamped."

"And the neuralcomp? Remember, the neuralcomp is important. It keeps them in line."

Alvarez had never before heard that the undead needed to be controlled.

"Jeremiah, I have important news. Word in from Mercury that a major solar flare is on its way."

There was a long moment of silence while Cory worried that Jeremiah had detected the deceit in his voice. "What does that mean?"

"Massive doses of lethal radiation to anyone caught outside, or if the magnetics go down, which they won't. ETA fifteen minutes."

"I'll call everyone in."

"I have to shut done all non-protected electrics. If power and data cables are fried…" He left the sentence hanging, allowing Jeremiah to work out the rest for himself.

"How long will it last?"

"An hour, maybe two. Hard to tell because we'll need to wait for the all clear from Mercury."

"That could be days?"

"Yes. Maybe…"

Another longer moment of silent contemplation followed.

"Very well, Brother Cory, you can shut down. Keep me updated on developments as they occur."

Alvarez terminated the call. He wanted to smile in his deceit but he couldn't. There was no solar flare. He just wanted everyone inside so he would know where everyone was.

He got to work quickly, re-set all the security sensors so they would loop old feeds from the previous evening, and disabled every alarm on the base. Then he waited through twenty minutes of awkward roll-call, as each base individual was called for and asked to respond. Beth was even called for once.

"Wait here," he said to Beth, who had spent her time in the corner spewing the defrosting gases in her mouth and skin. He locked her in the server room, found the nearest airlock, suited, then disappeared outside.

The sun was setting. The undead were slowing down, resembling statues rather than automations. Again he ignored them, and moved straight to Jeremiah and Charity's habitat.

When he reached the metal hull, he unlatched his suits stethoscope, and listened through the metal. The first voice he heard was Charity's.

"Do you think he suspects anything?"

"No, how could he? He's just upset, that's all."

"He's an ungrateful atheist," Charity literally hissed that last word out from what Cory could only imagine were clenched teeth. "I still don't know why you let him and his cheap whore into our community in the first place. I don't believe they were really married either."

"Charity, please," Jeremiah said in his best sermon-giving voice, "the woman paid for her unbelief and now serves the will of God, in death if not in her sinful life."

Then Jeremiah said seven words that bounced around in Alvarez's head, doing damage and causing pain, like a bullet ricocheting inside his skull.

"We gave her cheap existence a purpose."

As stunned and as furious as the realization of what those words meant filled Cory, he kept on listening. His brain, like a cold yet functioning machine, kept on deciphering the words.

"As soon as we can get a true believer here that can do the job of Mr. Alvarez, we'll have him join his slut and the rest of the undesirables," the Director said.

"Dear God, let that day come soon." His fat wife said, no doubt around a mouth stuffed with more than her fair share of the colony's slim supplies.

"Charity, the Good Lord moves in mysterious ways, and sometimes it takes a while, but He always provides."

Cory did not realize he had fallen until his spacesuit-clad ass hit the red Martian dust. How long he sat there, he did not know. The next thing he became aware of was a constant beeping inside his helmet. It was the warning that told him he only had ten minutes of oxygen left.

He stood without turning off the alarm, without thinking at all, and then moved in the general direction of his habitat. He stumbled in the now complete darkness that was nightfall on Mars, yet he still did not think to turn on his helmet light. Thinking was beyond him, he was pure, motorized instinct and nothing else.

Romero 2.0

Then he walked face first into a wall.

The sudden, jarring stop brought some semblance of himself back up from the depths of the subconscious hole it had crawled into and Cory looked around. He finally thumbed a button at his left wrist to turn off the oxygen alarm and toggled another to switch on his exterior suit light. He saw that he had run into the fencing that surrounded the dead compound, and just inches away on the other side of the fence stood one of the lifeless laborers.

Alvarez could not place the dead man's face, because most of the flesh had been ground away to the bone by numerous sandstorms. Although the atmosphere on Mars was thin, the blowing grit was like fine sandpaper, gently but constantly rubbing. Sooner or later anything that was once soft and supple would be worn away. Only plastic lenses, that all outside workers eventually had installed, saved the thing's eyes and what tiny bit of humanity it had left.

Even without a face there was something eerily familiar about the corpse before Cory. No, it wasn't the worker itself, but something the reanimated man was doing. It was opening and closing its mouth, clacking its jaws and what few teeth it had left, over and over again. This wasn't completely uncommon; sometimes the dead would sort of lock up in a movement loop. Most dead techs chalked it up to a misfiring of rotting synapses and a lot of the walking dead had minor twitches like this guy's snapping jaws, or a ceaselessly nodding head, perhaps a spasmodically flexing finger or two. If the twitch was more severe and interfered with work then it was Cory's job to use the server hub, locate the malfunctioning worker on the grid, and reboot them through remote access with their neuralcomp.

But now, staring at the dead man's mouth opening and shutting, opening and shutting, a memory stirred inside Alvarez. One that caused him to grin mirthlessly, turn from the fence and begin sprinting towards home. He couldn't put his finger on it, but he knew there was something there, tickling the underside of his memory. By the time he reached the airlock he was breathless with a scant three minutes of air left in his suit's tanks.

The cycling of the airlock, which had been so routine as to become unnoticeable, took a maddening long time now as thoughts and plans raced through Cory's mind. He wanted nothing more than to rip the vacuum suit from his body and find the sliver drive that he could all but see in his head. It was old, made of cheap red plastic, a product of Earth in both design and the contents it held. The faceless worker Cory had literally bumped into had stirred up foggy memories inside of him. He knew there was something there, something he could use, but while the details eluded him, he knew the answer was the worn sliver drive Beth had brought with them to Mars.

At last the green light shown and the door to his habitat hissed open. All but tearing the vacuum suit from his body and leaving it in a heap in the floor, he first went to the entertainment hub and began to frantically search. He naturally assumed the sliver he sought would be there with all the other interactives and holo slivers, but it wasn't.

No, of course it wouldn't be there, he chided himself. It was old, bought on a lark one rainy night from a street vender in Mexico City for a few credits.

The memories of those early days with Beth welled up inside him, crushing him. They were so vivid and now so painful.

Shaking his head, Cory purposely turned his mind back to finding the sliver drive. The views it contained were old, late Twentieth Century at the latest. That was long before holos and interactives. They were barely able to be free-projected and even then they would only play in flat mode. Their historic novelty had quickly faded for Cory, but Beth still loved the old views, or movies as she called them. She would occasionally still put the sliver in the player to give some slice of the past a view, usually when he was out fixing workers in the field. In fact, Cory had all but forgotten about the sliver until last week when he happened to see it while looking for something else…in the junk drawer!

Taking six long strides from the entertainment hub to the kitchen, Cory pulled open the drawer that had collected bits and pieces of odds and ends over the Martian year they had been in Salvation Point. There, sitting next to a splicer and an unopened deck of cards, was the red sliver drive with *400 Classic Movies* written on it in worn black letters.

Cory snatched it up, stepped back and slid the sliver into the player. He set the unit for 2D mode and started wanding his way through the list of old views one by one. The one he was after he had only seen once, late at night and with him more than half asleep. It was even before Beth and he had left Earth, because Cory associated the foggy memory with the sound of rain on their tiny apartment's only window and their lumpy, third-hand couch, but he knew he would recognize it

ROMERO 2.0

when he saw it. The title was catchy, strong and memorable, just not to him right now.

The list of titles flickered past his eyes on the flat-field holo as he waved his hand up and down until his wand finger stopped at one that read; *1978 – Dawn of the Dead – Dir. George A. Romero.*

"That's it, that's the one." Cory said to the empty room as he flicked the title, sat down in front of the shimmering curtain of lights, and began to watch. Fifty minutes later, and not even at the view's halfway point, Cory got up and headed for the server hub.

~*~

The small room was exactly how he had left it, empty save for Beth, who was standing motionless in the corner. When Cory entered the small space, she immediately began to shuffle toward him, raising her arms.

"Hey baby, do you recognize me?" Cory said. When he had first brought her into the room from outside she had stumbled around like an automaton and hadn't reacted to him at all, but now…

"Maybe all you needed was some warming up?" Cory said to both himself and the lurching woman before him. "Maybe it was the antifreeze kicking in, or just getting you in from the cold?"

The logical part of his brain, the one that was full of facts he had learned when he studied to become a dead tech, dismissed such notions as impractical, emotional wishing. Cory chose to ignore those thoughts. Even the slights glimmer of hope was better than none.

"You know it's me, don't you? You know it's Cory?"

The cold dead thing, leaking a thin river of green antifreeze from its left nostril and staring blankly through its one remaining, unfocused eye, opened its mouth. Then it snapped her jaws shut with a loud *clack*. The shell of Beth opened and snapped shut her mouth again and again as her hands grabbed Cory at the shoulders and tried to pull him into an embrace.

"…g… …em," he thought he heard her say.

His eyes looked her up and down twice. He swore she had spoken to him.

"…g… …em," the sounds erupted from her desiccated throat.

Cory shuddered. "Did you say 'Get them'?" He stared for a long time at Beth's mutilated face. Her jaws were working themselves up and down. "Damn right you are if you did." Images of the faceless man outside chomping away at nothing blurred with bloody scenes from the old horror view he had just been watching reminded Cory of his pain, his rage, and his plan.

"No, you're not Beth. Not anymore." He whispered and pushed the dead woman away. The cold thing rather meekly took a few steps back, lowered its arms and stared at him, unmoving. Then the loop started anew and she raised her arms back up, opened her mouth, and took a step forward.

"…g… …em," she mumbled again.

"Damn it, come here" Cory said as he grabbed her by the arm a little too roughly, causing the top layer of her recently thawed flesh to slough off in his hand. He led the half-blind reanimate to a corner of the room, picking up a couple of bungee tie-downs as he went, and then strapped her to a tool cabinet.

"I'm sorry, but I've a lot of coding to do, so I need you to stay put." He said as he picked up a rag and wiped her dead skin from his fingers.

Cory took a seat at the hub computer and brought up the central worker grid. He chose one of the dead at random, as they were only represented as a series of numbers, and dove into the 'guts' of its neuralcomp.

When Beth and Cory had arrived on Mars, he had taken a three week course in the care and programing of the recently, but no longer immobile, deceased. It covered just after death prep for them joining the Martian workforce, preventive maintenance, repair and how to maintain structural integrity, and basic programing of the neuralcomp and the Ethernet grid it was connected to. That's where the class ended. The new dead techs, as almost everyone called them, knew just enough about the technical side of things to keep the corpses moving and to do minor trouble shooting, but not enough to get into any real trouble. For the big fixes, like an entire grid crashing and frying all the neuralcomps linked to it, the Sandhouse Consortium would send out a very costly technician to put everything back in order, and those bastards guarded their technical secrets like the rich guarded their credits.

"Well let's see what you don't want us to see," Alvarez said to himself as he fell back on his old skills that he had employed years ago for fun and profit as a gifted high school hacker. "And let's see how I can break it."

Romero 2.0

Cory rushed past the basic command prompts and into the heart of the program that controlled the dead. It took hours, and all the technical mojo he had learned over fifteen years of building, repairing, and sometimes tearing down the codes that made computers do the things they do, before he had breached the three firewalls and two logic traps that had been erected to keep the nosey out of the neuralcomp's inner workings. Once inside he found dead end file trees with headings like 'military' and 'home service'. He uncovered strings of code that regulated 'compliance protocol' and provided 'deep stem suppression'. There were subprograms and slave programs that had titles like *Friend/Foe, Instinct Nullifier*, and one with the cute name of *LockJaw*. There was, in fact, far too much to learn in one sitting, and time was against Cory. A new Martian morning was only a few hours away, and Director South would want his slave labor ready for work as soon as they thawed.

Alvarez reached into the left drawer of the desk, pulled out two military grade *No Sleep* poppers, and snorted both down. Once the buzz hit him, his fingers danced over the holokeys that floated between him and the projected screen. He was creating a virus, which struck him as both funny and appropriate considering the old view——correction——the old *movie* that had inspired him. Keeping with that bit of blackest humor, when he was done some five hours later he gave his new creation a proper name.

"Go get the bastards." Cory said and dramatically fingered the floating enter holokey that launched his virus, *Romero 2.0*, through the grid and into the heads of all thirty-two undead workers in Salvation Point.

~*~

Dawn broke on Mars and Cory was waiting. While his fellow unbelievers, infidels, and undesirables thawed in the rising sun, Cory was hard at work making sure his poetic justice would be perfect. If simple revenge was all that he wanted, he could have easily hacked the safety overrides on the airlock controls and opened them all up at once and without warning. That would have been just as difficult a hack, considering the numerous safety overrides built into Martian habitats. The resulting explosive decompression would have had everyone choking on the poisonous atmosphere of Mars and their blood boiling in the depressurized atmosphere within seconds. Instead, after opening the gates to the worker's pens, he sounded the alarm that warned of a leak in the habitat.

Cory turned to the projection at his side. He had easily busted the cheap program that Director South used to give him, and only him, access to the outpost's many security cameras. He saw the faithful, and now fearful, residents of Salvation Point spring out of bed and quickly don their vacuum suits. It was an emergency procedure they had all practiced many times.

Cory smiled then wanded the picture to another camera. This one showed the worker pens and he saw the dead shuffling out of the now open gates. Cory had implemented a new nav-point program along with his other tweaks to the corpses' neuralcomps. It was set for the main doors to the living quarters. Once the dead reached that point it would shut down and then they would be free to wander as they saw fit, not to mention them following other changes that *Romero 2.0* had liberated in them.

As he was locking down the doors to the garages that housed the outpost's rovers and released the dirigible into the skies unpiloted, to ensure no one drove or flew out of the outpost, Cory's datacom started to buzz. He answered without looking at the ID.

"Yes, Jeremiah?"

"Damn it, Alvarez, what's going on? Do we have a leak in the shell somewhere?"

Cory wanded back to the internal cameras to check that people were in their vacuum suits. "You could say that. Is everyone accounted for and in their suits?" he asked as he switched from camera to camera, doing a visual headcount for himself.

"Yes, Charity says everyone has reported in that they're safe, but what's going on? My screen in here says pressure is normal inside the habitat. And why is the dirigible floating away?"

"Well how about now?" Cory said as he activated the program he had waiting that opened all the airlock doors.

"Dear God, what was that?" Director South shrieked into the datacom in panic. Cory hoped the fear the older man felt was at least equal to the terror that Beth had no doubt known when the bastard had plunged his multi-tool between her ribs.

"Director South, do you believe in God?" Cory calmly asked.

The director could only answer in disbelief at the question, "What?"

ROMERO 2.0

"Do you. Believe. In God?"

"Of course I do." The director spat angrily.

"Good, because it's judgment day you sanctimonious son of a bitch! I know you murdered Beth, just like you killed all the others. Everyone that wasn't useful. Everyone that didn't follow your narrow-minded beliefs. Hell, everyone you and your fat-assed wife just didn't like. You played God, Jeremiah, and then to drive the point home, you even resurrected your victims so they could be your slaves in death just as you wanted them to be in life."

"No, wait...I...we didn't...you've got it wrong, Cory. There's been a terrible mistake and we can——" the director stammered before being cut off.

"Just shut it." Cory yelled. "You've been telling lies so well and for so long that even you may believe them now, but I know the truth, Mr. 'God always provides'. You took the one thing I cared about in this world——in any world——and you killed her. You threw her away because she wasn't like you——or just because you could do it, you egomaniacal asshole.

"You didn't know my Beth. You didn't know how wonderful, how caring she was. How beautiful inside and out. How she could always make me feel better no matter how bad the day went. You didn't know a God damned thing about her, but you murdered her for what, another puppet to control?

"Well motherfucker, I'm going to teach you something about my Beth. Did you know she loved movies? Not views, not holos, old fashioned movies from Earth. She said they were just made better back then. Well here's a blast from the past, and the best part is that I couldn't have done it without you."

"Cory, my God, what are you raving about?" the Director asked, his voice equal parts fear and confusion.

"Take a look out your eastern ports, towards your slave pens."

Cory waited for the few seconds it took Jeremiah to cross his quarters and look out the window.

"Oh...shit..."

"That's right you bastard." Cory said. "I've made a few programing changes to your workforce so you can get a little taste of what hell's going to be like."

The director began to shriek his protests, but Cory silenced him with a click of his datacom. The first of the dead had reached the main

223

doors of the outpost and Cory had a new horror movie to watch.

~*~

The movie was over.

It had been suitably bloody and frightening, but surprisingly short. The claws of the dead workers, many of which had been reinforced with wire and metal, tore through the vacuum suits of the colonists with only a little bit of effort. The people inside instantly began choking on Mars' carbon dioxide atmosphere while their blood vaporized in the thin atmosphere, but they didn't have to gasp for long. Once the dead had ripped a hole in the suit wide enough to shove their faces through, their snapping teeth went to work. Gapped-toothed jaws tore through night cloths, flesh, and the muscle beneath. Chunks of meat were savaged from thrashing, bleeding bodies, chewed in the most mechanical of ways, then forced down dry throats, or simply fell from gaping maws when the dead went in for another bite. The ravaging teeth of the dead workers quickly turned gasps for air into shrieks of pain, and then into silence. Cory was positive that not one person died of open exposure to Mars.

With only wall mounted security cameras to provide visuals, Cory thought the action was much tamer than Mr. Romero's earlier works, but still effective. Even kept at a distance, he thought the actors in his little drama portrayed the terror and hopelessness well. Some of the colonists went down fighting, but with no weapons allowed in the habitat, and Cory locking the doors to the armory, such resistance was as fleeting as it was futile. Others tried to barricade themselves inside their quarters, only to have Cory override their door locks when the dead were near. The ones that Cory liked to watch the most were those that fell to their knees and prayed for salvation that never came. Cory liked those precious few not in a cynical way, but because they seemed to have real honest to goodness faith. They still died screaming but they died practicing what they preached.

The same could not be said for the stars of the show; Charity and Jeremiah South. As soon as the dead entered their private compartment, Jeremiah shoved his plump wife into the group of three shambling workers to distract them. His sacrifice was accepted and it allowed him to squeeze past the dead as they immediately started to tear into the quivering fatty folds of Charity's flesh. But just like

Romero 2.0

so many other sacrifices throughout history, the benefits of doing so were debatable, because Jeremiah found all the halls blocked by the dead and nothing more to offer up.

The once proud and sure director of Salvation Point had his final moments hiding in a small utility closet, with several of the dead banging on the door. Sadly there was no camera in the closet, so Cory remote hacked the door, only to be surprised that when he opened it, the dead did not rush in to finish off the director. Instead they stood around aimlessly for a few moments before wandering off in different directions. As the shambling corpses cleared the camera's view, Cory saw why they had left; the dead only ate the living, and Jeremiah was no longer that. The purportedly pious bastard had chosen the relatively quick and far less painful death of using a hand cutter to open up both his vacuum suit and his neck. The fact that his suicide would damn the director's soul for eternity, if you believed such things, made Cory smile. The only thing that would have made Jeremiah's ending more perfect was if he had used a multi-tool to do it.

As satisfying as the villain's death scene was, there were some elements of the movie that pushed Cory to his limits, scenes that caused him to look away from the screen or cover his eyes. They were the parts of the show that he didn't expect, or more accurately; the ones he had forgotten about.

They were the children.

He had not taken into account the three families living in the outpost when he had crafted his revenge. It was an honest mistake, he told himself. He never worked with any of their parents and Beth and he had no friends here. The children had simply slipped his mind. It was an accident and it was not like he could do anything to stop what happened after he set it in motion. Once he saw the kids cowering in corners, hiding in their closets, or crying for their parents as the dead mauled them before their eyes, he would have stopped it if he could.

For one fleeting moment, he considered if he was any better than the psycho who snaps one day, takes out a gun and goes on a killing spree in the streets, shooting dead anyone who comes into sight.

He dismissed that thought quickly.

Unfortunately the truth of *Romero 2.0* was that it didn't so much reprogram as it did smash the old program to bits. That included all the safety protocols that Sandhouse had put in place to rein in the 'natural tendencies' of the dead. That's why standard dead tech protocol was to attach the neuralcomp as soon as possible to the recently deceased. While the Sandhouse serum gave a corpse some semblance of life, the corpse still rotted away, albeit more slowly, and the most susceptible organ to decay was not coincidently the most complex; the brain. As it rotted, the refinements of evolution were lost to putrefaction until only the most basic of functions and drives remained. Like the ability to move, sense its surroundings, and the need to feed.

Cory Alvarez found all this out too late, over the next few days he spent locked in the server hub. Most of it he inferred from the lines of code and safety programs that was stuffed into the neuralcomp. The sort of things he had sliced through in haste to get his revenge movie up and running before that first bloody dawn. Such severed ties could not be repaired and each of the workers would need a whole new neuralcomp. That meant they were now all roaming wild and free and under no one's control.

Then there were the forty-seven newly risen dead. The colonists that had died at the hands and teeth of the workers joined their reanimated ranks once their own Sandhouse Serum kicked in. Those new walking corpses had never even had neuralcomps installed.

There were now close to eighty walking death machines at Salvation Point, and while Cory could have waited until dark for the dead to freeze up to make good his escape with one of the rovers, that still left two big questions he just didn't have the answers to.

First, there was Beth. She looked fully gone. The rotting brain inside her skull degenerated so much that no neuralcomp would ever control her, not that Cory wanted that done to her. But the question was; what would he do with her? Could he bash the woman he had loved so completely in the head over and over again until the decomposing slush that was her brain finally stopped working in an effort to free her? Was there even anything of Beth left inside that rotting husk to be freed? Or should he just leave her like she was now?

Cory didn't think he could do the latter.

Then there were all the others. Everyone on Mars had taken the Sandhouse Serum, so everyone would become like Beth once they died. It was easy to agree to the unthinkable when you were poor, hungry, and desperate enough, but to see what became of the dead first hand… Could Cory allow that to continue?

Cory turned from his snarling, teeth snapping former love to the projection hovering in front of him. It had held the same blank screen

ROMERO 2.0

and single line of text for the past two days.

UPLOAD ROMERO 3.0 Y/N?

Over the past days, Cory had refined his creation. He made it sleek and stealthy. While all the neuralcomps at the outpost were down, the grid was still up, running, and connected to the master hub at Sandhouse Station One. Cory was confident that his virus could sneak past the scrubbers all along the grid, to the mainframe, and then to all the workers on the grid. That meant every single walking dead on Mars, all 14,736 of them.

But could he do it? Could he kill tens of thousands to hopefully stop the hundreds of thousands that were already lining up to come to here?

Was Mars ready for the inevitable sequel?

"...g... ...em."

He turned surprised that someone was talking to him when he was all alone now.

"...g... ...em."

It was Beth, and this time Cory was certain she was talking to him. It had sounded like she was trying to say 'get them'. Get them all, but he already had, and he had done so for her, out of revenge.

"...g... ...em."

She looked sad, if that was possible. He raced to her side, placed his ear as close to her rotten mouth as he dare, and listened again.

"Forgive them."

Cory convulsed. Repelled he stumbled backwards until his back was pressed against a wall.

"...g... ...em."

What had he done? What kind of person had he become?

Was he the director now, he thought as he looked at the video feed of the lifeless colony all around him. The wandering corpses of children were the most accusing in their undead stares.

"Am I the director?" he asked himself. "What scene must I create next?"

Undead and Unbound

MOTHER BLOOD
By Scott David Aniolowski

A cold sleety drizzle fell, painting everything the sheen of whale skin. Neither rain nor snow, the icy precipitation stung as it spattered solemn faces deep in contemplation, stabbing the back of necks to cause unpleasant icy jolts. Warm, foggy breath curled up into the November night, carrying guarded whispers. Jagged red neon tore through the monochromatic darkness, casting glaring blood red streaks across everything.

In a short dark alley just off a busy street the small assemblage stood gathered in a circle, studying the grisly tableau before them. A woman lay motionless at their feet, clothes and hair plastered to the pavement. There was an unsettling sense of peace about her, eyes staring into the night sky, arms outstretched as if wings readying for flight. With legs outstretched she would have looked for all the world like someone making snow angels in the accumulating slush, were it not for the savage red smirk in her sizeable stomach; a body like a great eyeless face wetly grimacing, eager to tell its secrets. A tongue of dark organ meat hung from her split-open belly, drooling redness which the incessant drizzle had all but washed away.

The first responders mumbled amongst themselves. A few scribbled messy notes on wet notepads. All wondered the same thing: who had done such a thing? The woman's baby——still glistening with gore from being ripped from its mother's womb——was found only yards away, its throat torn. A man——presumably the husband—— was found in a heap in a doorway, his throat also ripped and coat deep with blood. Despite the hour, there was ample foot traffic on the main streets of Chinatown, yet no one claimed to have seen or heard anything from the dirty little alleyway. A crowd of obvious tourists perched at the edge of the bright yellow police tape, gawking and straining to glimpse the carnage. None of the locals hesitated for more than a moment, however, pulling their collars up and hurrying into the monotone darkness, shaking heads the only response to inquiries.

"What do we got?" asked a plain but pretty middle-aged redheaded woman in a long black coat.

"Homicide. Husband and wife from the looks of it. Tourists. He's over there," the young patrolman gestured toward the bloodied man humped in a dark doorway. "Baby was ripped out of its mother. It's over there," he nodded at something small that was being covered with a sheet by another officer.

"Jesus," spat Detective Angela Hodges. In her nearly ten years in big city homicide she'd never seen anything as brutal as this. "It's Jacobs, right?" She was vaguely familiar with Jacobs——he was known as 'Baby Boy' at the station because of his boyish features and blond hair, his naivety, and for the excessive amount of cheap cologne he wore like some high school kid out on his first date.

"Yes, ma'am," nodded the baby-faced policeman.

"Witnesses?" she asked, absently running a hand over her own belly.

"Nothing yet," the bleary-eyed patrolman shook his head, shaking slush from the brim of his hat. He looked entranced by the awfulness of the scene.

"What about you? You see anything?" Hodges asked, brushing wet hair out of her eyes.

"No. Patterson was first on the scene," he gestured to an older uniformed cop.

"Something down here was sparkling. That's what caught my attention," Patterson explained. He was older than officer Jacobs and doughier, and wore a thick reddish moustache on his washed-out face.

"Sparkling?"

"Well, flashing. Twinkling. I don't know. Like little sparks," Patterson tried to describe what he'd seen.

"Maybe like fireflies?" Officer Jacobs suggested.

Angela Hodges shot young Jacobs a quizzical look and he looked away like he was embarrassed.

"When I was a kid we used to camp a lot in the summer. You know. To get out of the city," Jacobs tried to explain. "Used to see fireflies. They were cool."

"Well, it wouldn't have been fireflies. In the city. In November. In this freezing drizzle," cut Hodges' partner, Sal Difranco as he brushed the drizzling slop from his coat. The mustached, soft-bellied man moved to the doorway and the man's body.

"Of course not," Jacobs agreed. He absently gazed at the ground, unable to make eye contact with the older man.

Patterson smirked and let out a deep chuckle at Jacobs' expense.

"No. So, what did these flashes turn out to be?" Detective Hodges asked.

"Don't know. Soon as I came down here I saw them," Patterson gestured to the bodies, "and I called in backup. Didn't see anything else. I mean, whatever was flashing."

"Probably just the streetlights on the rain," Detective Difranco said.

Camera flashes lit up the alley with bursts of cold white light to preserve the scene in pictures. Gloved men gingerly searched trashcans up and down the alley with sharp blue-white flashlight beams, gathering suspect items in envelopes. "Strange," said one of the men.

"What's that?" Angela Hodges asked as she pulled on rubber gloves.

"Here's his footprints," the officer shone the beam of his flashlight over a set of tracks in the slush that led to the doorway and the man, "and there's her's," he illuminated the woman's tracks, "but there aren't any others leading away. Looks like just ours. No perp tracks."

"Maybe they were attacked out there and made it this far before…" shrugged Detective Difranco. "Just take the pictures. We'll get it figured out."

Detective Hodges stooped down next to the eviscerated woman. Gently she slipped bags over the woman's hands and felt in her coat pockets. "Wallet and keys," she said, extracting the items and handing them to someone to bag. "Check for I.D.," she said.

"Florida driver's license," came the response, "Julie Webber. Looks like a couple hundred bucks. Definitely a tourist."

"Donald Webber here," replied Detective Difranco. "He's got a couple hundred, too. And a nice wedding band. Wasn't a robbery. This neck is the only wound I see. Nasty. Looks like a bite. Have to see what the medical examiner says."

"Looks like she's been bitten, too," Hodges said as she delicately examined the wide rip in the woman's abdomen. "Doesn't look like a cut. It's like this was chewed, not cut. One on her neck, too, like the husband."

"Baby, too. Neck was all chewed up," added patrolman Patterson.

"Jesus. What the hell happened here?" asked Detective Difranco.

Undead and Unbound

"What kind of freaks we got in this city now?"

As the sleet-drenched bodies were bundled onto stretchers for the ride to the morgue, Jacobs slid up to Detective Hodges and bent his head to whisper into her ear. "You better come with me, Detective. They just found another one in there," he nodded with his head toward a neighboring building. She bobbed her head in acknowledgement and motioned for Difranco to follow them.

The building in question housed a Chinese apothecary and a souvenir shop. An old woman bundled in a flannel coat stood in the side doorway smoking, politely nodding to the law officers as they passed. Her skin was the color of old parchment and her eyes thick with the fog of cataracts. She smiled at Angela Hodges and lightly brushed a skeletal beige hand against her stomach. "Bayi," she nodded. "Bayi."

Detective Hodges looked to the patrolman.

"Baby. It's Malaysian for baby," Jacobs explained, studying the old woman. "There's a pretty big Malaysian population in this neighborhood. This building's mostly all Malaysian. And mostly old folks. Most of them right from the old country."

"Yes," Hodges answered the foggy-eyed crone, surprised that she'd noticed. Instinctively she put a hand to her stomach. The old woman grinned a toothless smile at her and nodded again as she passed.

The building's cramped entranceway was barely big enough for Hodges, Difranco and Jacobs to all maneuver in, and it was all they could do to keep from falling over each other as they brushed the frozen rain from their coats. There were three floors of apartments above, a dim narrow stairway wound up into flickering sallow light and the sounds of tenants. The odor of some pungent exotic spice hung thickly in the stairwell——an unrecognizable mixture of culinary and medicinal scents. Three rows of mailboxes were mounted just inside the entranceway, a snow shovel and trashcan on silent watch next to a closed door with a sign pinned to it.

"Jauhkan?" Difranco read the sign.

"Means 'keep out,'" the young policeman interpreted.

Outside, the elderly woman stood staring through the glass of the door at the investigators, smiling widely and sucking on a nub of her cigarette. "Penanggalan," she said, "penanggalan."

"What's she saying now?" Difranco asked.

"Penanggalan? It's an evil spirit," Jacobs translated.

Angela Hodges had to look away. Something about the little figure unnerved her. She absently rubbed her stomach again. Noticing her unease, the young patrolman waved at the old hag, gesturing for her to go away.

Jacobs opened the door and headed into the gloom of the basement. "It's down here."

The rickety wooden stairs creaked and cracked as the three descended into the cellar. A chill breeze blew up the stairs, suggesting that a window or a delivery door was open down there. The basement opened up into a surprisingly large space otherwise crowded with boxes, water boilers, furnaces, and typical basement accoutrements. The damp mustiness was palpable and made Detective Hodges' skin go clammy. A handful of low-watt bulbs weakly washed the room with pale ghostlight; the shadows were thick and long and were reluctant to give up their secrets. Water pipes knocked and furnaces roared, and the familiar night-songs of the city filtered in through a small broken window that breathed in the night's icy dampness. Above the mustiness hung a strong sour smell, stirred by the late autumn breeze squeezing in through the glassless pane.

A second policeman stood, arms folded, in front of a pile of boxes. He was significantly older than officer Jacobs, and had the look of weary experience carved into his chestnut brown face. "She's over here," he said. "Ain't pretty."

Rounding a mound of boxes, the detectives saw the headless body of a small elderly woman lying on the damp cellar floor, arms folded serenely across her chest. The hands sported long manicured nails and jade rings, and she was dressed neatly in intricately embroidered silk. Although the head was missing, there was no blood anywhere on or near the body. Sitting near the corpse was a large basin of clear liquid.

"You think this is connected with that out there?" Difranco mused, almost to himself.

"Yeah... I don't know. This is different. Wounds are different. M.O. is different. This one looks like she was laid out. Those outside were chased down. No blood. She wasn't killed here," Hodges said.

"There's no I.D. on her. Must have been someone important, though. Look at the way she's dressed. Not what you usually see around here," added the older cop.

"Maybe she's a visitor. Detective Hodges is right. She definitely wasn't killed here. Someone put her here," said Difranco.

"Yeah. Very carefully, though. Not a drop of blood anywhere.

Clothes are immaculate. And what do you make of this?" she asked, squatting down near the bowl of liquid.

"Who knows? In this area it might be some kind of offering or ritual," the older patrolman injected. "These people in Chinatown stick pretty close to old-world traditions. They believe in all that ghosts and gods mumbo jumbo."

"Smells like vinegar," sniffed Detective Hodges.

"Worse than Baby Boy's Old Spice," Sal Difranco slapped Jacobs on the back and snorted, making fun of the young man's signature cheap cologne.

The boyish policeman blushed and said, "Spirit Festival," in an attempt to change the subject away from himself. Hodges knew that Jacobs had become used to the whole 'Baby Boy' thing but didn't like it, and didn't like being the center of attention. He seemed to prefer to just fade into the background.

"What?" asked Difranco.

"Spirit Festival. It's this time of year," young Jacobs answered.

"And what's that all about?" asked Difranco.

"Offerings are left for the restless ghosts who visit in the night."

"Mumbo jumbo. Like I said," the older officer countered.

"How do you know so much about this stuff?" Difranco asked the younger man.

"Don't know. Just working this neighborhood long enough, I guess. Get to know the people and their customs," he explained.

"Well this is probably just a homicide. Awful, maybe, but probably nothing more. Could be ritualistic, though, I suppose," Difranco said.

"Yeah, I don't know Sal. Anyway, get some pictures before we move her," Hodges said.

As Detective Difranco busied himself with the body, Hodges examined the broken window. It was about eight inches square and was at the back of the building. There were no shards of glass on the basement floor or on the ground outside, so it had been broken prior to this evening. She did find several serpentine drag marks in the slush outside the window, however, like a mass of wires and cables had been pulled through recently. She also found what appeared to be a strand of long grey hair stuck in the wood of the window frame. The detective carefully collected and bagged it for testing.

"Holy Christ!" cried Difranco.

Angela Hodges hadn't heard Sal's voice take such a tone often.

Mother Blood

"What?" she spun around.

The seasoned detective was on his hands and knees crouched in front of the corpse, camera dangling from a gloved hand. He was staring into the stump of the neck, his faced flushed with a mix of disbelief and repulsion. "She's empty," he said.

"What?" Hodges crossed the damp floor to where her partner almost lay near the body.

"I didn't believe it at first. I saw it through the camera and then I shone my flashlight in there. There's no guts. None that I can see," he said incredulously.

"Empty?" Hodges couldn't really grasp what she was hearing.

"Old lady's empty," Difranco insisted. "I mean, as far as I can tell. We need the M.E. to look at her as soon as possible."

~*~

Angela Hodges gulped down a cup of thick, black coffee. It wasn't very good, but it was hot, and that's all that mattered to her. It had been several hours since they'd come in from the crime scene, and still she felt chilled through. Hodges and Difranco had propped a rickety old space heater between their desks in a futile attempt to dry out and warm up. Her skin still felt clammy and her feet were like ice.

"Shitty night," said another detective as he passed Hodges' desk.

She just nodded. She wished now that she kept a change of clothes in her locker like most of the men did. Of course, her clothes didn't fit her anymore, and it would only get worse until the baby was born. This was to be their first. She and Carl had been trying for a few years and had just about accepted that theirs was to be a childless marriage when they got the little surprise. Carl had immediately wanted Angela to stop working, but she convinced him that staying on the force for the first few months wouldn't hurt her——that it would be good for her to stay active. Grudgingly he agreed, with the stipulation that Angela promise to put in for desk work until it was time for her to go on maternity leave. That hadn't quite worked out yet, but she kept assuring her husband that she'd take a desk job. Soon. The detective had to admit that that time might be sooner than she'd thought; this standing in freezing rain and running around the streets was starting to get to her. Her back ached and her feet were screaming and no amount of pain reliever would quell her pounding headache. This might have to be her last active case outside until after the baby came. She could still work——she could follow up leads on the computer and over the phone. There was always checking to be done. Research. It was usually deadly dull and she hated it, but at least she could still work. Still help fight the good fight.

"Okay. So this is weird," Sal Difranco said as he tossed a manila folder on his partner's desk.

Angela jumped, startled. "Christ!" she sucked in air with a gulp.

"Sorry. Didn't mean to scare you."

"I didn't hear you come in. Must have been thinking about something."

"And what's with that?" Difranco shook a finger between Hodges' coffee mug and the bottle of pain relievers sitting next to her keyboard.

"Get off me," she said. "I gave up cigarettes and wine. Anyway, what you got?"

"Take a look," he pointed to the file. "I thought there was something familiar about all this. Just like a case Wendt and Hanley had last year."

Detective Hodges opened the folder. It was the report of a headless body of an elderly woman being found in Chinatown the previous year. The eight-by-ten photographs of the scene were eerily familiar; they showed the headless body of a small woman in similar clothing. There was no blood at the scene——a fact both shown in the photographs and recorded in the written report. Some of the photos also revealed a large bowl of liquid resting near the corpse. Although the background was different, Hodges thought this could have been the very same crime scene they'd been to early this evening.

"It's the same M.O.," she said.

"Look closer," Difranco pointed to the pictures.

Detective Hodges studied the pictures for a moment before it suddenly jumped out at her. "The rings. It's the same jewelry as our Jane Doe."

"Looks that way."

"So it is some sort of ritual or cult?" she studied the pictures closer.

"Yeah, I don't know. But it's spooky how similar they are."

"I looked up Jacobs' Spirit Festival," she offered, since they were discussing the weird.

"Yeah. And?"

"It's called the Spirit Festival or the Water Lantern Festival. At sundown lanterns are lit and then floated down the river as offerings to restless spirits," she explained.

"That don't sound like anything to do with this."

"And didn't Jacobs say the area was mostly Malaysian?"

"Yeah," Difranco nodded.

"Well, this is a Chinese holiday. And it's already gone by. And that 'penanggalan' thing the weird old woman said is some kind of female Malaysian vampire that feeds on pregnant women and babies. Supposed to soak in vinegar or something. I don't know, I haven't finished reading the article."

"Oh, vampires now? Spooky," Detective Difranco waved his hands and feigned a scared look. "The three in the alley were chewed on. Maybe it was a werewolf," he made the scary face again, "and we had a headless old gal in the basement. We got a vampire that eats heads?"

"I'm just saying these people are very superstitious and apparently believe in this stuff. I'm going to go back to it later and see if there's anything useful."

Their discussion was cut short by the telephone on Difranco's desk. He picked it up and spoke to someone for a moment before putting the caller on speaker. "Go ahead, Doctor. Detective Hodges is here, too," he said, his face the color of confusion.

"Detective Hodges, this is Rob Roslof. Listen, I've been examining your Jane Doe and there's some strange stuff here."

"Yeah?" Hodges asked.

"Well, first of all, there's almost no blood present. And most of her internal organs are missing."

"Yeah, we thought that," Difranco injected, eyebrows knitting in perplexity.

"That's not the strangest part," the medical examiner said. "This is hard to believe and I have no explanation…"

"What?" Hodges rolled her chair to Difranco's desk.

"I've had her in here before," the doctor blurted.

"What?" Detective Hodges didn't understand what Doctor Roslof was saying.

"I mean, this person——this old woman——this body——has been in the morgue before," the incredulous doctor said.

"What are you saying, Rob?" Difranco asked.

"I'm saying that this corpse was here in the morgue over a year ago. I checked the finger prints against the one I saw last year. They're a match. And there are autopsy scars down the front of her. It's all the same."

"But how can that be?" Hodges looked at Difranco and they both stared at the phone.

"I have no explanation. There isn't enough decay to this corpse for it to have been dead for a year, even with embalming. But I'm telling you it's the same one. I've checked and double checked. It's the same."

"Well what happened to the body last year?" Hodges asked.

"I thought it had been buried in Potter's Field with all the other unclaimed John and Jane Does."

"Then how did it get in that basement? And how come it's in such good shape?" Difranco asked the questions they were all wondering.

"I don't know," the doctor sighed deeply. "But I tell you, it's the same person who was dead and laid out in my morgue over a year ago."

"Okay. Well, um, thanks," Detective Hodges said.

"I'm going to do some more tests and I'll get back to you. But that's what I have so far. I don't know what else to say. I just don't know," Doctor Roslof said and then hung up. For a moment Difranco and Hodges stared at each other in silence before she spun back around to her desk and leafed through the file photos again.

"This makes no sense," Hodges shook her head. "It just can't be. It's not possible. Roslof must be wrong."

"He sounded pretty sure of himself," Difranco fell into his chair. "And those pictures there."

Detective Hodges just stared at the pictures, unable to believe what they were telling her.

~*~

The sloppy drizzle had finally stopped and the cool autumn sun was climbing steadily in the blue-grey sky. The neighborhood looked completely different in the light of day. Surprisingly, it looked dirtier, dingier. The cold yellow wash of sunlight exposed every bit of trash and swirl of graffiti that the night had kept hidden. In the light of day the neon that had glared so fiercely in the night looked bleached out and faded. Throngs of people——locals going about their daily routines and tourists rubbernecking the sights——swarmed in and out of shops and up and down the noisy, crowded street. The teeming populace was oblivious to the bright yellow police tape that still cordoned off the alley crime scene, passing by without as much as a glance or a word. Puffs of grey-white steam rolled up out of sewer drains and car exhausts, mingling with the misty breath of the people and exotically-perfumed chimney smoke from atop of rows of tightly-packed buildings. A foggy mix of scents hung in the air like incense, eclipsed only by the orchestra of chattering voices and car horns. Grey, grime-etched storefront windows reminded Angela Hodges of the foggy cataract eyes of the old Asian who had smiled so strangely at her.

    She stood in front of the building where they had found the headless woman, watching the clientele moving in and out of the apothecary and the souvenir shop: mostly locals in the former and tourists in the latter. Detective Hodges noted the varied and exotic array of herbs and animal horns and bottled substances lining the shelves and counters of the apothecary shop. Several serious-faced people of presumed Chinese descent tinkered behind counters, attended to customers and concocted their remedies. Through the garish, trinket-jammed window of the other storefront she could see typical Chinatown tourist souvenirs: little plastic Buddhas, paper fans and lanterns, cheap kimonos and t-shirts printed with touristy slogans, ceramic dragons, tea sets and an unguessable hodgepodge of other over-priced junk. The only similarity between the two disparate stores was the strands of thorny vines Hodges noticed looped around all the windows and doors.

    Detective Hodges walked around the side of the building and saw the same spiny stuff strung in most of the apartment windows. In the back she saw more thorn-lined windows, and rusty scaffolding that had been erected up the old brick building to the roof. Bricks and tools were stacked at the top of the scaffolding in preparation to make repairs to a crumbling chimney. Hodges made a mental note to contact the building department or the local fire station to report that some of the windows were completely blocked. This was a blatant violation of building and safety codes. In a fire the tenants would be unable to escape out their windows.

    The detective walked the far side of the building and back out to the street. Most of the windows on this side were decorated with the prickly garland of leaves and thorns, too.

    "Detective Hodges," came a man's voice. The redhead turned to the street. Crossing through the continuous stream of traffic was baby-faced Jacobs. Someone in a delivery van honked and waved at the young policeman and he smiled and waved back.

"Thanks for meeting me here," she said.

"No problem," he smiled.

"So I wanted to go over the scene again and speak with some of the tenants. Since this is your beat and you know these people, I figured you'd be a lot of help."

"I'll try. Where's your partner?"

"Downtown. At the morgue talking to the M.E."

The pair moved into the cramped entryway with the rows of mailboxes. The basement door was closed and sealed off with crime scene tape. Detective Hodges studied the entrance door and the basement doorframe.

"What's with all the thorny stuff around the windows and doors?" she gestured with a thumb toward the street-side of the building and the storefronts. "Nothing on these doors, but I saw most of the apartment windows have the same stuff. There wasn't anything around that broken basement window."

"Local superstition. They're prickly leaves from something called Mengkuang," Jacobs casually explained. "Supposed to keep away evil spirits."

"Like this penanggalan thing?"

Jacobs shot her a surprised look. "What that old woman said last night?"

"Yes. I looked it up on the internet. A vampire. Always female. Drinks the blood of pregnant women and babies. And the vinegar——what they use it for. Pretty gross, the whole thing."

"Like I told you, these people are very superstitious."

"And these prickly vines are supposed to keep the vampire out?"

"Yes. Supposedly," he said. "But you don't really believe…"

"No! Give me a break. But these people believe in this stuff, so maybe our perp is taking advantage of that," Hodges explained.

"So what have you found so far?" Jacobs asked.

"I'm not sure. It doesn't make any sense. I don't know what I'm even looking for."

"Well, you probably want to talk to this lady," he pointed to a name on a mailbox.

Detective Hodges ran her finger under the name.

Mother Blood

"Najwa binti Shaqir. She's an old Malaysian midwife. Right from the old country, like a lot of them. If there's anything you want to know about this neighborhood, she's the one to ask."

"She speak English?"

"Uh, no. Not really. A little. But I can translate a little. Maybe enough. Worth a try," he scratched his head and shuffled a little, studying his watch. "Well, let's go talk to her first. She's not always available to see people."

"Yeah. Alright," Hodges agreed.

The pair ascended the dim, narrow stairway. The pungent mixture of thick exotic smells and Jacobs' infamous aftershave made Hodges a little nauseous. Handbills were stuck to the walls; although she was unable to read any of them she assumed they were for local businesses and entertainment. Somewhere music played——the sort of sharp, high-pitched tones of the Orient. An elderly couple passed them going down. They smiled and nodded at Jacobs and then chatted amongst themselves in their native tongue as they exited to the street. As they continued to climb the officers passed graffiti that appeared to Hodges to be Islamic symbols and the same two words: 'Darah Ibu.'

The detective thumped the graffiti with a finger without saying anything.

"Darah Ibu? Means 'Mother Blood,'" young Jacobs translated. "Probably because Cik Shaqir——that's Miss Shaqir, I mean——is a midwife and delivers babies."

"Or maybe someone is trying to scare people?" Detective Hodges wondered. "Perpetuate this whole vampire legend."

"But why?"

"I don't know, Jacobs. Maybe there's something bigger going on here and our perp is trying to scare people away. Drugs, maybe? Illegal weapons?"

"Yeah, well there is a fair share of that stuff down here," Jacobs grudgingly admitted.

They reached the top of the dirty staircase and turned down a short dark hallway heading to the back of the building. The only window on the corridor had been covered in black plastic, presumably to keep out the cold, but it cast a sickly grey-black shadowlight. The blond patrolman stopped at the last door on the hallway and knocked.

"This is the one," he said. "Sharifah," he called and knocked again. "She's a princess," he said with the pride of knowing someone important.

"Is she?" Angela Hodges dug in her coat for her notepad. As she was wondering what an alleged Malaysian princess was doing living in such a dingy place the door swung open. A small, elderly woman peered out. She was more intent on studying the pairs' clothing than their features, but waved them in.

The tiny apartment was dusky and still, its windows covered similarly with black plastic but without the standard vines of leaves and thorns adorning most of the other windows in the building. Detective Hodges could tell that these were the windows that had been blocked by the building materials on the scaffolding. She made another mental note about contacting the proper authorities and to have the landlord fined for putting his tenant in such jeopardy.

Despite the gloom, the detective could see that the old woman was very attractive and stately-looking. Her long black hair was thickly streaked the color of pewter and she wore elaborately-decorated silk. The apartment was chilly and a sour smell hung thick in the still air.

"Detective Hodges, this is Sharifah Najwa binti Shaqir," Jacobs extoled with flourish through a wide boyish grin as though he had just introduced the president or some iconic celebrity.

Angela Hodges extended a hand but the old woman simply smiled thinly and bowed her head. It was when she returned the polite bow that the detective noticed the familiar jade rings adorning the woman's withered hands. Wordlessly she reached out and gently took the old woman's hands to better see her jewelry. "Such beautiful rings. May I?" she asked.

Hodges was surprised at how firm Miss Shaqir's hands were, but they were also icy-cold. There was no doubt in her mind, though, that these were the same rings that were on the headless corpse——and in the file picture from last year's similar crime scene. Perhaps the link was a family member or a religious sect? Admiring the jewelry, Hodges softly turned the woman's hands over. Immediately the old woman curled her fingers into her palms, making little upturned fists.

"Darah Ibu," said Jacobs. The old woman looked at him and then slowly opened her hands. Her fingers were smudged with something black, like ink.

Angela Hodges' cell phone rang as she was processing what she was seeing, still unaware of what it all meant. It was Sal Difranco on the line. "Angela, this is Sal. Listen, you're not going to believe this, but our Jane Doe is gone. They don't know what happened to her or…"

As Detective Hodges cut off the call and reached for her firearm she heard a wet squelching noise, viscous and deep.

With a blood-chilling shriek the old woman's head separated from her neck. Her body fell to the floor, head floating in the air with glistening entrails still hanging from it like a mass of giant bloated worms. Eyes blazing like burning coal, fang-filled mouth drooling, the disembodied head and gut swooped at Angela Hodges with a banshee wail. The dangling organs writhed and squirmed like tentacles, reaching for the detective, little flashes sparkling in the twisting bloody mass like fireflies.

"Jesus!" screamed Angela Hodges. She grabbed Jacobs firmly by the arm and pulled him back out into the hallway, slamming the door. "Don't let her out!" she yelled. The young patrolman grabbed tightly to the doorknob to try to keep it closed.

"What the…" the detective blurted. Her heart raced and her mind was an explosion of incongruent thoughts. The online article had said that penanggalan detached their head and entrails from their body to feed. That they moved——flew——on their own, and that after glutting themselves on blood they soaked in vinegar so the entrails would shrink and fit back into the empty body. Sunlight didn't bother them when they were whole, but stunned the disembodied head. They couldn't make eye contact. Smelled of vinegar. Sparkled as they flew. Couldn't cross anything sharp. It was bizarre. Horrible. Something out of an ungodly nightmare. But it was all folklore. Legend. Fairy tales. Such things didn't exist. Couldn't exist!

Something was pounding and squirming from the other side of the door, and it seemed to be all the boyish officer could do to hold his ground. It must all be an illusion. There was some other explanation for what she thought she saw. If not, then she must be losing her mind.

As Detective Hodges worked to compose herself and think of what to do, a figure appeared at the top of the stairs shuffling in their direction. It was the smoking old woman from the night before. She saw the pair and smiled. Pointing she said, "bayi, bayi."

"Stop!" Hodges ordered.

The old woman continued slowly shambling down the murky corridor toward them, heedless of her warning.

"Stop! Stop, goddamnit!" she brandished her firearm.

"Menghentikan!" shouted Jacobs. "Menghentikan! Darah Ibu!"

Undead and Unbound

The withered old crone stopped in her tracks and stood gazing at them through her hazy cataract eyes, her smile thinning.

Dividing her attention between the apartment door and the old woman, Detective Hodges fished out her phone. "I'm calling for backup," she said through clenched teeth and pressed the autodial for her partner. She tried to clear her head, to put everything into perspective and make sense of it all. The door shook again, and Hodges heard something wet thud heavily against it. "We can't hold this door much longer," she listened to the phone ring. There was just a normal perp on the other side of that door. Her mind had played tricks on her, or she had been drugged——that strong smell in the air. Maybe it was some sort of hallucinogenic. The old hag stood swaying just a few yards down the hall, a curious expression painted across her face.

"Yeah. Angela?" came the welcoming voice over the phone.

"Sal! Jesus, I have a mess here. I have our perp but I need backup," Detective Hodges rambled breathlessly into the phone. "I'm at the apartment building from last night. Top floor. We can't hold her much longer…"

"On my way," her partner scrambled. "Listen, Angie, that's what I was going to tell you when you cut me off. We got two perps. The M.E. says there are two sets of bite marks on our victims. There are two of them…" the phone fell to the grimy carpeted floor.

"Two?" Detective Hodges mumbled. "Two," she turned her head to the tottering old woman behind them. "The old lady," she whispered. "It's the old lady."

"Close," came the voice from behind her, "Sharifah has shared a lot with me," he grunted. With a disgusting moist sucking sound, something thick and wet wrapped itself around Hodges throat and squeezed, and babyfaced Jacobs' headless body fell at her feet with a thud. His disembodied head floated into view just at the right side of her face, eyes glowering and mouth wide with a hungry toothy smile. A mass of raw entrails flailed and writhed from beneath Jacobs' neck, sparkling like fireflies. The ghastly apparition sank its shark-like teeth into the detective's neck, tasting the expectant mother's blood. Jacobs' twisted face flushed deep red as he drank in the warm liquid, entrails thrashing like a nest of frenzied snakes.

Detective Hodges crumpled to the floor, head swimming and vision starting to blur. As she fell she pulled a heavy, wet mass with her, bloody tentacle-like entrails still twisted around her neck like the string of a ghastly balloon. She was aware of the apartment door swinging open, of something else squirming into the hallway. Teeth began tearing into her belly, savagely digging for her unborn child; two brimstone-eyed writhing shadows scuttled around her. Pain began to fade to numbness——light to darkness. A shadow at the end of the hall turned and moved away saying, "Bayi. Bayi."

The last thing Angela Hodges was aware of over the sound of gruesome slurping was a familiar voice ringing in her fading ears; "Penanggalan aren't always women," Jacobs said.

Undead and Unbound

THE UNFORGIVING COURT
By David Schembri

There is a fear of things that dash from tree to tree,
In haunted places where creatures bear no breath.
To be caught seeing their skin, scarred and pale,
Is an Omen for certain Death.

—Umschlagplatz, Warsaw Ghetto, 1941.

The boxcars loomed in the distance before a sea of petrified faces. Fabiane's hand was hot in Edmund's grip as they were forced along the flow of the crowd. Helina, their daughter, cried in-between them, clasping her suitcase to her chest. The whistle of the black, steam locomotive pierced the air. German infantry and SS officers had begun to penetrate the masses. Edmund looked on in horror as everyone was being divided. Machine gun fire cracked as warning shots were blasted into the sky. "Stay close!" Edmund yelled to his family.

The condemned were being sent to the left and right of the platform. Edmund saw the boxcars, normally used to transport cattle, being filled with terrified civilians.

"What is happening?" Fabiane cried.

Edmund looked deep into her eyes. He had never seen her so pale, so frightened. "Help us, papa?" Helina begged and he drew her close and kissed her hard on the forehead.

The division had reached them.

"No!" Fabiane screamed when her shoulder was grabbed.

Edmund held his grip firm and Fabiane surged towards him. A soldier's gloved fist met her jaw. Edmund looked on in terror as the trooper shoved her away. He cried with Helina as they watched Fabiane scream back at them, her arm raised to the sky as if she were drowning. "*Edmund! Edmund! Helina!*"

"I love you!" Edmund cried, but before he knew it, Helina was snatched from him also, shoved into the flow that claimed his wife. Edmund was forced to follow a surge of countrymen to the right. He could still hear their screams when he was loaded onto a truck.

~*~

The treacherous journey went on for what seemed like days. It was enough to shake one's bones to the point of breaking. Two German troopers, clad in winter coats and rifles strapped over their shoulders, rode against the tailgate. They stood against the backdrop of a red dawn that felt like the entrance to hell itself.

The crank and squeal of the breaks shook everyone. Startled from a somnolent daze, Edmund looked upon the bemused faces of his countrymen. The two troopers leapt off the tailgate and their boots hit snow. Edmund looked upon the snow as it fell from the heavens.

The heavens that had forsaken them all.

He could hear German voices in the surrounds. A gate was opened. The truck's engines were throttled again and barb wired fence posts passed by. Through the haze of falling snow, Edmund could see troops closing the gates. The truck stopped and the engine was killed. His head ached at the sudden absence of the roaring motor that thundered his ears for so many long hours. The tailgate was dropped and they were ordered to get out.

Edmund was seated close to the rear, so he was one of the first to exit. They were all lined up, hands on heads, along the length of the beast that had taken them so far. They were before four soldiers. Edmund looked beyond their helmets to see a decent occupation of German Military. Mostly infantry soldiers, either marching along the boundaries, or towards what looked to be a large, two story building. The haze of snowfall clouded the hefty swastika flags that waved lazily from the rooftops, and the flag of Nazi Germany centered between them; high and proud atop a small bell tower.

Edmund was scared to his very marrow. He wondered what Fabiane and Helina would be seeing at that same moment. One of the soldiers marched toward them, selected two from the line up and led them out of sight. Soon, two more troops appeared escorting an SS officer. He was tall, thin, and wore a face of distaste. His coat was double breasted

The Unforgiving Court

and secured with gold buttons and a thick, black leather belt. A Luger automatic pistol was holstered to his hip, along with accompanying pouches, housing ammunition no doubt.

He walked slowly to Edmund's end of the line up with his hands casually behind his back. He walked down the line up with eyes of piercing inspection.

"I am SS Commandant Gotifried Harrer. This is my Weimar Headquarters. To the south of this site, is the labor camp of Buchenwald. Here, we need laborers. You have been brought to me because you are all farmers!" he said and reclaimed his position.

The two countrymen returned, rolling a large, freshly sawn slab of a pine tree. An axe was dropped onto the wood and the men hurried back in line.

"Each of you will take it in turn to chop this wood. You will be given two attempts. Once you have taken your turn, step back into line at once!" called Harrer.

In that moment, a soldier grabbed the first man in line (the man next to Edmund) and thrust him before the slab. The man grabbed the axe in trembling hands. Edmund looked on as two quick thrusts were made. The countryman dropped the axe and ran back into line.

It was Edmund's turn.

Shoved towards the slab, he held the axe as firmly as he could. In all of his fear, he looked at the slab as it was being lightly covered in snowfall. He eyed the knots in the grain. Edmund had chopped many slabs of wood in his time and knew where to aim. He feared that two attempts would not be enough.

"*Hacken!*" ordered Harrer.

Edmund quivered and raised the axe and put as much might into his first attack as he could. He aimed where the knots weren't, and created a deep fissure in the left quarter of the pine. He steadied his footing, with the faces of his family embedded in his mind, and swung again. Splinters flew as the left portion of the slab was cut clear. He kept his eyes shut and exhaled, almost crying, and he let the axe fall from his grasp. To survive would leave hope, no matter how small, to see his family again.

Before Edmund reclaimed his place, Harrer shouted, "Halt!"

Edmund frozen.

"*Gesicht mir!*"

Edmund obeyed and turned, his trembling hands instinctively

raised above his shoulders.

Harrer gestured a harsh finger, ordering for Edmund to stand aside. Edmund did so and was held clear of the soldiers before the line-up. Then the echoing voice of the Nazi shouted, "*Feuer auf mein Kommando!*"

Edmund whimpered instantly, as he had learnt how to speak German from his father. Having traded with German farmers it was customary to learn the language. He knew what Harrer had just ordered. The soldier behind him shoved his shoulder as if to silence him, yet Edmund continued to whimper.

"*Feuer!*"

The crack of rifle fire erupted, reducing the countrymen into a line of motionless bodies in the snow.

Edmund's vision was a blur through his tears. Harrer stepped before him. "Your duties here will be to collect and chop wood to feed the fireplaces within the Headquarters. Store your wood by the rear door in the provided bucket for the house attendants to retrieve. If you are seen doing anything other than your duties, if the attendants complain of not having sufficient wood, you will be executed. Food and water will be supplied once a day. Your quarters are located to the west behind you."

Edmund nodded before being left alone, cold and petrified.

It took several moments before he had the courage to roll the pine west. As he labored with the wood, he burdened himself with the axe beneath his arm. Edmund eyed the building to his right. Its geometric architecture looked newly built with perfect ninety-degree angles. White boards, and a tall tiled roofline with four chimneys reaching for the angry sky. The further he pushed on, the more he thought of Fabiane and Helina. It had been over two days since he last saw them.

He reached the rear of the house and stood gasping. A shelter, little more than a shack fit to house firewood, stood before him. He slid open the door, stumbled in and looked at the interior. There were holes in the roof and the walls were made of rusted sheeting. His heart sank further when he saw a make shift bed to his left, crudely constructed from timber. Upon it was some damp bedding——a single army blanket and a small pillow. He noticed some writing on the outer paneling of the door painted white in large letters.

Arbeit Macht Frei

THE UNFORGIVING COURT

He understood it to say *work brings freedom*.

The floor of the shelter was the ground itself, muddy with melted snow. He felt the wind whistle through the many holes in the walls, and he wrapped his arms around himself and shivered. Before long, he decided to inspect the exterior. A small port, with a single piece of sheeting for a roofline, housed an old wood cart and a small assortment of rusted saws.

He then braved the wood bucket by the rear of the Headquarters. He trudged his way there and noticed to his left that soldiers were walking in and out of a single story building. Their barracks, he guessed.

To his surprise, the bucket was full by the rear door. He couldn't help but think that someone else had died to fill it. He then noticed the nearby woodlands further south. He knew with heartache that Fabiane and Helina were imprisoned within the distance.

He spent hours thinking of the sign that was painted crudely on the boxcars that had swallowed them.

Buchenwald, it read.

Edmund kept working until night and cold demanded he stop. He was exhausted when he entered the darkness of his shelter. He dropped to the bed that may as well have been made out of a slab of stone. He listened to the thud of his broken heart, the ache of his bones, and the painful rumble in his stomach.

~*~

The sounds of commotion shook Edmund from his troubled sleep. Light glared in through the many holes in his shelter and he rose. Many voices shouted from the barracks. The young soldiers were yelling words like, "*Dämons!*" and, "*Abschaum!*"

He rubbed his eyes. He didn't know how long he had lain down before sleep had finally taken him. He struggled to his feet and cautiously looked out the door to see soldiers rallying.

Something was disturbingly wrong.

He hauled himself out the door. With his strength waning, he wheeled the wood cart towards the barracks, darting glances back and forth from the Headquarters to the commotion. He paused when he noticed two soldiers drag out something from the barracks——a body? He quickly went to the bucket when he saw Harrer appear with his escorts. Edmund hurriedly busied himself with the wood.

He didn't dare turn his head for fear of being caught spying, but he listened.

"*In den Wald sofort!*" Harrer ordered after seeing what the soldiers had dragged out.

Immediately, at least two dozen soldiers followed their Commandant's orders and charged into the nearby woodlands. Edmund's heart was pounding. He listened to the Commandant grunting distasteful theories to other SS officers who greeted him before he entered the Headquarters. Notions of "*Polish Resistance*" gritted through his teeth, and "*Worthless guerilla operations, we will find and burn them all!*"

Within moments, the courtyard behind the Headquarters was deserted. Edmund feared to venture forth, but he couldn't help but investigate what had spooked the great army. He wheeled his wood cart over to the crude figure in the snow and gasped. What he thought was a charred corpse, was nothing of the sort, and it left him filled with dread and confusion.

The object in the snow was a life size wooden carving of a man. There was no face, just the grain, but the mimicking of limbs and head were in accurate proportion. The etching into the wood looked to have been crafted with fine, sharp tools. The grooves worked in all directions across and through the grain, suggesting to him that the carving had been done in extreme haste. He did not know what to make of it.

He wheeled his cart back to the shelter when he heard distant gunfire from the forest.

~*~

Edmund spent the next hour chopping the pine slabs that were scattered behind his shelter. He was running low and had no idea how he was going to obtain more. He was too petrified to enter the woods for fear of being shot. His entire duty seemed hopeless to him. When he turned, there was Harrer and his men, watching him.

He dropped his axe and stood to attention.

"*Essen! Wasser!*" Harrer spat.

He understood that food and water had been brought.

"Your supply is obtained in the Ettersberg Hills behind you! You

The Unforgiving Court

will have a guard with you at all times. Attempt to escape and you will be shot!"

A third soldier then marched from behind the trio and stood to attention before the Commandant.

"The prisoner is to bring in three carts of wood before nightfall. If he fails, you are to shoot him in the courtyard before the barracks!"

"*Ja Commendant!*" the soldier yelled.

Harrer and his escorts departed leaving Edmund alone with his possible executioner.

~*~

The journey into the Ettersberg Hills was slow. It was almost impossible for him to push the old cart through the dense scrub. He looked towards the tangled woods ahead and sighted a fallen tree. He rested for a moment, eyeing the soldier and the rifle he held in gloved hands; the same weapon he had seen in the hands of most German soldiers.

"*Umzug auf!*"

The soldier stabbed north with his weapon.

Edmund's tree was up a small rise to the west. He had to say something, so he spoke in German to the young man, the boy.

"I must leave the cart here and roll wood down to it. I will take my saw up with me."

The soldier's face grew pale.

"*Nein!* North!"

Edmund threw his hands in the air.

"North!"

He quickly moved his cart north and continued the laborious journey. He couldn't set eyes on a boy so polluted by obvious hatred.

When Edmund found more fallen trees, he rested his cart and went to work.

For hours he cut and chopped for his life. The surrounds of the forest were disturbingly still; compared to the strong winds he would suffer when returning a cartload to the shelter. The small portions of bread and water were hardly enough to keep up his strength, but he pressed on.

As he cut into a second tree, he caught the soldier looking at him eagerly, as if interested in his labors. The soldier would behave dismissively in those instances. Edmund sensed humanity in the boy, and kept an eye on him.

When he had emptied a second load and ventured back, the commotion of the returning infantry stopped him in his tracks. The soldiers were rallying into the courtyard. Their captain stopped and noticed Edmund's guard and yelled. "The barracks! Fifteen minutes!"

Edmund's face went pale and chills covered him.

He knew he would never fill the cart in that time. It was over. Having any chance of surviving to see Fabiane and Helina again were gone. He had failed and he suddenly fell to his knees and broke into tears.

The soldier stood over him and ordered him to stand. When he didn't move, the boy gripped his shoulder and lifted him to his feet. Edmund was shoved towards the woodlands and could feel the butt of the soldier's rifle pressed against his back. Edmund thought that he was to be shot in the courtyard, but what did it matter… Back at the work site Edmund turned to face his executioner, whom had shouldered his weapon. "You can still fill your cart," he began. "I can help you. *Schnell*, it will be dark soon!"

The boy didn't wait for him to utter a word. He positioned himself on the other end of the saw that was wedged in a trunk, and waited for him to take his position.

"*Schnell!*"

Edmund was shocked at the sudden benevolence of the boy. He soon took his place and they worked together.

By twilight the cart was back at the shelter for inspection like nothing had happened.

~*~

The following morning; the same commotion.

Edmund didn't venture out into the courtyard, but witnessed the same events take place. Another carved figure was dragged out of the barracks, accompanied by the panicked voices of the armed Hitler youth. Yet again, Harrer ordered his infantry to raid the forest in search of the guerrillas. The Nazi seemed more furious and his voice was full of the aggression of a madman.

Edmund noticed that a soldier was marching his way, and he knew that it was his guard, his savior… When the soldier stood to attention before him, he said. "The same drill as yesterday. *Schnell!*"

They ventured back into the Ettersberg Hills. At the work site they heard the distant crack of gunfire. Edmund felt compelled to say something.

"Is the compound being raided by a resistance?" he asked as he steadied himself before the saw.

The soldier took a few moments, looked about himself as if to make sure there were no onlookers and immediately shouldered his weapon.

"There is *no* resistance," he whispered.

"*Nein?* Then an army, *ja?* Invaders?"

"Invaders. *Ja.*"

He drew back his saw and began to cut. He stopped and looked at the boy watching him.

"My name is, Edmund. What's yours?"

The soldier looked about himself again.

"Julius," he whispered.

"Your orders were to kill me, Julius. Why didn't you?"

Julius shrugged, but Edmund knew the answer. Julius was just as ensnared as a soldier as Edmund was a prisoner.

"Thank you, Julius. It was very kind of you."

Julius looked at him and displayed the hint of a grin. "I can help, *Ja?*"

Edmund nodded.

Julius stepped down to the other end of the saw keenly and they went to work. They cut pine together into the dying morning. They rolled the slabs to a more level part of the forest floor for Edmund to chop. Of course, Julius showed interest in having a turn with the axe. "Have you ever used an axe before?" Edmund asked him.

"*Nein.* I grew up in Berlin. I have never been on a farm."

"Be careful."

Suddenly, they paused to a disturbing sound in the west——a scream? They could hear sounds of someone whimpering in-between bursts of agony. Edmund and Julius looked at each other and went down the pathway they had grooved through the forest. Edmund stared up the hill, to the very first tree he had wanted to cut. The screams were heard again. They were close, just on the other side.

Edmund motioned to venture up.

"*Nein!* Don't go up there!"

"Someone sounds hurt, Julius. We must try and see if they need our help?"

"*Nein!* We can't go *near* there. It's a haunted place!" Julius whispered harshly.

"I don't understand. How do you mean, haunted? The person suffering could be one of your friends. What has been happening at the barracks, Julius? You seem to know something that no one else does."

"It has been happening for weeks. Soldiers are being kidnapped. Taken from their bunks. Left in their place, beneath their blankets, is a wooden carving to mimic them. The Commandant believes it's the work of a Polish guerrilla operation. So do the men, but not me."

"What do *you* think is happening to——"

Suddenly, the scream again, and Edmund walked up the hill.

"We must keep out of sight!" Julius whispered from behind.

They reached the fallen moss covered log and kept themselves hidden. Heard from beyond were different noises, which accompanied the torment. The sounds suggested that swooping ravens were cutting the air. Edmund and Julius stared at each other and shared their trepidation. Edmund decided to peer over the log to get a view of the activity. At first he saw nothing but forest. Then, he noticed a road dwindling off in the distance, which appeared to be nothing more than a track. The forest was clearer down that way, leading into a field of earth mounds.

Edmund was protected from sight by the cover of long grasses from the other side, that in turn, obstructed his view of the swooping and suffering. He leaned in carefully and separated the grasses with his hands and looked upon a sight that nearly made him collapse.

It *was* a German soldier. He was stripped of his clothing from the waist up. Tied to a tree, his hands were bound over his head. His torso was covered in bloodied, deep lacerations, and his legs shook and twitched to his obvious misery. Edmund then saw the bird-like creatures swooping from the treetops, and every time, they left the soldier with another cut to his chest and belly.

"Don't let them see you!" Julius urged, tugging at Edmund's coat.

"They are only birds,"

"*Nein!*"

Edmund looked closer and his head swam.

They were not birds. Some settled on the soldier's chest, with their talons dug into his flesh.

The Unforgiving Court

The creatures looked to be humanoids of small stature. They were pale skinned, naked, and had wings of a transparent, veined and crude nature. More of them suspended on the soldier's body, hanging from his skin and began to rip at it, boring into him. The screams of the soldier intensified as the malicious (*daemons?*) all flocked and covered him. The voices coming from their fang-filled little mouths resembled the sounds of enjoyment, as if their actions were designed for entertainment.

The creatures perched on the soldier's head plucked out his eyes. The screams were cut short. Edmund dry-retched as he witnessed the humanoids rip open the soldier's belly, and began mercilessly and playfully pulling out his intestines and stomach. The others that were swarmed on his head soon had it dislodged from the neck and were bathing in the fountain of blood from whence it sat. The humanoids continued to strip the corpse, revealing rib bones and spine, their little mouths feasted merrily. Their faces held an angelic beauty that was hauntingly seductive, even as blood covered them. Delicate little tongues licked. Glowing eyes gleamed beneath perfect brows.

"Not birds," Julius whispered.

"Nein. Not birds… but what?"

Edmund felt winded due to the horror he witnessed. Scarcely able to stand, Julius held his arm as they walked back to the work site. He slumped down on the ground, resting his back onto the trunk of a tree. Julius offered him his canteen. "Finish it. I can get more later."

He drank slowly and already felt better as the cool liquid flowed down his dry throat. Julius searched one of the larger pouches on his belt and produced some bread. "Here, eat."

"I——I don't want to get you into trouble, Julius,"

"Who will know? Eat. You need it."

After Edmund had eaten the small portion of bread, more than his normal ration, he felt his strength returning.

"What are those creatures?"

Julius sat next to him and brought out a small leather bound book, which was tucked beneath his trousers. He opened it and flipped through several hand written pages.

"Yours?" Edmund asked.

"My fathers. This is his journal. My father is a poet and a professor of Celtic folklore. I share the same passion."

"You want to be a poet?"

"*Ja.* I wish I could be studying now, but the war started. My father gave me his journal to read, so I can remember that the world is full of different things...magical things."

"Magic?"

"Listen;

"*In a dark time within heaven's skies,*
"*In burned the angel's rebellion to threaten God's power,*
"*Banished from the white gates, now said to be locked,*
"*In their corpse's graves 'tis said they cower...*"

"What does that mean?"
"Do you believe in faeries, Edmund?"
Edmund huffed.
"Just imagination. Old stories of make-believe."
"Do you really believe that after what you saw?"
"Tell me what I saw?"
"They used to be alive, Edmund. Like you and me. They were people that had met a horrible death. In the west, did you see a clearing in the forest?"
"*Ja.*"
"Burial mounds, Edmund. Mass graves. The people buried there died not long ago and God has closed the gates on them. Heaven is only for pure and peaceful spirits."
"How can our maker deny our passage home?"
Julius flipped through the book again. "My father wrote here, and he quotes from an old English scroll, that centuries ago, the angels rebelled against him. God banished them and any others he suspected. The ones who are buried in those mounds are full of more than just sorrow, but also, anger and grief. They are bound to it, and God knows this and has locked them out. So, denied passage, and not being evil spirits, they were also denied entry into hell. Caught in-between, these spirits descended back to earth and are bound to their burial site. Reincarnated from denoted angels, into the creatures you saw feasting."
"Faeries?"
"*Ja,* but of a different kind... There are many sorts, but these are written about here in my father's journal. They are not spirits, and they are not alive, but they are physical."
"Julius, none of this makes any sense. They were angels, and now

they have been reincarnated, but they are not alive? What are they?"

"Edmund, they are the undead breed of the Unforgiving Court."

Edmund rose from his place and looked west to where he saw the creatures. Another horrific thought suddenly struck his mind, ringing his ears.

"When you told me that bodies are buried in those mounds, then where have they come from?"

Julius directed his eyes out towards the northern sky, to the smoke that rose from Buchenwald. Edmund looked there too.

"They are bodies that couldn't be burned in the crematorium of the concentration camp."

"Crematorium? Harrer said it was a *labor* camp!"

Julius nodded his head mournfully. "*Nein, Edmund.* I was stationed there for a year before coming here. People die in Buchenwald every day. Many are executed or worked to death in the quarry. Bodies are piled and burned, and when the corpses are too many, they are loaded onto trucks, and buried in the mounds."

"My wife and daughter are in that camp!"

"I am so sorry, Edmund. I wish I could do something. If only I could..."

Edmund cried into his hands. Julius went to him and placed a hand on his shoulder. "You should not give up hope. They may yet still be alive. You must hold onto that."

Edmund wished he could believe it, but for the warning in his heart, that told him hope was lost.

Julius put his book away. "Edmund?"

He looked up with a swelling face of devastation.

"We are losing daylight. *Schnell...*"

Edmund wiped his face and got up.

"Julius. If you were ordered to kill me, would you?"

Julius shrugged.

They worked and met the quota.

~*~

A soldier named Anton was the next to be taken. The day after that was Rommel. Then came Albert, Fritz, Karl and Hermann. The piles of wooden stand-ins were burned after the number had reached a dozen. Julius said that the custom behind the crude carvings were the indicators of the faeries' prankish nature.

"To toy with the living is a common source of enjoyment, but with the Unforgiving Court, they have far more deadly behaviors."

Edmund and Julius continued their labors every day for the next three weeks. They talked about the details of the journal, and Edmund came to understand more about the undead; the winged creatures that had chosen the barracks as their playground.

"Make no mistake, the Unforgiving Court have no sides. They would kill anything, anyone," Julius said during a break.

"So they are not vengeful? You would think they would be."

"The spirit that went to heaven was not the same one that was stuck in-between worlds. *Nein, Edmund.* They are the remainders of the spirit. The bad part. They are left bound to their mounds, to the Otherworld they have burrowed beneath the earth."

"They live underground?"

"It is their territory. They would harm anyone who goes near them. Anyone who sees them, anyone who touches the earth they deem sacred."

"What do you think will happen? Will they just keep taking one soldier at a time, or start doing worse?"

"My father quoted from old Scottish folklore that this court are familiar to the *Unseelie Court* faeries. They have a shared liking in bringing harm to humans for entertainment, and that they are *trooping* creatures."

"Like an army?"

"*Ju, Edmund, ja!* These creatures are just playing, soon they will——"

"They are going to attack the compound?"

"That would fit their customs. It may happen soon."

"They will kill all of us."

Julius stood and stared down at Edmund. "Not if you have the deterrents."

"You can repel them?"

"Just wear any item of clothing inside out."

"Sounds ridiculous."

"Any faerie creature, be it spirit, angel or undead, would regard this as being detrimental. I wear all of my under garments backwards. They work just like a protective charm!"

Julius retrieved a slice of bread from one of his pouches and gave it to him.

"Thank you," said Edmund.

"No! Don't eat it!"

"Why not? I am starving."

"Keep *that* piece of bread in your pocket. The prototype of food, a symbol of life, is also another protection against them!"

"Is this why you have not been kidnapped?"

"I would like to think so."

Edmund tucked the bread into his coat pocket.

"There is another thing all faerie creatures have in common. They are all bound by one weakness."

"I cannot imagine what."

"To utter a faeries name could summon it to you and you could force it to do your bidding."

"Even these flesh eaters?"

"*Ja, Edmund.* But, of course, one would need to get close enough to hear them speak and live to tell the tale, but I don't think anyone has…"

Edmund remembered the feasting creatures and their little voices. He couldn't recall any words that meant anything to him. Edmund and Julius resumed with another hard day of labor.

Screams echoed in the distance.

~*~

Edmund stopped dead in his tracks.

Harrer and his escorts were waiting. Julius stood to attention before them. Harrer stepped before Julius and looked him up and down with grimace. "Do you take me for a fool?"

"*Nein, Commandant?*"

Harrer immediately stepped before Edmund and threw a hard, closed fist into his jaw. Harrer, all the while, had his eyes locked on Julius' face and could see the boy jolt.

"We are at war! Yet you mingle with the enemy? Do you believe in your country and your *Führer!*"

"*Ja, Commandant!*"

Harrer stepped back and ordered Edmund to face the forest on his knees with his hands behind his head.

Edmund trembled into position.

"Do you realize that we are under attack! Rebels are taking your fellow countrymen and skinning them alive! *Savages!* And I receive intelligence that you are mingling with this prisoner! I have no time for the weak minded. Do you hear me?"

"*Ja Commandant!*"

Through the movements in the snow, Edmund could sense that Julius was forced to remove his helmet and stand behind him, a few steps away.

"*Feuer auf mein Kommando!*"

A trail of urine streamed down Edmund's leg and he cried as Julius' breaths became rapid. A gun, perhaps a pistol, was heard being drawn from its holster.

"*Feuer…*" Harrer's voice was heard, but only in a whisper.

"Please, Commandant," Julius whimpered. "I can't…"

"*Feuer!*"

"I just want to go home to my father…to my——"

A single gunshot pierced the air.

A splash of something warm draped the back of Edmund's neck. He then felt the weight of a body drop over him. Edmund cried to see Julius' beautiful face stare lifelessly up at the twilight sky.

Harrer shoved Edmund down to the snow and landed a hard boot into his belly. "Bury this mess in the mounds," he ordered as he holstered his pistol.

Edmund stared at the blood flowing out of Julius' head.

His young friend's body was stripped of his weapon belt, helmet, coat and boots. Edmund was then left alone with the corpse as if it were a molested doll. The journal was gone; it would no doubt find a home in one of the fireplaces. A life-long account of histories about the unknown would be for no eyes to see. He knelt down to Julius, who was face down in the snow. It was the first time Edmund had seen his hair, as Julius had never removed his helmet. Julius' fine, golden strands swayed lazily in the cold breeze.

Edmund cried and stoked them before loading him into the cart.

~*~

Edmund chose to bury Julius at the work site. The place where they became friends. He didn't dare go to the mounds as he knew he would not return. He buried Julius beneath the pine they were cutting

The Unforgiving Court

together. He even carved a small memorial into the wood.
Julius the Poet, 1941.

When night came, Edmund laid down on the make shift bed within his shelter for hours. He tried to focus through his sorrow. He tried to remember. He thought about the little snarling creatures feeding on the soldier's corpse. He tried to remember what was spitting from their tiny, bloodied tongues.

Edmund mouthed and mouthed for hours. He was whispering the same grouping of letters over, and over again.

Faf-nir. Faff-nirrr… Fafnir…

Was it right, he thought?

Was he uttering a faerie's name?

Edmund was startled in the darkness, only pierced by a few beams of moonlight. He heard a scratch at the iron and he jolted again. He fell back into his bed and pulled the blanket up to his chest.

The scratching continued all around him, as if something were circling the iron structure with the tip of a bayonet. Edmund trembled as his eyes followed the rapid assault on his walls. It stopped suddenly.

Through a hole near the roofline above his feet, he saw two sets of tiny claws. He held his breath at the emergence of a small head. It glowed with the aid of the moonlight. The tiny face of womanly beauty tilted sideways as its eyes caught sight of him. A small squeak, with likeness to a rat, came from the creature before it pushed itself noisily through the hole and hovered down to his legs. When it landed, its crude wings fluttered to a stop and folded behind its hunched back.

Edmund feared these Unforgiving Court creatures of the damned, but having one creep over his stomach, was another horror altogether. Its pale skin glowed in the dark and was mapped with scars. Yet, the matted flesh weaved into a smooth, almost delicate, draping of skin over its shoulders and neck. The face did look female, yet no other features on the creature could determine sex. No breasts or any detail between its legs. Edmund was shocked he had the courage to allow his eyes to wander. Its thin line of blue lips was parted slightly to reveal a hint of tangled jaws, gleaming. The hair on its head was dreaded with dirt and clotted blood. It approached in a quick succession of steps until it was at Edmund's nose. He tried not to yelp as the creature hissed, *Fafffff-nnnnnniiiirrrrr!*

Edmund shook where he lay with the faerie panting. It soon let out a small growl of impatience, its beauty transforming, and thrashed a claw at his right cheek, drawing blood. Edmund jolted timidly and Fafnir squealed and flew up out of reach. As Edmund stood, he looked about fearfully, shielding his face the whole time with his forearm. After a moment, Fafnir hovered down slowly from the darkness and settled before him.

Fafff! Nnnnirr!

Edmund lowered his arm from his face. Fafnir's gaze was hypnotic; replaced again by the slender façade. The creature was doing something to him. He felt a heat in his chest and throat, then in his skull. A sensation like nothing felt before was moving through his body like a warm haze. It settled his nerves and sorrow. All he could think of then was what his heart truly desired.

Fafnir...

Edmund gulped. "I-I command you to sa-save my wife and daughter."

Fafnir's face grimaced, growled and hissed as if in protest; its face of horror returning, as if it was turned inside out. Edmund felt the warmth of the faerie's magic leave him and then the weight of his sorrow returned. He felt that Fafnir's response could only mean that the task was not possible. Fafnir circled, hissed and flew out a larger hole in the shelter.

He listened to the creature's departing flight as it entered the darkness of the Ettersberg Hills.

~*~

Dawn.

Edmund went back to the work site and did nothing. He simply sat at Julius' grave. He picked at the snow. He cried for his family. He listened to the branches above creak eerily. He listened to the distant gunfire as soldiers searched for the guerillas.

When the day finally died he walked back to the shelter with his empty cart. He expected to find Harrer and his escorts. But there was no one.

He could not help but wonder.

~*~

Edmund jolted at a knock at the iron door. He could see the beams

The Unforgiving Court

of a flash light pierce the darkness from the outside.

He got up guessing that his execution had been saved for the night. He took a breath and slid open the door. The man before him was an SS officer, but no one he had seen before. Whoever it was, he said nothing. He simply stood in the doorway with a torch in one hand and something else in the other. Edmund thought it was a pistol, but then the officer brought it up to his mouth and drank from it. He swayed slightly as he wiped his mouth. "Where is your hospitality? Stand aside."

"This shelter is not fit for your grace."

The officer huffed and stepped in. Edmund slid the door closed as the officer dumped the torch on the ground. They stood within a meter of each other. The officer's breath smelt of whisky. He slumped down on the hard bed and grunted in disgust. Edmund stood silent. The officer took another sip from his silver flask and burped. "Your name?"

"Edmund."

"Your *full* name!"

Edmund's heart raced.

"E-Edmund Mieszro Adamski."

The officer seemed to relax again and took in another drink.

"I, am Commandant Von Ludendorff."

"Heil Hitler…" Edmund said. He didn't know what else to say and his gut churned when he said it. He extended his right arm straight in front of himself to mimic the Nazi salute.

Ludendorff stared.

He then burst out into laughter. Edmund's arm lowered slowly as he watched the Commandant snort and chortle. This display made Edmund fear every passing second. He felt belittled and was expecting to die at any second.

"Do you know why I am drinking?"

"*Nein, Commandant.*"

"To honor my family. I have four children. A wife too. They are in Heidelberg…safe. I had leave planned for a month to see them… it has just been denied by the Chancellor. I am to continue my duties for the war effort. It has been two years since I last saw my family. My youngest son has just turned five years old… My government can't even give me one month…so, forgive me if I do not return the greeting."

Ludendorff took another drink.

"I take it that you have your own tragedies to bear?"

"*Ja.*"

"Mine would seem small in comparison, I know. But, I didn't come here to offload my burdens, I have come for your help."

"Help, Commandant?"

"*Ja.*"

Ludendorff tucked the flask beneath his belt and straightened himself. He looked up at Edmund seriously. "Not only *work* can set you free. The truth can do that too."

Edmund gulped.

"The head of this compound, Gotifried Harrer, has a history. It has been circulating amongst the ranks that he has lost touch with the international convention of war."

Edmund stared blankly.

"He has broken the rules, Edmund. To dispense ones infantry to their death is one thing, but to directly murder ones infantry, is something else altogether. Do you know of what I speak?"

Edmund stood silent, too petrified to move a muscle.

"I have been given some intelligence that Commandant Harrer murdered a German soldier yesterday. I was also informed that *you* were present. Can you account for this, Edmund?"

All Edmund could see was the distant stare of Julius' eyes. He nodded.

"You saw this happen?"

"It happened behind me, Commandant. I still have the soldier's blood on the back of my neck. I was ordered to bury him in the woods."

"You can account for the whereabouts of this grave?"

"*Ja, Commandant.*"

Ludendorff nodded, rose to his feet and straightened his coat and hat. "I will need you to testify this incident in a trial. Tomorrow, I will return and relieve Commandant Harrer of his position. After that, I will see what I can do to secure your freedom."

Ludendorff motioned to leave.

"Commandant?"

The officer stepped back before Edmund curiously. "Speak."

"I would rather something else, Commandant."

"Pardon?" Ludendorff said with a hint of outrage.

Suddenly, Ludendorff was taken off balance slightly, displaying a

The Unforgiving Court

sudden discomfort within him. His hand went to his chest and his head as if following a trail of pain.

"Commandant?"

"It must be the whisky… I-I feel a warmth in me."

Ludendorff looked up at Edmund instantly.

A scratching noise.

Edmund caught the sight of a crude shadow whisk past one of the holes from the outside.

"What did you want to ask me, Edmund?"

"If my wife and daughter are alive to save, I wish you to free them in my place. They were put on the train bound for Buchenwald."

Ludendorff straightened. His hand quickly went to his belt and collected a little black book. He also withdrew a small pencil.

"Names?"

Edmund gulped.

"Fabiane Emilia Adamski. My wife,"

"Age?"

"Thirty-five, Commandant."

Edmund feasted his eyes on the swift fashion that Ludendorff penciled his wife's beautiful name.

"And?"

"Helina Florentyna Adamski. My daughter. She is fourteen."

"Any illnesses?"

"*Nein, Commandant.* They were healthy when last I saw them. That was over a month ago."

Ludendorff finished writing, slid the pencil back with precision, closed the book and tucked it back into his belt. He hesitated, then retrieved his silver flask and tossed it onto the bed.

"Keep it. It will keep you warm."

Ludendorff gave Edmund the slightest nod before leaving him.

~*~

The sorrowful past bound the Ettersberg Hills. Edmund stared at them at dawn and embraced hope. He chose to try and do his duty, although he had no energy. All that lurked in his stomach was the whisky. He kept the silver flask in his coat pocket along with the stale bread. He noticed activity by the front of the Headquarters. A car was leaving the gates. A long, black sedan, bearing the red flags of Nazi

Undead and Unbound

Germany on either sides of its hood. Ludendorff taking his leave, he thought. Perhaps to search for his family, among other matters.

Edmund listened to the foolish soldiers charge into the woodlands. The recent ritual of the Harrer barracks. However, something caught his attention. From the treetops nearby, things flew and swooped. Undesirable things. Dangerous things.

Trooping things.

Edmund went back into his shelter.

It didn't take him long to turn his trousers and coat inside out.

Edmund waited until he saw Ludendorff's car return. It was an hour before he had the courage to empty his wood by the rear door. He was startled by raised voices from within the Headquarters. He heard both Harrer and Ludendorff arguing. He went to a nearby window and could hear everything.

"The regional leader has condemned your actions! You have been allowed the opportunity to give yourself up for arrest!"

"You have no authority in my Headquarters!"

The intense war of political insults even drew the attention of some of the soldiers.

"I claim *seizure of power* to this compound!"

"Leave before I arrest and sentence you!"

"You swore an oath to the *Führer* to abide by the rules of war, and I——"

A single gunshot.

Then, a scatter of machine gunfire, which came from different directions from the inside. Ludendorff had personal guards too, so that evened out the exchange. Edmund gasped. He thought fearfully if Ludendorff had the chance to search for his family.

Harrer suddenly burst out of the rear door, pistol in hand and barrel smoking. He carried a wound to his left arm.

Soldiers noticed and hesitated. Harrer then saw Edmund and his face contorted with revulsion.

"Seize him!"

Edmund was frozen with fear. Two soldiers threw him at Harrer's feet; he felt the pistol being pressed against his temple.

A scream.

Sounds of breaking glass suggested that the barracks was under machine gunfire.

More screams and counter attacks.

The Unforgiving Court

Harrer lifted his pistol and locked his eyes to his panicked infantry. Edmund could hear the creatures.

Squealing. Hissing. Swooping.

They had come.

Harrer stepped away and yelled orders to form ranks. The Unforgiving Court charged into the yard like an enormous swarm of ravens. The squealing was deafening. Edmund gripped his ears and saw many others do the same, even the Commandant. Edmund watched as soldiers were lifted from the snow and torn apart. He then looked at Harrer who was aiming his pistol at him.

He fired.

Edmund coughed as his lungs filled with blood.

Harrer stood over him and aimed at his right eye. He was suddenly gripped and clawed and his pistol dropped from his grasp. Edmund watched as claws dug into the Nazi's left ear and right eye socket. His body shook as he screamed in horror. More of the Court were upon him and they ripped at his coat and exposed his chest. His torso was then clawed and stripped of its covering to expose his white, blood soaked ribs.

Edmund's final glances were of the Commandant's gut and throat being eaten. Edmund could hear the crunching of bone and before long, two of the Court raised the Nazi's rib cage from the foundations of his corpse and hovered it above the slaughter.

Epilogue

Weimar, Central Germany, 1987.

Erich had never been requested to take a group of visitors out this far. The memorial of Buchenwald was further north, but this group directed him onto the winding tracks to the west. They were a party of four. Erich smoked his cigarette as the cold mist slowly consumed them. He eyed the surroundings.

He'd heard of many such sites, which all were deserted like this one. The grass had not fully concealed man's intrusion over time. There were the foundations of a building and the remains of a fence boundary. Erich felt uneasy as he stared at the forest hills. He'd heard rumors that it was a haunted place. He had read enough history to know that the U.S. bombing in 1945 destroyed most of what was built

Undead and Unbound

for the German war effort. But, there was something else about *this* site to the west. A slaughter happened, so it was written, but nothing was ever known of the cause.

The group returned from the mist and he drove them onward to the Buchenwald memorial.

An hour later Erich returned to the overgrown grasses of the site, later researched as belonging to SS Commandant Gotifried Harrer. Erich found the remains of an old iron shack. He noticed a small bunch of flowers and a note.

To my dear father, Edmund.
I understand the sacrifice you made for us.
We will love you always.
Your family, Fabiane and Helina.

A lump developed in Erich's throat.
Then, he heard something scratch at the iron.

NORTH OF THE ARCTIC CIRCLE

By Peter Rawlik

The little men bring the two bodies they found on the ice for me to examine. This place is so remote that few men have the fortitude to make the journey. Indeed, I suppose that is one of the reasons that I find myself here. A kingdom of my own is all I asked for. I had no intention of finding this great and ancient city of ice and basalt, of awakening its small, dark-skinned inhabitants, of assuming the role of master with all the associated privileges and duties. To the Zwarte-Piet I am their master, or at least they treat me as such, so they bring the bodies to me for examination.

They are dead, or nearly so. The spark of life is strong in the one who is monstrous in both size and appearance being eight feet tall with skin of yellow and huge watering eyes that glowed in the shadows. I order him taken to the great hall where the hearth will serve to warm him and perhaps sooth the anger and angst that I know permeate his psyche and his brief life. The other is frozen solid, beyond the pale that men know, but I reach inside and I kindle what little spark remains. It shall be enough to sustain him for my needs. The body spasms and arches and steam rises from the extremities. My diminutive servants scatter like rats running for the shadows. All these centuries and they still fear my power, as if I were as wrathful and capricious as my father.

He convulses and coughs, tries to speak but finds his throat still too stiff to utter but the most base of sounds. I raise my hands in a calming gesture and he relaxes letting the Zwarte-Piet cautiously creep back bearing fur blankets, hot food and warm coffee. I watch the bearded aristocrat as he slowly revives and my encyclopedic mind recalls his name, his childhood of privilege, and his chosen occupation.

It takes time but the combination of warmth, sustenance and my shoddy necromancy eventually restores him to a semblance of health, enough so that he rises to give me thanks but I cut him off before he can utter a word. "Your thanks are unnecessary Doctor. My hospitality is given freely to all, but you…and your creation are most welcome in these halls."

He stands there flabbergasted for a moment but then recovers. "You have me at a disadvantage sir. You know who I am and what I have done, but I do not recognize you."

I flash a smile, "When I come to them, few adults recognize me for who I am, but I assure you that most children know me for who I am. Still, no fault of your own, if you must you can call me Nicholas. I shall call you Doctor, given your current condition there would be some irony in calling you Victor."

My guest pauses to take a sip of coffee. "I had thought you a myth, a story to keep children well behaved."

I rise from my hoar frost throne and let my crimson robes tinged with ermine flow around me. "I assure you, Doctor, that I exist, and have for millennia, though not always in this role, but I have always been known as a gift-giver." My stride quickly brings me to his side. "Walk with me, Doctor, and tell me of your problematic creation."

For a dead man he has no problem keeping pace with me. "If you know of his existence then you know what I have done. I have no excuse for my actions, I thought in my pride, in my hubris that I had the knowledge and power to create life from the lifeless. I was a fool and though I succeeded in giving life to my base creation it was a degenerate thing, knowledgeable yes, but amoral and violent. When I refused to reproduce my deplorable act and create for it a mate, it swore vengeance on me and destroyed those I held most dear. My creation is nothing more than a monster and I shall hunt it down and destroy it."

I laugh, deep belly laugh that instantly offends my guest. "My apologies Doctor, it is just that I have some experience with rebellious children. I wonder if perhaps you expect too much, too soon of your creation." We pass through the tunnel leading past the workshops where the Zwarte-Piet labor on their trinkets and toys.

"How do you mean?" His voice holds some incredulity.

"Let us consider the human infant, horrible things, voracious, demanding, with no thought or consideration for anything but their own needs. If they had any strength at all they would be dangerous. Toddlers are little better, oh they have some self-control and can be somewhat reasoned with, but left to their own devices they'll be more than happy to pull their parent's hair and throw a tantrum at the drop of a hat. As they age, they learn, but most often the hard way. They tease dogs and cats until they are bitten. They'll happily pull the wings off of insects until the wasp stings them back. They secretly plot the death of one parent so they may usurp that position. It takes a decade of learning, if not more, for children to learn how to control themselves, not only mentally, but emotionally and physically as well. Even then some remain little more than walking and talking toddlers, hell-bent on satisfying their own desires regardless of the cost to others."

The incredulity spreads to his face. "How exactly is this relevant to my current predicament?"

I shake my head and chuckle. "My dear Doctor, your creation may have been proportioned as a man, but he was in both his emotions and mentality nothing more than an infant. Yes he could stand, and run, and if need be take drastic, even horrible action, but he had no clue as to what he was doing, or that it was wrong. You brought him into the world but then you failed to instruct him in its rules and the consequences of breaking those rules. What did you expect him to do? You didn't even teach him to speak."

I pause to allow him to counter but he remains silent so I continue. "Do you think you were the first father ever disgusted by the appearance of their newborn? All men, or at least a good portion, are reviled by the squealing thing covered in blood and excrement that their wives deliver to them. Yet it is only a rare few that run screaming into the night disavowing their offspring. You did so for years. And when the creature finally comes to you, the only being to which it can refer to as father and begs you to create for it something to which it can relate as an equal, something to love and be loved by, you unilaterally deny it and curse the day you created it. How did you not expect that it would seek vengeance?"

A tear comes to my guest's eye but he still doesn't speak. We come to the balcony overlooking the Great Hall and I force my guest to look down on the scene below. It only takes a moment before he is on his knees, hanging his head in shame. Below us is the nursery, where the coal-black children of the Zwarte-Piet are frolicking with their new friend. He towers over them, his hands and feet alone are larger than some of the children, and yet neither they nor he show anything other than playful joy.

I place a comforting hand on his shoulder. "It will take time, but he can be redeemed."

The mad doctor's tearful eyes stare up at me. "But what of myself, Nicholas, is there any road to redemption for one such as I?"

I raise him up and smile gleefully. "Would you agree, my friend, that my task here is a noble one?"

He fights through the tears stammering out his agreement.

"The world is changing," I tell him. "Once it was only the children of eastern and northern Europe that expected a visit from Saint Nicholas or Sinter Claus." I turn and take a step away. "Soon the legend will spread, first to the colonies in America, then throughout Europe, in a century children on every continent will know of Father Christmas, and all shall be expecting a gift, whether they have been naughty or nice. My abilities shall be pushed beyond their limit, unless you help me."

His face screws up in puzzlement. "How can I help?"

I hold out my hand. "You will repeat your act of creation, not once but countless times. You shall build me an army of new men who shall, under my command, fill the skies each Christmas and deliver my gifts to children throughout the world. Your will through creation of this charitable legion, be not only redeemed but also forgiven."

Doctor Victor Frankenstein takes my hand and rises up. "I will need equipment, supplies, and parts...things that would be considered illegal if not blasphemous."

Suddenly there are dozens of Zwarte-Piet swarming around us. "My minions shall see that your every need is met." The small men take him by the hands and lead him away down the hall and to the workshop where he shall toil. Their tiny voices buzz and whisper like flies as they disappear into the darkness.

A heavy footfall on the balcony causes me to turn. "Some say that on Christmas Eve, the Devil himself is bound to serve Santa Claus." The creature's voice is deep, cultured, refined even.

I bow my head and spread my hands before me accepting his observation. I try to speak but he beats me to it. "He may not see you for what you are, but I still can. What shall I call you: Father Christmas, Santa Claus, Nicklaus, Woden, Prometheus, Light-Bringer, or Nahash?"

I look up slyly. "I have many names, one is as good as another, but am I not always the bearer of gifts? Have I not given your creator the greatest gift of all?"

The creature known as Adam roars at me. "That man, my creator, may still walk and speak, but he has the stench of death on him. Even now he slowly rots, and you have him teaching your servants how to create more things like myself. Tell me what great gift did you give him?"

I throw my head back and cackle loud enough to shake the room. "I have given him what I give every child who believes in me, what every child needs, and soon what I shall cover the world with. I have given him hope. It's a lie of course, but what more can you expect from one such as I?" I turn and stalk triumphantly down the hall, casting a final look at the thing Victor Frankenstein has created as it rages against the invisible chains that hold it in place. "If you must call me something, I suggest you use the name my own creator chose for me, it's as good a name as any; call me Lucifer."

And as I leave him behind, the only being that can claim the title son of Frankenstein falls to his knees, and tears of pity flow forth for the sad undead thing that was once his father.

CONTRIBUTOR BIOGRAPHIES

SCOTT DAVID ANIOLOWSKI'S fiction and poetry has appeared in several magazines and anthologies including Barnes & Noble's omnibus *365 Scary Stories*. Scott has edited five fiction anthologies and has been writing for *The Call of Cthulhu* role-playing game since 1986. He is an active member of the Horror Writers Association.

GLYNN BARRASS lives in the North East of England and although Undead, is more Unhinged than Unbound. His work has been translated into Japanese, French and has appeared in a number of magazines and anthologies. Details and news of his latest fiction appearances can be found on his website Stranger Aeons: www.freewebs.com/batglynn

GUSTAVO BONDONI is an Argentine writer with over eighty stories published in ten countries. His first two books were published in 2010: a collection of Gustavo's previously published stories, *Tenth Orbit and Other Faraway Places* was released in October, and his short novel *The Curse of El Bastardo* in November. His third book, *Virtuoso and Other Stories* was published in 2011. He can be found on his website at www.gustavobondoni.com.ar, and his blog, located at http://bondo-ba.livejournal.com/.

DAVID CONYERS is a science fiction writer and editor from Adelaide, South Australia. He has published more than forty short stories worldwide and been nominated for various awards including the Aeon, Aurealis, Ditmar and Australian Shadows. His first collection co-authored with John Sunseri was *The Spiraling Worm* from Chaosium was published in 2007. He is the editor of anthology *Cthulhu's Dark Cults*, co-editor with Brian M. Sammons of the anthology *Cthulhu Unbound 3*, as well as being a contributing editor to *Albedo*

CONTRIBUTOR BIOGRAPHIES

One and *Midnight Echo*. His latest publication is *The Eye of Infinity*, a Lovecraftian science fiction novella from Perilous Press. www.davidconyers.com

DAVID DUNWOODY is the author of the *Empire* series of novels and short stories, as well as the horror collections *Unbound & Other Tales* and *Dark Entities*. Dave lives in Utah and can be visited on the Web at daviddunwoody.com.

CODY GOODFELLOW has written three solo novels——*Radiant Dawn*, *Ravenous Dusk* and *Perfect Union*——and three more——*Jake's Wake*, *The Day Before* and *Spore*——with John Skipp. His short fiction has been collected in *Silent Weapons For Quiet Wars* and *All Monster Action*. As editor and co-founder of Perilous Press, he has published illustrated works of modern cosmic horror by Michael Shea, Brian Stableford and David Conyers. He lives in Los Angeles. www.perilouspress.com

JOHN GOODRICH is so awesomely manly that Wilum Pugmire once called him a crybaby. His bookshelves groan under the weight of hoarded esoteric ephemera. His stories from his unclean mind appear in *Cthulhu Unbound 1*, *Dead but Dreaming 2*, and *Cthulhu's Dark Cults*. Sample his madness at qusoor.com

DAMIEN WALTERS GRINTALIS lives in Maryland with her husband, two cats, and two rescued pit bulls. She is a member of both the HWA and SFWA, an Assistant Editor of *Electric Velocipede*, and her novels are represented by The McVeigh Agency. For more information, please visit her blog: http://dwgrintalis.blogspot.com.

MARK ALLAN GUNNELLS is 37 years old and holds a degree in English and Psychology. He is the author of the Sideshow Press titles *A Laymon Kind of Night*, *Whisonant/Creatures of the Light*, *Tales from the Midnight Shift Vol. I* and *Dark Treats*, the Zombie Feed novella *Asylum*, and the digital collection *Ghosts in the Attic* from Bad Moon Books. A small town boy at heart, he still lives in his hometown of Gaffney, South Carolina, with his partner of ten years. He blogs semi-regularly at http://markgunnells.livejournal.com/.

Undead and Unbound

C.J. HENDERSON is the creator of both the Piers Knight supernatural investigator series and the Teddy London occult detective series. Author of some 70 books and/or novels, plus hundreds and hundreds of short stories and comics, and thousands of non-fiction pieces, this questionable personage of dubious lineage is one of the laziest lumps of flesh on the planet, which is why he became an author. To tell him what you thought of his story, to read more of his fiction, or to have the opportunity to check out one of the most antiquated websites of all time, go to www.cjhenderson.com and have at him.

TOM LYNCH is a longtime devotee of the horror genre, but very new to being published in it. He is descended from a line of family that enjoys a good nightmare. Is it any wonder he writes horror? By day, Tom is a graduate student and runs Miskatonic River Press.

GARY MCMAHON'S short fiction has been reprinted in both *The Mammoth Book of Best New Horror* and *The Year's Best Fantasy & Horror*. He is the British-Fantasy-Award-nominated author of the novels *Hungry Hearts* from Abaddon Books, *Pretty Little Dead Things* and *Dead Bad Things* from Angry Robot/Osprey and *The Concrete Grove* trilogy from Solaris. www.garymcmahon.com

WILLIAM MEIKLE is a Scottish writer with a dozen novels published in the genre press and over 200 short story credits in thirteen countries. His work appears in a number of professional anthologies. He lives in a remote corner of Newfoundland with icebergs, whales and bald eagles for company. Check him out at http://www.williammeikle.com

PAUL MUDIE is a horror illustrator from Edinburgh, Scotland. Qualified in Scientific and Technical Graphics from Edinburgh's Telford College, Paul is best known as a cover artist for various horror anthologies and collections, including *The Black Book of Horror* series for Mortbury Press, *No Man and Other Stories* and *Passports to Purgatory* by Tony Richards, and *To Usher, the Dead* by Gary McMahon, amongst others. He was shortlisted for the British Fantasy Society's 'Best Artist' award in 2011. *Undead and Unbound* is his first cover illustration for Chaosium. www.paulmudie.com

Contributor Biographies

BOB NEILSON lives in Dublin. In partnership with his wife he runs a successful retail business. His short fiction has appeared extensively in professional and small press markets and he has had two plays performed on RTE and one on Anna Livia FM. He also presented a radio show on Anna Livia for a year. He has had two short story collections published, *Without Honour* (1997, Aeon Press) and *That's Entertainment* (2007, Elastic Press) as well as several comics and a graphic novel. His website and blog can be found at www.bobneilson.org.

ROBERT M. PRICE, a fan of H.P. Lovecraft since the Lancer paperback collections of 1967, began writing scholarly articles and humorous pieces on HPL and the Cthulhu Mythos in 1981. His celebrated semi-pro zine *Crypt of Cthulhu* began as a quarterly fanzine for the Esoteric Order of Dagon Amateur Press Association in 1981 and made it to 109 issues. In 1990 he began editing Mythos anthologies for Fedogan & Bremer and Chaosium Inc., and still does! His fiction has been collected in *Blasphemies and Revelations*. Centipede Books will soon be issuing his five-volume annotated edition of the fiction of H.P. Lovecraft. The premise of this tale was suggested to him by his then eight year old pal Martin Stiles.

PETE RAWLIK'S literary criticism routinely appears in the *New York Review of Science Fiction*. His fiction has appeared in *Talebones*, *Crypt of Cthulhu*, *Morpheus Tales*, the *Tales of the Shadowmen* anthologies, *Dead But Dreaming 2*, and *Future Lovecraft*. His collection of Lovecraftian material has been deemed socially unacceptable and on occasion has raised the eyebrows of authorities both secular and religious. His therapist believes that given time and a proper regiment of pharmaceuticals he may become competent enough to stand trial for his anti-anthropocentric literary crimes.

OSCAR RIOS began writing material for the *Call of Cthulhu Role Playing Game* in 2005, branching out into writing fiction in 2010 with an appearance in *Cthulhu's Dark Cults*. He worked in the cemetery industry for 10 years. He is married with two children and a proud native New Yorker.

BRIAN M. SAMMONS has been writing reviews on all things horror for more years than he'd care to admit. Wanting to give other critics the chance to ravage his work for a change, he has penned a few short stories that have appeared in such anthologies as *Arkham Tales, Horrors Beyond, Monstrous, Dead but Dreaming 2* and *Horror for the Holidays*. He co-edited the upcoming anthology *Cthulhu Unbound 3*, has his first novella coming out, "The R'lyeh Singularity", co-written with David Conyers, and is currently writing for and editing a whole mess of upcoming books. For more about this guy that neighbors describe as "such a nice, quiet man" you can check out his very infrequently updated webpage here: http://brian_sammons.webs.com

DAVID SCHEMBRI has had stories published in *The Big Book of New Short Horror, Zero Gravity, Dark Things,* and *Black Box*. His new collection, *Unearthly Fables*, edited by Paula B. of *The Writing Show*, will be published in 2012. David lives in Melbourne, Australia with his lovely wife and children. www.screamingink.org

MERCEDES M. YARDLEY wears red lipstick and writes whimsical horror. She has been in several delightfully diverse publications and is the nonfiction editor for *Shock Totem Magazine*. Visit her at www.mercedesyardley.com.

Selected CHAOSIUM FICTION titles

CALL OF CTHULHU® FICTION

ARKHAM TALES
#6038	ISBN 1-56882-185-9	$15.95

STORIES OF THE LEGEND-HAUNTED CITY: Nestled along the Massachusetts coast is the small town of Arkham. For centuries it has been the source of countless rumor and legend. Those who return whisper tales of Arkham, each telling a different and remarkable account. Reports of impossible occurrences, peculiar happenings and bizarre events, tales that test sanity are found here. Magic, mysteries, monsters, mayhem, and ancient malignancies form the foundation of this unforgettable, centuries-old town. 288 pages.

CTHULHU'S DARK CULTS
#6044	ISBN 1-56882-235-9	$14.95

CHAOSIUM'S *CALL OF CTHULHU®* IS AN ENDLESS SOURCE of imagination of all things dark and mysterious. Here we journey across the globe to witness the numerous and diverse cults that worship Cthulhu and the Great Old Ones. Lead by powerful sorcerers and fanatical necromancers, their followers are mad and deranged slaves, and the ancient and alien gods whom they willingly devote themselves are truly terrifying. These cults control real power, for they are the real secret masters of our world.

ELDRITCH EVOLUTIONS
#6048	ISBN 1-56882-349-5	$15.95

ELDRITCH EVOLUTIONS is the first collection of short stories by Lois H. Gresh, one of the most talented writers working these days in the realms of imagination.

These tales of weird fiction blend elements wrung from science fiction, dark fantasy, and horror. Some stories are bent toward bizarre science, others are Lovecraftian Mythos tales, and yet others are just twisted. They all share an underlying darkness, pushing Lovecraftian science and themes in new directions. While H.P. Lovecraft incorporated the astronomy and physics ideas of his day (e.g., cosmos-within-cosmos and other dimensions), these stories speculate about modern science: quantum optics, particle physics, chaos theory, string theory, and so forth. Full of unique ideas, bizarre plot twists, and fascinating characters, these tales show a feel for pacing and structure, and a wild sense of humor. They always surprise and delight.

FRONTIER CTHULHU
#6041	ISBN 1-56882-219-7	$14.95

AS EXPLORERS CONQUERED THE FRONTIERS of North America, they disturbed sleeping terrors and things long forgotten by humanity. Journey into the undiscovered country where fierce Vikings struggle against monstrous abominations. Travel with European colonists as they learn of buried secrets and the creatures guarding ancient knowledge. Go west across the plains, into the territories were sorcerers dwell in demon-haunted lands, and cowboys confront cosmic horrors.

    Ed. William Jones; Authors include Tim Curran, Lee Clark Zumpe, Darrell Schweitzer, G. Durant Haire, Stephen Mark Rainey and many others.

MYSTERIES OF THE WORM
#6047	ISBN 1-56882-176-X	$15.95

"H.P. LOVECRAFT — LIKE HIS CREATION, CTHULHU — *never truly died*. *He and his influence live on, in the work of so many of us who were his friends and acolytes. Today we have reason for rejoycing in the widespread revival of his canon.* . . . *If a volume such as this has any justification for its existence, it's because Lovecraft's readers continue to search out stories which reflect his contribution to the field of fantasy.* . . . *{The tales in this book} represent a lifelong homage to HPL* . . . *I hope you'll accept them for what they were and are — a labor of love."*   —Robert Bloch

Robert Bloch has become one with his fictional counterpart Ludvig Prinn: future generations of readers will know him as an eldritch name hovering over a body of nightmare texts. To know them will be to know him. And thus we have decided to release a new and expanded third edition of Robert Bloch's *Mysteries of the Worm*. This collection contains four more Mythos tales–"The Opener of the Way", "The Eyes of the Mummy", "Black Bargain", and "Philtre Tip"–not included in the first two editions.

    By Robert Bloch, edited and prefaced by Robert M. Price; Cover by Steven Gilberts. 300 pages, illustrated. Trade Paperback.

NECRONOMICON
#6034	ISBN 1-56882-162-X	$19.95

EXPANDED AND REVISED — Although skeptics claim that the *Necronomicon* is a fantastic tome created by H. P. Lovecraft, true seekers into the esoteric mysteries of the world know the truth: the *Necronomicon* is the blasphemous tome of forbidden knowledge written by the mad Arab, Abdul Alhazred. Even today, after attempts over the centuries to destroy any and all copies in any language, some few copies still exist, secreted away.

Within this book you will find stories about the *Necronomicon*, different versions of the Necronomicon, and two essays on this blasphemous tome. Now you too may learn the true lore of Abdul Alhazred.

Authors include Frederick Pohl, John Brunner, Fred Chappell, Robert A. Silverberg, Manly Wade Wellman, Richard L. Tierney, H. P. Lovecraft, L. Sprague de Camp, Lin Carter, Frank Belknap Long, and many more. 384 pages.

THE STRANGE CASES OF RUDOLPH PEARSON

#6042	ISBN 1-56882-220-0	$14.95

PROFESSOR RUDOLPH PEARSON MOVED to New York City after the Great War, hoping to put his past behind him. While teaching Medieval Literature at Columbia University, he helped the police unravel a centuries' old mystery. At the same moment, he uncovered a threat so terrifying that he could not turn away. With the bloody scribbling of an Old English script in a dead man's apartment, Rudolph Pearson begins a journey that takes him to the very beginning of human civilization. There he learns of the terror that brings doom to his world.

Gathered here are the weird investigations of Rudolph Pearson. This compilation of cosmic horror and Cthulhu Mythos tales brings to life a world full of the grotesque and the malefic, set against a backdrop of an unknowable universe. Progress can be horrifying.

TALES OUT OF INNSMOUTH

#6024	ISBN 1-56882-201*4	$16.95

"Right here in our own state of Massachusetts, in February of 1928, agents of the U.S. Treasury and Justic Departments perpetrated crimes worthy of Nazi Germany against a powerless minority of our citizens . . . When the dust of this jack-booted invasion had settled, no citizens {of Innsmouth, Massachusetts} were found guilty of any crime but the desire to live peaceful lives in privacy and raise their children in the faith of their fathers. The mass internments and confiscations have never been plausibly explained or legally justified, nor has compensation ever been so much as attempted to the innocent victims of this official hooliganism." {Senator Kennedy, speaking to the Miskatonic University Class}

—Brian McNaughton, "The Doom That Came to Innsmouth"

A shadow hangs over Innsmouth, home of the mysterious deep ones, and the secretive Esoteric Order of Dagon. An air of mystery and fear looms... waiting. Now you can return to Innsmouth in this second collection of short stories about the children of Dagon. Visit the undersea city of Y'ha-nthlei and discover the secrets of Father Dagon in this collection of stories. This anthology includes 10 new tales and three classic reprints concerning the shunned town of Innsmouth.

THE THREE IMPOSTORS

#6030	ISBN 1-56882-132-8	$14.95

SOME OF THE FINEST HORROR STORIES ever written. Arthur Machen had a profound impact upon H. P. Lovecraft and the group of stories that would later become known as the Cthulhu Mythos.

    H. P. Lovecraft declared Arthur Machen (1863–1947) to be a modern master who could create "cosmic fear raised to it's most artistic pitch." In these eerie and once-shocking stories, supernatural horror is a transmuting force powered by the core of life. To resist it requires great will from the living, for civilization is only a new way to behave, and not one instinctive to life. Decency prevents discussion about such pressures, so each person must face such things alone. The comforts and hopes of civilization are threatened and undermined by these ecstatic nightmares that haunt the living. This is nowhere more deftly suggested than through Machen's extraordinary prose, where the textures and dreams of the Old Ways are never far removed.

THE WHITE PEOPLE & OTHER STORIES

#6035	ISBN 1-56882-147-6	$14.95

THE BEST WEIRD TALES OF ARTHUR MACHEN, VOL 2. — Born in Wales in 1863, Machen was a London journalist for much of his life. Among his fiction, he may be best known for the allusive, haunting title story of this book, "The White People", which H. P. Lovecraft thought to be the second greatest horror story ever written (after Blackwood's "The Willows"). This wide ranging collection also includes the crystalline novelette "A Fragment of Life", the "Angel of Mons" (a story so coolly reported that it was imagined true by millions in the grim initial days of the Great War), and "The Great Return", telling of the stately visions which graced the Welsh village of Llantristant for a time. Four more tales and the poetical "Ornaments in Jade" are all finely told. This is the second of three Machen volumes to be edited by S. T. Joshi and published by Chaosium; the first volume is *The Three Impostors*. 294 pages.

CHAOSIUM SCIENCE FICTION

EXTREME PLANETS

#6052	UPCOMING	$TBA

Introduced by Hugo and Nebula Award-winning author David Brin. Featuring stories from David Brin and Gregory Benford, Brian Stableford, Peter Watts, G. David Nordley, Jay Caselberg and many more.

> *"A stellar line-up of writers presenting the most exotic worlds imaginable—prepare to have your mind blown!"* — *Sean Williams, Author of Saturn Returns and Twinmaker*

TWO DECADES AGO ASTRONOMERS CONFIRMED the existence of planets orbiting stars other than our Sun. Today more than 800 such worlds have been identified, and scientists now estimate that at least 160 billion star-bound planets are to be found in the Milky Way Galaxy alone. But more surprising is just how diverse and bizarre those worlds are.

Extreme Planets is a science fiction anthology of stories set on alien worlds that push the limits of what we once believed possible in a planetary environment. Visit the bizarre moons, dwarf planets and asteroids of our own Solar Systems, and in the deeper reaches of space encounter super-Earths with extreme gravity fields, carbon planets featuring mountain ranges of pure diamond, and ocean worlds shrouded by seas hundreds of kilometers thick. The challenges these environments present to the humans that explore and colonise them are many, and are the subject matter of these tales.

The anthology features 15 tales from leading science fiction authors and rising stars in the genre:

"Banner of the Angels" by David Brin and Gregory Benford

"Brood" by Stephen Gaskell

"Haumea" by G. David Nordley

"A Perfect Day off the Farm" by Patty Jansen

"Daybreak" by Jeff Hecht

"Giants" by Peter Watts

"Maelstrom" by Kevin Ikenberry

"Murder on Centauri" by Robert J. Mendenhall

"The Flight of the Salamander" by Violet Addison and David Smith

"Petrochemical Skies" by David Conyers and David Kernot

"The Hyphal Layer" by Meryl Ferguson

"Colloidal Suspension" by Geoff Nelder

"Super-Earth Mother" by Guy Immega

"Lightime" by Jay Caselberg

"The Seventh Generation" by Brian Stableford

Extreme Planets is scheduled for release in late 2013 in both trade paperback and online e-reader formats. Edited by David Conyers, David Kernot and Jeff Harris with cover illustration by Paul Drummond.

A LONG WAY HOME

#6049	ISBN 978-15688236387	$15.95

THIS IS THE STORY OF SEAN MCKINNEY, a young farm boy from the medieval world of Brae who longs to escape the family farm. On his way to begin study at the university, Sean stumbles into a fire-fight between troops of the local tyrant and Congressional Marines trying to overthrow Brae s corrupt and brutal government.

Saving the life of one ambushed Marine, McKinnie is taken aboard the Congressional Starship cruiser Lewis and Clark and is befriended by the starship's crew -- becoming an unofficial ship's mascot. His new friends realize that though McKinnie comes from a backwater world and is ignorant of interstellar politics, he is highly intelligent and might become a valuable asset as a covert Congressional agent. They teach him about Congressional history, including how humanity's home world was destroyed in a collision with an asteroid.

Surviving pirate attacks and deep personal losses, McKinnie grows from an innocent country bumpkin into a civilized young man, and develops a relationship with Lt. Alexandra Andropova, a young nurse in the ship's medical department.

His training complete, McKinnie embarks on several missions to primitive worlds including a return to his home world of Brae. He discovers that slavers kidnapped members of his own family, and others from Brae, to be sold to an alien machine-intelligence. Pursuing the slavers, Lewis and Clark and her crew must battle machine-controlled starships and a massive machine-controlled deep-space station in a desperate attempt to rescue the kidnapped humans.

All titles are available from bookstores and game stores. You can also order directly from www.chaosium.com, your source for fiction, roleplaying, Cthulhiana, and more.